PRAISE FOR
"BENEATH THE ROCK"

"This is one of those books that I wish I could give more than five stars. It is well written, and moves along at a good pace. The character development is outstanding."

Amazon Reader Review (authorpholloway)

"The first 6 chapters were very intense. I was worried that there is no way the rest of the book could keep up this pace. I was wrong. The way this book pulls you into the characters' story lines is amazing. The plot had a number of twists and turns."

Amazon Reader Review (Adam)

"Intriguing and thought provoking. I, my parents in their eighties, and my college student nieces can all gain from this read."

Amazon Reader Review (jhs65)

"This book is a great read. Starts out exciting from the get go. It will probably hit home with a lot of former vets and their families. Definitely recommend it."

Amazon Reader Review (Patrick M. Phelan)

"Thought provoking and meaningful introspection and lessons within a story of action and suspense. In other words, the reader is compelled by an unpredictable plot, while experiencing the raw emotions and life-changing choices of characters battered by war and overwhelming odds."

Amazon Reader Review (M. A. Fitch)

"Beneath the Rock is a story of generations of men going to war. It is the story of the secrets held from times at war, and the serpentine route it takes, with its demonic secrets that destroy lives even when the wars have ended. And at its center it is a vastly moving story of guilt, love & redemption."

Amazon reader Review (Mary Beaulieu)

Also by Tommy Birk

Beneath the Rock

ZERO GOD

A NOVEL

TOMMY BIRK

CALUMET EDITIONS
Minneapolis

**CALUMET
EDITIONS**
Minneapolis

SECOND EDITION DECEMBER 2022
ZERO GOD

This is a work of fiction. All of the characters, names, incidents, organizations, and dialogue are either the products of the author's imagination or are used fictiously.

10 9 8 7 6 5 4 3 2

ISBN: 978-1-959770-98-5
Book and cover design by Gary Lindberg

To my brothers and sisters, in order from oldest to youngest: Suzanne, Terry, Janet, Carolyn, (Tommy), Monie, John, & Kenny. They are my family, my best friends, & my best critics. There is a closeness among us, born of imperfect yet loving parents. I marvel at them. They are creative, intelligent, and accomplished, and they know the Schnitzelbank Song! LuvEmAll.

ZERO GOD

A NOVEL

TOMMY BIRK

CHAPTER 1

Few persons considered a run at 4:30 in the morning on a bone-chilling February day in Southwestern Indiana. Andy Balbach did, and so he normally had the Dubain Riverwalk to himself. Today he did not. He parked his Jeep alongside a Honda Civic hatchback in the lot at the Ruxer Golf Course, next to the Riverwalk's southern terminus. He laid his hand on the hood. It was warm and the engine clicked as it cooled. The new runner could not be far ahead. Andy skipped his own warm-up routine and started his run. A couple hundred yards in, he entered the Riverwalk's first wide curve and spotted a white-clad figure just entering the Riverwalk's woodsy stretch.

He inwardly laughed at himself. This runner dared to invade his solitary domain? He would soon find out who. Andy turned it into a one-side-only-knows-about-it contest and sped up. He spotted glimpses of the challenger along the meandering trail. Andy was strangely elated by the spookiness of it all—the darkness, the glimpses of the white ghost, and the woods, back-lit only by vacillating reflections of Dubain's streetlights off low-hanging clouds. He thought, *by golly, I'm catching up to him!*

The earthquake struck when Andy Balbach reached the Riverwalk's two-mile marker. He instantly sat down against a thick walnut tree, pulled his knees to his chest, circled them with his arms, and eyed the tree branches far above him. Ice in places along the banks of the Patoka River crackled while the river's surface water rippled and tumbled in confusion. Pieces of riverbank tumbled into the water. Ghostly branches of leafless trees swirled above. Limbs snapped and crashed around him. And underlying all this was an eerie undulating thunder, cracking and rolling far into the distance. Snippets of seismic talk raced through his head: "Wabash Fault… New Madrid Fault… 1812 quakes… the Great Midwest Earthquake?"

Ten seconds after it started, the shaking ceased and the thunder echoed away.

Andy rose, pulled out his cell phone, and dialed Rhonda to make sure she was safe. He terminated the call before the first ring when an animal, somewhere in front of him, started bleating. He ran forward, his tiny flashlight beam watching for downed limbs on the trail, until he encountered a confused canopy of branches laying across the Riverwalk, a young deer trapped under them, and the white ghost—a woman, to his mild surprise—struggling to lift them. What was probably the fawn's mama stood several yards west of the Riverwalk and upward from the river, glaring but showing no sign of attack. Several more deer stood behind her. Andy laid the light on the ground, waded into the branches, and helped lift. The fawn scrambled out and, with a slight limp, ran to its mama. Andy picked up the flashlight in time to watch the herd start up the hill. However, mama stopped, turned around and, ignoring Andy, stared at the woman. Then she and her fawn joined the others.

Andy turned the flashlight on the lady. It was his turn to stare. She, staring back, was about four inches shorter than he was. Her white running attire, although baggy, set off nicely against her dark hair. Andy didn't know the woman. He introduced himself and offered his hand. She made no move to take it or otherwise respond. Instead, she broke her stare and turned away to continue her run. Then she stopped, turned around, and said, "I know about you, Andy Balbach." She went on until she disappeared into the darkness.

CHAPTER 2

Jameel Shalih awoke in his top bunk to shouts and commotion. He grabbed one of the boys. "Where's everybody going?"

"Borgmann ordered us to get outside pronto. He said this could be the small one before the big one."

Jameel asked, "What big one?"

The boy asked, "You slept through it?"

"Through what?"

"We just had an earthquake!"

Jameel had been through several earthquakes as a child in Iraq and he wanted to brag that earthquakes didn't scare him, but he thought better of it. Instead, he told the boy that he would not leave his warm bed for the freezing temperatures outside.

"You're already in trouble with Borgmann, Shalih. You want more?"

Kurt Borgmann was the warden of Camp Morgan, a minimum-security prison for nonviolent young men, located inside Dubain County, two miles east of the town of Ferdinand, Indiana. One of Borgmann's favorite guards entered the barracks. "Need an engraved invitation, Shalih?"

"Yeah. Got one?"

"Lose the attitude, Muslim boy, and get your ass out of here before the roof falls in and kills you. Wouldn't wanna miss Ten-Cubed, now would you?"

Outside, Jameel focused on the six-foot-high wall that surrounded Camp Morgan, and then saw his friend, Jayden Ramirez, being led into the courtyard between Borgmann and another guard. Ten-Cubed had thinned him almost to the point of emaciation, but his eyes were bright and alert. A shiv had done double-duty. The guards had honed a spoon to a sharp point. They hid and then 'found' it under Jayden's mattress. Then they'd done the same to Jameel. Thus, Borgmann had cover for, first, Jayden's slow starvation and wasting of his strength in Ten-Cubed and, second, his disappearance under the guise of an attempted escape. Then it would be Jameel's turn.

Ramirez winked at Jameel and then nodded ever so slightly toward the wall. Jameel shook his head twice… too many guards with too many guns. However, Jameel watched Jayden and the positioning of the guards. There was no barbed wire atop the wall, unlike the wall that surrounded the Tigris River Prisoner-of-War Camp in Iraq. If Jayden made a move to escape, Jameel would have a split second to join him. Jayden's desperation made sense. He might be killed in an escape attempt, but there is no difference between being dead and being dead, and Ten-Cubed meant certain death. The confusion wrought by a small earthquake might mean their lives.

One-by-one the guards walked back to the barracks, leaving only Borgmann and the one guard with Jayden. By now, they should have escorted Jayden back to Ten-Cubed, the nickname the boy inmates had given to Camp Morgan's solitary confinement cell. Instead, the guards inside called the inmates back to their barracks. Jameel was certain that Jayden detected the setup.

Jayden made a run for it. The guard shot twice and missed. Ramirez jumped, tumbled over the wall, and disappeared. By this time, other armed guards were running from the barracks. They followed Borgmann and the guard over the wall.

There were several shouts of 'halt' and then gunfire. Someone screamed. Jameel saw a clear shot to the wall, but before he could move, a blow to the side of his head sent him to the ground. When he came to, he was on his back in his bed and tied down with restraints. Borgmann appeared.

"Congratulations. Your friend Ramirez killed a guard and escaped with his weapon."

Borgmann was lying, a trait he'd practiced and perfected at Tigris River.

In truth, Jameel knew his friend since Tigris River was dead, his body disappeared forever.

CHAPTER 3

Andy Balbach stumbled out of his house and started west on Orchard Lane. It was dark and drizzling but he didn't care. He had to see Stump. Stump could fix it. Andy slipped and fell on his right shoulder. The Jack Daniels had dulled the pain but spun his head. He managed to stand and take a few more steps. Then he stopped to take his bearings. There was the illuminated American flag atop All Souls Point, the highest elevation in Kundek Cemetery and Dubain, and north of St. Augustine Cathedral. Stump lived two blocks west of the cemetery.

The drizzle turned into sheets of rain. At times, he fell, forcing him to crawl in the streams of water until, with the help of a tree, stop sign, or lamp post—anything handy—he was able to pull himself up. He stumbled from sidewalks to streets and through yards. Horns blared when he stumbled into traffic. Two people called out from their homes asking if he needed help. He ignored them.

He reached the wrought-iron fence that formed the northern border of the cemetery. All Souls Point, now to his south and well above him, no longer mattered as a directional landmark, but he eyed it anyway. He grabbed the metal fence posts and walked sideways to the north gate. There he stopped and, for a moment, forgot about Stump. He entered the cemetery and crawled on all fours to the Balbach family plot, just inside the gate. The maple tree stood a little way uphill from there. He leaned back against Great-Great-Grandma Balbach's tombstone, laid his elbows on his knees, and closed his eyes. Occasionally he opened them to stare at the maple.

There was his dad's pickup. He tried not to see it. He envisioned a boy and a girl squirming in the back of the pickup. He tried not to see them. He failed at both and it didn't matter whether his eyes were open or closed.

Then he thought, maybe it hadn't happened. Maybe this was a nightmare. Maybe he wasn't drunk and it wasn't raining and he wasn't cold and he wasn't leaning on a gravestone in Kundek Cemetery and staring at the maple tree. He shook himself to wake up, but he failed because he wasn't asleep and this wasn't a bad dream. He felt the Jack Daniels rise into his throat. He fought it down once, and then again. Then he was on all fours facing uphill and retching. He sensed the rain washing his vomit to his trousers, so he turned to face downhill. His arms and shoulders quaked in weakness, but they held.

When he next opened his eyes he spied two blue-jeaned legs, one of which was artificial. Andy followed the legs upward until he saw Stump's face and an umbrella above that. Stump grabbed Andy's hand and propped him against another monument, that of Andy's older brother, Herman.

Stump sat beside Andy and covered both of them with the umbrella while Andy dry-heaved between his legs. "Easy Andy… easy there, son."

"Stump. Rhonda left me. She... she..."

"I know, Andy."

"She called... crying. I got home and her car... packed. Kitchen. I asked why she was crying. She said she was leaving. I asked where she was going. She said, 'India... napolis.' I asked when she was comin' back. She said nothing. I asked what's wrong. She... 'I'm leaving you Andy… I'm leaving you.' Why? Why? She ran outside... backed out. I tried… passenger door but... lock... locked it was. Couldn't stop her. Tried... cell phone maybe five times... no answer.

"Stump!" Andy sobbed and retched. "Ya gotta... fix this. You're her boss. Remember? She'll listen to you. Get... get her back!" For a few moments, the sobbing and retching overtook Andy.

"Easy there, Andy."

"Stump..."

"Not now, Andy."

"She chose Kincaid over me. Said I didn't approve… her... 'vestigation of Kincaid. I said... not true. We argued. Next thing she's in her car and driving away. Just like that. No fuckin' warning. No fuckin' nothin'. I'll kill that... bas... bastard... Kincaid."

"Can you stand up, Andy? My car's close. I'll take you home."

Andy shook his head, spit out more Jack Daniels, and gazed at Stump. His mind cleared for a few seconds. "Stump... how'd you know to find me... here?"

"I was coming to see you."

"At... my house?"

"Yeah."

"Why?"

"Rhonda told me she was leaving you."

"When?"

"Last week."

CHAPTER 4

Rhonda parked on the street in front of Stump's house and climbed the steps to the front porch. There she hesitated. The Beech Tree Boys were rehearsing "Danny Boy" in Stump's living room. Rhonda teared up. She told herself it was only a song but she knew that, for her, it was not. The song had many interpretations. To Rhonda, the beautiful yet mournful and soul-tugging tune was about two lovers, a girl-child lying in her grave before her time, and a boy-child, lost in sorrow, placing flowers on it. They longed for each other, but the barrier between earthly life and spiritual transcendence stood between them, their separation bridged only by haunting Irish lyrics embedded in a haunting Irish song.

Rhonda pushed the vision away and dried her tears. She had called Stump about an hour before.

Stump had answered, "Yeah?"

"Can I see you?"

"When?"

"Now."

"We're rehearsing."

"It's important."

"So is rehearsing. It takes time to beat it into these tone-deaf numbskulls."

"Please?"

"Be here in an hour."

Andy's brother, Al Balbach, nicknamed 'Clubby,' appeared at the door, frowned, and then led her into the hallway. He walked into Stump's living room and announced, "O'Malley's in the hallway."

Rhonda winced. Andy's family had turned frosty toward her after she left him. Al was the worst.

Stump ordered the others to keep practicing. "Remember, we got the gig at the Schnitzelbank when Rhonda interviews Lincoln Kincaid."

Stump owned and operated the *Dubain Courier Journal*. He wore his thinning hair in a military crewcut and carried his five feet eight inches with a military bearing. He'd lost his leg to a landmine in the first Gulf War. He had never married. He said that he was wedded to the newspaper, and that it was his life and reason for living. He had nicknamed Rhonda 'Tadpole' when she walked into the newsroom on her first day. Stump could be loud, impatient, and demanding. At first, his gruff demeanor intimidated her, but she soon uncovered a friendly and soft-hearted man with a quick sense of humor. Stump had supported her decision to leave the newspaper and launch a career in investigative journalism, but he told her in some way he would always be her boss. Stump had developed the Beech Tree Boys into a much-sought-after entertainment troupe. Stump knew his people. They had inherited their love for music, earthy humor, and 'gemutlichkeit,' from their Bavarian ancestors. He wrote the scripts for the Beech Tree Boys' comedy routines, many a bit off-color.

He met Rhonda in the hallway where she smirked and pointed at the frames on the wall. "They called you 'Firmus' when you had both legs. I like 'Stump' a whole lot more."

"Whaddya want, Tadpole?"

"Information."

"What kind?"

"Military records."

"Classified?"

"Maybe just a little."

"Tadpole, it's like pregnancy. Either you are or you aren't. A 'little' classified means classified. We'll talk about that later. For now, I want you to sing lead with Clubby. He's a bit off-key today… throwing the others out of whack."

It was no use arguing. She followed Stump and took her place beside Clubby.

"I don't need O'Malley's help."

Stump said, "You're off pitch, Clubby. Rhonda's higher overtones will force you back onto it."

"I'm on key. It's you, Peachfuzz, and Billups who are throwing me off." Then he turned to Rhonda. "So you can get the hell out of here."

"Whoa there, Clubby. This is my house and I decide who stays and who doesn't. Rhonda stays."

Stump chorded the key on the piano and they sang the first verse of "Lida Rose."

Clubby said, "I'll be back in a few."

Billups said, "Another bathroom break, Clubby? Better get your prostate checked."

"No pee break. Just checking on Andy."

Rhonda said, "Andy?"

"Yeah, O'Malley, your husband's sleeping off a Jack Daniels night in Stump's spare bedroom upstairs."

"Andy's sleeping in this house? Right now?"

"Did I stutter? Go up and see what you've done to him."

Rhonda had streaks of guilt over leaving Andy, but she would not put up with his cop brother's bullying and hypocrisy.

"What I did to him? Go look in the mirror, Al, and you'll see the guy who almost destroyed Andy."

"What're you talking about?"

"You know damn well what I'm talking about. I was there. I remember. You abandoned Andy after Herman died. He was a young teenager and the guilt was killing him. You only made it worse. It was the Piankashaw Indian who pulled him from the edge and nursed him back."

"I don't like your attitude, O'Malley."

"Put it in your fucking police report."

Rhonda stormed out of the house to her car. She was pulling away from the curb when Stump waved at her to stop.

Rhonda asked, "Why didn't you tell me on the phone that Andy was in the house?"

"I forgot to."

"Then why not when we were in the hallway?"

"I forgot to."

"You're either lying or you're in the first stages of Alzheimer's."

"Alzheimer's, maybe. Lies, yes."

Rhonda smiled. "Lying's a sin. Go to confession."

"White lies aren't sins, but I'll confess them anyway just in case I'm wrong."

"Thank you, Stump."

"For what?"

"First, for caring for Andy. Second, for 'Danny Boy.' I love that song. Third, for not calling me down when I threw it in Al's face. I just will not put up with his abuse."

"You hit back hard. Touched a nerve, I think."

"I told the truth."

"That you did. And don't forget that the Balbach family's history makes them right quick to circle the wagons around their own."

CHAPTER 5

Rhonda merged onto Interstate 69 north, which would take her to the south side of Indianapolis. From there she had an easy drive to her condominium in Speedway, a suburb. Normally, she stayed at her and Andy's house when she was in Dubain. However, Andy's dry-out at Stump's house gave her a strange sense that she would be trespassing had she remained in Dubain.

Stump was dead-on. The Balbach family's history of tragedy spawned a peculiar, though understandable, sense of collective Post-traumatic stress disorder, or PTSD, on the part of Andy's family.

The first was a series of events culminating in the Battle of the Piankashaws in 1968. Andy refused to talk about it, so Rhonda had wheedled the story from newspaper accounts and Father Paul Kessler who had divulged in detail the events leading to the articles and his personal role in them. The Balbach family was deeply rooted in the military histories of Andy's great grandfather, Andrew Balbach, in World War One, his grandfather, Ernie, in World War Two, and his father, Tim, in Vietnam. They'd left their wars but their wars hadn't left them, and so they were forced to live out in the woods at Piankashaw Rock. Andrew survived World War One trenches but had returned a broken man. He shot himself on December 7, 1941, after he learned of the Japanese attack on Pearl Harbor. Andrew's son, Ernie, saw action in some of the worst fighting in France in World War Two. He was the lone survivor of an SS massacre. Later, in a rage, he killed the French boy and his mother who had betrayed the patrol. Ernie's son and Andy's father, Tim, had joined the marines and fought in Vietnam. He returned with PTSD, made worse by his part in a massacre of Vietnamese villagers. A secret, neo-Nazi group had settled in Dubain after World War Two. They kidnapped and tortured Maria, Andy's mother. Tim, Ernie, and Father Paul had led the other Piankashaw men in a desperate attack on the Nazis and freed Maria.

Andy had no immunity against the wars of his fathers. He turned surly and argumentative when Rhonda raised the subject. These were pieces of history that not even Andy could digest.

The second event was another Balbach family tragedy with Andy at its core. Tim and Maria had five children: Shelly was the oldest; Al, nicknamed 'Clubby,' followed; and then Terri and Herman. Andy appeared as his parents' 'surprise bundle' seven years after Herman, who had died in a hunting accident at age nineteen. He'd taken Andy, then aged twelve, into the woods to teach him how to squirrel hunt. Andy tripped over a log and his gun discharged, killing Herman. Andy's grief and guilt were overwhelming, and no amount of his parents' love and forgiveness could relieve his despair. Rhonda, smitten with Andy after their first kiss not long before, had tried to help, but Andy cut her out. Herman's death hit Al so hard that he shunned Andy after the accident. But then there had appeared on the scene a mystical Indian who staked a claim on Piankashaw Rock as part of his tribe's heritage. The Indian's wise and gentle prodding pulled Andy back from the brink of self-destruction. With time, Al turned aside his grief, and he and Andy were reconciled.

It eventually occurred to Rhonda that, in loving Andy, she, too, carried these things.

Tim and Maria, now approaching their seventies, nourished a tight-knit family. There were barbecues and Thanksgiving, Christmas, and Easter get-togethers. The family wrapped its arms around daughters- and sons-in-law even when a marriage turned shaky. Rhonda loved spending time with Andy's family. She and Maria confided in each other about Andy. Rhonda loved jaunts in the Balbach's Coachman RV, owned equally in parts by Tim and Maria and their children. In retirement, Tim and Maria had turned snowbirds and spent winters living in the RV on a lot they owned in Fort Myers, Florida. Their children shared the RV for their own trips in spring, summer, and fall.

However, starting about six months before the separation, Rhonda ceased attending Balbach family events, and the family, with the exception of Maria and Tim, turned lukewarm toward her.

CHAPTER 6

Jameel Shalih lay on the cot in Ten-Cubed and stared into the blackness. Of these things he was certain: they would come for him, they would come at night, and they would come in their own good time. It might be a few minutes, a few hours, or maybe tomorrow night, or maybe the next. But they would come. They would say that Jameel had escaped Camp Morgan and that he was 'armed and dangerous.' They'd said the same about Ramirez.

Jameel looked into the past and saw Ramirez. He looked into the future and saw himself.

Borgmann announced to the entire camp that he was ordering Jameel to Ten-Cubed for the shiv and his 'attempt' to escape with Ramirez.

When the foot-square window with steel bars at the back of the cell let in its tiny shard of daylight, the solitary inmate could see that Ten-Cubed was about ten feet wide, ten feet long, and ten feet high. He could see that its walls were cement block and its ceiling and floor were concrete. There was a green cot with an army-issue blanket on one side, and a toilet and washbowl on the other. The cast-iron door hung in the wall opposite the window. There was one bare light bulb in the middle of the ceiling, but it was useless to the inmate because its switch was outside the door. There was no radio, no TV, no noise, nothing to read, no one to talk to, no god to pray to. It didn't surprise Jameel that his god had left him for good. After all, his god had mostly scooted when Jameel and Jayden served in the Military Police at Tigris River. Had Ramirez's god also dumped *him*? Maybe. Probably. Certainly.

Yeah, it was certainly. Ramirez took his chance and died for it. No god for Jayden. No god for Jameel.

How long had Jameel been in Ten-Cubed? Five days? A week? Ten days? Ten-Cubed did that to you. It scammed your life, sucked your soul, and stole what little god you had left. It made you want to cry, to scream, to beg, to babble. Other boys had given in to these. Jayden Ramirez—and so far Jameel—had not. However, there was more than no more god. Jameel felt the weight loss and body weakness brought on by Borgmann's slow starvation strategy. Had Ramirez tried, like Jameel, to conserve his strength for one last struggle? Had he promised his silence as a contract for his life? Had Ramirez been a slave to the waiting and fear? Indeed, Jameel had learned that, in Ten-Cubed, the waiting and fear synergized into a dread so raw and so relentless as to torture without mercy he who knows that other people considered his death much more valuable than his life—he who knows that his death will take place at night deep in a forest at a lonely place called Piankashaw Rock.

Piankashaw Rock was one of the few clearings in the Hoosier National Forest, three miles from Camp Morgan. Borgmann and his 'friends' loved the place. The boys hated it.

Sometimes a new boy, overhearing the others whispering to each other about Piankashaw Rock, asked about it. The others said nothing to the new boy because he was likely to suffer Piankashaw soon enough. He would learn that Piankashaw was a cliff formation two hundred yards long and thirty-five feet at its highest point above the forest floor. He'd see that Piankashaw had its own caves, cemetery, and river. He'd learn that a trip to Piankashaw was not a punishment, but a holy ritual in which he would play the Lamb to the Cradlers. He would learn that there might be other Lambs, and that the Cradlers would be Borgmann, some of the guards, and, at times, guests. Two such were George, the fat creepy dude from Las Vegas, and another man, his face covered and his pleasure expressed in grunting vulgarity. The boy would learn that it was at Piankashaw Rock, where, deep in the night—any night—a Cradler might tie him to a post and whip, beat, and sodomize him.

Two nights later the bulb flickered on. Jameel jumped from his cot and stood against the wall next to the door and opposite its hinged side. Keys rattled, the door screeched open, and the beer-bellied, African–American guard entered. Jameel pushed him toward the cot and then turned to run out of Ten-Cubed. He'd taken two steps when a nightstick, wielded by a second guard, of Hispanic roots, crashed against the side of his head. Jameel, stunned, went down to his knees and then fell face-first to the concrete, crunching his nose. The guards lifted Jameel, handcuffed his arms behind him, and shackled his legs. Then they half-walked, half-carried him to the prison gate. Borgmann stood there. He wore a .357 in a holster on his right hip and a sheathed, butcher-sized knife on his left. Jameel remembered that Borgmann was left-handed.

Borgmann and the guards normally joked with each other and taunted the boys, soon to become their pleasure, on the off-road Hummer ride to Piankashaw. But on this night they were somber, tense, and quiet.

Jameel saw a concrete block and rope in the far back of the Hummer. There flashed through his mind a scene of himself, tied to and weighted by the block, lying at the bottom of the Patoka River and rotting to the delight of snapping turtles. He imagined Ramirez, what was left of him, bobbing in the current beside him.

They dragged Jameel from the Hummer. The Hispanic guard lit a small Coleman lantern and hung it on a limb. The African-American guard ordered Jameel to stand at attention. Jameel's senses became super acute. Everything slowed, a trick of his mind to extend the last few seconds of his life. His head pounded, but he barely felt the blood from his nose running down his chin. The clearing extended east to the Patoka River. Jameel lowered his eyes to the crumbling crosses of the Piankashaw Cemetery by the river. He lifted his eyes to the waxing moon rising above the cemetery. Then he turned his head west to the sandstone and shale on the face of Piankashaw Rock. He morphed back some 25,000 years and watched the last glacier of the last ice age scraping the face of Piankashaw. He heard cicadas shrieking and frogs bellowing. An owl hooted. A coyote wailed from the direction of the Ohio River. Two more coyotes, one to the east and the other to the north, replied.

Jameel felt Borgmann's hot breath on his neck, and then heard him unsheathe his knife.

"Why? Why are you doing this? Is it be... because I know... him? I... I promise never to tell."

No one answered. The two guards, one on either side of him, held him, but each stood an arm's length away. Borgmann, standing behind Jameel, circled him with his right arm and pinned him to his body. Jameel saw the flash of the knife in Borgmann's left hand. He felt the cold tip of the blade on the right side of his throat and then a prick as it pierced his skin.

Just then, a man ran out of the woods from the north end of Piankashaw Rock toward Jameel and the Cradlers. In quick succession he shot Borgmann and the two guards. All three fell and lay still on the ground.

Jameel stared at the young man, more like a boy. He was close to six feet tall, thin, and his blue eyes glowed in the light from the Coleman lamp. He was dressed in black but his hair was blond, long, and braided. Jameel stumbled toward the woods as fast as his leg shackles would allow, but a woman, similarly dressed as the young man but with unbraided dark hair, emerged from the woods carrying a burlap bag. She blocked Jameel's escape.

Jameel managed to ask, "Who are you?"

"It does not matter," she said.

The young man got the keys from one of the dead guards and began unlocking Jameel's cuffs and shackles. The woman filled the burlap bag with the guards' weapons and Borgmann's knife. She handed the bag to Jameel and pointed downriver. "Go that way."

"But... downriver leads to Dubain. How can I hide there?"

"Do as I say."

Then both the woman and boy disappeared into the forest.

CHAPTER 7

Father Bernardo Estrada, thirty-nine years old, a Jesuit, the pastor of the Church of the Immaculate Conception in Ferdinand, and a counselor for military rape victims at the Richard Lugar Veterans Administration Hospital, raised the host in celebration of early mass. At the end of the mass, Father Bernardo spread his arms. "These are the days that the Lord has made. Let us give thanks and rejoice."

His cell phone buzzed before he reached the sacristy. The caller was Father Paul Kessler, ninety-two years old, in remarkable health, and still partially active in the ministry at St. Augustine.

"Bernardo, I need your help."

"Father Thaddeus?"

"Yes. Seems like he got the only serious earthquake injury in Dubain. That bookcase that fell on him damaged more than the doctors thought. Last night he went into atrial fibrillation, developed a blood clot in his brain, and lapsed into a coma."

"I'm hearing confessions this morning and then teaching at the hospital this afternoon. I'll drive over after that."

CHAPTER 8

From the Hangouts window, Garrett Jennings watched Polly Thompson disappear. He leaned back in his chair and stared out the window at the shirtless young men on the basketball court just beyond Oakenwald Hall's east ell. He shifted his gaze back to his laptop, lit a cigarette, and tried to push the young men out of his mind while pondering solutions to the Foundation's latest crises. The cigarette calmed his nerves and gave him focus.

He buzzed Earl Thompson, his boss and Polly's father. "Sir, I think you'd better come to my office."

Earl replied, "Can't it wait? The board meeting starts in thirty minutes."

"No, sir. We have two crises."

***

Earl entered. Despite the urgency of the moment, Garrett admired Earl's friendly yet authoritative bearing. Earl, at six feet, an inch shorter than Garrett, was seventy-one and had thick white hair, broad shoulders, sparkling teeth, and a deep tan.

Garrett closed the door to his office. "Sir, we noted a change in Polly's attitude after she moved to Indiana. Today she's in open rebellion. She and her group now call themselves 'Angels.' Your orders no longer bind them. They, and they alone, will choose their missions. It is right to dispatch Cradlers because they are evil rapists who deserve their fate. It is wrong to harm Lambs because they are innocent victims of the Cradlers. Polly said that she has 'nullified' your order to find and silence Jameel Shalih, a Lamb."

Earl said, "Refuse my orders? Notions of right and wrong? Evil and innocence?"

"Exactly, sir. I told her she has no authority to adjudge these things. Her only authority is the covenant among Jesus, the Foundation, and her group, and that covenant commands her to put out of the way both Cradlers and Lambs. She said they dissolved that covenant and entered into a new one. Their covenant is between the true Jesus and them."

"True Jesus?"

"'The true Jesus,' she said, and I quote, 'is adorned with the gospels, not stripped of them. This Jesus commands justice, and justice cannot be equal treatment of Cradlers and Lambs.'"

Earl stroked his chin and stared out the window. "She is right in one respect. Jesus does command justice, but in the form of obedience."

"Exactly, and I told her so. She replied that the Foundation has twisted the Jesus Equation to make a false Jesus, one who is complicit with the likes of Prime Minister Ponya of the Congo. She said that Ponya kills homosexuals and commits genocide on the ethnic groups who oppose him. I reminded her that you've prayed with Ponya and that he has promised to end these practices. She called your prayers 'hypocrisy.'"

"Hypocrisy?"

"She said that the Foundation's real goal was not to pray Jesus into Ponya's heart so he would stop killing. It was to bribe Ponya so he would award the gold, silver, and diamond mining contracts to a Congolese company controlled by Lincoln Kincaid's parents, Jackson and Rachel."

"That's preposterous!"

"It is, and I told her so. Then she sneered at me. Sir, her insolence so offended me that I responded rather strongly. I told her that all her actions—defiance of your orders, misuse of the Jesus Equation, and unilateral termination of a covenant—amounted to treason against the Foundation."

"Do they?"

"They do. Polly has broken her covenant of allegiance to the Foundation. Even worse, she has, in effect, replaced the Foundation covenant of allegiance with another to the Angels."

"Garrett, this is quite a shock. Polly has followed orders under covenants with skill and professionalism. She has never acted this way. This Polly isn't the Polly I designed. Something's happened to her. Do you know what?"

"Jesus sent her a sign. She refused to describe it and where and when it supposedly occurred."

"Do you know where she and her Angels—might as well use their term—are hiding?"

"Somewhere near Camp Morgan in Southwestern Indiana. It is forty miles north of the Ohio River and ten miles south of Dubain. I surmise that they're hiding in Dubain or somewhere close to it. Dubain is a white trash town of twenty thousand that stubbornly entertains high and mighty notions of itself. That nosy reporter, Rhonda O'Malley, is from there."

"Do the Angels pose a threat to us and Lincoln Kincaid?"

"Yes, indeed. However, sir, it's not as bad as it seems. The Angels had already worked through half of the Lambs on the list, and they continue to put away Cradlers. At some point, probably before Lincoln Kincaid is elected, but maybe after, they will have no place to go but to us and Oakenwald."

"I don't understand, Garrett."

"Polly has not thought this through. The Angels have forfeited both the Foundation's financial support and immunity against prosecution. They might obtain funds elsewhere, but they cannot find the type of legal protection offered by the Foundation. The Angels have committed serious crimes under the secular laws and could at any time face arrest, prosecution, and imprisonment… or worse. Indiana has the death penalty. It's only a matter of time before Indiana gets too hot for them. At that point, their only salvations are the legal cover of the Foundation and the sanctuary of Oakenwald."

"I agree. You said crises, Garrett. Russia and Ukraine again?"

Garrett lit another Marlboro Light even though he knew Earl disliked his smoking habit.

"Yes, sir, only this time they're on the verge of war. Fox reported that both sides have massed troops on the border and that there have been 'shooting incidents.'"

"Oil?"

"Exactly. Russia's main export is oil, and the world market price is dropping again. Economists say Trotsky will be forced to devalue the ruble for the third time in twelve months. There is already rampant inflation in Russia, and another devaluation will make it worse. He's desperate to turn the attention of the Russian people away from their lowered standard of living to what he calls the 'threat' of Ukraine."

"How bad is it?"

"The situation needs but a small provocation to set off a full-scale war between the two countries."

"What do you suggest?"

"Sir, we have three objectives. The first is to raise the Foundation's prestige. This leads to the second, the timber contracts with Trotsky. The third is saving Trotsky from himself."

"What do you mean, 'saving Trotsky from himself?'"

Garrett laid out his plan. "In my opinion, neither Trotsky nor the Ukrainians want war. Trotsky wants a diversion and nothing more. Ukraine wants Ukraine and nothing more. Trotsky fears a short war in which the much–improved Ukrainian military just might throw him back and out of office. Ukraine fears a long war in which they win the initial battles but ultimately lose to the much larger Russian military machine. However, neither side can unilaterally back away without losing face.

"These conditions, sir, give you an enormous opportunity and a clear path to the objectives. You mediate behind the scenes by convincing both the Russians and Ukrainians to move their respective forces say, ten to twenty miles from the border. This is close enough to hit each other with artillery, missiles, and air attacks, but it's far enough to avoid border incidents between soldiers. The situation moves from the brink of war to the noise of shouting. It will be understood by both sides that, after the withdrawals, the Ukrainians can shout all they want about their national security against the Russian threat, and Trotsky can shout all he wants about the Ukrainian–NATO conspiracy to attack Russia.

"In the process, both sides become more indebted to you and the Foundation. Trotsky ends the stalemate on the timber negotiations, and Ukraine looks the other way when we push the rules in its commodities exchanges."

Earl rubbed his forehead in thought, and then said, "Let's do it. I'll meet with Trotsky in the Kremlin and the Ukrainian leaders in Kiev. Arrange the flight and call with Trotsky."

"I've already done both. The Foundation's jet is waiting for you at Reagan National. Trotsky expects your call when you get in the air. Do you plan to raise the timber contracts in that call?"

"No. Trotsky will raise them himself after we pray."

Again, Garrett admired Earl's coolness under pressure. He had just learned of his daughter's treachery and come face-to-face with a world crisis that could explode and cost the Foundation millions. In a few minutes, he had to wade into a board meeting where he might face tough questions, even confrontation, over these things. Yet, there he stood, smiling at the prospect of a successful mediation. There was no panic in Earl Thompson.

Earl said, "There's still Polly."

"Leave Polly and the Angels to me."

Earl reached for the door but stopped. "Garrett, you've done well."

"It's my job, sir."

Earl told Garrett he wasn't needed at the board meeting.

Garrett returned to his office and dialed. "Rose, there's an emergency. I'm on my way."

CHAPTER 9

Garrett walked south on Oakenwald Drive toward the Fallout Shelter. Oakenwald Campus was a sixty-acre complex in Alexandria, Virginia. It fronted on Garfield Boulevard to the north and Old Dominion Road to the south. Oakenwald Hall faced north. It had two ells, one on its east side and the other on its west. Each extended south. From the air, Oakenwald Hall looked like a squared U. The open part of the U faced south toward Old Dominion and the north side faced Garfield Boulevard. A concrete road, Oakenwald Drive, provided access from both Old Dominion and Garfield. The south part started at Old Dominion, looped around the east ell to the front of Oakenwald Hall, and from there bisected the front lawn to Garfield Boulevard. Oakenwald Drive also accessed the parking lot between the ells. Earl and Imogene Thompson lived in the carriage house attached to the west ell. The acreage south of the Hall boasted three basketball courts, two softball diamonds, one football field, a number of tennis courts, and a heated, Olympic-size swimming pool. All the campus was meticulously landscaped except for five acres of dense woods located in the southwest corner. In these woods was the Fallout Shelter.

Garrett was half Anglo, half Cuban, and a catholic. He'd grown up in Florida, attended the University of Miami, graduated *Magna Cum Laude* from the Georgetown Law School, and then joined a mid-sized Washington, D.C. law firm. A year later, he had moved to Oakenwald. Two years after that he left the law firm to work full-time as Earl Thompson's executive assistant. He had known Polly Thompson since she was fifteen. Earl had sent her to the Fallout Shelter to train under Louis and Rose Cardova, a husband and wife team. There, Polly had excelled in the martial arts and knife fighting. She'd gone on to carry out the Foundation's clandestine missions with skill and determination. Yet, her courage had a grim quality to it, as though it was a burden she didn't want, but was fated to carry. In spite of her perpetual smile, Polly was cold, unemotional, and furtive. All this had changed an hour before when Garrett saw a non-smiling, rebellious, and self-righteous Polly.

Polly's father was another matter. Earl had taught Polly to hide behind her smile. What was he hiding behind his? For Earl Thompson held secrets of his own, and he had just lied to Garrett about one. Polly was dead right about payoffs to Ponya. Bribery, with a little Jesus thrown in, formed the bedrock of the Foundation's bid for world power.

Garrett's law firm had a client named Good Earth LLC. Garrett knew only that it was a Delaware company and it controlled many offshore bank accounts, a few in the name of Good Earth and most in the names of other companies. Much cash flowed in and out of them. The firm's partners had assigned Garrett the job of laundering the money, although they never called it that. It had become routine. Several days a month Garrett would find a small satchel full of cash—usually containing no less than a half million dollars—under his desk. An hour later, he'd be on a plane to the Cayman Islands, the money well concealed. There, he'd deposit it in eight Foundation business front accounts and wire the funds from the Cayman accounts to Foundation accounts in Hong Kong, Switzerland, Africa, Asia, and South America. Others, whose identities were unknown to Garrett, moved the money to accounts in other countries. Along the way, the money was commingled, split apart, and then bounced around the world. Most of the money was invested in assets such as buildings in Tokyo or New York, farmland in the Amazon Basin, precious metals, stocks, bonds, commodities, and the like. Garrett noted that the cash he deposited always exceeded the amount spent on investments. The partners disclosed to Garrett neither the sources of the money nor dispositions of the excess cash.

He had learned the truth shortly after joining the Foundation. On a hunch, he had entered special search commands that uncovered invisible Good Earth files on the Foundation's computer network. These contained names of Foundation members, the amounts of money paid in by them, the companies that fronted for them, and descriptions of the assets held by each company. Another column disclosed the gains or losses when those assets were sold. The Good Earth files linked to other files that uncovered the excess cash and its disposition to members of governments around the world, the amounts and dates of the moneys paid, and the purpose of each payment. The bribes ranged from paying off Chinese stock regulators to look the other way when Foundation members manipulated its exchange markets, to enriching a US Attorney to dismiss a felony charge for 'lack of evidence,' to funding Ponya's persecution of homosexuals by 'reimbursing expenses' of legislators who voted on the laws. The Foundation had granted five hundred thousand dollars to Ponya.

Garrett had fled his firm only to learn that he had escaped neither criminality nor the clutches of a machiavellian employer.

In less than ten hours, Earl would pray to Jesus with Trotsky in the Kremlin. That much was both true and farcical. The real prayer was the briefcase of cash in an amount north of one million dollars Earl would find on the plane and hand to Trotsky. No doubt Trotsky would see both the wisdom of nailing down the first of the timber contracts for the Siberian Project and pulling back from the Ukrainian border.

It paid to pay.

Earl Thompson knew Garrett had uncovered the Foundation's briberies. Of this much Garrett was certain. However, in the grandest of arrogances coupled with diabolical talents for duplicity and euphemism, Earl demanded that Garrett accept the lie as truth—except when it wasn't the truth—and, either way, to content himself with the built-in safety of the Jesus Equation. In the murky world of the Foundation, the Jesus Equation denied neither the bribery and money laundering nor the crimes for engaging in them. It simply made them irrelevant. Polly's real sin in Earl's eyes was not so much mutiny, but her brazen appropriation and bastardization of the Jesus Equation to assign the troubling notions of right and wrong to bribery.

Six months before, Earl had tapped Garrett to succeed him as the Foundation's executive director. Earl mentored Garrett as a loving father would a son. Outwardly, Garrett accepted Earl's friendship, confidences, and training. Inwardly, he'd grown uneasy. For it was Earl Thompson, of all people, who had spotted Garrett's homosexuality. Garrett thought he had hidden it. He had made no advances to anyone at Oakenwald, and he had been careful to meet his lovers in out-of-the-way hotels or, if they were not married, in their homes. He showered alone and averted his eyes when others entered and dropped their towels. So Garrett was shocked when Earl brought it up shortly after beginning Garrett's training. Garrett was more shocked when Earl, instead of throwing him out of Oakenwald, sent him to a clinic in Minnesota that specialized in curing homosexuals of their curse. Garrett had undergone the clinic's intense thirty-day rehabilitation program. He returned twice a year for three-day maintenance rehabs.

Garrett told Earl that the treatments had worked. Earl congratulated Garrett with a bear hug and assured him that his secret would remain between them.

But therein lay the start of Garrett's anxieties.

First, there were two secrets—the one between Earl and Garrett regarding Garrett's homosexuality and its cure, and the one between Earl and somebody else regarding Earl's discovery of it. No doubt Earl held the two secrets in counterpoint to each other, and, when it suited him, would use them to blackmail or expose Garrett. After all, had not Earl used his own daughter as a means to his ends? Had not he lamented her rebellion, not in the light of tender parental concern for a wayward child, but as a lost asset 'designed' by him?

Second, Earl rarely allowed Garrett to attend a board meeting. It was a strange dynamic. Garrett's appointment as Earl's successor required the board's approval and his success in the office entailed its support. His legal protection demanded its shield, for it was the board that supplied the Foundation's legal cover. Each of the nine board members had been carefully vetted and each held or had held a powerful position in government or business. Among the members were the Assistant Deputy Secretary of Emergency Communications of Homeland Security, the Director of the Executive Office for US Attorneys, the Director of Political & Military Affairs in the US State Department, the former Attorney General of New York, the former commander of the Texas Air National Guard, and the CEO of a Fortune 100 company.

Earl Thompson embraced secular law enforcement so long as said enforcement commended the Foundation and condemned the Foundation's enemies.

Third, three weeks before, Earl had prevailed on Lincoln Kincaid's presidential campaign organization, Kincaid For America, or KFA, to name Garrett as Campaign Manager. However, this only elevated Garrett's anxiety. Earl Thompson remained the unofficial *de facto* campaign manager who retained all the power and ran the campaign while Garrett, the official *de jure* campaign manager, had little power and practically nothing to do. Earl Thompson played this cozy arrangement like others between them—he set up Garrett to take the fall for his wrongdoing.

In all this, Garrett, of course, recognized that money laundering is a felony and that he had engaged in it dozens of times. 'My bosses made me do it' was not a defense for the accused. It was not unknown for partners in an unscrupulous law firm to assign unlawful tasks to a new and green associate. In the face of criminal prosecution, the partners could feign their own ignorance and simply allow the associate to take the fall. Garrett would face prosecution, conviction, prison, disbarment, and disgrace, and even perhaps be made to disappear by the firm's partners and the clients for whom he had rendered the services. A dead lawyer tells no lawyer tales.

At times like this, Garrett saw himself fated for some eerie and preternatural doom ordained and set into motion by Earl Thompson.

Secrets go both ways, however. Garrett had his own secrets and took glee in hiding them from Earl. Garrett had worked hard at the clinic because, he told them, he 'wanted to be straight.' In truth, he had been acting. Garrett had met a new lover before Earl sent him to Minnesota. The man was intelligent, sensitive, and, like Garrett, sometimes liked it rough. However, the man's prominence demanded discretion, so their trysts were fewer than either desired.

Garrett partly contented himself with the insurance he had built against criminal charges for committing crimes at the behest of the partners or Earl Thompson. First, he had written at least one invoice and one receipt for each transfer into the Cayman accounts as proof that the accounts and money belonged to legitimate businesses that were doing what businesses do—buy labor and materials, and produce and sell products. Second, at least once a week, he downloaded the Good Earth computer files onto flash drives. Third, he took advantage of the muddling inherent in money laundering to set aside, in small sums over time, about $250,000.00 of cash for himself.

He stored the invoices, receipts, and flash drives in safety deposit boxes, and deposited the money under false names in a maze of small banks in the Dakotas and Canada. If there ever was an investigation, he would buy time with the false paper trail. If Earl Thompson turned on him, Garrett would blackmail him with the flash drives. If Garrett needed or wanted to vanish, the cash would take him anywhere in the world and help him establish a new identity. This last precaution could give him life, literally. It was not written down and no one ever spoke of it, but it was there. You can join the Foundation and you can become a valuable asset for the Foundation, but the minute you leave it you are at best a neutral, more likely a liability, and probably in their crosshairs.

These were only parts of Garrett's exit strategy from the Foundation. By far the largest part, and that which would trigger Garrett's safest getaway, was the election of Lincoln Kincaid as President of the United States.

CHAPTER 10

Rose and Louis Cardova had an unhappy marriage. Both were overweight. Both smoked. Both drank heavily. On occasion, their fights brought the police. Twice, their daughter, Katie, had been taken from them. Sometimes there was an arrest. One such arrest brought them to the law firm of Garrett Jennings. Garrett's high-powered law firm defended white-collar criminals with deep pockets but snubbed its nose at trash mired in domestic disputes with no pockets. The Cardova's case was different because their cocaine business had generated the high retainer demanded by the firm. The State of Virginia charged Louis with domestic battery. It charged both Louis and Rose with possession of cocaine with intent to distribute and with neglect of a child. Louis spent several days in jail for the battery. Neither spent a minute in jail on the cocaine or neglect charges. The Foundation's legal cover motivated the prosecutor to drop the charges.

Garrett referred Louis and Rose to Earl Thompson. Earl prayed with them, bought them a gym membership, and asked them to come back in six months. When they returned they were changed people. They no longer smoked or drank alcohol. They'd changed their eating habits, lost weight, gained muscle and endurance, and learned the ways of Tae Kwon Do, knife fighting, and weaponry. Earl hired them to train young men and women destined for special roles within the Foundation. He expanded the Fallout Shelter to include a gym, a jail, and living quarters for the Cardovas.

They were in their early forties and in love, and doted on Katie, who was now at Bob Jones University.

Rose Cardova met Garrett at the Fallout Shelter side door and led him down several levels where they met with her husband. Louis, an inch shorter than Rose, sported a shaved head and a ponytail. Rose wore her naturally blond hair short.

Louis showed Garrett to a table. Garrett wasted no time on perfunctory greetings or small talk.

"Polly Thompson, and what she now calls her 'Angels,' have mutinied."

Rose asked, "What do you want from us?"

"A new group to counter Polly and her Angels."

Louis asked, "Why us? We don't go into the field. We train others to do so."

"That is no longer true," said Garrett.

"Then we'll talk to Earl himself."

"Go ahead. However, he'll speak to you as I will. Those cocaine charges can be resurrected."

Rose asked, "Code name?"

"Archangels."

CHAPTER 11

Polly, on the far left of the blackjack table, held at eighteen. Johnnie Christiansen, on the far right, split on two queens. The dealer, George Todrank, stood pat at nineteen and dealt a ten to one of Johnnie's queens and an ace to the other. Polly had lost but watched Johnnie pull in another five hundred dollars in chips, adding to the couple of thousand he'd already won. The assignment—or more accurately, for Johnnie, assignation—had nothing to do with his blackjack genius and the winnings it produced. Johnnie would have been just as cheerful had he been losing, instead of winning twenty-five hundred dollars. Polly had coached Johnnie in the art of tipping the dealer who dealt him winning hands. However, George's smile at Johnnie was motivated by prospects beyond Johnnie's generous tips.

Johnnie was relaxed and happy, and his eyes had begun to take on that peculiar glow when he approached the climax of an assignment—the saving of another soul.

Polly always researched her mission targets in detail, and she'd done so with George Todrank. Todrank had served under Lincoln Kincaid at the Tigris River Prisoner-of-War Camp in Baghdad. He'd grown up in the Bronx, done poorly in school, and run away several times. As a juvenile, he was arrested for car theft and possession of a stolen gun. The judge gave him a choice between adult prison and joining the service. George chose the latter. He was court-martialed for assaulting two male soldiers, but the charges were dropped when they refused to testify. His nearest relatives, his mother and a sister, still lived in the Bronx. Six months before, he'd gotten a road rage ticket for breaking the windshield of a woman who'd cut in front of him in traffic. He paid the fine but the Nevada Gaming Commission had placed George and his dealer license on probation, the step before suspension.

George was in his later thirties, mostly bald, of medium height, and beer-bellied. He publicly berated cocktail servers if he felt they were too slow in delivering drinks to his players. His strengths were his ability to size up gamblers and charm those most likely to tip him. His weakness was his bestial sexual appetite for young men, and this explained his friendly, help-ful, and empathetic behavior toward Johnnie and Polly. He was attracted to Johnnie and he knew he had to be nice to get him.

Polly and Johnnie, as 'brother and sister,' had arrived at the Las Vegas Hilton on Paradise Road the day before. That afternoon, Johnnie stayed in their room while Polly played blackjack at George's table and tipped him generously. George's shift ended and she had met him in the Lively Tempo Lounge. Polly introduced herself and said that she and her brother, Johnnie, were on their first trip to Vegas, that Johnnie was underage at nineteen, and asked if George could get a fake ID for Johnnie.

"No," he had replied.

"Do you know someone who can?"

"No."

"Well, I heard from friends that there're certain people in Vegas who provide false IDs," said Polly.

"I don't know nothin' 'bout that."

"I'm not from the gaming commission, Mr. Todrank. I'm not a cop."

"Don't matter. I don't trust…" George stopped to stare at a tall, blond, young man in the entranceway.

Polly said, "Johnnie, come in for a minute and meet our dealer."

George rose, "I'm very glad to meet you, Johnnie."

"Thank you, sir."

"Ms. Thompson, maybe I can help Johnnie." Within the hour, George had arranged fake identification for Johnnie and invited Polly and Johnnie to dinner in his suite on the eleventh floor. They declined, but Polly knew by the lecherous look in George's eyes that he was on their hook.

After the next day at George's table, Polly accepted another dinner invitation from George. She and Johnnie arrived at his suite just as dinner was being delivered.

George chewed a large chunk of Porterhouse steak and washed it down with a Black Russian. Polly fixed him another.

"I grew up in the Bronx. Where are you two from?"

Polly said, "Indianapolis."

"Well, I'll be damned. I know your governor personally. Lincoln Kincaid... served under him at Tigris River. I'll have me a friend in the White House. Whaddya think a' that, Johnnie?"

"Great."

"Goddamn it, Johnnie, it's more than great. It's fantastic. I'm a personal friend of the next President of the United States."

"Fantastic," said Johnnie.

"We Tigris River Cradlers gotta stay close."

"What are 'Cradlers?'" Johnnie asked.

"It's kinda hard to explain. I'll get to that later. However, I'm gonna tell you somethin' and don't you forget it. We showed those shit-smelly-sand-nigger-turban-heads who was in charge at Tigris. Then some bleedin' heart bastard snitched. They shoulda given a medal to that skinny woman—waz her name? Georgina? Yeah, named like me, George. She had the leash 'roun that greasy bastard's neck. Then some asshole talked. Goddamn press blew it up."

George wrapped his hand around Johnnie's bicep. "Whaddya say, Johnnie-boy. A little fun with those greasy-heads never hurt nobody."

Johnnie blushed.

Polly finished her meal and said she didn't feel like partying. She went to her and Johnnie's room and pulled the .357 Sig and the knife that she'd hidden in her suitcase. She loaded the gun, attached a silencer, and took the stairwell to the eleventh floor. She hid behind the soft drink machine in the ice and snacks room and waited for Johnnie. Five minutes later, she heard a door open and Johnnie calling to George that he'd be back with the ice in a minute. Johnnie whistled the first two bars to "Goodnight Irene," their prearranged signal that all was clear. She

gave the gun to Johnnie, slipped the knife under the shirtsleeve cover-
ing her forearm, and they entered George's suite. Polly shut the door
behind them. Johnnie stopped and she stepped around him. George had
stripped down to his large boxer shorts and was lying on the bed. Pillows
propped his head and shoulders, and his large belly lay over the top of
his boxers. Polly saw his pig-like eyes narrow. She strode to George and
shoved the knife up under his rib cage. George screamed. He was frantic
to pull the knife out until Johnnie shot him in the shoulder. George tried
to scream again, but the knife in his belly reduced him to puffing noises
and whispering.

"What the... what the fug... 'r you doin? Polly? Johnnie?"

Polly said, "We must cleanse your soul, George."

"My soul? Cleanse?"

"You shall die in a few minutes, George."

"Die? No! Stop! Both of you... fuckin' insane."

Polly crossed her arms. "No cursing, George. Accept your death."

George stammered. His face cried but there were no tears. "I'm only thirty-nine. It's because I'm a homo... sexual. Right? I'll change... get treated."

Polly said, "It's not your homosexuality, George."

"Then… what is it? I can… fix it."

"You can't fix it because it's already happened. You raped young men at
Tigris River. You are a Cradler. For this you must die."

Johnnie said, "We must cleanse your soul. Pray with me, George."
Johnnie began, "Our Father, who art in heaven, hallowed be thy—"

"Stop! We're... friends, Johnnie... got… you fake ID." George coughed
up blood and moaned.

"Johnnie is the best friend you will ever have," said Polly. "You will
meet God if you pray with Johnnie. You will meet Satan if you do not.
Johnnie, start over."

By this time, George's lungs were filling with blood faster than he could
cough it up. In between gurgles, he tried to mouth the words of the prayer
with Johnnie. These he punctuated with wild-eyed, gurgled pleas for his life.
By now, Johnnie was crying with him. When they finished, Johnnie said,
"George, tell God that you're sorry for your sins."

George puffed blood bubbles.

Johnnie pointed the .357 at George's head and shot. Then Johnnie wet his finger on his lips and made the sign of the cross on George's forehead right above his right eyebrow.

Polly and Johnnie turned to leave but stopped when they heard the door-knob turning. Polly took Johnnie's hand and led him to the other side of the suite. She switched off the light and they crouched down in the darkness behind a couch. The door opened and a man entered the room. He closed and locked the door behind him. He was a medium-sized, swarthy-looking Hispanic dressed in dark, ill-fitting, worn, and tattered clothes. His un-washed hair hung nearly to the base of his neck and his beard looked several weeks old. He reminded Polly of the hoboes she'd seen in history books of the Great Depression in the 1930s.

The man held a knife in front of him. His back waistband secured a pistol.

Johnnie whispered to Polly, "That's the man..."

Polly clamped her hand over Johnnie's mouth and gave him a stern look before turning back to the Hispanic. He bent his knees and then, almost duck walking, made his way to Todrank's bed. He stopped, looked over the bed, and then stood up. Polly saw the surprise on his face.

He stared at Todrank's body for what seemed like minutes and then softly spoke to it, "Some sonofabitch got you before I could. Burn in hell you butt-fucking bastard."

When he turned to leave, Polly took the gun from Johnnie. "Stop." The man dropped his knife and turned to face the voice while reaching for his gun. Polly raised the .357 and the man froze.

"Place your hands on your head." Polly walked to within ten feet of him. "Turn around very slowly. Yes, that's it. Now, with your left hand, remove the gun from your back and pitch it behind you toward me." Polly picked up his gun. "Turn around."

"What do you...?"

"Never mind us. You came to murder Mr. Todrank, didn't you? Tell the truth."

"Just let me go and I promise you won't see or hear from me again."

Polly ignored the man's promise. "You cursed the person who killed Mr. Todrank before you could."

"Who are you? What do you want?"

Polly said, "We are your friends, and we killed Todrank."

"Why?"

"Because he was a Cradler," said Polly.

"He was."

Polly lowered the .357.

"We know that Borgmann and Todrank repeatedly raped young soldiers, including you and your friend, Jameel Shalih, at the Tigris River Prisoner-of-War Camp in Baghdad. The army court-martialed both of you and sent you to Camp Morgan. But it turned out you and Mr. Shalih hadn't escaped either Borgmann or Todrank. Borgmann became the commandant of Camp Morgan, gathered you into his clutches, and picked up where he'd left off at Tigris River. At times, he invited his good friend, George Todrank, to join in the fun.

"Am I right?"

"Yeah."

Polly ordered Johnnie to come out of the shadows and stand beside her.

"Wait! It was you two who rescued me."

"Yes. My name is Polly Thompson and this is Johnnie Christiansen. We are Angels."

"My name is—"

"Jayden Ramirez," said Polly.

***

Early the next morning, before the others woke, Polly left the room and shopped. She returned with a blonde toupee, fake glasses, and an Armani suit. When he left the room, Ramirez had blonde hair, was dressed in an expensive suit, and carried his 'reading glasses' in his top pocket.

Polly said, "You are now a wealthy businessperson."

They flew nonstop to Louisville. On the drive from Louisville to Dubain, Ramirez asked, "How did you know that I would try to escape right after an earthquake? I didn't even know until I made a run for it."

Polly smiled. "We had been watching Camp Morgan and Borgmann. That's all I will say for now."

"They accused me of killing that guard with his own gun. But I didn't."

"We know that."

"Then who did?"

"Borgmann. He wrestled the guard's gun from him and shot him in the chest. Then he hid the gun. When the others caught up, Borgmann told them that he saw you kill the guard and that you had his gun."

"You two saved my life."

Johnnie smiled.

Ramirez asked, "Did he suffer?"

Polly had anticipated this question and knew it wasn't about the dead guard.

"Yes, Todrank suffered."

"Good."

CHAPTER 12

Garrett Jennings waited until the young women servers cleared the table, refilled glasses, and closed the door behind them.

He laid a Bible on the table in front of him. Opposite Garrett, at the other end of the dinner table, was Earl Thompson. Seated along the sides of the table were thirteen young men. They all lived at Oakenwald, all were from affluent families, and all had just finished dinner in one of Oakenwald's private dining rooms. Garrett caught Earl's nod. He handed the Bible to the resident on his right. That person passed the Bible to the person directly opposite him on the other side of the table. That person handed the Bible to the next resident across the table from him, and so on. In this way, each resident touched the Bible before it reached Earl.

Earl opened the Bible to Romans 13. "'There is no authority except from God, and those authorities that exist have been instituted by God.' What do you make of Romans 13, Carl?"

Carl had graduated from the Divinity School at Bob Jones University. "First, only God has authority. Second, God delegates part of His authority to leaders on earth. Third, only God can choose those leaders."

"George, can you name some?"

"President Joseph Trotsky of Russia, Prime Minister Ponya of the Congo, and President Sun-Yat of China come to mind."

"But, George, Trotsky exiles his political opponents to Siberian concentration camps above the Arctic Circle and hobnobs with the Russian mafia. Prime Minister Ponya imprisons or kills people he suspects are working against him. President Sun-Yat shot hundreds of pro-democracy demonstrators in Tiananmen Square. How can you apply Romans 13 and conclude that these men are chosen by God? It seems to me He'd choose someone else."

No one responded.

"Let's put this into a different context. This is a story about a man. He is the leader of a great nation. However, this is not enough for this man. He sends huge armies to defeat his enemies and then he massacres their soldiers. Still this is not enough for this man. He orders his soldiers to kill their women and children. Yet, he wants even more. So he hands the enemy's virgin women to his soldiers as prizes of war and tells them they can rape and torture and kill them as they please.

"What do you think of this man, Jacob?"

"He is evil."

"Was he chosen by God?"

"I don't think God would have chosen such a man."

Earl asked, "Who agrees with Jacob?" All except Garrett raised their hands. "And you are wrong. This is not a story. It's about a real person—Moses. Yes, Moses plundered and murdered. Did God punish Moses for these things? No. Moses carried out God's will. He led God's people out of slavery just as God commanded. We do not judge Moses. Why? Because Romans 13 tells us that God had chosen Moses and we are not to question God's choice."

Earl smiled at Jacob. "Don't worry, Jacob. Nobody gets the answer right the first time." There was laughter around the table. "But I'll give you a chance to redeem yourself. What would you say to Moses if there was a 'poof' and he appeared in this room right now? Do you say, 'Hey there, Moses, you rape and pillage and murder, but don't worry, God thinks you're a swell guy and so do we.' Would you say that?"

Jacob closed his eyes and held his fist against his forehead. Then he opened his eyes and lowered his fist to the table. "No! I'd say 'Moses, thank you for doing God's will,' and that's all I would say."

"C'mon, Jacob. You'd actually thank the murderer who's standing here and smelling up the whole room?"

"God chose Moses," Jacob replied. "What happens after that is between God and him."

Earl bore into Jacob's eyes, and then said, "Jacob, you are exactly right." There was laughter and some clapping. Earl laid the Bible down.

"Let's bring it alive. You are Moses. You've been lucky. You were born into slavery at a time when the Pharaoh ordered that all newborn male Hebrews be put to death. Your mother hid you along the Nile River. The Pharaoh's sister found you and raised you in the royal household as a prince. Servants wait on you. They serve you the best food and drink. They hand you the most beautiful women for your sensual pleasure.

"However, the slavery of your family and people doesn't sit well with you. One day you see a master beat a slave. You've seen this many times, but this time your temper gets the best of you and you kill the master. You flee to a place called Midian. One night God appears to you in a dream and commands you to free the Israelites from the Pharaoh. You do not want to do it. Midian is almost as good as the Pharaoh's house. 'Why,' you ask God, 'must I throw all this away, return to Egypt where I'm a marked man, and somehow free my people? Choose somebody else.' God says, 'But I have chosen you.'

"'But, but, but...' you sputter. God says, 'You shall do as I command. You shall go back and hide amidst your people as a slave.' And so you do. However, the slave life is damnable. You struggle in the rock quarry and you're always tired. You don't get enough to eat and you're always hungry. Your water is infested with filth and you're always thirsty. Time passes, and you think *God wasn't really serious, so I'll just sneak back to Midian.* That night, you roll and toss because it's hot and sweaty, and the mosquitoes are biting and you itch, and your mom's snoring is atrocious. But God has read your thoughts. He comes to you and says, 'I am the Lord Thy God. You shall remain here and carry out my commands.'

"You reply, 'But God, I know nothing of plotting and leading slaves into revolt.' God says, 'I will guide you. Aaron, Joshua, Caleb, and your mother will help you.' You say, 'But God, Aaron is an idiot who thinks he can turn rods into snakes. Joshua goes around and blows a horn all day. Everybody but me hates Caleb because he's a thief and all-round scoundrel. My mother is insane.' God says, 'Have faith. They shall rise with you, and be at your side, for I have chosen them as I have chosen you.'

"You get a little mouthy and say, 'Good luck with that, God.' God likes you so he lets this pass."

The residents laughed.

"You know the rest of the story. It happens just like God said it would. Just think of it! Moses, a lazy and pampered prince, and those ignorant misfit slaves—Aaron, Caleb, Joshua, and Jochebed—plot the escape, stare down the Pharaoh with the ten plagues, and make good their getaway.

"How did they do this?" Earl paused. "They had something that no one else had. What?"

Jacob said, "A covenant."

"Which arises out of…?"

"The Jesus Equation."

"Right. Let's review. A covenant binds a small number of people to each other and they achieve great things. Just look at what Moses' group did with their covenant. We have some modern examples. Mao Zedong went to his illiterate cabal of followers and said 'we must free China,' and they said 'we're in,' and they hiked over five thousand miles and freed China. Mussolini gathered his black shirts and told them 'we must march on Rome, throw out the inept government of democracy, put ourselves into power, and save Italy,' and they did. Hitler, Goering, Goebbels, and Himmler got together, made a covenant, and came close to conquering the world.

"Moses abides in our collective consciousness. This is not worthy of him, of us, or of God. We must raise Moses above the collective to the personal. Moses shall revisit.

"You cannot prepare for it. Do not even try."

Garrett said, "Let's say we light up the courts and play some hoops."

CHAPTER 13

Andy lay on his couch, a glass of Jack Daniels in his hand. The decision was gut-wrenching—either watch Rhonda's nationally televised interview of Indiana Governor Lincoln Kincaid, or don't. He sipped the drink and decided to let Jack choose. It would either make him too drunk to watch, or too mellow not to.

Well-meaning people urged him to forget about Rhonda O'Malley and get on with his life. None of them understood the paradox. A man cannot push someone out of his mind when the mere attempt to do so demands that he conjure up that someone.

The front door opened and his brother, Clubby, still in his police uniform, walked in.

Clubby asked, "Do you plan to watch Rhonda?"

"Me and Jack haven't decided yet."

"Let's decide now. Come on down to the Schnitzelbank and watch her with the rest of us."

"I don't know."

"You can take Jack with you."

"In your cop car?"

"We make the rules. We can break them. Just don't spill any."

Andy and Jack hitched a ride with Clubby.

Andy took his usual seat on the corner stool in the Schnitzelbank barroom. Beside Andy, moving down the bar, were the Beech Tree Boys: Clubby, Stump, Billups, and Peachfuzz.

Kim Seaton, the Schnitzelbank's head bartender, served Andy a boiler-maker—a beer with a shot of Jack Daniels in it.

The Beech Tree Boys took their places in front of the bar. The crowd quieted. Peachfuzz closed his eyes, bowed his head, and lowered his hands as if in prayer. For a few seconds he moved his lips but made no sound. Then he asked Stump if he could hear it.

"Hear what?"

"My grandma."

Stump said, "Your grandma's been dead over twenty years. I did her obit."

"She knows that. But her spirit's here and she says you gotta buy me an Irish beer so Rhonda does good. She says Guinness Extra Stout. She also says—"

"To buy Guinnesses for me and Clubby, too," Billups interjected.

Peachfuzz said, "Yeah, she did. How'd you know that, Billups?"

"Me and Clubby been listening in on you and your grandma."

Stump said, "Clubby can't drink. He's in uniform."

"There ain't no law against it."

"I know that, but a cop drinking in uniform just goes against my morals."

"The same morals you had with Josie?" asked Clubby.

"Leave Josie out of this," said Stump. "And Peachfuzz, tell your grandma to buy the beers for you yahoos."

"I'll try, but she won't like it."

Peachfuzz, Clubby, and Billups folded their hands and bowed their heads. Peachfuzz talked to his grandma in muttered gibberish and then raised his head.

"Grandma says she can't buy us beers cuz there ain't no money in heaven."

"Well, that's just too—"

"Wait! She's saying something else. What is it, Grandma?" Peachfuzz muttered, and then raised his head. "Stump, Grandma says she didn't like the obituary you wrote on her. She says you lied."

Stump responded, "About what?"

Billups started humming the melody to "Amazing Grace."

"She says you called her a prostitute when you wrote that she was a 'Grand lady of Dubain.'"

Stump said, "Tell her I apologize. Prostitutes charge. Your grandma didn't."

Billups sang in a low undertone, "…how sweet the sound, that saved a wretch like Stump…"

Stump pointed, "Billups, you're the only wretch what needs saving."

Clubby said, "I'll arrest your ass if you don't watch it, Stump."

"For what?"

"Littering. Your newspaper's trash."

Clubby took over "Amazing Grace" from Billups.

Peachfuzz asked, "How ya doin' with the ladies now, Stump?"

Stump said, "How many times I gotta tell you jackasses a gentleman don't—"

"Kiss and tell," the other three Beeches chimed in a minor chord.

Clubby said, "Stump don't tell cuz his last girlfriend was good ol' Senator Josie. Hey, Stump, think she'll be watching Rhonda and the governor tonight?"

"Course! Told me this afternoon she'd be glued to her TV. Now listen up you yahoos," said Stump. "We gotta give Rhonda positive energy."

Stump pitch-piped the lead note. The others took theirs on key. Stump raised his right hand, index finger pointed, and then dipped his arm. The four voices jazz-hummed into the chorus of "My Wild Irish Rose." "…*the sweetest flower that grows. You can search everywhere, but none can compare…*" They sang two verses and three choruses. The Beech Trees took in the applause and formally bowed.

Kim whistled and pointed at the monitors.

Andy guzzled the boilermaker and ordered another.

CHAPTER 14

Rhonda O'Malley and Indiana Governor Lincoln Pennington Kincaid faced each other in straight back chairs. Rhonda wore a blue skirt that hung below her knees, a white blouse, and a pink jacket. Kincaid wore a blue business suit, white shirt, and red tie. Between them was a small table with a pitcher of water and two glasses.

"Governor Kincaid," Rhonda started, "you're basing a large part of your campaign for the presidency on your record as a two-term governor of Indiana. Why?"

"Because I can. When I became governor, I made it clear that I would not be shackled by Indiana's history of conservatism... that I would move Indiana forward no matter what. And I did."

"How, Governor?"

"I'm a creative person who is well-grounded in common sense. I surround myself with like-minded people. It pays off. Our teachers told us that 'Indiana is the crossroads of America.' It turns out that our teachers were right. We took a careful look at the state's infrastructure and, after much thought and planning, we built more interstates, upgraded our crumbling railway system, started Indiana's high-speed rail program, improved existing airports, and built more. Today, Indiana is fast becoming the 'Hub of Commerce' for America."

"Governor, your school initiatives have gained national attention and, in most cases, national acclaim. Do you intend to impose your Indiana model on the rest of the country if you are elected president?"

"No one school program can fit a country as complicated and diverse as America. However, know this—schools are about resources, standards, teachers, students, and parents… nothing else. We stopped the private school vouchers and put that money back into public schools. We started year-round school. We raised scholastic standards and made it clear that students are in school to learn and teachers are in school to teach. The results are there. Indiana's test scores steadily rise, and the number of math and science students has increased by fifteen percent."

"Governor, you often use the phrase 'stewardship of earth.' Why?"

"Our world is a gift from God. It is also fragile. I believe every generation has a God-given duty to make sure that the world is a better place when they leave it than when they came into it. I can sum it up. We have not inherited earth from our ancestors. We have borrowed it from our children."

"Soaring rhetoric, Governor."

"Maybe so, but words count. Wouldn't you agree?"

"I ask the questions here!"

They both laughed.

"Let's turn to the international scene. How can the US handle the crisis that is brewing between China and Russia?"

"We cannot sit on the sidelines. China has long had its eye on Russian Siberia and is building a twenty-million-man army along its border with Russia in order to get it. President Trotsky has made it clear that Russia will use nuclear weapons against China if it invades. China says it will retaliate with its own. We cannot allow any of this to happen."

Rhonda said, "President Harding is running for reelection. Senator Josie Carter Lodge is leading the charge in the Republican Party to defeat Harding in the primaries. What do you say to Senator Lodge?"

"I won't speculate on the Republican nominee, and I cannot speak for Senator Carter Lodge. I know her, and I can say that she is a decent and intelligent person. But, she is, and will remain, a Republican. She can neither run nor hide from that. She will have to answer for her party."

"President Harding has accused you, and I quote, 'Lincoln Kincaid is a wild-eyed liberal whose secret goal is world government.' Do you support world government?"

"Sarah Harding has little credibility, if any at all. I do not support world government. I support world cooperation."

"How would a Kincaid administration deal with Russia's threat to Ukraine?"

"We cannot tolerate Russian expansion into Europe any more than Chinese expansion into Russia. Sarah Harding has squandered any goodwill that existed between China and the United States. Instead, she has stumbled into the Eastern European crisis with Russia."

"What will you say to President Trotsky of Russia?"

"I am not president, Rhonda, and I cannot engage in hypotheticals. But I believe I can voice the feelings of a strong majority of Americans who would say, 'President Trotsky, there is a line, and you must not cross it, and if you do you will be eyeball-to-eyeball with NATO and, by extension, the United States.'"

"Are you threatening war?"

"No. An American president does not threaten. He states facts. So, I want to be very clear on this—a president's first job is to protect the American people. I will not hesitate to order military action when it is necessary to do so."

"Let's turn to the political scene. You have strong support from the Democratic Party and social conservatives. This coalition has been unheard of until now. How will you hold it together?"

"I have asked the Democratic Party for its nomination and I am working hard to be worthy of it. If the Democratic Party sees fit to so honor me, I intend to lead it to victory in November."

"You poll much higher with women than with men. Is this because of your good looks?"

Kincaid laughed. "I'll let the voters be the judge of that."

"Good answer."

"Thank you, Rhonda."

Rhonda poured two glasses of water, offered one to the governor, and drank from hers. She set the glass down and, for a few seconds, stared into the governor's eyes.

"Governor Kincaid, did you live at a place in Arlington, Virginia, called Oakenwald?"

Kincaid's smile faded, and then came back. "Yes. It was during my first assignment at the Pentagon and before Marian and I married. I lived at Oakenwald because the rent, room, and board were cheap."

"However, there's more to Oakenwald than rent, isn't there, Governor?"

"I don't understand your question."

"You lived at Oakenwald for four years. Certainly you knew that it's owned by an organization that calls itself, simply, the Foundation."

"Rhonda, I didn't do a background investigation on Oakenwald before I moved in."

"What do you know about the Foundation?"

"I know almost nothing about it."

"Let me refresh your memory. The Foundation has been described as a group of wealthy and powerful men—members of the present and former administrations, high-ranking military men, senators, congressmen, prosperous businessmen, and well-known clergy from the megachurches. They operate behind the scenes while using the name of Jesus Christ to gain world influence and, along the way, grow even wealthier. Their membership is—"

"Rhonda, what is your question?"

"Are you a member of the Foundation?"

"I most certainly am not!"

"Do you agree with the Foundation?"

"Of course not, Rhonda! You know me better than that."

"Then why are you running your campaign from the east ell of Oakenwald Hall, the very center of the Foundation and the place where you lived for four years?"

"Kincaid For America is only renting space from Oakenwald."

"There are other places to rent. Why Oakenwald?"

Kincaid smiled. "I suppose I have to ask my campaign people about that. Let's move on, Rhonda."

"I shall. In 2003, you commanded the 800th Battalion Military Police that ran the infamous Tigris River Prison in Baghdad. Prisoners were tortured, sodomized, and humiliated. Some even died. American soldiers raped other American soldiers. You've maintained that you had no knowledge of these things. However, many ask, how could you, as commander, not know?"

"I was fully exonerated of dereliction of duty at Tigris."

"So you were, but via an army investigation that many believe was white-washed to protect the officers… you included."

"Rhonda, you have been misinformed."

"Am I misinformed about the Congo?"

"The Congo?"

"When you were in Congress, you were the ranking Democrat on the House Foreign Affairs subcommittee for Africa. The Congo was wracked by civil war. It was no secret that the forces of the government, under Prime Minister Joseph Ponya, had committed atrocities, including rape, torture, and mass murder, against villagers suspected of sympathy with the rebels. The United States had limited its involvement to humanitarian aid. However, you got to know Mr. Ponya."

"I met with many leaders of African nations. It was my job."

"Was it also your job to invite Ponya to the National Prayer Breakfast sponsored by the Foundation?"

"I recall that he prayed at one of the breakfasts."

"To God?"

"Of course he prayed to God. Who else do you pray to?"

"In Ponya's case, it was to you and members of your subcommittee."

"This is getting way out of line, Rhonda. Let's move on to—"

"To the private, off-the-record meeting between Ponya, you, and the members of the subcommittee who supported him. The meeting took place at Oakenwald right after the prayer breakfast."

"The subcommittee met with many leaders from Africa in many different places."

"How hard did Ponya pray?"

"I don't understand where you are going with this."

"I think you do, Governor. Ponya drank his tea, ate his breakfast roll, listened to the speaker, and prayed like the dickens. Six months later his prayers were answered, not by God or Jesus or Allah, but by you. Did Ponya's prayers have anything to do with the half-billion dollar military aid package that you pushed through Congress?"

"I did push it through and I stand by it. The Congo civil war had to come to an end because it was spreading to other African nations. Prime Minister Ponya did, in fact, end the war."

"I did my job, Rhonda."

"However, part of the military aid to Ponya included artillery."

"Of course it did."

"Ponya put down the rebellion as you said, but in the process he got even more blood on his hands. He designated a safe area for several hundred thousand people displaced by the fighting but whose loyalties were unclear. He waited until the people moved into the safe area, and then massacred them with a barrage of artillery you had given him. Ponya said the bombardment was an accident. The survivors say he's lying."

"Rhonda, what is your question?"

"Couldn't it be said that you were partly responsible for the deaths of the people in the 'safe' area inasmuch as you led the push to give Ponya the artillery with which he massacred innocents?"

Kincaid's eyes narrowed and his face flushed. He looked down and took a long drink of water. When he looked up, he'd regained his composure. "No, it cannot be said. I'm shocked, Rhonda, that a journalist of your caliber would take such a tragic event and twist it toward some sinister personal agenda. The truth, had you bothered to look, is that Ponya is not lying. Some shells fell among the refugees by mistake. Prime Minister Ponya made amends to the families of those who were killed or injured."

Rhonda paused for a few seconds, her eyes never leaving Kincaid's.

"Do you have any more questions, Rhonda?"

"No. Thank you for your comments, Governor."

"Thank you, Rhonda."

A mixture of puzzlement and anger buzzed in the Schnitzelbank. One man asked Andy why he couldn't control his wife's big mouth. Another answered that Andy had no cojones and that's why Rhonda and her big mouth had left him.

"That's enough, gentlemen," Kim warned.

A woman said, "O'Malley set him up with the 'good looks' comment and then attacked him. You'd expect better from an Indiana reporter."

"Lady," Andy responded, "Lincoln Kincaid is a two-faced asshole."

"Are you jealous?"

"Fuck you."

"Well, whaddya know," said another man, "the big high-falutin' lawyer is standing up for his ex-wife by attacking another woman."

"She's not my ex-wife, buddy."

"Oh, sorry, just your soon-to-be ex-wife."

"Go fuck yourself."

"That's more in your line, Balbach, seeing as your loud-mouthed bitch isn't doing you anymore."

"You bastard!" Andy jumped off the stool but Clubby grabbed and restrained him, and then led him out the door.

CHAPTER 15

Rhonda was on a barstool in the St. Elmo Steakhouse in downtown Indianapolis. She wore faded jeans, a worn Indianapolis Colts long-sleeve T-shirt, and old running shoes. She wore no makeup and had brushed her hair forward, so as to hide much of her face. She slouched on the stool with her arms crossed and resting on the bar. Last night she'd been a national figure on Fox News. Today she was an anonymous beer drinker at an upscale and historical restaurant and bar. She had to keep it that way.

Marian Kincaid had asked Rhonda to lunch via a text message sent two hours after the interview. The message was friendly, the timing less so, and the signals much less so. Marian would stand by her man and confront Rhonda for breaching the trust of their friendship. It might be possible for Rhonda to patch up the bond between them, but only if they had true privacy. A meeting between the wife of the next president and the journalist who had shaken him only the evening before on a national broadcast would be a sensational story. There could be no reporter jumping from his lunch table, no texts or tweets, and certainly no gone-viral YouTube video of them together.

Rhonda O'Malley and Marian Arancha Vicario had met at New Mexico State where both majored in journalism. Marian, from Phoenix, Arizona, and Rhonda, from Dubain, Indiana, had been thrown together as roommates when they arrived on campus the first day. They shared their love of journalism and its companion, deep curiosity. They became best friends, were maids of honor at their weddings, and talked at least once a week. After graduation, Marian worked for the *Washington Post*. She was researching the Iraq disarmament crisis and the Pentagon assigned Captain Lincoln Kincaid to meet with her. Kincaid, a native of Indiana and former standout quarterback at West Point, was clearly on his way up. They married less than a year later at the Washington National Cathedral.

From all appearances, their marriage was idyllic. They were a loving couple in public. They had three children, Gerardo, age nine, Kaitlyn, six, and Shandra, age two. Theirs was the All-American family, the kind that Americans approved of and voted for. Captain Kincaid had served his country, while Marian worked as a roving reporter. He received high marks for his work at the Pentagon and his command at the Tigris River POW Camp in 2003. After Tigris River, Lincoln resigned his commission, and he and Marian moved to Indianapolis. Lincoln ran for Congress, served two terms, and then was elected governor of Indiana. He was now into the last year of his second term as governor and heating up his campaign for the presidency.

But Rhonda had long detected a dark side to Lincoln Kincaid.

Rhonda finished her beer and then signaled the St. Elmo bartender for another. He was a medium-sized man with long sideburns and a short neck, and he smelled of cheap after-shave and cigarette smoke.

Rhonda said, "Thank you."

He stood in front of Rhonda and smiled. "Please call me Wilbur."

Wilbur didn't move.

"Can I help you with something, Wilbur?"

"No, ma'am. It's just that you look sorta familiar."

"I've never met you."

Just then a man entered the barroom. Rhonda picked him up in the mirror behind the bar and watched him walk along the line of stools toward her. She noticed Wilbur watching him also. Rhonda studied his reflection. His ponytail highlighted his trim and muscular body and his chiseled face. He moved with an air of stealth, like an inward looking cat on the hunt. He took the last stool around the corner from Rhonda and next to the restrooms. Wilbur had walked away and taken a seat next to the man. There, in a quick and coordinated movement, Ponytail slipped an envelope to Wilbur and Wilbur slipped a bulging grocery bag to Ponytail. Ponytail carried the bag into the restroom.

Rhonda watched two of Marian's security people enter the restaurant and didn't notice Wilbur walking back to her until he was standing right next to her. She turned to him and said, "That guy you were talking to is quite handsome. What is his name?"

"Jethro. He's a new waiter here. This is his second day."

CHAPTER 16

Rhonda and Marian sat opposite each other at the small table in the room St. Elmo's set aside for their lunches. Rhonda studied her friend. Marian had lost weight and along with it most of her figure, normally trim and athletic, but now more boyish than feminine.

Jethro entered and introduced himself. He served shrimp cocktail and set the bowl in the middle of the table.

Rhonda said, "Thank you, Jethro, but we didn't order shrimp cocktail."

"They're on the house in honor of Ms. Kincaid, the next first lady. Ms. O'Malley, enjoy your lunch with Ms. Kincaid."

Rhonda looked puzzled. "I took care that I wouldn't be recognized. When did you first identify me as Rhonda O'Malley?"

"When I walked into this room." Jethro smiled. "I'll serve your main entrees in about ten minutes."

Jethro turned to leave but Marian stopped him. "Jethro, could you find a seat cushion?"

"Certainly."

Rhonda thought it best to start gently with her best friend. "Marian, I'm sorry about the interview."

"No, you're not."

"Okay, I'm not," Rhonda shot back. "What do you want me to say?"

"I want you to say, 'My name is Rhonda O'Malley. I'm a very good investigative journalist. I do my job the way I do my job. If Lincoln Kincaid doesn't like it, that's just too bad.'"

"You're not angry with me?"

"Of course not. The facts are there. Lincoln did live at Oakenwald. The Foundation exists and Oakenwald is tied to it. Lincoln's campaign managers were stupid enough to confirm this by renting space in Oakenwald Hall. Lincoln did command at Tigris River when soldiers under him abused those prisoners and raped other soldiers. Lincoln's opponents have raised Oakenwald, the Foundation, and Tigris River in every one of his campaigns. However, you were the first to confront him on the Congo and Ponya's massacre of his own people. Your questions were relevant and pointed... some softballs, some open-ended, and some leading. You were good, Rhonda. Lincoln was not."

Rhonda folded her hands on the table. Marian reached over and covered them with her own. The door opened and one of the security people handed Marian a cushion. Rhonda saw her wince when she slid the cushion under her. Then Jethro served their entrees. He left the shrimp cocktail.

Marian took a small bite of her tuna salad sandwich. "Rhonda, President Harding and her Republican Party—if you can even call it that—have run this country into the ground. Harding will not get the nomination, and that leaves Senator Josie Carter Lodge. However, the senator has the Republican rock around her neck. Lincoln nailed that in the interview. Lincoln has a good record as both a congressperson and governor, and his lead in the polls has been steady. In spite of his stumbles last night, this is Lincoln's election to lose."

"I agree. Senator Josephine Carter Lodge is a hard campaigner but the fight between her and Sarah Harding is bitter and is rending the Republican Party. The senator will win the nomination, but it won't be worth having."

Marian didn't respond. She looked down at her plate while nibbling on a shrimp.

"Marian, what is it?"

Marian raised her head and looked into Rhonda's eyes. "I get the feeling that this election—like all of Lincoln's elections—is being handed to him. I can't feel, see, or touch it, but it's there. He's getting special help from somebody buried deep behind the scenes." Marian sipped her coffee. "You asked questions of Lincoln that have been nagging at me for a long time. Is Lincoln a member of the Foundation? What really happened at Tigris River?

Did Lincoln know or even suspect that Ponya would kill his own people with the very weapons he'd helped provide? My God! What if he did?"

Rhonda said, "Honey, Lincoln denied membership in the Foundation. He was exonerated of dereliction of duty at Tigris. Sometimes a commander's soldiers go behind his back and do terrible things. Lincoln was right when he said that the Congo civil war was spreading to other African nations. He took responsibility and did his job. Both houses of Congress and the president agreed with Lincoln. Ponya might have purposely shelled the people in the safe area. However, Lincoln could not have known that would happen. Had Lincoln done nothing, it's possible that more millions of Africans would have been slaughtered."

A security man opened the door. "We have to leave for the zoo in ten minutes."

Marian leaned over the table. "All those things may be true. However, you shook him last night. Not only did he bumble his answers, he flashed anger."

"Marian, even governors and soon-to-be presidents have tempers. An occasional lapse is okay. It makes them more human to the voters."

"Lincoln? Human?"

Some of the beer in Rhonda's stomach turned into quicksand. "Marian, I've never heard you talk like this. What's wrong?"

"It's the presidency, Rhonda. The friggen presidency for Christ's sake!"

Rhonda let the comment go. Jethro served more water and coffee.

Marian said, "I believe Lincoln lied about the Foundation. I think he is a member. Oh, I know they don't keep membership lists and they're secretive because the Bible says to not brag about good works and blah, blah, blah. However, somewhere along the way there has to be an understanding, a wink and a nod sort of thing that says, 'Welcome aboard the Jesus Ship.'"

"Have you asked Lincoln about all this?"

"No."

"Why not?"

"I can't risk it."

"Risk what?" Rhonda fought the urge to lean forward.

"Has your Andy ever lied to you?"

Rhonda fought the bile rising in her throat. "Andy's incapable of lying. His voice and face give it away. He does tell white lies, mostly to get me to laugh."

"Do you?"

"Not always. Andy's a complicated man."

"Embrace your complicated man! He's honest, decent, and loving. Andy would have stopped the mayhem at Tigris River. He wouldn't have set foot in Oakenwald, cheap rent or not. He would have told the country that he knows much about the Foundation and that he stands solidly against it. If Andy ran for president—if he ran for anything—he'd earn his votes with integrity and character, not simply rely on his good looks and shady people to get them for him."

"Andy's not running for president. He's not running for anything. If anything, he's running away."

"From what?"

"Himself."

"I don't understand."

"He blames himself for our separation."

Marian asked, "Why?"

"I laid it on him."

"How?"

"I told him that he doesn't support my career."

"Do you believe that?"

"Yes."

"Well, I don't. Rhonda, you're so lucky! Many women would give a year of their lives just to spend a day with a man like Andy, complicated or not, supportive or not."

A security man said, "Five minutes."

Marian went on. "You said in the interview that the Tigris River Report was a cover-up. Was it?"

"Like I said, some people—"

"Don't give me that 'some people' crap, Rhonda. Was it or wasn't it?"

Rhonda looked out the window. A pigeon sat on its ledge. She had to decide then and there whether to lie or speak the truth. She chose the former even though she sensed that Marian didn't buy the army's report any more than she did. "I don't believe it was."

"But you asked Lincoln the question anyway. Why?"

"I guess it was one of my leading questions." Rhonda smiled. Marian did not, and so Rhonda added, "And don't forget that Lincoln denied all of it."

"Did you expect him to tell the truth?"

Rhonda needed to change the subject. "Your autobiography sparkles."

"Yes, well, Kincaid For America trashed it."

"Why?"

"They said that the sole purpose of my autobiography is to get votes for Lincoln. So, this Marian Kincaid," she pointed at herself, "cannot be the published Marian Kincaid. They've demanded that I rewrite the book to make it 'softer'... talk more about my love for Lincoln and the children... how happy I am cooking for them, cleaning for them, praying with them, and on and on. I blocked their emails, texts, and phone calls. However, a few days later a young lady named Polly Thompson appeared at the mansion and said that her father and Lincoln's de facto campaign manager, Earl Thompson, had sent her to help rewrite my book."

Rhonda had uncovered Polly in her research. She wondered whether Marian knew that Earl Thompson was also the head of the Foundation and that Polly worked for it. Rhonda pictured Marian as a prisoner of war, responding to her captor's questions with name, rank, serial number, and distortions.

Rhonda lied. "Polly Thompson? Doesn't sound familiar." She didn't know whom she could trust.

"She's actually very friendly and helpful. She seems to understand my predicament."

"So you're revising the book?"

"Yes."

"That's a positive."

"Maybe. Turns out that Polly is just another mystery. She disappears for up to several days at a time for 'personal business.' When she's in the mansion, she makes and receives calls but she goes into another room, presumably so I don't hear what she says. I, well, eavesdropped a few times. She argues with a man she calls 'Garrett' about strange things like 'lamb,' 'cradler,' and 'Jesus plus zero.' What do these mean?"

"I don't know," Rhonda lied again. "Where are you going with all this, Marian?"

Marian pushed back the hair that had fallen in her face. "I need your help."

"For what?"

"I want the truth! ...the truth about the Foundation, about Oakenwald, about Tigris River, Ponya, Lincoln, the people around him, the people behind him. Will you help me?"

"Marian, what could I possibly find about Lincoln that you don't already know?"

"I hope nothing. I hope my suspicions are proven wrong."

"I'll help," said Rhonda, "but I don't think anything's there."

Marian asked, "Can you start with Polly Thompson?"

"Yes." That bought her some time. She wanted to believe Marian was sincere.

Jethro entered with the check and Marian signed for it.

"Thank you for the tip, Ms. Kincaid."

Jethro turned to go but Rhonda stopped him. "Jethro, you're a talented server. How long have you worked here?"

"Going on two years, ma'am."

CHAPTER 17

When Rhonda was certain that Marian and her security had left the St. Elmo, she returned to her barstool and ordered a beer.

"Wilbur, where do you take your smoke breaks?"

"In the alley behind the restaurant."

"Can I bum a cigarette?"

"Sure, ma'am."

"When are you taking your next break?"

Wilbur handed Rhonda a cigarette. "In about five minutes."

"Can I meet you in the alley?"

He shrugged. "Sure."

***

Rhonda walked to the alley behind the St. Elmo. She reached into her purse, pulled out a brush, pulled her hair back from her face, and then applied makeup. She rarely smoked, but this time she lit up.

Wilbur emerged, lit up, and leaned against the building. He looked Rhonda over. "You are that reporter from TV last night. O'Malley. Am I right?"

"Yeah," said Rhonda. "Rhonda O'Malley. I just had lunch with Marian Kincaid. I want information."

"I ain't saying nothin'. It might end up on TV."

"Do you like your job, Wilbur?"

"It's a paycheck. Why?"

"Because, unless you give me what I want, I'll walk back into that building and in five minutes get you fired and then jailed."

"I ain't sayin' another word."

"Then I will. Let me spell it out for you. I'll find your boss and tell him that you lied about Jethro. You said he was a new waiter. Jethro told us he'd been here for two years. In fact, he does not and has never worked here. You somehow got him into our dining room. Jethro could have been an assassin intent on killing Marian Kincaid. However, you didn't care. All you wanted was the money he paid you. Yeah, I saw that. It's in an envelope in your left pants pocket, in case you forgot. It doesn't matter so much to me how much Jethro paid you. The police'll get it out of you one way or another."

Wilbur's face went red. He looked up at the sky with watering eyes and was about to speak, but Rhonda cut him off.

"However, you see, Wilbur, you don't have to talk to me. I already have my story. So, after I get you fired from here, I'll tell the whole world that you're a lying, cheating, bribe-taking asshole. Then nobody'll hire you. You'll live on the streets and in mission houses the rest of your life."

"You... you fuckin' bitch. You're blackmailing me."

"'Blackmail' is a little harsh, don't you think? I prefer incentivizing."

Wilbur lit another cigarette, took a long draw, and slowly exhaled the smoke.

"Whaddya want?"

"Have the dishes from our lunch been washed yet?"

"Probably not," said Wilbur. "Slop line's slow today. What are you looking for?"

"Oh, nothing." Rhonda smiled. "I just need to examine them so I can... well... look for nothing."

"They'll fire me if I get caught... think I'm stealing from 'em."

Rhonda threw her cigarette down and ground it with her shoe. "Wilbur, either you get caught and get fired, you refuse me and get fired, or you get those dishes out here without getting caught and without getting fired. Your choice."

"Your dishes may still be in the bussing tub. Give me a few minutes." Wilbur threw his cigarette on the concrete and entered the restaurant.

While she waited, Rhonda thought about Marian. She had lost more than weight. The dark circles under her eyes added to the aura of profound tension and bone-tired fatigue that imprisoned her. Marian, normally cheerful and outgoing, was bitter, and she directed it toward no less than her husband, the leading candidate for President of the United States. Was there a connection between Marian's request for a seat cushion and her husband? Rhonda tried not to think about it.

Wilbur emerged with the tub and the dishes, said "Five minutes," and then reentered the restaurant. Sixty seconds later, Rhonda found the tiny transmitter under the shrimp cocktail serving dish. It took all her willpower not to whistle into it and call the listeners assholes. She put it into her purse and went to her car.

CHAPTER 18

Garrett and Earl entered the dining room. It was one week after the first lesson. Garrett started the Bible's journey for Lesson Two by handing the Bible to the resident on his left. Its journey ended at Earl.

Earl asked, "How many of you vote?" Everyone raised his hand, including Garrett and Earl. "Why do you vote? Joseph?"

"So I have a say in our government."

"That's interesting." Earl rubbed his chin as though he was groping for the next question.

"Joseph, what gives you the right to vote?"

"The Constitution. Our laws. It's... well, it's democracy."

"Did God write the Constitution? Does he write the laws?"

"No. Men wrote the Constitution and men make the laws."

"Where is God in the Constitution?"

Joseph said, "Nowhere. In fact, the First Amendment excludes God."

"Right," said Earl. "However, millions of people vote in this country. Millions around the world vote in their country's elections. What do you say to them? Desmond?"

"They disobey Romans 13. Only God has authority to choose our leaders."

"Right. Romans 13 has no exception for democracy. It says that only God can choose leaders. It follows that God, indirectly through his chosen leaders, writes the laws. Garrett, what about this democracy thing?"

"Democracy is an insult to God because it intrudes on His domain. Besides, God is wiser than any person chosen by a bunch of foolish voters."

"But, Garrett, we still vote. Why?"

"God knows that we mortals have to deal with His world as it is. The affront that is democracy is a part of that world. God chooses his leaders, but we, the Foundation, have to lead the fight to ensure that God's choices actually get to leadership."

Earl paused to let this sink in. He then asked the group, "Where is Jesus in all this?"

Carl said, "He is God's son. But there's bound to be more to your question because the answer I gave is too easy!"

"Right. The world has had Jesus wrong for centuries. Liberals—also known as 'secular humanists'—have hijacked the Gospels and in doing so they've hijacked Jesus. They tell us that Jesus lived with the poor, prostitutes, and sinners, and that he gave worth to these. They attest to miraculous moments when Jesus cured the sick, made the blind see, the deaf hear, and raised Lazarus from the dead. They say that Jesus spoke out against injustice, which they first and foremost define as the poor versus the rich.

"All this is bunk." Earl looked around the table. "Jesus didn't make loaves and fishes to feed the poor, he didn't turn water into wine for them to drink, and he certainly didn't walk on water for their entertainment. Deep down, the secular humanists know all this. Yet, they hide their duplicity so they can inflict upon the world a Jesus who commands high taxes and redistribution of wealth. They will never understand the Foundation because they don't want to. Government, not Jesus, is their god. Taxes, not good works, are their mantra. Jealously, not dedication, is their guiding light.

"But we are bound to take Jesus as he really is. Jesus isn't about piety and meekness... he's about power and obedience. Piety and meekness produce saints. Power and obedience produce His Kingdom. However, Jesus also said 'whatsoever you do to the least of my brothers, that you do unto me.' To whom was he talking?"

Joseph said, "Certainly not the least of his brothers. That wouldn't make sense."

"Of course it wouldn't," said Earl. "Let's look at this another way. At this very moment, not too far from here, there are poor and destitute people who live in ghettos. You desire to help them escape their misery. Do you go to the ghetto and say, 'Hey, I want to help you folks. Here's a bunch of hundred dollar bills, make your lives better... problem solved,' and then walk away?"

Jacob said, "No, the problem is made worse. They'd smile and thank you for the money and wait until you leave. Then they'd spend it on alcohol, drugs, prostitutes, and gambling. The next week you go back expecting to see all the trash gone and people painting their houses. But we see none of this. Instead, there are the very same people holding out their hands for another round of hundred dollar bills."

"So," said Earl, "back to Jesus. We know that Jesus was a man of the world. He was wise. He knew that the poor of his time would simply throw Roman coins away on fleeting pleasures, just like those of our time throw away dollars. So we're back to the question. Who was Jesus talking to when he said to care for the least of his brothers?"

Desmond said, "The people with the resources, the wealthy and the powerful."

"Right," said Earl. "Jesus, while in the company of the wealthy, admonished them to care for the poor. But under what circumstances?" Earl searched up and down the table. "Did Jesus walk up to a bunch of wealthy people at a picnic on the Jordan River and say, 'Hey, you rich people, you have to care for the poor,' and then walk away?"

Desmond smiled and said, "No. Jesus delivered one-liners but he did so within the context of his teachings. Besides, whoever heard of picnics on the Jordan River two thousand years ago?"

The residents laughed.

"Desmond?"

"It's really the other way around, isn't it? Jesus didn't spend his life among the poor with an occasional sermon to the wealthy. He spent his time among the wealthy and preached to the poor."

"Exactly, Desmond," said Earl. "In his own inimitable way, Jesus delivered his messages to the right people at the right times and in the right places. With respect to 'the least of His brothers,' He laid down three principles. One, you help the poor by way of the wealthy. Two, you assign to the wealthy the ways and means of doing so. And three, you minister first to the needs of the wealthy because they carry burdens far heavier than those of the needy. Why this last message? Garrett?"

Garrett said, "The ghetto people know nothing about interstates, social security, health insurance, defense, government financing, money supply, or the Constitution… and they never will. They lack the intelligence, drive, and morality to learn about them. So, someone must do it for them, and that someone is us. However, we pay a price for this."

"And," Earl followed, "that price is our well-being. We run the businesses, invest the money, advise the government, engage in high finance, pay most of the taxes, and build homes, sewers, bridges, and shopping malls. At the same time, we work hard to earn money so that it is available for those less fortunate. It is we, not the ghetto people, who carry the weight of the world. There is logic in this. Jesus salves our burdens by treating us first. Then, and only then, do we have the strength to care for the less fortunate. In short, Jesus takes care of us so we can take care of them. We'll leave it at that for tonight. It's basketball time."

CHAPTER 19

Rhonda lay propped in bed, a glass of wine on the nightstand beside her, a legal pad on her lap, and a tablet computer on the bed. She picked up a pen, laid it down, and reached for the wine.

She reproached herself for not sniffing out the mission of Ponytail from the get-go. Her anxiety over a possible stealth reporter had blinded her to the implications of Wilbur, Ponytail, and the exchange of the envelope for the bag. Ponytail's mission was screaming in front of her from the first time he entered the room with the shrimp cocktail 'on the house in honor of Ms. Kincaid, the next first lady.'

Rhonda had been investigating the Foundation, Kincaid for America, or KFA, Lincoln Kincaid, and Oakenwald for months. They were so intertwined with each other that she lumped all under 'Foundation.' Her research, and the intel from her informant, a person inside the Foundation, had confirmed her intuitions and justified Marian's suspicions. She started with the murky history of Oakenwald's owners going back decades. The key owner was Frederick Thompson. Frederick built the fallout shelter shortly before the Cuban Missile Crisis and added the ells some years later. When the building was expanded, they named it the Fallout Shelter... not very creative. He had served the Foundation as its executive director for decades. His son, Earl, had succeeded him.

Rhonda had read the army's report on the goings-on during Lincoln's year of command at Tigris. The report blamed privates and non-commissioned officers. The commissioned officers, from second lieutenant up to

Captain Lincoln Kincaid, had received only one paragraph of bureaucratic mumbo-jumbo to the effect that there was no evidence of dereliction of duty or participation by them. The report stated that the "Guilty persons had hidden the attacks and intimidated the victims into submission and silence. No blame is to attach to the officers for not uncovering their deeds."

The informant explained 'Cradler' and 'Lamb' to Rhonda. Modern civilization supposedly started in the Tigris River Valley. Historians call it the 'Cradle of Civilization' for that reason. At the beginning of the Iraq War, the US military built the Tigris River Prisoner-Of-War Camp in Baghdad next to the river. The rapists hijacked the term, 'Cradler,' from 'Cradle of Civilization.' Along the way, they anointed their victims as 'Lambs.' These terms reigned from 2003 through the closing of Tigris River. The Cradlers returned to civilian life and continued to rape Lambs, now expanded to include civilian victims.

On the legal pad she scribbled three questions:

(1) Who employed Ponytail, a.k.a. Jethro?
(2) Who was the target of the bug?
(3) How much had Ponytail's employer heard?

The answer to the last question was easy. Right now, somebody somewhere was replaying Marian Kincaid's condemnations of her husband: *"I get the feeling... he's getting help from somebody buried deep... Human? Lincoln? Lincoln lied about the Foundation. Somewhere... a wink and a nod... I want the truth! ...about the Foundation... the people behind him."*

The answer to the first question was harder. Who pulled Ponytail's strings? Senator Carter Lodge's reputation for honesty and integrity eliminated her as a suspect. Sarah Harding, on the other hand, did spy on her 'enemies,' as she called them. Harding no doubt considered Lincoln Kincaid an enemy. However, Harding was fighting for her political life against Senator Carter Lodge, not Governor Lincoln Kincaid. Moreover, Harding could not alienate the social conservatives who were leaning toward the Democrat, Kincaid, but who would likely vote the Republican ticket in the primaries.

The Foundation had employed Ponytail.

The target was either Marian or Rhonda, or both.

It was unthinkable that the spouse of a presidential candidate would deep-six his campaign and cost him the election. However, the Marian she'd been with that day—angry, confrontational, and, worst of all, contemptuous of her husband—made it thinkable. *"It's the presidency, Rhonda... the friggen presidency!"*

Why would Lincoln Kincaid, the leading candidate for President of the United States, bug his own wife? The answer was, he probably had not. The Foundation, via Earl Thompson, probably had. If so, Thompson would, no doubt, hand Lincoln a transcript of their lunch conversation. This made sense, given the Foundation's misogyny—a man should control his wife... much more so when that man was running for the most powerful position in the world and that wife could make or break his election.

Rhonda had assumed that Marian was the sole target until she spotted the black Ford Transit Wagon tailing her after she left the St. Elmo. She lost the tail near the Indianapolis Motor Speedway and drove to her condominium on Moller Street. A minute later, the Wagon appeared and parked along the curb on the west side of Moller. When it U-turned, she snapped a photo of its license plate. It headed north and she lost sight of it.

She clicked a special search engine and matched the Ford's license plate to that on her photograph. The vehicle was registered to a Delaware company, Good Earth LLC, an innocent enough sounding name. She then entered commands and various passwords and hacked into a special grid on the dark net. Rachel and Jackson Kincaid owned the company. It listed the Transit Wagon as its only asset. It reported no liabilities and, apparently, conducted no business. Rhonda had discovered several months before that Rachel and Jackson Kincaid were members of the Foundation. They, then, formed the connection between the Foundation and Good Earth. But why set up a Delaware limited liability company for the sole purpose of owning a vehicle?

The tail confirmed that Earl Thompson, or at least Garrett Jennings, took Rhonda seriously. Why? The first explanation was that Rhonda's investigation of Lincoln Kincaid and the Foundation was no secret. They'd probably been monitoring her movements for a while. But, after the interview, they'd stepped up from watching to intimidation. She smiled at this. Other targets of other investigations had tried intimidation and some had come to regret it. Even so, Rhonda was mildly surprised that the Foundation hadn't tailed her before the interview.

The second explanation went deeper. Rhonda had carefully raised, subtextually, a darkness, both behind and inside Lincoln Kincaid. No doubt Lincoln's campaign managers had detected this and well knew that other reporters were now digging into Lincoln Kincaid's fitness for the presidency. Rhonda's questions and Kincaid's stumbling responses had set into motion powerful forces that neither Earl Thompson nor she could control.

Rhonda concluded that the Foundation was targeting both Marian Kincaid, the candidate's wife, and Rhonda O'Malley, the candidate's nemesis.

Her last question had caught Lincoln Kincaid unprepared to explain his connection to President Ponya of the Congo and his massacre of his own people in the 'safe area' he'd designated.

Rhonda thought through the charged conversation at the St. Elmo. She knew that Marian hadn't been candid with her, and realized that Marian knew she hadn't been candid with Marian either. Marian had to know of Rhonda's investigation. Earl Thompson certainly followed Rhonda's research and knew of the friendship between her and Marian. He would pass this to Lincoln, who would throw it in his wife's face, and maybe order Marian to leverage her friendship with Rhonda to call off the investigation. Marian did the exact opposite when she prodded for the seamier evidence acquired by Rhonda and then, when Rhonda fibbed, asked for her help to get it.

Underneath Marian's thin facade was the unspoken question: *Is my husband as big a sonofabitch as I think he is?*

Rhonda admitted that all this could be conjecture. However, it fit the circumstances. Had she been the unscrupulous Earl Thompson she would have bugged the meeting for the same reasons as he: First, to keep tabs on the candidate's wife, who was less than enthusiastic about electing her husband and bucked him on her biography to prove it. Second, to check whether said wife ordered her reporter friend away from her investigation. And third, if said wife failed to do so, or the reporter resisted, glean the extent of the reporter's knowledge and where she intended to go from there.

There was another factor well beyond the bug, tail, and intimidation. The Foundation broke a cardinal rule of politics—never ever allow your candidate to go into an interview unprepared. Lincoln had fielded the questions in elections going back several years. Yet, last night, he'd stumbled over them. His campaign managers failed to prepare him. Were they that stupid? Had they made a mistake? Or, was something else going on? Lincoln's smooth and professional campaign, until last night, belied stupidity. For now, however, Rhonda would go with mistake.

Rhonda wanted help and knew where to get it. She texted Andy and asked him to meet with her at the Schnitzelbank Restaurant Saturday evening.

CHAPTER 20

Rhonda received a Facebook message from JSGold. "Can we meet? It's important."

It was the fifth such message Rhonda had received in the past two weeks. Again she checked his homepage and again the only information given was that JSGold was a male, lived in Montana, and was born on December 31. He had no friends, photos, or interests.

She Googled 'JSGold' and got five hits. Two were deceased, and one each lived in California, Arkansas, and Florida. There was no Montana JSGold. Why would someone set up a Facebook page, lie about his location, and post no personal information? He was probably a troll, a person who friended Rhonda only to post vicious and threatening comments about an op-ed she'd written on her wall. She hovered the mouse pointer over the 'block' option but hesitated. There was a faint echo of desperation in the 'Please do not block me.' JSGold probably feared discovery. However, assuming he was messaging in good faith, he evidently wanted her help with something. If so, what?

Curious, and willing to take the risk, Rhonda replied to his message. "There is no JSGold in Montana. Who are you?"

"Thank you for replying to my message."

"You're welcome," Rhonda responded. "I'd like to know more about you. Where do you live?"

"Send stoan liv hi up see your house orchard see all over born 1867."

Rhonda studied the message but it made no sense to her. "I have no time for your games."

"No game."

"Then clarify."

JSGold responded, "Think."

"About what?"

JSGold did not respond.

Rhonda thought and accepted JSGold's Facebook friendship.

CHAPTER 21

The sight of Rhonda entering the Schnitzelbank Bar caused the familiar heart tug in Andy. He watched her greet friends with handshakes and hugs and ignore angry stares from other patrons. His eyes swept the packed barroom. She was searching for him, but his pride wouldn't let him wave to draw her attention. He turned away from her when the bartender served him his second boilermaker. When he turned back, she was gone. He combed the room but didn't find her. Then he felt a tapping on his shoulder. He turned and there she stood, smiling. His libido stirred at the sight of her. There were those large, blue-green eyes. Her streaked, brown hair brushed her shoulders, and her dark lipstick accentuated her eyes. She wore a red skirt that hung just below her knee and was slit halfway up her tanned, left thigh. The top two buttons on her blue and white striped blouse were undone, exposing ever so slightly the swell of her breasts.

Andy Balbach helped his estranged wife, Rhonda O'Malley, onto the barstool beside him. She'd asked for his help on what she called a 'special project.' They had agreed to meet at the Schnitzelbank that evening, but Andy had warned her that it would be a Saturday night on the Fourth of July, the Beech Tree Boys Barbershop Quartet would be performing, and the Schnitzelbank would be crowded and noisy.

Rhonda ordered a dry martini with two olives.

"Does this special project involve your investigation of Kincaid?"

"Not so loud, Andy," Rhonda replied. "Yes, it has to do with Lincoln Kincaid."

"What about him?"

"We can't do it here, Andy. We'll talk about it later at the house."

Andy said, "Didn't know you were staying the night."

"Well, I am. It's my house too, you know."

"Whatever." Andy didn't know what to expect when they got home. She'd built her Kincaid investigation into a wall between them. Andy hadn't wanted the wall. It wasn't necessary and he'd told her so. She'd come back with the 'you don't support my career' routine. Andy could say or do nothing to change Rhonda's mind. He loved that she was beside him and evidently planned to spend the night in their home, if not their bed. However, he was irritated. She had some nerve asking for his help on the very subject she'd lashed him with.

There were cheers from the Schnitzelbank's dining room. The Beech Trees had just sung "Happy Birthday" to America. Then they entered the bar.

Peachfuzz bellowed, "Set us up, Kimmy!"

Joe Billups, the base singer, an African-American, gay, married to a man, and extremely conservative, pointed to Rhonda and Andy. "Hey there, Rhonda, ol' buddy. Gonna buy us that high-class liberal beer like ya did last time?"

"I might, Billups," said Rhonda. "But you have to ask real nice."

The Beech Trees, now with Schnitzelbank mug beers, lined up in front of the bar. The noise dropped.

Clubby, the baritone, said, "Billups, you queer, black, tea party asshole, they shoulda kept you locked up in that log cabin."

Stump, the first tenor, cut in, "Clubby, the politically correct terms are 'African-American,' not 'black,' and 'gay,' not 'queer.'"

Billups said, "Thank you, Stump."

Clubby said, "What's your problem, Stump? Think you're smarter'n everybody cuz ya only got one leg?"

"Stump ain't smart," said Clubby. "He been a-singin' a quarter step low all night."

"Clubby," said Stump, "you don't know the key of C from a cow. I been right on pitch. It's you singing sharp."

Peachfuzz said, "Clubby's singin' sharp cuz he's got his knickers in a twist and they're squeezing his pair."

Stump said, "Clubby ain't got a pair. He only gotta the one."

"Got three, you one-legged, hop-toad, Pabst-swillin' know-it-all."

"Clubby," said Peachfuzz, "you're too ignorant to count to three."

Billups said, "Get off Stump's back, Clubby. Newspaper sales are down. PBR is all he can afford."

Stump said, "Billups, you gotta get out more. PBR's makin' a comeback with the college crowd."

Clubby retorted, "I be a-choppin' off Stump's other leg if he don't stop insultin' me. And Peachfuzz, you're so dumb you drink your own bathwater."

Peachfuzz said, "I take showers, not baths, numbskull."

Stump threatened, "Clubby'n Peachfuzz, I'll wrap this artificial leg around your necks and then write an editorial tellin' the whole world what assholes you are."

Clubby retorted, "We'll hire my little brother, Andy, and sue your ass for slander."

Andy forced a smile.

Stump said, "It's libel, genius, not slander. Besides, truth's a defense. I'll prove that you and Peachfuzz're assholes. Not even Andy could win that lawsuit for ya. Besides, Andy's my lawyer so he can't go a-lawyerin' for you. Conflict of interest. Billups is the only lawyer dumb enough to take your case."

Peachfuzz said, "Billups is a cheatin' lawyer."

"Got your ass outta many a jam, Peachfuzz," said Billups. "Let's see." Billups began counting on his fingers. "Breaking the peace, two drunk driving, littering, jay-walking, and the time you mouthed off to Clubby one too many times in the Strassenfest beer garden."

Clubby confirmed, "I arrested Peachfuzz in the beer garden. Drunker'n a hunnert bucks he was."

"Peachfuzz's deadbeat ass ain't never paid me a dime," said Billups.

"Give it up, Stump," said Clubby. "Everybody knows you got your leg cut off on purpose just so people'd call you Stump 'stead of Firmus."

"Stump," said Peachfuzz, "you oughta shoot your parents for namin' ya so stupid."

"They're already dead, bird-brain," said Stump. "Clubby, I gotta talk to your old man."

"'Bout what?"

"He shoulda let you run down your momma's leg."

Clubby said, "That's awfully personal, Stump. My old man'll bust your head for it."

Kim Seaton, the Schnitzelbank's head bartender, finger-whistled from the other end of the bar. "Rhonda just told me that if you pea-brains shut your ignorant mouths for a minute, she'll buy you the next round."

Clubby, Peachfuzz, and Stump turned to Billups.

"Stay off your red-neck politics, Billups, and the lady'll buy us a beer," said Clubby.

"In case you didn't notice, Mr. Blithering Idiot, I can't get a red neck. It stays black."

"Whatever. Point is, the liberal lady always beats your black, tea-party ass."

Stump stifled Billups' retort with a hand over his mouth.

Kim served the drinks.

"Well, chalk one up for the tree-hugging, bleeding-heart, high-taxes, liberal, Kincaid gal," said Billups, raising his free beer.

Then Kim yelled, "Quiet!" She turned the music down and cranked up the wide screen TV monitor behind the bar. The announcer was saying, "...shot in the stomach at Camp Morgan a week ago. St. Mary's hospital has released a statement on the condition of Kurt Borgmann. 'Mr. Borgmann's doctors have upgraded his condition from grave to fair. They predict a full recovery.'"

Borgmann was popular as the long-time St. Augustine choir director. Some in the bar cheered at the news. Kim again shushed them. A blown-up photo of Jameel Shalih's face appeared on the monitor. "This is Jameel Shalih. In his statement to police, Borgmann said that 'Shalih somehow obtained a pistol, most likely from his gang friend, Jayden Ramirez. Shalih killed the two guards, and wounded me. He took the keys from one of the dead guards, unlocked the gates, and escaped.'

"Viewers might recall that Jayden Ramirez escaped from Camp Morgan several months before Shalih and has not been apprehended. The FBI became involved when the search for the fugitives turned nationwide. The FBI warns that both are armed and dangerous and says to call 911 if you spot either of them.

"Mr. Borgmann issued another statement thanking St. Augustine Parish for the masses and prayers, and says that he looks forward to returning as the choir director."

Rhonda nudged Andy and pointed to the screen. The station was running footage of the murder scene in slow motion.

"Are you getting all this, Andy?"

"No."

"Shalih is innocent."

"They're all innocent, Rhonda, and none of 'em ain't ever had more'n two beers."

"How many beers did Shalih have?"

"What do you want from me?"

"First, is security that lax at Morgan, or were the escapes set up? Second, how could they have possibly coordinated their escapes, as the FBI claims? Ramirez had already escaped and there is no evidence that he had contact with Shalih after that. Third, Borgmann was gut-shot, lying on the ground and bleeding, and probably unconscious or close to it. Yet he says he saw Shalih take the keys, unlock the gate, and escape."

"Has nothing to do with me."

"Yeah, Andy, it does."

CHAPTER 22

Rhonda turned off the shower, opened the door, and yelled down to Andy, "Are you cooking my favorite breakfast like you promised?"

"Yeah."

"Be down in five."

They'd left the Schnitzelbank around midnight, taken a shower together, and then spent the night together. Their lovemaking was mostly gentle and sometimes frantic, but never rough. She was surprised at her own desires and responses. She was more surprised at the tenderness that wrapped around them and seemed to lift them upward. She could not recall the last time they'd been this close.

Rhonda took her customary seat at the small kitchen table. Andy had set it with china, crystal, and their best silverware. She smiled when he handed her a steaming cup of strong, black coffee. Then he turned back to the stove and hummed tenor and baritone harmonies to "A Whiter Shade of Pale" coming from Dubain's NPR station. He passed eggs, hash, a mound of bacon, and orange juice to Rhonda.

Rhonda said, "The breakfast is wonderful." Then she leaned forward and grinned. "I love the table settings."

"Thought you hadn't noticed."

They laughed at Andy's white lie. Rhonda remembered the good times of their marriage when they'd been happy and easy together, just like now.

Andy poured more coffee. "So, what's up?"

"It's about Marian. She asked me to review the first draft of her autobiography and I did. Marian's passion comes through. She worries about her children and the world they'll inherit from us. Then she moves into ecosystems and global warming, and on to the elimination of weapons of mass destruction. She rails against the far right wing—the fundamentalists, evangelists, the 'family values' and 'god, guns, and gays' people—who have taken over the Republican Party and managed to elect the likes of President Sarah Harding."

Rhonda went silent. Andy asked, "What is it?"

"Andy, the Marian we know didn't write this book."

"Who did?"

"An angry and bitter Marian. She's written two stories. The first is in the prose. The second is in between the lines, or rather the lack of them."

"What'd she say about her husband?"

"That's just it, Andy. She hardly talks about him. Worse, she never moves from 'Governor Lincoln Pennington Kincaid' to making the case for 'President Lincoln Pennington Kincaid.'"

"At least she didn't write fiction. If you and Marian had left me alone I woulda busted that Scotch-swirling, strutting, arrogant, swell-headed, I'm-better-than-you, low-life's face of his."

Rhonda rolled her eyes. "Christ alive, Andy. That fracas was at their wedding."

"So my timing was a little off but I had a good reason. When he made fun of my beer, he insulted every red-blooded beer drinker in America, including the ladies. I was just doing my patriotic and chivalrous duty."

"You were a patriotic and chivalrous jerk." Rhonda couldn't hide her smirk. "Then she received KFA's version of her life. KFA's book is a trip down nutso lane. They transformed the bright, smart, and high-spirited Marian we know into a Snow-White-and-the-Seven-Dwarves idiot Marian. I don't even recognize her in it. The jaw-dropper was, and I quote, 'I saved myself for my handsome and loving husband.'"

"I'm gonna throw up."

"Marian hurled it back in their face. She told KFA that she might consider using the handsome husband virginity thing if KFA allows her to publish the loss-of-virginity stories of its top ten people in KFA."

"Good for her."

"KFA did offer an olive branch when they sent a young woman, Polly Thompson, to the governor's mansion to help Marian revise her version. I thought, *here comes Marian Kincaid Lite.* However, Marian says Polly's a pleasure to work with. I've met Polly and agree with Marian. There's more about her in the banker's box."

Andy mused. "You turned the Foundation and Kincaid's ties to it into a national story. I remember several years back when they tried to cover up the extra-marital affairs of several of their members. Got caught with their pants down."

"Literally." They laughed. "There's much research in the banker's box, but I can't seem to sort it all out. You might see something I don't. That's why I'm asking for your help."

"You know you have it."

Rhonda went upstairs. Andy gathered the dishes from the table and placed them in the dishwasher while his mind jumped all over Rhonda's words. They'd made love the night before and she was now asking—almost begging—for his help on a very sensitive investigation that involved her best friend. Was Rhonda signaling that she wanted to come back to him? Could he not exact a price—as yet vague and ethereal—for it? His lawyer instincts told him not to push it.

Andy turned on the dishwasher and placed the banker's box on the table. He put his hands behind his head, leaned back, and stared at the ceiling in thought.

Then he frowned.

Rhonda walked into the kitchen with her suitcase.

Andy said, "Here's what I don't get. The Foundation is far right wing. Sarah Harding should be their girl. However, they're hell-bent on electing a liberal, reform-minded governor from Indiana. Why?"

"That's the one-hundred-thousand-dollar question. Marian asked me, in so many words, to find the answer."

"Did your investigation come up in the conversation?"

"No."

"I didn't think so, and this leads me to another point—Marian also has secrets. There's no question in my mind that she's aware of your investigation through her lily-livered husband. At the same time, she's asked for your help. Marian is holding something back. She's sandbagging, as lawyers say."

"Don't come down on Marian. She's—"

"Your best friend. I get that. But she didn't ask you to find the truth. She's asked you to confirm it. There's a thin line between a friend who wants help and a mafioso who wants a hit man."

"Rhonda, what's going on?"

"I don't know. Not yet. That's the reason I asked for your help."

Andy looked away and down. In an undertone he said, "I'm proud of you."

"Oh, really? You're proud of me?"

Andy jumped up. "Spare me the sarcasm, Rhonda. When have I never supported your career?"

"Let's drop it, Andy. I shouldn't have brought it up."

"But you did." It had all changed in a few seconds. The give and take of their conversation had evaporated, as had the comforts of hope and the detached lawyer. A different temper suffused the kitchen. This had happened before—she could read his damn mind!

"Andy," she said, "I appreciate your help. I really do. However, I don't want you to get the wrong idea. I have a new life and I like it."

"Goddamn it to hell!"

"Andy, we've been through all this."

"No, Rhonda, not all. You've thrown me away."

"I have not. I separated myself from you. There's a difference."

"There is not."

"Andy, you've never left your father's pickup truck. You're happy there. You're safe there."

"We were high school seniors. You certainly enjoyed it, at least after—"

"My hymen broke. It was lovely and precious. However, you have to move on."

"Move on? That's meaningless. Our past—including the pickup truck—is part of us. If we drop what happened then, we lose ourselves now."

"I have no response to that."

"Of course you don't. That's the part you don't get."

"C'mon, Andy. You're dreamy, and romantic, and fun. You're highly intelligent, and remarkably intuitive. You're charismatic, creative, and willful.

You're a great person, Andy. People love you. They're attracted to you, and you genuinely love them back. You're decent, and tenderhearted. However, in so many ways, Andy, you've never grown up. In so many other ways, you have lifetimes of wisdom. You were born with these. They're instinctive to you. But you pay a price. You carry a weight, a sadness, that you cannot lay down. You try so hard to trump these with your off-the-wall sense of humor, but sometimes you fail.

"You have too many sides, Andy, and I get lost in them. You told me one time that if you didn't laugh, you'd cry. It's not selfishness on your part. It's just a different kind of loneliness than mine."

"Andy Balbach, the sonofabitch."

"Stop the self-pity, Andy. If you were a sonofabitch, this would be easy." Rhonda hesitated and then said, "There's something else, Andy. I can't say no to you. No one can say no to you. This gives you great power but also great responsibility. You have to understand this."

"Now you're talking gobbley-gook." Andy stood. "Fuck this." He walked to the back door and turned the knob.

"Stop, Andy."

"For what? It's obvious that your 'Andy doesn't support my career' is a facade. Nice, clean, convenient, and cliché-ish. I suppose last night was just more of all this."

"Andy, I'll say this as gently as I can. We both needed it, we both wanted it, we both loved it. However, I misled you. Now, I've hurt you even more. I'm so sorry, Andy."

"Gee, Rhonda, I can't tell you how fucking much it means that you're sorry."

"I'll leave the banker's box."

"Fuck the banker's box."

CHAPTER 23

Rhonda needed a safe place to cry. She backed her Toyota Camry onto Orchard Lane and headed west. She saw the steeple of St. Augustine Cathedral about a mile away, but it disappeared as she went down the steep, long hill on Orchard. At the bottom, she rolled through the stop sign, turned right onto Jackson, and parked behind an abandoned factory. She laid her head on the steering wheel and cried.

What price, Andy?

They'd known each other since kindergarten. In sixth grade, they sneaked from the playground of St. Augustine's School to the church steeple. There, behind the bushes, they kissed, and this sealed them together. They married two months after Andy graduated from Michigan Law School, and then set up their home in Dubain. Rhonda went to work for Stump's newspaper, the *Dubain Courier Journal*. She built a reputation for small-town investigative reporting and human interest stories while Andy became one of the best trial lawyers in Southern Indiana. Rhonda and Andy laughed much, cried together at sad movies, and finished each other's sentences. Rhonda mostly played to Andy's impulsiveness and the many predicaments in which he landed. At times, she'd try to scold him, but she couldn't hold the straight face required to do so.

In one of their girl-to-girl talks, Maria told Rhonda that her son Andy, like Peter Pan, treated life as an 'awfully big adventure.' Rhonda and Maria laughed at the remark. Only later did it register with Rhonda that Maria had planted in her the seed of profound insight into Andrew Joseph Balbach.

Andy's 'Peter-Pan' approach to life was the only one that made sense to him, indeed sustained his will to live. Andy pondered too much, felt too much, and knew too much. He was one of those rare souls fated to enrich the world around him with intuition, creativity, and conviction, but at the price of his own peace. Andy thought in dimensions, times, and places unknown and unknowable to her, or anyone she knew.

Rhonda loved the song, "Turn, Turn, Turn" by the Byrds. The song and lyrics spiritualized the message in Ecclesiastics: 'To everything there is a season.' There were times to be born and die, weep and laugh, gain and lose, love and hate, and so on. Andy hated the song and turned it off when she played it. Out of her anger at Andy's impulse, it dawned on her that Andy disdained notions of time and chronology, that his world had no beginnings, middles, or ends. He lived in a place where all seasons applied all the time. To others, this amounted to chaos. To Andy it was simply a piece of the universe in which he dwelled.

Andy fought his emotional pain with his sense of humor, wit, charm, willpower, and one hundred MPH go-at-life attitude. He once told Rhonda that his greatest fear was not dying, but boredom. Andy exulted when he found or made adventure, whether it was in a courtroom, at a movie with Rhonda, camping at Piankashaw Rock, hollering himself hoarse at a Big Ten football game, spouting inane comments, singing with the Beech Tree Boys, or exploring the ruins of old towns in the Hoosier National Forest. Andy charmed Rhonda to his will. He charmed juries, and clients, and the media. Andy charmed everyone, it seemed, to his will. He sensed he was different, but he rarely dwelled on it. He never asked Rhonda to accept him on his own terms as a price of her marriage to him. It never occurred to him. He had some self-awareness, but not much. He was like a ship that had lost its anchor and merely floated in the vastness of the oceans. But his descent into depression and his irritable moods of hypomania exacted a price on their marriage.

In the end, the charmer that was Andy could not charm himself.

Rhonda tried—oh, how hard she'd tried—to rescue Andy when the heartache overtook him. She held him when he spiraled down, and then she struggled to pull him back up. However, depression spawns melancholy. As time went on, Rhonda struggled more and more for herself, and less and less for Andy. She sensed the first inklings of separation when she realized that she had a choice and she could use it. She began weighing the cost of Andy Balbach, and marriage to him, against the value of her own peace.

Andy sensed Rhonda's change, but was helpless to stop it and the widening void between them. Andy denied the estrangement. Whenever she raised her frustrations, he would change the subject or simply walk away. When she persisted, he became angry.

But their separation had changed little. Before their breakup, life's circle always connected her to Andy. After their separation, the circle hadn't changed. She couldn't escape Andy's gravitational pull. Did she even want to? The previous night's lovemaking was much more than physical for her, much more than she'd told Andy. Instead, she lied to a man who was incapable of reconciling his loss of her with her stated reasons for it. In Andy's case, there was no acceptable point between lovers once and 'just friends' next.

Some people aren't meant to be happy. They're meant to be great. Was this her Andy? Was this his tragedy? She'd seen his sad side, but also his happy side.

However, an unfamiliar feeling had been moving into her since last night. It sprung on her now. What if there were times when Andy was acting? What if, by sheer willpower, he swallowed despair and showed happiness, not for his sake but for hers? Why was she suddenly baffled by all this? She'd been with Andy most of her life. Could it be that there were parts of him that she hadn't seen, hadn't even thought of, until after she left him?

Then she pictured Andy at the table, drowning himself in Jack Daniels and popping Valium tablets. My God! He could be on the edge of suicide and there was no one there to protect him. She could drive back to the house and stay with him, but eventually she'd have to leave, hurting him even more. Besides, she was struggling to escape the Andy circle, not be drawn farther into it. She called Maria and Tim, but there was no answer. She tried Al and Shelly, but neither would take her call. She finally reached Stump who said he'd look in on Andy.

Rhonda dried her eyes with a Kleenex and drafted a text message to Andy: "Please forgive me."

She didn't send it.

CHAPTER 24

Andy sat at the kitchen table. He'd turned to his latest best friends, Valium and Jack Daniels. He called them Val and Jack. They called him Andy. His psychiatrist said don't mix Val and Jack and Andy. Bad combination, he said. So, either Val or Jack should leave. No! Only two things counted—the pain, and then not the pain. Besides, Jack, Val, and Andy were intimates. It'd be a shame to separate them.

Andy introduced Remington, a.k.a. Andy's Remington 12-gauge shotgun, to Val and Jack. Wrong move. Val and Jack despised Remington for killing Herman Balbach. Remington told them they didn't have the guts to kill anyone. Remington rebuked Andy because he hadn't shot Remington since the accident. Andy threw it back. "You bastard," he pointed at Remington, "you clicked off the safety and couldn't wait for me to stumble over that log."

Andy turned away from Remington to the box of Rhonda's research lying on its side on the floor by the refrigerator. The top was partly off and half its contents lay on the floor. He thought about kicking the box again, and then again and again, until it and everything inside it was destroyed. He placed the box on the table and flipped through the first notebook. It was in Rhonda's handwriting and one sentence captured him: 'Jameel Shalih is innocent.' Farther down the page was another sentence: 'Andy will defend Shalih.'

"No!" he yelled. The notion of defending Shalih, of defending anybody, made him ill. At one time, Andy loved courtrooms. He loved their smell, the court reporters, the jury boxes, the judge's bench, even the opposing lawyer. He loved questioning witnesses and arguing to juries. He loved the combat, the sheer challenge of taking a hopeless case and winning it. He loved looking into the jurors' eyes as he persuaded them, one-by-one, of the righteousness of his client's cause.

After he and Rhonda started to have problems, Andy couldn't go near a courtroom. He'd lost his voice, his passion, his grasp of the law, and his confidence. The most insignificant hearings on simple issues, like pretrial motions and settlement conferences, made him sick to his stomach. One time, he'd had to excuse himself from the courtroom, run to a restroom, and vomit. He hardly ever worked these days. Some mornings he couldn't pull himself out of bed because he was either drunk or hung over. Clients fired him. Judge Townsend threatened to hold him in contempt for missing hearing dates.

No one could break through his isolation and despair. From some losses there was no returning.

Andy let his phone go to voicemail. It was Stump. He wanted to borrow Andy's lawnmower because his was in the shop for repairs. "Call me," Stump had said. Andy wouldn't. Instead, he thought about the peace of the next world. Certainly it was there. Val, Jack, and Remington would help him get there if he asked. Andy pushed the box away and moved Remington closer to Val and Jack. You decide, he told them. They commenced arguing, so Andy had to wait before jumping into the blissful abyss of oblivion.

Hey, that sounded neat—blissful abyss of oblivion. He said it aloud, "Blissful abyss of oblivion!" Andy laughed. It was so good he decided to use it at his next appointment with the psychiatrist. When the check-in lady asked for his insurance info he'd say 'blissful abyss of oblivion.' When the shrink asked how he was feeling he'd say, 'blissful abyss of oblivion.' He'd answer every question with 'blissful abyss of oblivion.' When they sent him to the loony bin he'd say 'blissful abyss of oblivion, blissful abyss of oblivion, blissful abyss of oblivion.'

The joke faded and Andy sobbed. He'd never make it to his next appointment. He'd never make it anywhere. After all, if he left the house somebody would get hurt and it would be his fault because nobody, except for Remington, could say no to him. He'd never asked for this power. He didn't want it. He knew not how to rid himself of it. There was only one way out. He looked at Val, Jack, and Remington and ended their argument. Andy chose Remington and explained. "It's an upside for both of us. You're one to zero against Balbach's. This'll improve your record to two to zero."

He fed Remington a 12-gauge shell and chambered it.

Someone knocked on the door. It was Stump. Remington was pissed but Val and Jack clapped. Andy hid Remington in the closet, but didn't remove the shell.

Andy drafted a text to Rhonda: "I love you."

He didn't send it.

CHAPTER 25

Rhonda's informant inside the Foundation, Imogene Thompson, sat across from her in a booth inside a dinky, out-of-the-way restaurant in Harrisonburg, Virginia. Rhonda had come to like Imogene, a courageous woman who struggled with alcohol and her husband's misanthropy.

Rhonda asked, "What did you say to Earl when you left this evening?"

Imogene, with a wry smile, said, "I told him I was attending an Alcoholics Anonymous meeting."

Rhonda held back a laugh. Imogene had called on a prepaid cell phone to set up the meeting.

"The Angels have revolted."

"Against whom?" Rhonda asked.

"The Foundation. Polly said that Lambs are innocent victims of the Cradlers and the Angels would no longer follow orders to 'put them out of the way.'"

"Polly defied her father?"

"Yes."

"Why?"

"It has to be something momentous, maybe even biblical, for Polly to take the risk."

"What kind of risk?"

"Polly—shall I say—is well versed on the reactions of her father when he detects a threat to the Foundation or Lincoln Kincaid's election. The Angels now pose just such a threat, if for no other reason than their revolt places them outside Earl's authority. Put another way, he no longer controls them, and an Earl Thompson without control is an Earl Thompson who resorts to extreme measures."

"Imogene, what are you telling me?"

"The Foundation formed a new group called 'Archangels.' Their job is to carry out the missions that the Angels have refused and end the revolt with extreme prejudice."

"Extreme prejudice means killing."

"Yes."

"Earl Thompson would kill his own daughter?"

"Of course. He'd kill me if he discovered my disloyalty." Imogene sipped her drink. "Earl Thompson is an evil man who hides behind his smile."

Rhonda couldn't get her head around the vulgarity of someone who would murder his own family for personal benefit. She ordered two whiskeys on the rocks, a single for Imogene and a double for herself.

Rhonda asked, "Who leads this group—'Archangels?'"

"Louis and Rose Cardova. They live in the Fallout Shelter and train young Foundation members. They trained Polly."

"Louis Cardova doesn't happen to have a shaved head and a ponytail, does he?"

"He does."

"Marian Kincaid and I met for lunch at the St. Elmo's in downtown Indianapolis. He posed as our server and bugged us. Earl, no doubt, ordered a written transcript. I need a copy. Marian… made a number of statements that were less than complimentary of her husband."

"I'm ahead of you." Imogene reached into her purse and handed a flash drive to Rhonda under the table.

"Thank you."

"There's more. The Archangels will recruit a spy among the Angels."

"That won't work."

"It will," said Imogene. "The Archangels will choose the person and then make an offer he can't refuse."

"Money?"

"That and the spy-to-be's life. The last is an Earl Thompson lie. He'll kill the spy after he's done with him."

Rhonda and Imogene hugged in the parking lot.

Rhonda asked, "Can you drive?"

"Yes. I have a high tolerance for alcohol."

"Earl might smell it on your breath."

"I'll respond like I always do. 'Honey, I stopped at a bar after the AA meeting and had a few.'"

Rhonda laughed. "Thank you, Imogene."

"I'm not done."

"I hope not," said Rhonda, "but these meetings are dangerous for you."

"You misunderstand. There's more information on that flash drive."

"About what?"

"Polly's birth." Imogene's eyes watered over. "And you," she pointed at Rhonda, "are probably on the list Earl keeps in his head, along with Polly and others."

"Earl Thompson wouldn't dare harm me. I'm too visible."

"They'll disguise it as a freak accident, or suicide."

CHAPTER 26

Her father had created a killer, and it was she.

On her first day of school he had told her she was a special little girl of Jesus, and special little girls of Jesus are quiet and do not have friends. When she was ten, he had told her she was special to Jesus and must never let anyone but Jesus know what she was thinking. At age thirteen, he had said she was so much smarter than all the other kids and so from now on she would attend school at home. Her mother would teach her, but she and Jesus and he would have a secret. Okay? Okay. He told her that her mother was not like her. He told her to take fully of her mother's intelligence and knowledge, which she has in abundance, but to know that her mother wastes her life in alcohol. "Your mother loves smiles. Hide yourself from her behind yours."

Two years later, he said she was a special young lady, and he introduced her to a man and a woman. "These are my friends," he had said, "Louis and Rose Cardova. Their home is the Fallout Shelter and it shall be your new home. They will feed and clothe you, run and lift weights with you, and teach you the dominion and glory of Jesus." He introduced her to another man, Garrett, and said he was his assistant and would oversee her.

He told her that one day Jesus would give her special powers of mind, body, and soul. Yes, that day would come, but only if she hid herself from all but Jesus. At age seventeen, he had said she was a special young woman and special young women have no boyfriends. She remembered the Young Life Camp she'd attended at age fourteen, and wanted to say that she'd already decided to have nothing to do with any boy, but she hid this behind her smile, just as he had taught her. At university, she watched other girls and saw their foolishness. A girl fell in love and then was jilted and sorrowful. The anger of a girl bred ridicule and abandonment. Unattractive girls wallowed in the miseries of rejection by others. Before, she'd had no time for happiness or sadness, anger or indifference, empathy or cruelty, hope or desperation. Now, she realized, she had no appetite for them. To keep to herself and Jesus was to be safe, and she was safe. She had graduated at the top of her high school class and then attended Purdue and Bob Jones University, where she had also reached the top of her class and had graduated with a degree in Systematic Theology. She would have spurned pride and joy had she felt any, but she did not. However, at the graduation ceremony, her mother allowed herself both a vodka bottle and a cry.

She came home. Her father greeted her and said she belonged to the Foundation and would dedicate her life to it. The Foundation was the wellspring of a covenant with the real Jesus. The real Jesus was not the liberals' Jesus. Theirs was the weak and sad-looking fool who spoke in parables and uplifted the poor at the expense of the wealthy. The real Jesus was a muscular carpenter, tough in mind, body, and spirit, and well-versed in the ways of wealth and power. He had explained the mission of the Foundation. The real Jesus had handed them the brilliance of the covenant, and anointed them His chosen people. For this, however, He exacted a price and the price was a task, stupendous in nature and glorious upon attainment. He commanded them to bring about His Kingdom on earth and then rule under it in joy and majesty. In this, He had handed them two cups. The first was fine and sweet. Most of the world will accept their rule, for what can be greater to a man than His Kingdom on earth? The second was bitter. There was a vastness of fire, trial, and suffering between what is and what shall be. The wicked, the blasphemous, the non-believing, and the homosexuals—most definitely the homosexuals—would rebuff them, spurn them, bear false witness against them, and inflict cruelties upon them. These have long since chosen the kingdom of Satan. They must be destroyed. He explained that the defeat of these people would be the glory of the Foundation. His last words were, "We dare not fail the command of Jesus."

Once more, Polly disappeared into the Fallout Shelter. Jesus bestowed on her the special powers her father had promised. She mastered the martial arts and excelled in the ways of the knife and garrote, the gun and explosive, the stalker and attacker. She learned how to kill, where to kill, when to kill, and who to kill. It was on these bases that she formed her own covenant with Jesus. Her mother, spineless, unguarded, and drunk, told her that her father was wrong and she need not accept her fate. She smiled at her mother but did not tell her that her fate was unalterable and that there was not now, nor had there ever been, an issue of her father's wrongness or rightness. Jesus and the Covenants were all right with her. She needed not the faculty of critical thought. She had the freedom of one who revels in action and need never question it.

Then came a time when she lost this freedom. A new and unfamiliar Jesus spoke to her at 4:45 a.m. on February 7, on the Dubain Riverwalk. An earthquake rolled under her feet, and a helpless fawn bleated for her help. It was innocent and suffering, and Polly had lifted the tree limbs to free it. There had been more than gratitude in the face of the mother.

Polly pondered this. However, from that moment, Polly Thompson's life of mindless obedience to her father began to slip away and a life of feeling—sadness, joy, anger, empathy, love, and hate—began to replace it. There became two of her. At first, her point of reference was that of the old Polly. Old Polly watched new Polly, and gradually old Polly began to fade. Slowly, painfully, she finished the journey from the old to the new.

She'd gained a new vision of her life and those around it. She saw her father manipulate and distort Jesus for the greater honor and glory of himself and his cronies. She'd watched him guide Imogene into a bottle. She grasped that he'd kidnapped her at birth and fed her to a culture of assassination. Her mother had tried to save both Polly and herself, but Polly wouldn't listen and her mother had failed.

It was the first time Polly remembered being afraid.

CHAPTER 27

Andy opened another file from the banker's box and again it popped out at him: X = Jesus + 0. He glared at it. Rhonda had said it made sense to someone but certainly not to her, and she'd asked Andy to unravel it. Andy loved the challenge but not the frustration.

He placed a legal pad in front of him. He considered the equation from two points of view, mathematics and theology. He listed bullet points:

- X = Jesus + 0. Stated in English: X Equals Jesus Plus Zero.

- Mathematically senseless. Zero neither adds to nor subtracts from Jesus. Zero added to anything equals that anything.

- Theologically senseless. Theology is all words, a few numbers, and no math.

- Remove the zero and you have "X Equals Jesus."

- Something equals Jesus?

Andy stared at his words, and then wrote, *Where the hell is this going?*

There was a knock and Stump entered. Andy motioned him over to Rhonda's kitchen chair. He'd started on the banker's box two days after his bout with Val, Jack, Remington, and Blissful Abyss of Oblivion. Stump had pulled him from the edge and actually proposed that Andy admit himself to the psych ward at St. Mary's Hospital. This Andy would not do. Stump stayed at Andy's house through the next morning and then drove him to Tim and Maria's house. Andy stayed for two days and then returned home. It was then that he dove into the banker's box.

Stump waved his arm around the kitchen. "Paper, files, flash drives all over. Your kitchen's a mess."

Andy smiled. "No, it isn't. It's organized chaos."

"How do you cook?"

"I don't. McDonald's serves low-fat Big Macs and fries."

"How far have you gotten?"

"A little over half. Rhonda's research on this outfit is scarier than hearing about it from her."

Andy pulled another folder from the banker's box and handed it to Stump.

"Don't know if I can help."

Andy said, "I don't either but I thought I'd try you out."

"What's the pay?"

"Ten cents per hour, liberal vacation time, beer benefits, and the Courier's greatest story of all time."

"Sign me on."

Andy said, "Look at the first page. Rhonda wants info from the government."

Stump read, "List of names US Army—need military records US Dept. Defense."

"Can you help?"

"Don't think so. It's classified. However, I recognize some of the names."

Two hours later they opened beers. Andy printed off his X Equals Jesus Plus Zero bullet point list and gave it to Stump.

"See anything that makes sense?"

"No," Stump replied. He laid down Andy's bullet points and opened a notebook he'd been reading. "Says here that the Foundation has been around since the 1930s. Anti-Roosevelt, anti-communist, anti-New Deal, anti-everything except what makes them more money. Their Jesus is not a deity to them, he's their buddy."

Andy stood up and paced. "Stump, picture the scene. This Thompson guy and his friends and Jesus... drinking buddies... sitting around the poker table. Earl Thompson says 'Five card stud, fellas. Ante a million.' Thompson deals the cards. Jesus has four aces but George has a straight flush and wins. He gets the millions. Earl says, 'Hey, Jesus, get us another round of beers, will ya?' Poof, and every man has another cold Bud in his hand. 'Thanks, Jesus. You're a helluva guy. Great gettin' to know ya, man-to-man.' Then Thompson gets sly. He looks at Jesus. 'Hey, Jesus, you threw the gamblers out of the temple just to fool everyone, didn't you?' Jesus says, 'Damn, Earl, thought you'd never figure that one out.' They all laugh like hell. Then Earl promises, 'Jesus, we'll pray ten Our Fathers, pay you royalties from the contract you got us, and beat the shit out of a queer before the cock calls three times. All in your name, Jesus Ol' Buddy.'"

They laughed.

Stump got serious. "They hate homosexuals. Remember when they hobnobbed with Vladimir Putin some years back? Got him to outlaw 'homosexual propaganda'—whatever that means. Good old Vladimir 'I hate queers' Putin. Must be in his upper eighties. Probably got him locked up in a special Russian 'Dacha For Senile High Up Russian Bastards With Blood On Their Hands.' Maybe Stalin and Khrushchev are in there with him. Not Lenin cuz he's stinking up the inside of that glass bubble."

Andy said, "Hmmm, in the olden days, they prayed with Putin and the top kahunas in Uganda. Today they pray with Russia's president and Congo's prime minister. What do Uganda, Russia, and the Congo have in common, other than their hatred of homosexuals? In the end, the motives are usually sex, money, or drugs. I'll rule out drugs for now. So, unless this Earl Thompson guy, Trotsky, and Ponya are in a love triangle, it's money."

"Siberia has enormous untapped natural resources."

"Right. The Chinese have had their greedy eyes on Siberia for centuries. Lincoln Kincaid brought up China and Siberia in his interview with Rhonda."

"Andy," said Stump, "why can't it be us? I mean, what more could a man want? All the Siberian gold he can steal and nobody trying to sodomize him."

They laughed.

Andy said, "They're talented in other ways. They use cash and offshore accounts. No paper trail, no proof, no taxes, no FBI, and no prosecutions.

Second oldest profession, Stump. In the first oldest profession, one person takes money from another person and screws that other person. In the second, a group of persons takes money from another group of persons, kicks back to them, and screws everybody else."

"Why are they so ate up about privatizing government?"

Andy said, "It's too good a gig, Stump. They direct the privatizing contracts to their members. 'Wanna run that school? Sign this contract and you're the boss. Get rid of the union, fire the highest paid teachers and aides, put a hundred kids in every classroom, and make a ton of money. That county hospital's going under because they treat too many people who don't pay. Here's your contract. It gives you authority to turn away the want-it-all-for-nuthin-mama with black eyes and a kid running a hundred-and-five-degree temperature. You got friends in high places so overbill Medicare and Medicaid and the insurance companies, and you get away with it.'

"Here's another. The governor of the brand new state of Candy-Ass says they need more interstate lanes around Bumblenuts, their capital city. 'See this here contract about a foot thick? Don't worry. It's nothing but a bunch of legal hocus-pocus-dominocus. Most of it don't mean shit. The stuff that does is hidden. The deal is you add the extra lanes. In return, you get a ninety-nine-year lease on the roads.' Oh, the kicker. 'You collect the tolls. Pay your investment and pocket the rest for yourself. Stick it to the toll-paying whiners who are too cheap to pay the taxes for better roads.'

"The bastards love vouchers. They take money from the public schools and give it to the private schools. Great setup. Starve the public schools so they get worse. Then get the people to support more vouchers and—"

"The upshot is more profits to the Foundation's friends," said Stump.

"The greater upshot is you get uneducated kids who turn into uneducated voters who fall for the Foundation line. The greatest upshot is that you weaken government itself."

Stump asked, "Does any of the money make it to the Foundation itself?"

"Kickbacks. Going both ways. The Foundation owes former Senator Dingleberry because he guided an appropriation for that school in Minnesota that cures homosexuals. So they offer him a sweet contract. 'Senator Dingleberry,' they say, 'go run this private school and you'll get rich.' Now, Dingleberry's mom didn't raise no dumb ass. The devil set up the sweet deal and Dingleberry must pay the devil his due. So he kicks back to the Foundation. Nothing is said. Nothing is written down. No checks, no money orders, no wires, no banks. Only cash and a little cooperation from the Cayman Islands banks."

"This Foundation outfit," said Stump, "ain't your grandma's fundamentalists."

"Yeah. Creepy, isn't it?"

"It's more than creepy, Andy. They're gunning for a fascist state ruled by them."

"Right, Stump. They have the contacts and the money. They've infiltrated our governments. They talk the talk and walk the walk of traditional fundamentalist Christianity. That's okay. We can handle that. But they're nothing of the sort. They can do no wrong because they own Jesus. Their ends justify their means. They kill people in the name of Jesus yet they're free from sanction.

"The worst is that no one pays attention to this side of the Foundation because they know nothing of it, yet the Foundation creeps are out there for everyone to see. They go to traditional churches, pray, coach little league, barbecue with their neighbors, take their families to Yosemite, and bore the hell out of you with photos of their kids and grandkids on their smart phones. They drink a beer after mowing their lawns, get artificial hips, bitch about the government, and get flu shots. They hide in plain sight but they're snakes in the grass.

"No one can stop them except—"

"Rhonda." Stump finished Andy's sentence.

Andy stood and walked to the sink.

"Andy, I'm worried about her too."

"She's in danger, but she won't listen to me."

"I was her boss. Still am. Maybe I can get into that stubborn Irish head of hers… get her to take some precautions."

CHAPTER 28

Polly Thompson had chosen Dubain as a base of operations for the high-stakes and dangerous mission her father had assigned to her and Garrett Jennings a year before. He said that they had at hand a leader, chosen by Jesus, who would command vast forces to bring about His Kingdom. They must protect him. Her father said to choose her base of operations carefully. Garrett was versed in strategy but unfamiliar with tactics. Polly was superb at both. Dubain, located in the center of Southwestern Indiana, came more and more into focus. Polly had rented a hotel room and spent a week exploring the town and the territory around it. On the one hand, Dubain offered less cover than a larger city. On the other hand, it was within easy driving distance of the Indianapolis, Louisville, Evansville, and Nashville airports. It was close to Camp Morgan, a minimum-security prison and a hive of Cradler targets for the Angels. The Hoosier National Forest, to the east of the city, offered both escape routes and the hideaways of Raven Rock, Piankashaw Rock, and Hemlock Cliffs. Therefore, she'd chosen Dubain and centered her operations in a place long forgotten to the Dubain townspeople.

Before the tremor and the fawn, Polly had sent her underlings on missions around the country and sometimes outside it without a thought to their dangers. She viewed them as interchangeable parts and valued them only to the extent they were mission successful. If one of them failed to return, she marked the name from her list, notified her father, and awaited the replacement. They were mere assets, and the loss of an asset was no more and no less than just that. After the tremor and the fawn, she ached for their safety and deliverance. She perceived them as extraordinary persons who saved innocents. She named them her Angels, entered into a new covenant with Jesus, and defied her father. Garrett Jennings had responded with the Archangels. Thereafter, Polly sent the Angels against Cradlers only when the target's immorality was clear, the menace from the Archangels minimal, and she could accompany them.

Polly had an advantage over Garrett and his Archangels. Rhonda O'Malley shared with Polly the numbers and dispositions of the Archangels. Rhonda gathered this information from a source inside the Foundation. Rhonda never disclosed the source to Polly and Polly never asked.

Polly's favorite Angel was Johnnie Christiansen. Johnnie's special weakness was his inability to perceive danger. At one time, this had concerned Polly insofar as it risked the loss of a highly valuable and hard-to-replace asset. Then Jesus spoke to her on the Dubain Riverwalk. The fawn was innocent. Johnnie was innocent. She saved the former and would protect the latter. From that moment of clarity, she cared nothing of Johnnie the asset and deeply for Johnnie the innocent.

Johnnie Christiansen had grown up in San Francisco. Two years before, when he was seventeen, his family, concerned about what they called 'homosexual tendencies,' sent Johnnie to their friend, Earl Thompson, and asked him to rid Johnnie of any such desires. Earl placed Johnnie in Polly's charge and training. Several months later, she assured Earl and Johnnie's parents that Johnnie had no homosexual leanings and was probably still a virgin. It was just that Johnnie's good looks and palpable innocence attracted both women and men.

What she told Earl, but not Johnnie's parents, was that she had Johnnie tested at the Children's National Medical Center in D.C. The doctors told her most of what she already knew or suspected. Johnnie had visual acuity in the 99th percentile, the maturity of a twelve year old, High Functioning Autism Spectrum Disorder, and Savant Syndrome, a rare condition little understood but highly manifested in a person who possessed it.

The doctors had told her that Johnnie had a photographic memory and considerable mathematical, mechanical, and spatial skills. They said he would excel at complicated sciences such as quantum physics. One pulled Polly to the side. He told her that Johnnie was a sure winner at a blackjack table because he could memorize, or 'count' cards already dealt, and calculate the probabilities of the fall of cards still in the deck. However, Earl did not send Johnnie to Purdue University, Polly's school prior to Bob Jones University, which was, Earl mused aloud, "the cradle of astronauts, quarterbacks, and cutting edge research." He instead enrolled Johnnie in Foundation University, "the cradle of Jesus, obedience, and covenants." There, Johnnie excelled. He was a winner at blackjack, a deadeye shot in basketball, and a dead-on sniper with firearms. The Foundation had some use for the blackjack, little use for the basketball, and great use for the shooting.

When Johnnie's father, Fredrick Christiansen, saw Johnnie on the range hitting one bullseye after another, he proclaimed that he knew for sure that Johnnie was not a homosexual, because "no queer can shoot that well."

Polly tried to explain her metamorphosis to Johnnie. He didn't understand, or so she thought. Johnnie said nothing, but he disappeared for the rest of the day. The next day he came to her with a notebook whose pages he'd filled with various Bible passages and numbers. She could make little sense of it. There was something about a fault and certain dates going back more than two hundred years. The rest were mathematical symbols.

Johnnie explained as best he could explain anything. He said the recent tremor had been spawned by a dangerous fault called New Madrid. The fault started in Arkansas and Tennessee and ended in Indiana, near Dubain. The New Madrid fault had spawned the largest earthquakes in North America. There were three major earthquakes in 1811 and 1812. They were felt as far away as Boston, New York, New Orleans, Minneapolis, Washington, D.C., and South Carolina. They terrified the early settlers in Indiana. Black clouds of coal dust blotted out the sun. The dust came from coal seams near the surface of the earth. The quakes caused the ground above the seams to open and slam shut. When the ground opened, the coal seam was exposed. When the ground slammed shut, the top of the coal seam shot into the air. Water tables rose to make quicksand out of previously dry land. Rivers spilled their banks. The Mississippi River flowed backward for several days. Giant oaks, over three hundred years old, toppled. The chimneys attached to settlers' meager cabins broke apart. Johnnie said that some settlers in Southwestern Indiana kept diaries of the time, and that he had found them on the Internet. They said that, right before each earthquake struck, game had become more wild and then more scarce, and that these phenomena were most pronounced in deer. The settlers interpreted all this as a sign from Jehovah that the end times were here, and that they must repent of their sins.

Johnnie had written down the times of the three quakes. The first occurred on December 16, 1811, at 3:15 a.m.; the second on January 23, 1812, at 10:15 a.m.; and the third and last, on February 7, 1812, at 4:45 a.m. The recent tremor had occurred on February 7, at 4:45 a.m., the precise time and date of the last earthquake in 1812.

Johnnie had added the dates of the three: December 16, 1811 = 12 + 16 + 11 = 39. The next two were 1 + 23 + 12 = 36 and 2 + 7 + 12 = 21.

Johnnie summed the three numbers: 39 + 36 + 21 = 96. Then he opened a Bible.

The number 96 has great significance in the Bible, he explained. It was used only two times. It was the sum of the occurrences of all numbers in the New Testament that are multiples of eight. There are 365 numbers in the Bible. Of those, 269 are even numbers and 96 are odd numbers. Dividing 96 by 8 equals 12.

The biblical signs were unmistakable. Polly had encountered two deer, moments after an earthquake that was triggered by the same fault on the same date and time as the latest of the earlier quakes. February was the number two month of the year, and seven denotes completeness and perfection, both physically and spiritually. It was no accident that the sum of the three dates in 1811 and 1812 was 96, and that 96 equals 8, which symbolizes a new order, times 12, the perfect number.

The biblical significance of the numbers derived from the 1811 and 1812 earthquakes and the recent tremor—96, 12, 8, 7, and 2—meant that the Angels, not the Foundation, were God's New Chosen. The real Jesus is that of the Gospels in which He, like Polly and the fawn, set multitudes free. The terrified pioneers in their cabins in 1811 and 1812 had it wrong. The quakes were not signs of the end but of the beginning.

To Polly, this was the voice and words of the new Jesus. She formed a new covenant called 'Angel Covenant.' Polly gathered her Angels around her and proclaimed that the times and dates of the last quake in 1812 and the recent tremor centered the Kingdom of Jesus not in Washington, D.C., but in the gently rolling hills of crops, pasture, woods, and poultry farms in

Southwestern Indiana. The small tremor was but a prelude to a much larger earthquake. Jesus would speak again, and when he did, a good part of the American Midwest, centered near Dubain, would be devastated with great loss of life and property. It would be from the ashes of this disaster that the new Kingdom Of Jesus, led by Polly and the Angels, would arise.

Polly named the Angels' hideout in Dubain '7-12,' the numbers for perfection and a new order.

CHAPTER 29

Stump met Rhonda at the door and led her into the hallway.

"Tadpole, the Beech Trees are entertaining at the Schnitzelbank this Saturday evening. Andy's agreed to lead it."

"Is Andy here?"

"No. I'd like you to team up with him. Can you do it?"

"I can if Andy's okay with it."

"He is. There'll be a large crowd due to the high school band contests in town. Kimmy'll whistle the crowd and then hand the stick to Andy. Andy'll do his humble declining act until the crowd begs him to lead it. Then you'll jump in to get the crowd into the chorus. The quartet will sing backup."

"I'm out of practice."

"It's your lucky day, Tadpole. We're rehearsing it next and you can sing lead with Clubby. After that, you're having supper with us... ham sandwiches, potato salad, and beer."

"I'm here to get information, not fight Clubby and get drunk."

"Clubby's cooled considerably and I've never seen you squeamish about a drink. We'll talk after supper." Stump walked into the kitchen, returned with a beer and handed it to Rhonda. "You're tense as hell, so here, start early."

Clubby and Rhonda said hello to each other and kept their peace.

Rhonda had written an article on the "Schnitzelbank Song." It was an energetic and humorous tune with German lyrics. The song was named after a woodworking tool, called, appropriately, *Schnitzelbank*. German immigrants in the 1800s brought the tool to Dubain in order to take up carpentry, the trade they'd left behind in Germany. Rhonda and the men filled their paper plates, opened their beers, and took seats around Stump's dining table.

Clubby asked, "Stump, who you gonna vote for? Kincaid or your old girlfriend, Josie Carter Lodge?"

"None of your business."

"Aw, c'mon Stump," said Billups. "We heard you and Josie were hot and heavy at Indiana University."

Clubby asked, "Stumpy, why'd she come all the way from Maine to go to IU?"

"IU School of Business. Top ranked."

"How long did you date?"

"Two years."

Clubby said, "Give us the details, Stump."

"You don't need the details. Besides, I'm a gentleman."

Billups persisted, "Don't leave us hanging, Stump. Besides, you're not that much of a gentleman."

"Billups, you know nothing about nookie with a woman."

Clubby asked, "Did you ever visit her in Maine?"

"Yeah."

"Did her family like you?"

"Yeah."

"Did she visit Dubain and meet your folks?" Billups asked.

"Yeah."

"Did she like Dubain?"

"We never talked about it."

"Course not," said Clubby. "You were too busy getting the nookie."

Rhonda cut in, "Let's drop the subject. Okay, guys?"

CHAPTER 30

Rhonda got another beer for Stump, poured a glass of wine for herself, and then took a seat at the kitchen table opposite him. For a moment, Rhonda remembered another kitchen table when she had sat opposite Andy.

"That's the sixth drink for a woman who came here for information and not to get drunk."

"Didn't know we were counting."

Stump lit a cigarette, offered one to Rhonda, and then lit hers. "What do you want, Tadpole?"

"Information," said Rhonda.

"What kind of information?"

"Important information."

"How important?"

"Extremely."

"Go on."

"The information is classified."

"Why?"

"Privacy."

"Target?"

"The government."

"Which government?"

"Federal."

"Which part?"

Rhonda said, "Department of Defense."

"Weapons systems, battle plans, national security 'for your eyes only' type stuff. The government frowns on people who bust their firewalls and get into these things."

"I don't want national security secrets."

"What do you want?"

"Information on certain people."

"Go look in the phone book."

"They don't make them anymore. Where have you been?"

"Damn," said Stump. "Next thing you know a man's gonna hafta buy toilet paper."

Rhonda said, "I have a list of fifteen names."

"Where?"

"In my shirt pocket."

"Part of your Kincaid-Foundation investigation?"

"Yeah."

"Glad to hear that. I was afraid this was about you entering the Mars Astronaut Corps."

"This is serious, Stump."

"See me laughing?"

"No."

"Show me the list."

Rhonda smoothed it out on the table.

"Impressive bunch," said Stump.

"Do you know them?"

"Sort of. There are five names I recognize—Jameel Shalih, Jayden Ramirez, Kurt Borgmann, and those two guards that Shalih's been accused of killing. Who are the other ten?"

"Dead people. What do you mean, sort of?"

"I mean sort of. Are you in their wills?"

"No." She looked puzzled.

"Did you know any of them?"

"No."

"How did they get dead?" Stump asked.

Ronda turned toward the window. "I don't know."

"Tadpole, I fell off the turnip truck."

"You did? When?"

"Not yesterday."

"They were most probably murdered."

"When?"

"First murder on the list was a little less than a year ago."

"Who murdered them?"

"I don't know."

"Do they have anything in common, other than that most are dead?"

"All of them served in the military. I need their enlistment dates, branches, posts, and discharge dates."

"Going back how far?"

"Sometime in 2003. Most on the list served then. The rest served at various times since."

"Any particular place?"

Rhonda said, "The Tigris River Prisoner-of-War Camp in Baghdad, Iraq. Can you help me?"

"Do I look like General Von Friggen Kluckhead to you?"

"No."

"Good, but maybe I can help anyway."

"Maybe?"

"Not 'maybe.' More like I already have." Stump placed another list on the table.

Rhonda said, "These are the same people on my list, but with the information I needed. How—"

"I made a few phone calls, Tadpole."

Rhonda said, "Andy."

"Andy?"

"You and Andy. How much of the stuff in that banker's box has he shown you?"

"He keeps me posted on what he learns as he goes through it. I helped him go through part of the box several days ago, in fact. He found a copy of this list. You'd scribbled the data you wanted on the back. Andy asked me to look into it."

"I told Andy that the banker's box is confidential."

"It is."

"Make sure it stays that way."

Stump glared at her. "Why'd you ask Andy to go through your research?"

"Andy's smart and I wanted his take on this."

"Bullshit, Tadpole. You could have asked any number of people, including me, but you didn't. You asked Andy. Know what I think?"

"I don't care what you think."

"Yeah you do or you wouldn't be here. There are two possibilities. Either you're using Andy for your own glorification, or you're still in love with him. Which is it?"

Rhonda glared back. "Go to hell, Stump."

"You haven't answered my question."

"I don't have to."

"Yeah, you do. I'm still your boss."

"No, you're not."

"Reconsider that answer, Tadpole, like real quick."

"Okay. You're my boss."

"Glad that's settled." Stump got another beer from the fridge and poured Rhonda a glass of wine. "I got another one for you. You took a helluva chance when you told Kincaid in the interview that the Tigris River investigation was a cover-up. You didn't know that and you weren't sure how he'd respond. Remember the first rule about a live telecast interview. Never—"

"Ask a question that you don't already know the answer to. I did take a chance."

"You got lucky, Tadpole."

"I did."

"Well, you just got luckier. I know the general who investigated Kincaid and Tigris River."

"Personally?"

"Yeah. Talked to him yesterday, as a matter of fact. He sat in the same chair you're in now."

"He actually flew in to see you?"

"Come off it, Tadpole. I thought you knew more about Dubain. It just turns out that General David Hernandez grew up in French Lick. When the army, in effect, kicked him out because he told the truth about Tigris River, he and his wife retired to a home here. Yeah, right smack dab in that fancy-dancy subdivision on MacArthur Drive. The guy's got an axe to grind with the army. He wants to meet with us."

"Can you schedule it?"

"Way ahead of you, Tadpole. You, Andy, and I will meet him and his wife at the Schnitzelbank for dinner Saturday evening before the entertainment starts. If you impress him, he might stay to watch you and Andy perform the Schnitzelbank Song."

"Thanks."

"It doesn't take a genius to see that you intend to expose both the Foundation and Lincoln Kincaid. Kincaid is the more vulnerable. His story starts when he lived at Oakenwald, and then it moves to Tigris River, his terms in Congress, his little prayer-dance with Ponya, and his 'maybe connection' to Ponya's massacre of his own people. Then it moves to the governorship. Now he's running for president and if the election were held today he'd win it big time. In all this, you've established a pretty strong connection between Kincaid and the Foundation and you likely have multiple sources to back this up."

"I do."

"By the way, I wouldn't stress the massacre. Kincaid's an asshole, but he's not a mass murderer."

"I agree."

"Good analysis. Now, listen up. This Foundation crowd is a bunch of first-class pricks, but a smart and dangerous bunch of first-class pricks. Seems that anybody who knows too much about them or Lincoln Kincaid ends up in the morgue or at the bottom of some lake. My guess is that most of the fifteen people on your list knew too much. Take care you don't find yourself inside a cooler with a tag on your big toe."

"I won't live in fear."

"Fear is sometimes necessary. It tends to keep people like you alive. There's another thing, Tadpole."

"What's that?"

"Andy. The stuff in that banker's box places him in danger if they find out about it."

"Stump, I never intended to place Andy in danger. Do... do you think they'll find out? Wait! You know about the box, too. I opened a can of worms and I never intended to put Andy or you at risk."

"I know you didn't." Stump lowered his voice. "Andy and I have talked about this. We're big boys and we both know the risk, which is quite small."

Rhonda pulled Kleenex out of her purse. "I know that, but now I feel so guilty. I was so insensitive to Andy."

"The man you still love?"

Rhonda finished her wine and stood.

Stump asked, "Where are you going?"

"Indianapolis."

"You've had too much to drink. It's my guestroom for you tonight."

She searched in her purse for her car keys, then she searched her pockets, and then looked at Stump. "Where are my keys?"

"They're safe."

"Give me my keys."

"I will. Tomorrow morning."

Stump went into Rhonda's bedroom with fresh towels. He wore sweats and a T-shirt.

"Still awake?"

"Yeah."

"Thanks for shutting down the Josie talk at supper."

Rhonda rolled toward Stump and he sat on the bed. "I've known you for years, Stump, and learned only today that you and Josie Carter Lodge had a fling."

"It wasn't a fling. We were engaged."

"What happened?"

"She wouldn't move to Dubain and I wouldn't move to Maine. That's all."

"Do you stay in contact?"

"That's a professional secret."

"It's also a 'yes,'" said Rhonda. "Do you still have feelings for her?"

"I put Josie behind me a long time ago."

Rhonda stared at Stump. "No, you didn't."

"'Danny Boy.'"

"'Danny Boy?'"

"'Danny Boy.' Josie loves that song."

"You're still in love with Josie. After all these years, you're still in love, aren't you?"

"Are we talking about me or you?"

"How long does love last, Stump?"

"If you're lucky, the rest of your life."

"Are you lucky?"

"Maybe." Stump grinned.

"Love hurts, Stump."

"Yeah."

"Do you stay in touch?"

"Yeah. Had a little chat with her last week, in fact."

"About all this?"

"Confidential. Priest-penitent thing."

"You're not a priest."

"Damn. Missed my calling."

"Stump?"

"Yeah?"

"I'm not using Andy."

"I know you're not, but methinks you still hold the torch for him. You took it up in grade school and you never put it down. I ask of you one thing."

"What?"

"Don't make the same mistake I made with Josie."

Rhonda raised and kissed Stump on the cheek.

"Good night, Stump."

"Good night, Rhonda."

"You mean 'Tadpole,' don't you?"

Stump left the bed. He turned around in the doorway. "There's something else."

"What?"

"You've given Andy the greatest gift any man in his position can wish for."

"What's that?"

"You've given him an enemy."

"How can that be a good thing? He's a lawyer. He already has enemies. They're other lawyers, some of his clients, and judges that upset him."

"Correct, but those enemies change colors for Andy. Over time, they mostly turn into non-enemies, and then mostly friends. However, he sees

Lincoln Kincaid and the Foundation differently. To Andy, they are black and evil, and they will not change. He need not concern himself with shades of color. He can slash and burn and maul them without the least pang of guilt. I've seen it. Andy has turned his anger, frustration, and hurt on them and away from himself."

Stump closed the door.

Rhonda got off the bed, removed all her clothes, and slipped between the sheets.

CHAPTER 31

Garrett clicked the Polly icon and she appeared on the large-screen, three-dimensional monitor in the boardroom. She stared at Garrett and said nothing. *Go at her head-on*, Garrett reminded himself.

"Let me introduce two former friends of yours." The Cardovas appeared on the screen with Garrett. "Louis and Rose are heading up the new group, Archangels. I assume you've heard of them."

"No."

"Now you have."

Polly said nothing.

Garrett continued. "We now have a square—Cradlers, Lambs, Angels, and Archangels. Great symmetry, don't you think?"

Polly said nothing.

Garrett said, "Maybe it's not clear to you. The Cradlers are homosexual rapists. The Lambs are the Cradlers' victims. The Angels' mission is to eliminate those Cradlers and Lambs who jeopardize the election of Lincoln Kincaid. This changed when you led the Angels in mutiny. Now we have the Archangels. Their job is to finish the Angels' mission and put down the Angels' rebellion. Louis and Rose are the Archangels' field commanders."

Polly stared back at Garrett.

"Your father has issued the following orders. The Angels shall disarm themselves and return to Oakenwald within seven days. Their disobedience of this order will condemn them to a state of treason and they shall suffer the consequences."

"Put my father on the monitor."

"He's not here."

"Where is he?"

"Doesn't matter. He has directed me to pass on anything you have to say."

"Then tell him this—the Angels, including his daughter, do not recognize his or the Foundation's authority, and have no intention of returning to Oakenwald."

"Do you wish to reconsider that statement?"

"No."

Garrett hesitated but kept eye contact with Polly. No one dared to disobey a direct order from Earl Thompson. It was unthinkable—until now. "The penalty for treason against the Foundation is quite severe."

"The penalty is death, Garrett. There's no need to wallow in your sordid euphemisms."

"There must be no misunderstanding. Your family connection does not exempt you."

"My family connection has never exempted me. My father buried a daughter at her birth and resurrected a killer. He never considered that the daughter, too, would resurrect, but she has. Today, I am alive."

"You talk in circles."

"I'm free to talk any way I want. I'm also free to ask questions. Where is my mother?"

"I believe Imogene is in the residence."

"No one's seen her in months. Why?"

"She's been drinking heavily."

"Why hasn't my father put her into rehab?"

"You've ignored Imogene for years," said Garrett. "Your father's had to deal with her drinking alone. You haven't lifted a finger to help him."

Polly only smiled. A profound anxiety gripped Garrett, and he could not be certain that he'd hidden the chill that had rushed through his body. Polly was a highly skilled assassin and he, Garrett, was no bystander. She'd gone renegade and was making up her own rules. *Could he appear on her assassin list? Was he already on it? If so, could she get close enough to kill him? Was she hiding this behind her smile?* Garrett hesitated. Then Earl Thompson appeared on the lower right corner of the monitor.

Earl said, "Hello, Polly."

"Where's my mother?"

"She's at the Lakeside Treatment Center in North Palm Beach, Florida."
Polly nodded.

Earl continued, "You dare defy the Foundation and me and then you
brush away the consequences? Something has changed you. What is it?"

"Jesus speaks here, in Indiana. His Kingdom is here, in Indiana. It is not
there, in Washington, D.C."

"Nonsense!"

"Where does the killing end, Father?"

Garrett said, "Explain yourself."

"The Angels kill Lambs and Cradlers. The Archangels kill Lambs,
Cradlers, and Angels. This will end someday. What happens to the Angels
and Archangels still standing? They know too much and they might talk.
Mustn't they be killed also? Who murders the murderers?"

"Come in, Polly," said Earl. "It's your only option. Time is running out.
Come in before it's too late."

Garrett slept little that night. Polly had asked "who murders the murderers?" He'd raked over the same question for months. The simple answer
presented itself—murderers murder the murderers.

CHAPTER 32

For JSGold, it was always a 'they' who came for him. When he was a child in his native Iraq, 'they' were the Shi'a who came for him and his family because of their Christian faith and friendships with Sunnis. When he was a teenager in Detroit, 'they' were the police who came for him, a member of a family of confused immigrants, and falsely accused him of stealing in order to protect the real thief, the son of one of the cops. When he was serving his adopted country in uniform at Tigris River in Baghdad, 'they' were his commanders who had come for him for stealing food and selling it on the black market. Another 'they' were coming for him now because he knew too much about them. If it was a double-cross, they'd be coming for him right now, in the middle of a hot summer night, and right here, in the cavernous loft of St. Augustine Cathedral.

JSGold had acquired an intimate knowledge of the history and structure of St. Augustine. He'd studied its past on a tablet computer stolen from St. Augustine school and Wi-Fi commandeered from the church. At night he explored the building, looking for nooks and crannies where he might hide if the need arose. When he stood on the floor of the cathedral and looked up, he could count eighteen hemispherical arches, six on the south side, six on the north side, and six in the middle. Each was white with red stripes. Each stripe started at the base and met the other stripes at the topmost point of the hemisphere. Stained glass windows dominated the north and south walls. When he stood on the two-foot-wide catwalk nailed to the ceiling rafters of the church and looked down through a hole he'd found in the northwestern-most dome, he could see the cathedral's floor 115 feet beneath the catwalk. One step off the catwalk meant a plunge through the balsam-like material of a dome to a death on the floor or over the back of a pew.

The steeple on the east side of the cathedral had five sections. Section one, the lowest, rose from the steeple's foundation to the utility landing. This landing marked the steeple's halfway point and flushed with the catwalk leading into the loft. Section five, the highest, was the golden cross, the top of which was 294 feet above ground level. In between were section two, the belfry, which housed four bells, each weighing twelve tons; section three, the steeple's clock unit; and section four, the Lookout Room. The Lookout Room, 270 feet above the sacristy, was a cube, each dimension about twelve feet. There were four, square, open-air windows, one each facing north, south, east, and west. The north window opened to Kundek Cemetery, the south toward the Dubain County Courthouse, and the east toward Apple Hill about nine blocks from the church. The west window looked out over the top of the cathedral to St. Augustine School and, beyond it, to St. Mary's Hospital.

The catwalk began at the utility landing and extended 307 feet to the cathedral's west wall. Wooden beams were attached to every sixth ceiling rafter and ran upward at an angle to the church's roof rafters. The utility landing housed the electrical circuits for the clocks and bells in the steeple.

He stood on the catwalk near the west side, or back of the cathedral, and peered through the hole into the church. The cathedral's immensity swallowed up the flickering candles on the main and side altars and the bit of street light that prismed through the stained glass windows. However, there was just enough light to eye the entrance doorway on the east side near the front of the church. At night, this door alone allowed entrance into and exit from the cathedral. Town bums came through it to sleep under the pews in the back of the cathedral. Other Dubain people entered to pray or perhaps to silently confess a sin that had stolen their sleep.

His backpack lay on the catwalk beside him. In it were the tablet computer, one charger, two loaded pistols, and extra ammunition. He carried a third gun in the back of his trousers and a flashlight in the front. It was uncomfortable but he needed both arms free. He'd practiced escape routes. If they came for him from the west side, he could escape via the catwalk onto the utility landing and down the steeple staircase to ground level. If they came for him from the utility landing, he could escape down the west wall. If they came from both sides, he'd shoot his way out.

He checked his watch. Three minutes.

A tall but stooped-shouldered man with a cap pulled low on his face entered. He shuffled more than walked, and he held onto something in his right pocket. A pint of whiskey or a gun? He made his way down the aisle and disappeared into the darkness in the back of the church. Exactly fifty-four seconds later, the south door swung again and his subject stepped inside the church. She genuflected before the main altar, glanced over her shoulder toward the darkness that had swallowed the man, and then disappeared behind the altar.

It could be a setup. He slipped on the backpack, got down on all fours, checked the gun, and then began to crawl on the catwalk toward the utility landing. He would confront the danger there.

CHAPTER 33

Kundek Cemetery lay to the north and northwest of St. Augustine Cathedral. The top of the cemetery, All Souls Point, was the highest elevation in Dubain. From All Souls Point, the cemetery sloped down on all sides to flatter land and the wrought-iron fence that guarded its borders. An American flag flew above All Souls Point. At night, the flag, illuminated by floodlights, was visible to most of Dubain and to some areas outside it. However, the floodlights were timed to turn off at midnight.

It was now 12:45 a.m., and All Souls Point was dark. Rhonda had scheduled the meeting with JSGold at 1:00 a.m. She wore dark farmer-type overalls, a long-sleeved black T-shirt, and a black cap. The cap was pulled low over her face and covered her tied-up hair. The side pockets of the overalls were filled with energy bars, and the breast pocket held her smart phone. She started into the cemetery from its north side and walked uphill toward All Souls Point. She stopped behind Herman Balbach's monument in the Balbach family plot to get her bearings and lost her concentration when she recalled the gravesite rites for Herman so many years before. She'd been there. Andy, sitting between his parents, had cried inconsolably. She next turned her eyes to the maple tree, slightly uphill from the Balbach dead, and remembered another hot, midsummer night, twenty-some years before. She and Andy had pulled off a risky stunt on a challenge from their high school classmates. The flush of their triumph was consummated on the bed of Andy's father's pickup truck, parked under the tree. It was the first time for both. She remembered the pain, and then the pleasure, of their couplings that night.

Rhonda scanned the area for the shadow or movement of a would-be follower, someone ill disposed toward JSGold, Rhonda, or both. Strangely, and a bit annoyingly—but then not so much of either—she longed for Andy... not to allay fear, for she felt little. Not to add confidence... she had enough. She just wanted him there, with her, in the cemetery. She wanted his warmth and intelligence, his whispered off-the-wall humor, his ease in this, the cemetery of their ancestors. Andy would get the mission. He'd grasp that JSGold could be obvious danger and yet intuit the paradox that the mission's greatest risk lay in its success.

Funny, Rhonda thought, how the dead below evoked memory and passion in the living above.

She crept uphill to All Souls Point. After another quick reconnoiter, she picked her way down the south slope, slipped through the gate opening, and sprinted to the safety of the bushes and trees surrounding the steeple on the east end of the cathedral. She crept around to the evergreen shrubs next to the steps leading up to St. Augustine's south entrance. Her watch showed 12:55 a.m. There was no vehicle in the cathedral parking lot to the south. The steps blocked her view to the neighborhood west of the cathedral, but she saw that the houses to the south and east were dark. The only sounds were the occasional car on the highway, about one hundred yards to the east, and faint thunder from the west.

She was about to jump on the steps to the door when a drunk, holding a pint in the right pocket of his jacket, appeared in the parking lot. He stumbled up the concrete steps and, with his other hand, pulled his cap low over his face. He entered the church.

About a minute later, Rhonda followed him through the doors. She genuflected and glanced over her shoulder toward the back. The drunk had disappeared. She slipped behind the altar into the sacristy, located the door to the steeple, and stepped into the spiral staircase. She turned on her cell phone light. The staircase was the first leg of the climb to the Lookout Room, 270 feet above her. She climbed the staircase to the utility landing, walked a few steps onto it, and then stopped. The light from her phone only slightly penetrated the darkness.

"JSGold?" she called softly.

No answer.

"I'm alone."

No answer.

She turned back toward the stairs to resume her climb. She'd taken two steps when a bright light framed her from behind, and she heard the click of a hammer cock on a pistol.

"Do not turn around." It was a young man's voice. "Do exactly as I say."

Rhonda said, "okay."

"Turn off that light and lay it on the floor. Yeah, just like that. Put your hands on your head."

Rhonda did so.

"Turn around, and look into this flashlight."

Rhonda did so.

"Did anybody follow you?"

"No."

"That tall drunk-looking guy has a gun."

"That tall drunk-looking guy is a drunk, and I believe has been for a long time. He stinks, he has a pint of cheap whiskey, and I'm pretty sure he has no gun."

"Do you have a gun?"

"No."

"Your pockets have bulges."

"They're energy bars—for you."

"Take them out and drop them on the floor. Then put your hands back on your head."

"No."

"No? I'm givin' the orders here."

"Not any more, JSGold." Rhonda put her arms to her side.

"Lady, you're not in any position to—stop!"

Rhonda had reached to the floor and picked up her cell phone. "Uncock that revolver and get that friggen flashlight out of my eyes."

JSGold hesitated.

Rhonda said, "Do as I say, or I'll go down that staircase and never come back. You'll be on the run until they find you and kill you."

"You know nothing about running and killing. You know nothing about me."

"I know plenty about you, Jameel Shalih."

CHAPTER 34

Rhonda watched Jameel light a small Coleman lantern and place it near a corner of the Lookout Room. He waved her to one of two small chairs beside a crude table. There were two large cans of baked beans and a jug of water stacked against the south wall. Over them leaned what looked like a 30-30 rifle. Next to these were a fork, a spoon, a large butcher knife, two cell phones, a radio, extra battery packs, and an ancient electrical outlet. An extension cord ran from it to a laptop computer. In another corner lay a mish-mash of clothing. Rhonda spotted coats, blue jeans, flannel shirts, T-shirts, and a folded burlap sack.

Jameel took the chair opposite Rhonda and laid the butcher knife on the table. Rhonda made eye contact and tried to ignore the knife.

Rhonda said, "I've met other people in hiding, but I've never met one hiding near the top of a church steeple. Why?"

"Why? That's the real question, isn't it?" Jameel exclaimed. "Why should I trust you?"

Rhonda said, "A little late for that, don't you think? It was *you*, alias JSGold, who messaged *me*, remember? It was you who sent me your location with that screwy message—'send stoan liv hi up see your house apples treez see all over born 1867 jsgold.' Clever... took me weeks to break it. You did your research. Translated... 'I am JSGold. I see your house on Apple Hill because I live high up in a place built with sandstone. Its cornerstone was laid in 1867.' Construction on St. Augustine Cathedral began in 1867 with the placement of the cornerstone. You were high enough to see our house in Orchard Acres across town with those binoculars. It could only be this steeple. I'm the only person who knows you're here, Jameel. Borgmann, you, and I are the only people who know that the guards and Borgmann were shot somewhere other than inside the front gate of Camp Morgan."

Jameel picked up the knife and stared at it.

"How could you know this?"

"I had a hunch."

"A hunch?"

"Yeah," Rhonda smiled, "but I wasn't certain about it until right now."

Jameel's eyes flashed anger. "I don't like tricks."

"That's too bad," Rhonda shot back. "Let's get something straight, Mr. Shalih. You will tell me everything, and all of it had damn well be the truth. I'm good at this. No—correction—I'm *very* good at this. I'll know if you lie, so don't give me this crap about 'tricks.' Are we clear?"

"Yes."

"Now, stop acting the fool and put that knife away."

Jameel laid the knife on the floor with the other utensils.

Rhonda asked, "Why?"

"Why... What?"

"Why do you live up here? If someone climbs up here, you have no escape. Besides, your enemy, Borgmann, is the choir director and is familiar with this church."

"Makes this room an even better hiding place, don't you think? Whoever heard of a Muslim hiding out in the steeple of a Christian church? Borgmann and his friends want me dead, but will never suspect I'm holed up in the steeple of St. Augustine's Cathedral."

Rhonda asked, "Where's your prayer rug?"

"I don't have one."

"I thought all Muslims had a prayer rug."

"Most of them do, but not me. I'm a Christian. Borgmann and the guards at Camp Morgan just assumed I'm Muslim because I'm from Iraq and have a Muslim-sounding name. They called me 'Muslim Boy.' In Iraq, we got along well with both the Sunni and Shi'a Muslims in our town."

"Why did you leave Iraq?"

"I was eight years old. I left because my family left. Why did my family leave? You must understand, Ms. O'Malley, that, in Iraq, the Shi'a outnumber the Sunnis. Saddam Hussein was a Sunni. He persecuted the Shi'a. He put them in prisons, tortured them… burned them alive. When the Americans invaded, there was chaos. The Shi'a's saw their chance. Overnight they started persecuting Sunnis and Christians." Jameel turned and stared out the north window. "They did to Christians what Hussein did to them." He turned back to Rhonda. "We fled our village and Iraq and came here. I'm a US citizen."

Rhonda said, "A US citizen with a bad scar on his neck."

"Yeah."

"How did it get there?"

Jameel's sullenness returned, and he said nothing.

Rhonda let the question hang. She turned around, shined her cell phone light in the corner, moved it up about two feet, and saw the date she and Andy had carved in the wood—July 1, 1995.

"Look at this, Jameel."

Jameel said, "It's just a date carved in the wood."

Rhonda said, "It's more than just a date. My boyfriend and I carved it in the middle of the night."

"Why didn't you also carve your initials?"

"It was a Saturday night, the summer between our junior and senior years in high school. My boyfriend had bought—illegally, of course—seven large Roman candles."

"Yeah," said Jameel, "except they're not candles. I saw some when I was a kid in Iraq."

"So you know that they shoot up about a thousand feet and then explode in a starburst."

Jameel nodded.

"That night, we and our friends planned to shoot them from the cemetery over downtown. Then a friend suggested shooting them out of the steeple. They dared us, and we took them up on it.

"Andy—that was my boyfriend—and I climbed up here, carved the date in the corner, and then set off candles from each window. We heard the sirens and made it out of the cathedral just before the cops arrived. The police suspected that the episode was a high school prank. The next day, the police interviewed Andy, me, and others from our gang. We stuck to our denials. Nobody talked. For about a year after that they locked all the cathedral doors at night."

Jameel stared at the carved date. "So you know something about running away, Ms. O'Malley."

"Yeah," Rhonda replied, "but our escape was thrilling, and fun, and mostly innocent. Yours was none of those."

Jameel said, "I know something about carving initials. See your 'July 1, 1995?' Move your light down into the corner. What do you see?"

"'J.S.' is a bit reckless, don't you think?"

"No. My life has two choices. The first is to live until I'm ninety. The second is to die young by Borgmann's hand. If it's the first, I can show the 'J.S.' to my grandchildren and great-grandchildren. If it's the second, I'll have the pleasure of telling the bastards that I was here all along, right above their noses, but they were too stupid to look up."

"True courage with unaffected attitude is rare."

Jameel softened. "Thank you, ma'am."

Rhonda asked, "What happened to Jayden Ramirez?"

Jameel said, "They said he escaped, but I don't believe it. I think they killed him… just like they were going to kill me."

"They?"

"Borgmann. The guards."

"When did you and Ramirez first meet Borgmann?"

"Two years ago. Me and Ramirez were at the Tigris River Prisoner-of-War Camp in Baghdad. Borgmann was in command," said Jameel. He put his head down and spoke to the table. "Borgmann and his... his 'friends' called themselves 'Cradlers.'"

"I'm aware of the term and its meaning."

Jameel lowered his head. "They stole the name. They stole everything."

"Oh, what would that be?"

"They sold American military equipment on the black market—bullets, guns, mortars, night goggles, uniforms—anything they could get their hands on. The buyers used the weapons to kill Americans."

"What else did they steal?"

Jameel rose and stared out the west window. "That storm's getting closer." Then he turned and faced Rhonda. "I'm not sorry those two guards died. I am sorry that Borgmann didn't."

"Did you shoot them?"

"No."

"I don't believe it."

"It's the truth."

"If you didn't, who did?"

Jameel again turned and stared out the window.

Rhonda allowed a minute of silence to pass, and then said, "Answer me."

"You'll laugh." Jameel sat down. "Do you know that me and Ramirez were court-martialed for stealing food from the army and selling it on the black market?"

Rhonda said, "Yes, I do. However, you didn't do it for the money. You did it to get caught."

Jameel's head snapped up. Then he laid his hands palms-down on the table. "If you know that, then you know why."

"You had to get away from Borgmann and his henchmen. You said they stole something else, but you didn't say what it was."

"Yeah."

Rhonda said, in a gentle voice… mother-like, "You and Jayden had to get away because Borgmann and his friends—the Cradlers—were raping you." Rhonda remembered the comfort of Marian's hands over hers. She closed her hands over Jameel's. Jameel stared at her hands, but made no move to withdraw his. Then he slowly nodded.

"Yeah, but how do you know this? Don't tell me it's another of your tricks."

"I'm a good researcher, Jameel, and I can put two and two together. But there's some things I don't know, and even more I don't understand. I need your help so I can help you. You and Ramirez pled guilty. That makes sense if your goal was to get away from Borgmann. However, how did you end up at Camp Morgan?"

"They gave us a choice. They said that we could get a less than honorable discharge or serve a year in prison and get an honorable discharge.

We chose the prison. There's some agreement where the army can place its non-violent offenders, like Jayden and me, in civilian prisons. That's how we ended up at Camp Morgan."

"More bad luck?"

"Yes. The governor needed a warden for Camp Morgan and appointed Borgmann. We couldn't get away from the bas—I mean Borgmann. Borgmann hired some of his Cradler buddies. They—"

"Borgmann and his cronies took up at Camp Morgan where they'd left off at Tigris River. They repeatedly raped you and Ramirez. Were there others?"

"Yes, Ms. O'Malley. Many others. At night, they would take two, maybe three, sometimes more, of us to a place they called Piankashaw Rock. Camp Morgan is northeast of Ferdinand, and about three miles away."

Rhonda said, "I've visited and even camped at Piankashaw Rock many times. My husband's dad, grandfather, and great-grandfather lived there—after they came home from their wars."

"Wars?"

"Yes, but that's another story. What did Borgmann do to you at Piankashaw?"

"Well, they beat and whipped us. Then they..."

She pointed to the pistol on the floor. "Is that the gun you used at Piankashaw?"

"So we're back to the 'who did the shooting' thing. Ms. O'Malley, I shot no one at Piankashaw. I didn't kill anybody."

"Jameel, you were defending yourself against deadly force," said Rhonda, remembering a similar case where Andy had successfully argued self-defense to the jury. "You didn't commit murder."

"I'm telling the truth, Ms. O'Malley."

"If you didn't shoot them, who did?"

"I don't know!" Jameel picked up the knife and turned it in his hands. "I was chained. The guards held me. Borgmann put this butcher knife against my throat." Jameel put the tip of the knife on his neck injury. "I felt it go in here. Then it happened."

Then Jameel checked his watch. "Bells at 2:00 a.m." He handed Rhonda a set of ear protectors. "Put these on. Quick." He slipped another set over his ears. Thirty seconds later the church bells chimed twice. "Without these, I'd be deaf by now."

Rhonda nodded. "You were saying that something happened."

"Yes. Somebody ran out of the woods and shot the three of them. He got the key and unlocked my cuffs and shackles. Then another person, a woman, came out of the woods holding a burlap sack." Jameel pointed. "It's over there. She filled it with two pistols, Borgmann's knife, that 30-30 rifle there in the corner, and ammunition.

"It... it was like they expected us at Piankashaw, knew Borgmann would kill me, and stopped it. But how could they know?"

"Can you describe the two?"

"He was weird-looking. Tall and thin. Long, blond hair. Pale face. He wore a long white robe and he was smiling. He looked... sort of like an angel. He said, 'We will help you' in a high-pitched voice, like a girl's."

"That's quite a story."

"It is. It sounds crazy. No, it doesn't sound crazy. It *is* crazy. Sometimes even I don't believe it, and I was there. However, I know it happened when I feel this scar. Ms. O'Malley, you have to believe me!"

"I do."

"You believe it?"

"Yes."

"Thank you, ma'am."

"So," said Rhonda, "Borgmann killed Ramirez. Then, several months later, he tried to kill you. Did he target anyone else?"

"No."

"Are you sure?"

"Positive."

"Why just you and Ramirez?"

Jameel stared at Rhonda as lightning lit up the Lookout Room.

"Answer my question, Jameel."

"Jayden and I knew too much."

"About the rapes?"

"About one of the rapists."

"One?"

"Sometimes Borgmann would take only me and Jayden to Piankashaw Rock. Another man—not from the Morgan prison—would be there. He'd take part. He disguised himself by dressing like a Muslim woman. You know… the veil she wears to hide her face. One night Ramirez ripped off the guy's veil."

"Who was this man?"

"They... they had to kill us because we saw his face. Goddamn Ramirez!"

"Jameel. The man. Who was he?"

Jameel's shoulders shook and he started to dry-heave and then sob. Rhonda moved around the table and took him into her arms. He'd lost his courage and turned into a confused and terrified boy on the run from the law for a crime he didn't commit, and from evil persons who cared little about the crime, but did care about seeing him dead.

"This man was behind Ramirez. He was grunting real loud. Then something happened to Ramirez. He went into a rage. That's when he turned and ripped off the man's veil. Jayden and I saw his face, and both of us knew we'd just been handed death sentences." Jameel stopped talking. He cried without tears, and heaved without vomiting.

Rhonda pushed Jameel's head into her neck. "It's okay, Jameel."

Jameel pulled away and stared wild-eyed at Rhonda. A shiver went through him. He put his hand to the scar on his throat.

"It's okay?"

"You can tell me when you're ready."

Jameel dug his face into Rhonda's neck. Her soothing words calmed him. His breathing eased. His retching and sobs went away.

He said, "I'm ready now."

"Fine."

"The man was Lincoln Kincaid."

Rhonda sat him on his chair and took her seat, but continued to hold his hands in hers. She said nothing.

Jameel said, "You don't seem shocked, Ms. O'Malley. Maybe you didn't hear what I just said."

"I heard you loud and clear, Jameel. I'm not shocked because I suspected it was Lincoln Kincaid, given his past and his friendship with Borgmann. I had to hear it from you to be certain. You should know that his wife,

Marian, and I went to New Mexico State together and are close friends. I despise her husband, and I'm fairly sure she knows it. He is a powerful but haunted and morbid man who will be elected president unless someone stops him. Do you recall the Tigris River scandal?"

"I heard about it when I was at Tigris, and I know that some grunts got court-martialed for it. What does that have to do with me?"

"Plenty. Lincoln Kincaid was in command. Kurt Borgmann served under him. Prisoners were sodomized and tortured. A few died. There were pictures of someone holding a prisoner on a leash, like he was a dog. The army prosecuted a few grunts, like you said, but whitewashed Kincaid and the commissioned officers under him. This included Borgmann."

"Ms. O'Malley, you know a lot about Kincaid and Borgmann and what they did—what they are doing. How can you help me?"

"By exposing all this in the media. After that, you can at least come out of hiding. I know a very good lawyer who'll defend you."

"Who?"

"My husband, Andy Balbach."

"You're divorcing him." Jameel smiled for the first time. "Yeah, Ms. O'Malley. I researched you. Your address is Speedway, Indiana, not Dubain."

"We are separated, Jameel. We are not divorcing." At least not yet, she told herself. "However, our separation doesn't matter. What matters is that Andy needs you as much as you need him." She said this for Jameel's benefit, but realized it was more for her own, and mostly for Andy's.

The storm moved on, leaving only the sounds of trickling water. Rhonda watched Jameel look through each window with the binoculars. He said that the best time to detect anyone was right after a thunderstorm, when everything quieted and the air was cleaner. He came back to the north window.

Jameel said, "There are electrical problems."

"There usually are after a storm like that."

"No. This is the opposite. Those lights—the ones at the top of the cemetery. They've come back on."

Rhonda saw the lights. Jameel handed her the binoculars. She adjusted them and focused on All Souls Point. "There are people standing there."

"Where?"

"Right under the lights. Look."

Jameel readjusted the binoculars, and then gasped. "Ms. O'Malley, he's—he's standing right there—by the flag. There he is."

"Who?"

"The angel. The one who saved me at Piankashaw. Wait! The girl's there too. The one with the burlap bag. She's in the middle. The shooter is to her right."

"Are you sure?"

Jameel handed the binoculars to Rhonda. "See for yourself."

It was Rhonda's turn to be shocked. Three drenched Angels, their robes stuck to their bodies, stood in a line and faced the steeple. Two had long blond hair and the third dark. Their faces were bright, almost shining, and Rhonda felt, rather more than saw, the Angels' eyes bore through the binoculars into hers.

The Angel with the dark hair was Polly Thompson, Marian's former writing assistant and one of Rhonda's investigative targets.

CHAPTER 35

It was the evening of Earl's third and final lesson. Garrett missed the usual banter and hijinks of the residents. They were quiet, reserved, and thoughtful.

Earl started. "Tonight's lesson is short." Earl summarized the previous lessons, and then moved into the last.

"Now I shall drive this home. Jesus lived a hard life on earth. Yet, he never complained of the burdens he carried, or sought acclaim for his good works.

"God commands us to so live. The moment you stepped on Oakenwald He forged His covenant with you. Your life as you knew it ended then. Why?"

Earl paused to look into the eyes of each in the class. "Because God chose you.

"God's covenant," Earl continued, "is hard and glorious. The time will come when He commands you to go forth and build the Kingdom of Jesus on earth. This will not be easy. People will bear false witness against you. They will fight you, slander you, oppose you, field armies against you, and try to kill you. You cannot waiver, you cannot bargain, you cannot give your burden back to God. No breaks for Moses. No breaks for you.

"It's too late for you now. You are in. You shall never get out."

Earl paused to drink from a glass of water.

"Prepare yourselves, each of you, for the Day. Certainly it will arrive and you shall know the Day is nigh by a sign He sends to you. The sign will not be a new Messiah. The clouds will not part. No set of hands will reach down from the heavens and rest on your head, and there will be no deep voice to give you confidence. Do not wait for a typed letter setting out your job description, salary, benefits, vacation time, and bonuses. God doesn't work that way. Just ask Moses. The sign will be something else. You may not recognize it at first, but God will bring you around to it.

"You shall go out from this time and place and await your mission. You shall pray to God every day, every hour, every minute, for the strength to take up your burden and lead when the sign arrives.

"God has placed you on call every minute of every day. He has your smart phone number, email address, website, social security number, credit score, medical records, passwords, report cards, blood type, fingerprints, and DNA. He can trace your family back to Noah. He's buried a GPS tracker in your body that is so small not even the best surgeon in the world can find it. He'll troll on your Google Plus, Facebook, Twitter, and Instagram pages. He's in on your thoughts, feelings, and motivations. He knows more about you than you do.

"You can't run, you can't hide, you can't say 'God, pick somebody else.'

"You are in the grip of the greatest covenant in history. You've made it with God Himself.

"You don't stand a chance."

Earl turned and left the room. The profundity of the moment ruled. No one spoke. Some folded their hands and lowered their heads. Others teared up. Still others sniffled.

No one mentioned a basketball game.

CHAPTER 36

Garrett needed to breathe. He entered his office and locked the door behind him.

He hyperventilated after every one of Earl's 'You don't stand a chance' last lessons. It was the Jesus Equation, and the covenant produced thereby, that bound each of them directly to God, he'd told them.

That the Jesus Equation was an abhoration to God, vulgar, and utter bullshit, he'd never tell them.

Did the residents get it? Did they realize that Earl talked literally when he said it was too late for them, that they were in and would never get out? ...that the cult of silence, democracy's affront to God, their membership in the New Chosen, had been twisted from bits of scripture stolen from their contexts and smoothed over by mathematics both unholy and false?

No, probably not. This was heady stuff coming from a man of legend who refeed their basketball games.

Earl Thompson forced the Jesus Equation into the Foundation's culture. He drilled it into Garrett, the board, Polly, the Foundation… everybody. He told Garrett that it was simple and innocent. It was neither. It wasn't religion, or spiritual warfare, or a principle of leadership. It was something else altogether—the product of Earl's genius and his means to attain the real power of the presidency, the invisible presence lurking behind the Lincoln Kincaid throne. Earl had thought it through to his goal—the Jesus Equation admitted of blackmail.

Garrett fingered the St. Christopher medal on a scapula around his neck. Did he have any right to ask St. Christopher for his help? He decided the right didn't matter. He silently breathed a prayer for protection and guidance.

Garrett opened the bottom drawer of his desk and pulled out a hammer. It was his hammer, the one he'd used during the summers between semesters at college and law school. Garrett imagined those days. It was Florida, it was summer, and it was hot. The Atlantic Ocean lapped at the beach. Sometimes it sent a breeze, but most of the time it didn't, and that was just fine with Garrett. He loved the heat, loved the sweat rolling off his face and back, and loved the chatter and clanging and the boss chewing out workers and yelling orders. He loved the smell of fresh two-by-fours, and the feel of this hammer in his right hand as he pulled nail after nail from between his lips and pounded them into the frame of what soon would be a condominium on the beach. Most framers used air-hammers, but some, including Garrett, did not.

An air hammer, like the Equation, had no soul. Garrett dared not drop, lose, or give up his hammer. It was part of him, and he of it. Deep, deep down in the innermost chamber of his heart, he fancied a tiny bit of soul in his hammer.

Garrett was Earl's air hammer, a valuable tool, one with high intelligence, deep insight, uncanny people skills, and a knack for solving problems. Earl Thompson employed Garrett, gave him a title, proclaimed him the next Foundation leader, praised him, shared confidences with him—and ripped his soul from him.

Marian Kincaid, like Garrett, was 'in,' but Garrett had not Marian Kincaid's courage to fight back. Polly had pieced the Equation's implications and used them to separate herself, not so much from the Foundation, but from her father. Would Polly take the next step, the one Garrett so desperately yearned for, and throw away the Equation along with the Foundation?

Garrett had been planning his exit for months. But where could he go? Where could he hide? What would he do? He wouldn't survive in a D.C. law firm. He'd considered law in another city, or maybe even a small town, like Dubain. Garrett worshipped the rule of law embodied in the Constitution and its built-in checks and balances, judges, juries, elections, and the Bill of Rights. Earl Thompson's rule of law was the Equation. He and it subsumed the real rule of law.

Garrett took no pride in the fact that he'd detected Earl's hypocrisy. Garrett served the Foundation in a leadership capacity and was therefore quite familiar with its sordidness. He envied Polly. She'd mostly escaped Earl

Thompson by bouncing the Equation off his face. However, Earl Thompson was no fool. A renegade Polly Thompson was a threat to the Foundation. A renegade Garrett Jennings was a *deadly* threat to the Foundation. Polly was on Earl's list. Garrett knew beyond a certainty that his jump from the Foundation would guarantee him a spot on the list also.

There was one silver lining. Garrett saw himself as a special assistant to the President of the United States, and the only one with the guts to wall off Earl Thompson.

Garrett admired his hammer at arm's length and then returned it to its place of rest in the bottom drawer. He would bide his time and be ready when the opportunity arose to free himself from Earl Thompson.

CHAPTER 37

Earl entered Garrett's office and said, "Let's get this done."

Marian Kincaid appeared on the Hangouts screen and held up a manuscript. "This is not my life. It depicts Marian Kincaid as the princess who lost her shoe. I don't even recognize myself in it. I never 'played with dolls as a young girl.' I read books. I do not 'pray to Jesus every day.' My family wasn't 'desperately poor,' and I certainly do not agree with Lincoln on all issues."

Garrett said, "I had hoped this wouldn't happen."

"Garrett, you're Lincoln's campaign manager and that's all you can say? Do you actually believe this nonsense?"

Earl said, "I can explain, Marian. This is politics, pure and simple. The voters choose the electors. The electors vote in the Electoral College. Lincoln must win 270 electoral votes. This means he must—"

"Earl Thompson, don't lecture me on the Electoral College. I can count. Lincoln must get votes. I get that, but I will not sacrifice Marian Kincaid in the process."

"No one has asked you to."

"Then what do you call this?" Marian waved the manuscript.

Garrett said, "Keep your eye on the ball, Marian. The ball is the presidency. Do you want to help or hurt your husband's chances?"

"That's a stupid question. Here's a smart one—why did you take Polly away from me?"

Earl said, "We assigned other duties to her."

"Why?"

"It's complicated, Marian."

"So let me simplify things for you. You're flunking Politics 101. The first rule is you don't tick off the candidate's wife. The next rules are about numbers and the opponent. I assume KFA can count votes, run polls, and read numbers, and it doesn't take a genius or a poll to see that Josie Carter is the candidate of a party that is unpopular and splitting."

Garrett said, "We get that, Marian."

"Of course you do. They're the easy parts. What you don't get is that it is not ideology but ideals—the kind that build coalitions—that will place Lincoln in the Oval Office."

"Of course we do. We've hired some of the finest political minds in the business."

"You've hired nincompoop men! The majority of voters are women, and they help decide elections as well. Lincoln's opponent will be a woman. Where are the women minds in KFA? They'd get it. Women have long ago moved past skirts, bras, thongs, tampons, Tupperware parties, and meno-pause to issues that will determine victories on election night. There is a profound intersection among Marian Kincaid's America, Senator Lodge, and Governor Kincaid. This is precisely the reason my book cannot be a fairy tale. First, I do not relegate myself to men. Second, my book will not lose votes that are already lost—it will gain votes that are sought. Third, a truthful Marian Kincaid is likely to solidify the women's vote."

Garrett said, "You have insight, Marian."

"Don't patronize me, Garrett Jennings. You are the one who is running a losing campaign. KFA subtly posits the American people as mere nuisances except on Election Day. You talk down to them. Americans deserve better, and they know it. They'll sense it and the polls will so indicate, beginning about two months before Election Day."

"That's hyperbolic, Marian."

"That's truth, Earl."

"Well, then, it's cynical."

"The truth is neither cynical, nor optimistic, nor anything else. It's the truth. It can cause cynicism or optimism. It can disappoint, terrorize, help, hinder, save or lose lives, lead to a full tank of gas, order your favorite pizza, and get you an MRI. KFA's strategy—and I use that term loosely—doesn't take into account the intangibles that Americans demand but rarely articulate. Does Lincoln Kincaid have it? Will he be controlled by an oligarchy of the few, or is he unafraid to surround himself with people smarter than him and demand their debate? Does he have the brains to distinguish a bunch of loud mouths in Russia from a bunch of quiet mouths in caves with a nuclear bomb? If it's the latter, does he have the guts to send America's young men and women into battle and then handle the caskets when they're unloaded at Andrews Air Force Base? Can Lincoln Kincaid take the 2:00 a.m. call and not have us in World War Three by noon? Is Lincoln Kincaid honest? Will he tell the truth? Can he make a mistake and admit it? Can he stumble, which is inevitable, and regain his footing, which is not?

"Does Lincoln Kincaid have a heart? Can he look past the mouthy, young prostitute to that which drove her to prostitution? Can he hug the smelly tramp under the bridge and withhold judgment on the hellfire and brimstone preacher who screws married women in his congregation? Does he have the tenderness to embrace and cry with the old man who'd lost his wife of sixty years in the tornado the day before? Can he calm a nation that's been devastated by a natural disaster?

"Then, gentlemen, ask yourselves these things in the context of my autobiography."

Garrett said, "We'll choose someone else to work with you. You should get a phone call in the next two days. Is that okay?"

"No, it is not okay. I don't need a helper. I'm a trained writer, remember? Polly got it, but you took her away from me. I can sum up my personal feelings this way. Josie Carter Lodge may lose the election, but she'll still be Josie Carter Lodge. If KFA's Marian Kincaid is published, the real Marian Kincaid will never again exist, win or lose."

Garrett said, "Marian, you need a lesson in First-Ladies-To-Be 101. Lincoln will certainly lose if the American people get the sense that his wife doesn't support him."

"Garrett Jennings, just what do you mean by that?"

Garrett turned to Earl who nodded. Garrett said, "Marian, listen to this." Garrett uploaded a voice file to the Hangouts window and clicked on it:

"Marian, even governors and soon-to-be presidents have tempers. An occasional lapse is okay... more human. Lincoln? Human? It's the... friggen presidency for Christ's sake! Lincoln lied... Foundation... he is a member... I can't risk it. Andy... protecting? Some of the officers... and Captain Lincoln Kincaid was the top officer. I need your help."

Garrett stopped the recording. "Have you heard enough, Marian?"

"You bastards! You bugged Rhonda and me. This is an outrage! It's the most lowdown, dirty... You... you actually bugged the candidate's wife and her best friend!"

"Actually," said Garrett, "it was your best friend, Rhonda O'Malley, who sniffed out the bug, but she's not told you about it. She's holding back on you, too, Marian."

"Did Lincoln know about this?"

Earl said, "Marian, it really doesn't matter what Lincoln knew. For the record, he had no prior knowledge of the bug. He has, however, listened to it."

Marian said, "Oh my God!"

Earl said, "God can't help you here, Marian, but I can. Take my advice and do not get in the way of your husband, the campaign, or the Foundation."

"Are you threatening me?"

"The Foundation doesn't threaten."

"Garrett Jennings, I pity you."

"I don't need—"

"You do. Can't you see that you're being set up? You're the named campaign manager, but you have no power because the real manager is your boss, the man standing next to you. If Lincoln loses, Earl will pin it on you. Get in the game, Garrett. Show some guts and demand real power from Earl or resign."

Earl nodded at Garrett, who terminated the session. Then he ordered Garrett to bug the mansion and Marian's cell phone.

Andy rose from behind Marian's computer and hugged her. "It's okay, Marian. It's okay. At least now we know they bugged your meeting with Rhonda."

"But, my book?"

"I don't put it past the Foundation to publish their version without your permission. It's a race. We have to make sure you publish yours as soon as possible."

"I'm in touch with several publishing houses."

"Good."

"What about—"

"The threat? I doubt that they would hurt you, but Rhonda may be a target."

CHAPTER 38

Garrett sat across the desk from Earl.

"Garrett, the only threat to Kincaid's election is his wife and her autobiography."

"I agree, sir. Her version is unflattering to her husband. This is not a surprise, given her own comments in the recording we just played for her." That is what Garrett told Earl, but he knew that wasn't the only threat. Lincoln Kincaid was a ticking time bomb.

"Do you have a plan?"

"Yes, sir. We publish our version first, and make sure she never publishes hers. The first part is easy. The second is very tricky."

"Can you handle it, Garrett?"

"I think I can, sir. First, we hire a cooperative publisher. Second, we work with the publisher to manufacture a trail that leaves Marian Kincaid neither a chance to publish hers nor room to deny ours as authentic. However, we don't have much time. There are many publishers out there who undoubtedly either have already or will soon offer Marian a hefty up-front payment and high royalties to publish her version."

"A publisher willing to take the risk for us would be hard to find."

"We have friends in the publishing industry who, with the right encouragement, will take the risk. I'll string Marian along on revisions."

Earl stared at the ceiling with his arms behind his head. Then he lowered them and eyed Garrett. "Maybe we can turn Marian Kincaid the pain into Marian Kincaid the asset."

"How's that?"

"Jesus Plus Zero."

"A covenant?"

"Yes."

"What kind?"

"The kind that will ensure the election of one Lincoln Pennington Kincaid. Americans can be so sympathetic."

Garrett closed his office door. He picked up the phone and dialed a private number.

"Garrett?"

"Yeah. Lincoln, we may not have much time. Earl and I just played part of the recording to Marian. Then Earl tried to intimidate her."

"Did it work?"

"Not at all."

"What did Earl say to her?"

"He told her to stay out of the campaign's way. She took it as a threat and said so. Earl replied that the Foundation doesn't threaten."

"I don't like it, Garrett. I told Earl to leave Marian alone. Threats only make her angrier."

Garrett asked, "Can you help?"

"I'll see what I can do. In the meantime, tell Earl to stay away from her."

"I can't tell Earl anything. You know that."

"Then I'll call him after I meet with Marian."

Garrett said, "That might work."

"It has to. I plan to be at the French Lick Springs in three days. Can you meet me there to talk through all this?"

"Yes. After all, I'm your campaign manager."

CHAPTER 39

If there was ever a person that Andy would accept as a second father, he was right here, in this private room at the Schnitzelbank, in the person of General David Hernandez, US Army, Retired. At sixty-nine, he was six feet tall, weighed around 180 pounds, and had broad shoulders. He carried himself with purpose, but without ego or arrogance. His thick white hair was short and layered, and he had that chiseled look that, in a younger version of him, would look good on recruiting posters. His wife, Louise, still attractive at sixty-five, complemented the general, but her spunk and sense of humor spoke of an independence from him.

General Hernandez quickly put his dinner companions, Rhonda, Stump, and Andy, at ease with army jokes and funny anecdotes of his career.

But Andy saw a bit of himself in the general's eyes. He read in them disappointment with a twinge of bitterness. Andy's immediate pain lay in his loss of Rhonda. The general's pain was rooted in a profound sense of duty, honor, and justice, qualities not altogether shared by others of his rank who had taken a keen interest in the general's investigation of the events at Tigris River in 2003.

After dinner, Stump explained, "General, the story of Tigris River in 2003 and your investigation of it will be published as part of a larger series in the *Courier Journal*. We expect to break the story in the next several weeks."

"You have my full cooperation."

"Rhonda's the investigative reporter. Andy and I will assist her."

The general grew stern and said, "First, I want you to know that I despise investigative reporters. They were always messing up my commands with their nosing around and pulling ridiculous stories from soldiers who had no business talking. You," he pointed to Rhonda, "are probably no different. Why should I trust you?"

Andy bit his lip and leaned back.

Rhonda pushed her shoulders up. Her eyes bore into the general's. "General Hernandez," she said, "there's absolutely no reason for you to trust me. However, you agreed to meet with me and… what?"

The general smiled, Stump snickered, Andy laughed aloud, and Louise playfully reproached her husband. Rhonda saw she'd been set up.

"Ms. O'Malley… Stump, Andy, and, it turns out, Louise, forced me into this... charade at your expense. I apologize."

"Apology accepted, General, but with three conditions."

"Oh?"

"First, please call me Rhonda. Second, after we're done here, you will buy us a round of drinks in the barroom. Third, you and Mrs. Hernandez will sing the Schnitzelbank with us."

"Fair enough."

"Actually, sir, my first question has nothing to do with the military. You grew up in French Lick. Did you know Larry Bird?"

"He's younger than I. I saw him around, but I really don't remember much about him."

Andy had seen Rhonda start an interview with seemingly innocent questions, and then either gradually or abruptly move into the real subjects. She'd set up Lincoln Kincaid with questions and answers that made him look good. And then, without warning, she had attacked. She wouldn't pressure General Hernandez, but she would ask pointed questions.

"How long were you in the Army?"

"About thirty-seven years, give or take."

"You graduated from West Point in 1970. Where did you serve?"

"Actually, it seems everywhere. I was in Vietnam toward the end of that war. Then I served in the First Gulf War in 1990-91, in Afghanistan in 2002-2003, and lastly in Iraq."

"When did you retire from the army?"

"In 2007, three years before the mandatory retirement age of sixty-two."

"Your rank?"

"Two-Star General."

The server entered. General Hernandez ordered two bottles of wine for the party.

Rhonda asked, "General Hernandez, have you ever disobeyed an order?"

"Yes. I've disobeyed two orders."

"What were the orders, and when did you disobey them?"

"The second time is right now. The higher brass ordered me to say nothing about the investigation. I am prepared to disobey that order by coming out with the truth about what happened at Tigris River in 2003. I am doing so with no less than an exceptional investigative reporter."

Rhonda blushed at the compliment. Andy smiled inwardly. Sometimes Rhonda's toughness with interview subjects was only a facade. Such was the case now, and she'd revealed her vulnerability.

"The first?"

"In 2004. The army chose me to investigate Tigris River but with a condition. I was to investigate only the privates and non-commissioned officers and let commissioned officers alone."

"Did you protest?"

"Many times, both verbally and in writing. Each time, they threatened me with court-martial should I disobey."

"But you disobeyed the order anyway."

"Yes."

"Even though you were warned of the consequences?"

"Yes."

"Why?"

"My conscience and the reality of the events at Tigris River in 2003 compelled me to disobey."

"But, General, I've read your report. It says nothing about commissioned officers."

"You did not read my report."

"I have a copy with your name on it."

"I'm sure you do. However, that report is not mine. The report you read is someone else's. They illegally used my name without my permission."

"Why?"

"The report that I wrote went to the core of one of the US Armed Forces' oldest and dirtiest secrets—rape. Sexual assault has been a constant in the United States Military, but the commanders have covered it up until recently."

"Why the cover-up?"

"Three reasons. Rapes in a command tarnish the commander's reputation, sometimes the commander himself engaged in these activities, and the military blamed the victim."

"How did they blame the victim?"

"It goes something like this. 'You! Private Ms. Lady. You invited the rape because you wiggled your ass in front of them.' 'You! Private Mr. Man. You invited the rape because you're queer or act queer.' Afghanistan and Iraq brought an upsurge in all this."

"Why?"

"America's military has been voluntary since the end of the Vietnam War. It held volunteers to high standards—no criminal records, stable personalities, high school diplomas, and good health. However, the army was forced to lower the standards when volunteer enlistments fell off during Afghanistan and Iraq. It enlisted felons, former prison inmates, and known gang members. These have turned the American army into a thug army. There was drug dealing, fights between members of rival gangs, theft of military supplies, an increase in black market activity, and, of course, a steep increase in rapes."

"Did you investigate the officers at Tigris River?"

"Yes."

"What did you find?"

"My team and I interviewed many of the enlisted soldiers at Tigris River in 2003. We started with the alleged abuse of prisoners of war and enemy combatants."

"Alleged?"

"Our investigation converted the 'alleged' into 'truth.' The 800th Battalion Military Police ran the Tigris River Prisoner-of-War Camp in 2003. We uncovered a pattern of abuse by members of the battalion. Prisoners were forced to strip naked and then were led around with leashes. Others were beaten, starved, and denied medical care. A few were sodomized. We noted two prisoners who probably died as a result of the mistreatment.

"All that was bad enough. However, we uncovered something deeper, darker, and uglier. Tigris River had taken on what I called in my report an 'ethos of rape and sexual abuse.' The victims were not only prisoners, but men and women in the ranks."

"Who infused the ethos?"

"The officers, along with some NCOs and a few enlisted personnel. However, it was the officers who led it, or otherwise knew about it and didn't put a stop to it. We identified a number of male officers who regularly raped the soldiers under their command, either singly or in gangs. The rapes almost always occurred at night. The rapists marched their victims to remote parts of the base and there did their business. The victims tended to be the weaker, more vulnerable, soldiers. However, some were strong men who could fight off one or two rapists, but not five or ten. The victims sought transfers from their hell. The army denied most, thereby forcing the victims to live and serve with their tormenters."

"Did you identify the officers?"

"Yes. I said in my report that it was impossible to chronicle the victims' ordeals without implicating the perpetrators, no matter their ranks."

"Were you punished?"

"Not at first. They called me in and said that 'only a few' of the officers at Tigris River were involved. This alone infuriated me. It was an admission that they knew something about the perpetrators *before* I investigated, but withheld the information from me and then forbade me to scrutinize them."

"What happened next?"

"They punished me but not by court-martial. That would have exposed the abuses and the perpetrators. I lost no rank, pay, or benefits. Instead, I was pushed to a worthless desk job with no responsibility. I had to endure hurtful comments such as 'traitor' and 'you should be breaking rocks at Leavenworth' and 'how can you live with yourself?'"

"Was that all?"

"No. The real sanction was much worse. They ostracized Louise and me. They no longer invited us to their homes, and they refused to come to ours. Even the spouses of the officers—mostly women but some men—gave the cold shoulder to Louise. You must understand, Rhonda, that these people were our best friends. Our kids babysat for each other, we had barbecues and beer on weekends, and we shared vacations. We served together in war zones and prayed for each other's safety and survival. In many ways, we were closer than family.

"However, the worst for me—the very worst—was my loss of confidence in the United States Military. As a military man, it is this confidence that sustains you through the hardest times… like when you're under fire, when a soldier under you is wounded or killed, when a firefight sneaks up on you, or when you disagree with a mission and you feel you must speak up. It was this loss that led to my early retirement.

"It also led me to Stump, and then to you, Rhonda. I want some good to come out of all this."

The server entered with the wine bottles sticking out of an ice bucket. After General Hernandez approved the wine, the server filled the glasses.

"I have only a few more questions, General Hernandez."

"That would be fine."

"You are aware that a number of the men, and a few of the women, who served at Tigris River in 2003 and since, have in the past year or so, disappeared or died in questionable circumstances?"

"It was Louise who saw the pattern in the military obituaries."

"Did you look into it?"

The general hesitated. "Yes."

"What did you find?"

"I have only supposition, and so what I am about to tell you is strictly background. You can use it, but not name me as your source. Is this okay?"

"Yes."

"I assume that they have to do with the rapes and prisoner abuse at Tigris River. I cannot identify the killers, but I do know that the murders are methodical, timed, and dispersed. This means that the killers are organized. I suspect they are protecting one or more persons up the chain of command. We have an example right here in Dubain—Kurt Borgmann. He was a colonel at Tigris in 2003. Two years later, the army appointed him the commander at Tigris River in spite of the fact that I had named him in my report. He is now the warden at Camp Morgan. The two boys who tried to escape

Camp Morgan—Jayden Ramirez and Jameel Shalih—apparently served un-der Borgmann at Tigris. Then Governor Kincaid appointed Borgmann, their tormentor at Tigris River, as Camp Morgan's warden.

"Those poor kids never had a chance. I don't buy Borgmann's stories about their escapes. I think he murdered them. Why? Because they knew too much.

"There will be more deaths around the country, Rhonda. The fact that you asked me about these poor people tells me that their deaths, too, are part of your research. I ask—no, I beg—that you expose all this as soon as you can."

"I do have one more question. Which officers are they protecting?"

"They're protecting several, actually."

"How high?"

"The highest—Captain Lincoln P. Kincaid."

CHAPTER 40

She knew since that morning that he would come to her bed that night. She'd seen the feral rage in his icy blue eyes and whiffed the liquor, for which he'd developed a high tolerance, on his breath. She met him at the front door of the Governor's Mansion and demanded, "What's wrong?"

He opened his briefcase and showed her a memorandum with other papers attached.

"We'll talk tonight."

Marian tucked the children in bed, said their night prayers with them, and then kissed them. She went to her bedroom to prepare. She sat on the toilet and forced a small bowel movement. There was nothing else there and she was glad that she'd only eaten an apple that day. She changed into cotton underpants and a light T-shirt, pushed the covers down, and then lay on her back.

Their whole marriage was a sham, nothing more than a globule of false companionship that, she thought, no one else could see. It was hypocrisy writ large when she wrapped an arm around his waist and waved with the other at cheering crowds on the campaign trail. Marian recalled her angst in the months after she had met Lincoln at the Pentagon. She was in love with him, she would tell him so, and he would respond in kind. She would act on her desires, initiate sexual affection, but he never responded in kind. There would be a quick kiss on the lips and then his escape from further foreplay, the prelude into the lovemaking that Marian so desperately wanted, indeed needed.

Their wedding day was a jubilant celebration of the union of tall and handsome Captain Lincoln Kincaid to the striking Marian Arancha Vicario. Rhonda O'Malley, already married to Andy Balbach, served as her maid of honor. She and Lincoln had exchanged vows in the Washington National Cathedral, then celebrated them afterward at the Hotel Palomar on Dupont Circle.

However, there were two unpleasant events. The first was a near fist-fight between Andy Balbach and Lincoln Kincaid the day of the wedding. They were contemptuous of each other, but they had maintained an uneasy peace for the sake of the two ladies. They met at the bar and managed to remain civil as their drinks were served. Then both turned and offered a toast to the bride and her maid of honor. All the people nearby joined in, and then laughed and clapped at this, another moment of jollity on a day full of such moments. Then the uneasy peace broke down. The two exchanged words and angrily squared toward each other. Marian and Rhonda separated them before their confrontation escalated.

The second occurred that night. Marian was lying naked under the sheets while Lincoln showered. She was enraptured when he emerged from the bathroom wearing only a lusty smile and a full erection. She turned to him with open arms when he entered the bed. But there was no taking in the joy of newlywed lovers' desires that night. Marian was shocked, humiliated, and trapped. She finally escaped the bed and her husband and ran into the bathroom, locked the door, and padded herself with toilet paper until she stopped bleeding. When she opened the door, Lincoln was sitting on the edge of the bed, sobbing into his hands. Marian lifted his head. Gone was the handsome and confident Captain Lincoln Kincaid who, eleven hours before, had promised 'I do' and then sweetly kissed her upon the minister's permission. Now, his face was a torn battlescape of devastation and self-hate. He begged Marian to forgive him. He promised it would never happen again. She lay in bed and calmed him into lying beside her. She took his hand. He stopped crying and fell asleep.

Lincoln never kept his promise. In time, Marian had to face the fact that he was incapable of normal sexual affection, and that she could not change him. She—and probably he—never knew when his dark side would emerge and take him to another place for sexual release, a place where the only sounds were his deep raspy snorting and animal-like grunts and her whimpers from the pain. Early in their marriage, it happened maybe three times a year. Always, when it was over, he cried and swore it would never happen again. It always did.

Marian had a respite when Lincoln took command of the 800th Military Brigade at the Tigris River Prisoner-of-War Camp in Baghdad. When he returned home, he was happy, relaxed, and upbeat, even as the goings-on at Tigris morphed into scandal. Their marriage intimacy even approached normality when, on occasion, Lincoln would react to her hand and mouth ministrations with an erection, and they would engage in vaginal intercourse. However, despite Viagra, he was prone to flaccidity and he had no interest in pleasing her orally. He'd been indifferent when she had mentioned children. Nevertheless, Marian persisted, and by marital assignations she could only explain as miracles, she'd conceived three children.

Then there occurred another near miracle. Lincoln was a good father who doted on their children. He filled the house with puppies and kittens. He took great pleasure in pulling the kids from their computer games and into other games that needed no computer. Their rambunctiousness sometimes exasperated Marian, but she said little and, on occasion, actually joined them in hide and seek, their favorite game. Lincoln looked forward to parent–teacher conferences. When he was not in Washington, D.C., he attended all the children's soccer and baseball games, and helped them with their homework. Lincoln reveled in and spoiled the children. He handed the disciplinary role, for which he had no capacity, to Marian. There were even times when, later in their bedroom when the children were asleep, Lincoln would gently chide her for a punishment he thought was too strong.

For several years, they were actually a happy family. It was the children who had preserved their marriage, who had stayed her hand against the divorce petition. However, beginning in Lincoln's second term as governor, the tempting whisperings of 'Mr. President' unleashed another darkness in his soul, that of power lust. It started as a glow in his eyes and a sharpness of his facial features. From there it escalated. He unleashed his sexual cravings on Marian more often with a stepped up intensity and abusiveness she could hardly tolerate.

Marian left their marital bed and moved into her own bedroom. She installed a strong wooden door and lock to keep him out and herself safe. It worked… up to a point. When he craved his release, he would beat his fists against the door until she let him in, lest he wake the children. When he was in an alcoholic stupor, she was safe. When he drank only enough to whet his revolting compulsion, she was not. He had long since ceased the post–act sorrow and never–again promises. However, Lincoln's affections for the children had not changed. He loved it when they went with him on campaign swings. He called their teachers from the Kincaid For America jet and even managed to make a couple of piano recitals. However, his temper was razor-sharp and unpredictable, and he would take it out on Marian in her bedroom.

Marian lay in her bed and focused on the Tonight Show. Then she switched to CNN where she saw Lincoln, in Columbus, Ohio, shaking hands and hugging women who'd broken through the rope to touch him and rip at his shirt buttons and sleeves. The video had been taken earlier that afternoon, which meant that Lincoln's plane would soon land at Indianapolis International Airport. Ten minutes later, she received a text: "leaving the airport." She switched off the TV, went to the bathroom, and then shoved as much lubricant inside her as she could. She washed her hands, placed the can of lubricant under the bed and within her reach, laid back down, and waited.

Her senses turned acute. She listened to the ticking of her old-fashioned, wind-up alarm clock. Then she heard muffled voices. The mansion's front door opened and shut very quietly. His briefcase thumped on the floor. His shuffling footsteps on heavy carpet started out faint, and then grew in volume until they stopped outside her door. Fingers scraped on the door. He tried to turn the doorknob but it was locked. She thought she heard sniffling.

"Marian, please open the door."

"Go to bed, Lincoln."

"Honey, I'm not tired and I really must talk to you now."

"We'll talk in the morning."

"Marian, something's come up and it's really bothering me."

He continued to scrape on the door and rattle the knob. By now, he was sobbing, and he'd started a litany of "Please open, please open, please open." She couldn't let the children see or hear him like this, so she rose, walked to the door, unlocked it, and then ran back to her bed. The door opened and Lincoln, slightly staggering and still crying, walked to her bed. He was carrying the memorandum.

"M… Marian, do you really think this of me?"

He handed her the papers. As she expected, they were a transcript of her and Rhonda's conversation at their St. Elmo lunch.

"No, Lincoln, I do not. Someone made this up. I never said those things."

"They... they bugged you. Don't deny it, Marian. It makes me feel worse."

"Lincoln, go to bed."

"No!"

His tears stopped and she saw the beginning of his escalation. She handed the transcript back to him but he backhanded it to the other side of the room. "You bad-mouthed me. You made me look like a fool, and a man in my position cannot be made to look like a fool."

"Lincoln, keep your voice down. You'll wake the kids. Why don't you close the door?"

He tore the blankets from her grasp and threw them to the bottom of the bed. "I don't give a fuck about the kids or the door."

"Then let me close the door." Marian started to rise but he grabbed her shoulder, wheeled her around, threw her down on the bed, and pinned her there with his arm.

"You aren't going anywhere."

Lincoln crooned as he took his pleasure. "You've known that O'Malley is investigating me and the campaign. Are you writing all this in that fucking book? Doesn't matter. The book that comes out won't be the book that you write."

He finished.

"Daddy, what are you doing to Mommy?"

Marian turned her head and saw Gerardo standing several feet inside the doorway. Lincoln released her hair and stepped out of the bed.

"Gerardo, honey," said Marian, "go back to bed. I'll tuck you in in a few minutes."

Gerardo ignored her and focused on his father. Kincaid calmly walked to Gerardo, stopped, and backhanded him on the face. The boy fell to the floor. Lincoln turned and left the room. He was still naked.

Gerardo lay crying on the floor. Marian pulled on her underpants and a long nightshirt. She rushed to her son, and then knelt beside him. Gerardo's upper lip was swelling and blood trickled from his nose. She took him to the bathroom and washed his face. Later, she lay in his bed and held a cold washcloth to his nose and lip until he fell asleep.

She held him for the rest of the night.

CHAPTER 41

General Hernandez bought the drinks in the barroom. Andy saw Rhonda tense up and stare at someone on the other side of the bar. Andy followed her stare and saw a swarthy-looking man with a shaved head and a ponytail. Andy then caught her eye. She mouthed, "Foun-da-shun." Then Rhonda ever so slightly raised her finger at Andy and shifted her gaze to an attractive woman sitting about ten seats away from the ponytail guy.

Andy glanced. It was the lady he'd met on the Riverwalk in February.

Andy downed his drink. "It's time for the Schnitzelbank. General, you and Louise please join us and help lead the chorus."

The general said, "I'm not good at that sort of thing."

"But you said you would!"

"Okay. Louise and I will sing from here at the bar."

Andy winked at Louise who smiled and gave a slight nod.

Andy loved leading the "Schnitzelbank Song" and, knowing he would do so in a few minutes, turned to the depiction of it on a wall in the barroom. The song featured twelve items, each with a German name and each entailing its own stanza. The first item was the Schnitzelbank, the traditional German woodworking bench. The last item, Gefaehrliches Ding, was a sort of dragon and, in loosely translated German, meant dangerous thing. One of the items in between was Hauffen Mist, or a pile of manure. Andy always sang 'Hauffen Mist' and the crowd always responded with 'horse-shit!' Andy used a ten-foot-long stick to lead the song. He pointed at each item and sang the name and lead-in melody for that item. The crowd followed with the refrain.

The Beech Trees and Rhonda took their places in front of the bar. Andy remained on his barstool. Kim handed the stick to Andy. He shook his head no. The crowd demanded that Andy lead the song. Andy raised his hands and quieted them.

"I want to introduce two special guests tonight. We have with us General David Hernandez, US Army Retired, and his lovely wife, Louise." Andy led the applause and then said, "I will lead the Schnitzelbank under one condition— General David and Louise must leave their seats at the bar and help lead it."

The general forced a smile but shook his head. The crowd clamored. Louise grabbed his hand and led him to the front of the bar.

Polly Thompson left her stool and joined the leaders in the front.

Andy pointed the stick at the first item and started.

Andy: Ist das nicht ein Schnitzelbank?

Crowd: Ja das ist ein Schnitzelbank!

Andy: Ist das nicht ein Langer man?

Crowd-Chorus: Ja das ist ein Langer man!

Andy and Crowd: Ei do shaney ei do shaney ei do shaney Schnitzelbank!

Andy: Ist das nicht ein Schnickel Fritz?

Crowd: Ja das ist ein Schnitzel Fritz!

Andy: Ist das nicht ein Hauffen Mist?

Crowd: Ja das ist ein **HORSE-SHIT!**

Andy and Crowd: Ei do shaney ei do shaney ei do shaney Schnitzelbank.

The song ended, the crowd whistled and cheered, and Andy, Rhonda, the Beech Trees, and Louise and General Hernandez bowed to the applause. Polly had already taken her seat.

Rhonda pulled Andy to the side. "That ponytail guy is Louis Cardova. The Foundation sent him. The girl is Polly Thompson."

"Sent him to do what?"

"To spy on us and probably the General."

"We should warn—"

"Omigod!"

Andy followed Rhonda to the private room where they'd had dinner. Rhonda said, "Place that chair on top of the table and hold it." Rhonda stood on the chair and searched the chandelier. She found a transmitter and handed it to Andy. "They got our entire conversation."

"Polly Thompson?"

"No. Louis Cardova. I'm going to confront the bastard."

"No," said Andy. "You leave that to me."

Cardova had left his seat and the barroom. Andy made his way through the crowd to the restroom. He entered and stood next to the washbowls. Cardova was peeing in a urinal. He zipped up, and then washed and dried his hands. Andy blocked his exit.

"What do you want, Balbach?"

Andy held up the listening device. "This is yours, I believe."

Cardova smirked. "Yes, it is."

"Pardon me for not returning it to you."

"No hard feelings."

"The reservations were under 'Balbach.' How could you know that we were meeting with General Hernandez—I assume he was your target—in that room for dinner?"

"Balbach, you're in the hunt for more trouble than you can possibly imagine."

"Not quite. I have a really big imagination."

"Get out of my way, Balbach. I can hurt you."

"Is that a threat?"

"Not really. However, you'd best warn your wife to back away. Oh, excuse me, your estranged wife."

"If you come after anybody, Cardova," said Andy, "you'd better stick with me. Rhonda O'Malley is way above your league."

The door opened and Clubby stepped in behind Andy. Cardova said, "I see it's now two against one."

Andy replied, "No. It's actually Polly Thompson against you." Then Andy stepped closer to Cardova. "Wish I was a betting man."

"Why?"

"I'd bet that Polly Thompson can whip your ass."

Cardova pushed past Andy and Clubby and left the restaurant.

***

Kim led Andy, Rhonda, Stump, and Clubby to the Schnitzelbank's main telephone switchboard. Clubby felt behind the wired box. He brought out an electronic device and handed it to Kim.

Kim asked, "What is this?"

Andy said, "Did you see that greasy looking ponytail guy at the bar?"

"Yes."

"He or someone he works with planted this."

"Why?"

"So they can listen in on the Schnitzelbank's phone traffic. They recorded us yesterday when I phoned in the reservations for our dinner with General Hernandez this evening. Ponytail then planted a microphone in the room and recorded Rhonda's interview of the General."

"I believe you'll find more of these throughout the restaurant," Clubby said.

Then Rhonda called General Hernandez, told him about the bug, and warned that he and Mrs. Hernandez could be in danger.

The General laughed. "See what happens when you disobey orders?" Then he grew serious. "I get it, Rhonda. We will load our guns and carry them with us. Thank you for the heads up."

CHAPTER 42

Imogene Thompson saw snakes. Polly's father had sent her to rehab so she would stop seeing them. Polly had never visited anyone in a hospital. Today she would do so at the Lakeside Treatment Center in North Palm Beach, Florida. Polly reached out to her mother, and her mother had asked Polly to come see her.

Polly and Johnnie were in the third to last row inside the Delta jet. Johnnie Christiansen, next to the window, was asleep with his head on Polly's shoulder. Johnnie had fallen asleep only minutes after the Delta shuttle had taken off from the Louisville airport. They had a two-hour lay-over in Indianapolis, where they would meet Marian Kincaid and Rhonda O'Malley. Marian had asked Polly to give her opinion on controversial statements in her autobiography.

Polly tried to warm Johnnie by moving her body closer to him, but he shivered in his sleep. She asked a flight attendant for a blanket.

Polly had sensed a widening of her world before she met the deer and Andy Balbach on the Dubain Riverwalk. It blossomed thereafter and led to the revolt. She accepted the pleasure and withstood the pain as the price for a genuine life. It bestowed on her new feelings, such as trust. She had discovered, however, that every new sentiment manifested only in counter-point to its opposite. Love and trust counterpointed hate and distrust. She'd taken Johnnie with her because she loved him as a big sister to a younger and clueless brother, and she distrusted the remaining Angels to care for him. It was no secret that Johnnie was her favorite. One of the Angels might take exception to this and avail herself of Polly's absence to harm Johnnie. The most likely danger was the Angel traitor that Rhonda O'Malley had warned her about.

Louis and Rose Cardova had trained all of the Angels. Many of these stepped up to Archangels. Archangels, like Angels, were learned in the ways of killing, whether by gun, knife, rope, or their bare hands. Archangels, unlike Angels, took to their new work unfettered by conscience. An Archangel close to fulfillment of his mission might stay hidden or appear as a nice and helpful person. Either way, they would strike without warning. In the confines of the passenger compartment, Polly was watchful.

The flight attendants served coffee, soft drinks, snacks, warmth, and smiles as they made their way down the aisle toward Polly and Johnnie. She watched them with the practiced eye of one who was certain of the reality of a mortal enemy that could turn deadly in an instant.

When the attendant reached her and Johnnie, one attendant handed a cup of coffee to Polly and said, in a low voice, "This young man is quite handsome. Is he related to you?"

"He's my brother."

"He's angelic."

"Thank you." Polly tensed and was on full alert.

"Can I get you anything else?"

"A blanket would be nice."

The attendant returned with the blanket. Polly turned down her offer to help wrap it around Johnnie. She waited until the attendant left and then covered Johnnie without waking him.

***

Polly and Johnnie met Marian and Rhonda at the Café Patachou in the Indianapolis International Airport. Marian's security detail sat at other tables nearby, but Polly's internal scanner for danger stayed on high alert.

Marian said, "I've hit a wall on certain statements I added to the middle chapters. Would you read them?"

Polly opened to the bookmarked page in the book. The episode was not prose but a peculiar series of mimeographed legal documents. Something slipped inside her when she saw her own name on the documents. She paged back and read them slowly and deliberately. Among them were two birth certificates. She was familiar with the first one that listed Earl and Imogene Thompson as her birth parents. She was not with the second one that showed Earl Thompson and Rachel Kincaid as her birth parents. Then, there were a series of papers concerning an adoption case. She started trembling when she saw the captions on the court papers: 'In Re: The Adoption of the Infant, Polly Thompson, Nee Kincaid.'

Polly looked up at Marian and Rhonda. "What... what is all... this?"

Rhonda placed her arm around Polly's shoulders. "Honey, your father and Rachel had an affair. You were the result. Jackson Kincaid still believes that he is your father. Rachel and Jackson gave up all parental rights in you. Earl Thompson is both your birth and adoptive father. Imogene Thompson is your adoptive mother."

"This... is the truth about my birth?"

Marian said, "Yes. Rhonda got it from a highly reliable source."

Polly read the documents again. "My mother—adoptive mother—is the 'highly reliable source,' isn't she?"

"Yes."

"She intended to give me all this information today, but asked you two to soften the blow, didn't she?"

"Yes," said Marian.

"This means that your husband, Marian, is my half-brother. Why didn't they raise me? They..." Polly went mute.

"Rachel and Jackson gave you away," said Marian, "because Earl Thompson and Benjamin Kincaid, a member of the Foundation's board of directors then and now, insisted. They said that all the attention and household resources of Rachel and Jackson must be dedicated to Lincoln."

"They threw me out because I was in the way of Lincoln?"

"Yes."

Polly started to cry. It was the first time in her life that she remembered doing so.

Johnnie placed his arm around her.

CHAPTER 43

Garrett Jennings and Louis Cardova sat in the Ford Transit Wagon in the parking lot of a cleaners in West Palm Beach, Florida. They were west of US Highway 1, a half mile from the Lakeside Treatment Center that fronted on the east side of the highway. The Atlantic Ocean loomed behind the center.

Garrett raised his binoculars and scanned the center. "Nothing yet."

"We've got another forty-five minutes," Louis Cardova replied.

Rose Cardova had called them earlier from the Indianapolis International Airport. She reported that Polly and Johnnie had boarded the Delta flight from Indianapolis to Florida.

Garrett asked, "Are you certain Polly didn't spot you?"

"Yes. I trailed them and observed the meeting among them, Marian, and Rhonda from another restaurant farther down the concourse."

"Was there any sign that Marian Kincaid's security detected you?"

"None whatsoever. I'm unknown to them. However, I saw Polly cry after reading something that Marian handed to her."

"What was it?"

"I don't know," said Rose. "I was too far away to tell. What are my orders?"

"Fly back to Oakenwald and get the Fallout Shelter jail ready."

"Roger that." Rose ended the call.

Louis said, "Polly never so much as shed a tear during even the hardest part of her training. What do you make of it?"

Garrett replied, "It's part of her mental breakdown."

"I wonder what she read."

"Probably an unhappy episode in Marian Kincaid's life."

Garrett knew better. Polly hadn't had a breakdown. She'd read something explosive and it wasn't about Marian's history. It was more likely about Polly's. Garrett had learned the truth of Polly's ancestry from Earl. He'd warned Earl that Polly was bound, at some point, to uncover the truth about her past. It was better that he break the news to Polly prior to that point. Earl, for reasons known only to him, had never done so.

At first, Garrett thought that it was the discovery of her true ancestry that had led to Polly's mutiny. However, in the Hangouts calls, she'd neither hinted at it nor backed away from her claim that she'd received a 'sign from Jesus.' Garrett surmised that Rhonda O'Malley had uncovered it. Garrett called Earl, who agreed with Garrett's assessment but said it didn't matter. Garrett wasn't so sure. A mutinous Polly was dangerous but mostly predictable. An outraged Polly was murderous and totally un-predictable. He shuddered in the Florida heat. If Polly had a list, Garrett could think of no good reason why he wouldn't be on it.

Louis asked, "Why did Earl send his wife to a rehab center this far away from Washington, D.C.?"

"This is a very good facility." In truth, Garrett had always felt badly for Imogene. Imogene had a PhD in International Relations and was lively and vivacious during stretches of sobriety. However, Earl Thompson dominated her in accordance with the Foundation culture that men rule and women serve. He treated his wife like a second-class citizen and belittled her in front of others. As far as Garrett knew, he had never apologized for the affair with Lincoln Kincaid's mother. Imogene could have no children so she had accepted Polly as her own daughter. She wanted a normal life for Polly, but it was not meant to be. Her husband overpowered her, and Polly disappeared into the Fallout Shelter. It was then that Imogene turned to alcohol.

Earl had committed Imogene to the Lakeside Treatment Center not because he cared for her. He didn't. There were larger issues. First, Imogene had been drunk and out of sight for most of the past year. The whisperings had begun. Earl, the Foundation, and Kincaid For America could not afford the rumors and the unwanted attention of the police. Second, he told Garrett, Imogene in treatment just might be the bait that flushed Polly into the open.

Louis said, "There they are."

He handed the binoculars to Garrett. Johnnie and Polly exited a taxi and disappeared into the center.

"Showtime, Louis."

CHAPTER 44

Polly talked herself and Johnnie past the receptionist and entered Imogene's room. Imogene raised her head from the book she was reading, placed it and her Diet Coke on the nightstand, and leaned back in the rocking chair. Polly saw that her mother's hair was longer and well brushed and her fingernails neatly clipped. She'd lost weight and wore no makeup although Polly doubted whether any application could have hidden the yellowish tint on her face. Her shrunken eyes, watering but not defeated, bore into Polly's. Most of her latest meal lay uneaten on the serving tray.

Imogene said, "You know."

"Yes."

Imogene put her finger to her lips and motioned Polly to search the room. Polly found two devices. Imogene whispered, "Outside."

Polly told Johnnie to go to the reception area and wait. Imogene asked Polly to carry a thick book with what looked like plastic pages. They sat across from each other on a picnic table and Polly laid the book in front of Imogene. She'd thrown the devices in the Atlantic Ocean.

"Mother, why hadn't you told me the truth of my birth before this? You've had years."

"I planned to break it to you after your graduation from Bob Jones."

"But you didn't. Why?"

"It was too late. Your father said he'd already chosen your life's work and it had nothing left for what he called, 'family sentimentality.' Your father never saw you as a daughter. To him, you were a high-functioning robot."

"Didn't I have the right to hear it from you?"

"You did. I'd planned to tell you today, but I feared that I wouldn't have the strength, so I asked Marian and Rhonda."

"It's okay."

Several herons squawked at each other on the Lake Worth Lagoon shoreline. Then they made peace and quieted.

"Why did he commit you to this facility? It's so far away."

"He didn't. I wanted a hospital. I needed rehab. The doctors said my liver was failing. Your father had made arrangements to commit me to a hospital in Arlington. I didn't want to be that close to him. Like you, I, too, had to escape. I found this hospital, flew down, and signed myself in."

"You defied him, as have I."

"I began to hope again when I heard that you'd left him."

Polly said, "He and the board haven't taken it lightly. Father has ordered me back to Oakenwald. When I said no, he threatened me. It wasn't an idle threat. I'm on his list."

"Then, I suppose, I'll make it on the list too. I'm leaving your father. I can't go back to Oakenwald. I can no longer abide the twisted 'covenants,' and the hypocrisy and corruption. Lincoln Kincaid is the most dangerous man in the world, far more dangerous than Sarah Harding. We know her. Nobody knows the real Lincoln Kincaid."

Polly had gotten to know him in one respect but she withheld that for now.

"Did father apologize to you for his affair with Rachel Kincaid?"

"No. A man of his ilk apologizes to no woman."

Polly looked away. A breeze off the Atlantic Ocean wafted through the palm trees. She watched a heron pluck a small fish from the sea. There were a few fishing boats in the distance. She'd never really known her mother and hadn't cared to know her. She did now. If only it wasn't so hard to find the right words.

Polly said, "My own father traded me for my precious half-brother, Lincoln Kincaid. He'd already planned my life without asking me. No one ever asked me."

Imogene said, "Polly, I lost you. We lost each other. You lost your life's timeline. I tried to save you from your father, but I wasn't strong enough. Please don't hate me for being weak."

Neither talked for several minutes.

Polly turned back to her mother. "Did... did Rachel love me?"

"No. After the adoption, Rachel Kincaid pulled me aside and said that she wanted no part of you. She didn't even want to see you again."

"I was only a distraction to them. This is my life, Mother! Lincoln got everything. I got nothing."

"It was your father and Benjamin Kincaid who made it happen."

Polly again turned away. "Why did you adopt me?"

"Because I wanted you. I could have no children, and your father was against adopting... that is, until you came along. It was the one time I defeated your father. He didn't want the scandal of an extramarital affair, especially one that involved the Kincaid family and produced a baby girl."

Polly turned back to her mother. "What is a life timeline? You said I lost it."

"Right, but I kept it for you in case... in case this day came. Your life timeline is in that book."

"Can I see it?"

"Of course."

Polly opened the book. It was a history of her life in bits and pieces and snapshots. The first two pages held Polly's baby pictures. These were followed by a number of photos of Imogene holding her. Birthdays were important to her mother. There were photos of cakes and Polly blowing out the candles. Curiously, there were other children in the photos. Friends? Polly flipped through the book. There were her school pictures and report cards. There were letters her mother had written to her over the years, but hadn't sent, and photos of Imogene and Polly. She flipped to the back. There was nothing after her graduation from Bob Jones. Her father was nowhere in the book.

Polly said, "You are the only human being who hasn't traded me, or used me, or thrown me away."

Two nurses helped another resident to a lawn chair where she sat and stared out over the ocean.

"I know Lincoln Kincaid," Polly said.

"What do you mean?"

"He raped me at a Young Life Camp. I was fourteen. He was a counselor. One night I left the cabin to visit the restroom. He grabbed me when

I walked out. His face was red and he smelled of alcohol. He overpowered me, gagged me, forced me into the woods, and stripped my shorts and panties. He raped me in my anus. When he finished he told me to get dressed and go back to the cabin. If I talked, he said he would hurt me." Polly rose and walked several feet away, her back to her mother.

"You never told—"

"I was father's robot. I… had no emotions. It was what it was and I put it behind me… until today." Polly turned to her mother. "My step-brother raped… sodomized me. I couldn't have known we were related, but he did. He had to know I was his half-sister."

Imogene pulled Polly's face to her bosom and held her there. "I'm so sorry, Polly. You are my daughter and I am your mother. I love you, Polly. I've loved you since the day I set eyes on you. I thought I'd never have the chance to say those words to you. I'd given up. Then you defied your father and I saw my chance."

Polly cried for the second time that day. She and Imogene wiped their tears.

Imogene said, "They must be stopped—your father and Garrett Jennings and Lincoln Kincaid and all their confederates. Lincoln Kincaid raped you. Who knows how many others he has or will victimize? Do we know the truth about Lincoln Kincaid and Tigris River? How could the commander not know what was going on? Did he himself participate in it? It seems that even Marian Kincaid opposes Lincoln. The Foundation seeks a world that is madness. Someone has to stop them."

"Is that someone me?"

"Polly, you must stop what you do... change who you are."

"Don't judge me, mother. If I am to stop them, I have to be like them. It's not the time to lay down my sword."

"You're wrong. There is in each of us good and bad and everything in between. You resurrected your conscience, Polly. I don't know how, where, or when, but it happened. You're in recovery too. The good inside will talk to you, honey. Listen to that voice."

"I'll listen, Mother."

"Do you know fear, Polly?"

"I've learned it in the past months."

"The Foundation is spying on me."

"I already know that, Mother. I found two of their bugs in your room. There are probably more."

"I'm not talking about listening devices. There's a black vehicle with tinted windows. It's mostly hidden, but I've seen it. I'm certain your father sent it to watch me."

Polly stood. "When did you last see it?"

"This morning right before you arrived."

"Oh My God!" Polly ran to the waiting area. Johnnie was gone. She searched Imogene's room and ran up and down the corridors.

The receptionist asked, "Are you looking for someone?"

"Yes. That young man who came in here with me."

"He left a short while ago."

"By himself?"

"No, some men came in and talked to him. He left with them. I thought they were part of your group."

Polly ran outside to her mother. "Johnnie's been kidnapped." Then her cell phone rang. It was Louis Cardova.

"We have Johnnie."

"You bastard!"

"Bastard? No, Polly, that's more in your line."

"Where is Johnnie?"

"Johnnie will be housed in the Fallout Shelter. If you want him back safely, you must obey your father. You must come in."

CHAPTER 45

Johnnie Christiansen sat at a table inside the small jail cell. Louis Cardova was beside him with Garrett and Rose on the other side.

Rose asked, "Do you want something to drink, Johnnie?"

"No. Can I go to bed?"

"Not now."

"I'm tired."

Garrett said, "We have a few questions. Then you can go to bed. Is that okay?"

"I guess so."

Garrett asked, "Do you like Polly?"

"Yes."

"Polly needs help. Do you want to help her?"

"Yes."

"So let's form a covenant to help Polly. Just you, Rose, and me."

"Okay."

"Where are the Angels hiding?"

"Polly said it's a secret."

"You just formed a covenant to help her. You must tell us."

"It's in a basement in Dubain."

"Which basement?"

Johnnie seemed anxious. He started to rock back and forth. Garrett glanced at Rose.

Rose asked, "Which basement, Johnnie? We won't tell anyone."

"It's under a large room. Don't remember the room."

"Does it have a name?"

"7-12. Can I go to bed now?"

"7-12. It's the large room, Johnnie. Try to remember it."

"Earthquake. Jesus spoke. Polly says there'll be more."

"Are you afraid of earthquakes?"

"No. Maybe just a little. Jesus sent it. I want to go to bed."

Rose asked, "Do you know Rhonda?"

"She's Polly's friend."

"Is she your friend too?"

"I'm tired. Blessed are the meek, for they shall inherit the earth. Blessed are the poor in spirit, for theirs is the kingdom of heaven."

"Johnnie, I don't understand."

"Blessed are the pure in heart, for they shall be... Jesus... Judge not, lest ye be judged. Jesus didn't judge. I'm scared."

"There's nothing to be scared of, Johnnie."

"I don't like this place." Johnnie started to cry. "Blessed are the peacemakers. Blessed are the poor... blessed, blessed, blessed."

Garrett asked, "What is the name of the building where the Angels hide?"

"No! Salt. You are the salt of the earth. Blessed be. Light of the world. Don't hide it under a bushel basket. It's a secret. Don't remember. Jesus came to fulfill the prophets."

Garrett slapped the table. "This is nonsense, Johnnie. Answer the question."

"I don't like you. Do not be angry with your brother. You are liable to judgment. Polly said the light of the world. I want Polly. Our Father, who art in heaven..." Johnnie gagged and then vomited over the table. "Go away! Go away!"

Garrett nodded at Rose. "Come, Johnnie, you can go to bed." She led him out of the room.

CHAPTER 46

Garrett cleaned up Johnnie's mess. Then he placed his feet on the table, lit a Marlboro, and took a long draw. He laid his head back and slowly blew the smoke at the ceiling. Then he called his boss.

"Sir, we can't get anything out of him other than he likes Polly and the Angels live in a basement in Dubain. He said he doesn't remember the name of the building. He got agitated, quoted material from the Bible, and then threw up."

"Any particular part of the Bible?"

"New Testament. Sermon on the Mount. These are Polly's teachings."

Earl said, "She's poisoning them with the 'love one another,' 'turn the other cheek,' 'before the cock crows' Jesus."

"Definitely, sir."

"What do you plan next?"

"Wait."

"For what?"

"Polly. Johnnie's her favorite."

"I don't follow you, Garrett."

"Sir, Polly will not walk into Oakenwald on your order. She'll attack. We are preparing."

"Attack what?"

"The Fallout Shelter. She'll try to rescue Johnnie."

"That makes no sense. Certainly Polly knows she can't take on the Archangels and win."

"We no longer know what goes on in Polly's head."

"Garrett, it's just not rational."

"The Angels will form a covenant to rescue Johnnie."

"You said you're 'preparing.'"

"We've placed motion detectors and sirens in three concentric circles around the Fallout Shelter and I've ordered around-the-clock surveillance. Three Archangels stay hidden in the woods at all times."

"What do you plan to do with Johnnie?"

"Keep him as bait for Polly. Then send him home to his family in San Francisco."

"That might be too much of a risk."

"What do you suggest, sir?"

"Another arrangement. It's better he be silenced. Anything else?"

"No, sir."

"The board is watching this very closely. They have confidence in you."

"Sir, I always do my best."

"They don't want your best, Garrett. They want your success. Do you understand?"

"Yes, sir."

***

Garrett walked back to Oakenwald in the dark. He stopped at the basketball courts. He found a basketball and started shooting around... some shots long, others short, some layups. He stood at the top of the key and imagined two opposing players guarding him. He made a drive for the basket while dribbling between his legs. Two points and a foul. He made the free throw. Then he practiced thirty-foot set shots.

He had suggested to Earl the possibility of a 'Save Johnnie Covenant' among the Angels. Earl had founded the concept of covenants. Did Earl actually believe in them or were they simply his hand-chosen motivators for others to do his bidding? The answers, Garrett surmised, were maybe the former but certainly the latter. In the twilight world of the Foundation, belief and motivation, like reason and unreason, sanity and insanity, morality and immorality, were relative terms, always changing, always negotiable, depending on the need at the time. Polly had changed, but not for the worse. She was gaining her soul, and thus freedom, founded on the notion that the universe assumed good and evil. Neither was negotiable. Neither was a euphemism for the other. The real point was that Polly's view made a lot more sense to Garrett than the Jesus Equation.

Earl Thompson had found in Garrett another talent. Garrett was an earthly black hole, one whose gravitation sucked in all that could otherwise be traced to Earl Thompson. Laundering money for his law firm client, Good Earth, seemed puny when placed beside kidnapping, extortion, and conspiracy to commit murder. Earl was always there, doing these things, but nobody saw him. They saw only Garrett Jennings.

There was one exception. Earl had negotiated a ceasefire between the Russians and Ukrainians and Trotsky had signed the contracts for the Siberian Project. Earl had stopped a war in Eastern Europe, but not to save lives and prevent destruction. He'd merely put the war aside until it was in his and the Foundation's interests to revive it. They'd need the revival of Russia versus Ukraine in order to divert Americans' attention away from the army Earl, via President Lincoln Kincaid, would be secretly amassing on the Mexican border.

Garrett hit three long shots in a row. Then he picked up the basketball and flung it at the opposite goal, sixty feet away. It went in. One good omen deserved another. He pulled a small digital recorder from his pocket, connected it to his smart phone, and uploaded his conversation with Earl to his personal cloud, the place where he kept all such recordings.

Garrett walked to his living quarters. There, he got down on his knees and prayed to his god, whether he existed or not.

CHAPTER 47

There were twenty-one of them: two truck drivers, three manufacturing technicians, one computer programmer, one chef, two mechanics, one bank president, one small town mayor, two construction workers, one lawyer, one airline pilot, two bartenders, and four were homeless. There were eleven Caucasians, one Native-American, one Jew, four African-Americans, two Hispanic-Americans, and two Asian-Americans. One had been on Iwo Jima, two had fought with the First Marine Division at Chosin Reservoir, seven had slithered with snakes in the jungle while hunting for—or hiding from—'Charlie,' and eleven had been up against, variously, the Taliban, Afghanis, Iraqis, and Al Qaeda. All were men. Eighteen were straight, two were gay, and one was scheduled for a sex change operation. They'd checked into the Lugar Veterans Administration Hospital that was a mile north of Interstate 64 next to the south side of the town of Ferdinand, Indiana. That morning, they were relieved of their luggage, then underwent rigorous physicals, and received their first psychological exams. Lunch was a ham sandwich, skim milk, fruit, coffee, tea, one-half hour long, and five minutes ago.

They sat on folding chairs arranged in a semicircle. Just outside the semicircle stood Father Bernardo.

Bernardo stared into the eyes of each of the twenty-one. Some returned the stare. Most met and then glanced away from it, and a few refused it altogether. During this time, two nurses pushed a wheeled table from a side door to a position about ten feet behind Bernardo. The items on the table were hidden by white sheets. Bernardo did not turn around.

Father Bernardo started. "The first lesson is that no doctor, nurse, counselor, or hospital—indeed the entire American medical system—have healed anyone. They never will. The patient must heal himself. Each of you is a patient. Only you can heal yourself. We shall facilitate your healing with treatments. The treatments are painful and gut wrenching. Some are downright ugly. When you leave this room today, none of you will like me and some of you will hate me. You'll leave this program in thirty days, and, if you're lucky, you'll love me.

"The second lesson is this—who you see here, what you hear here… when you leave here, let it stay here. All of you agreed to confidentiality when you signed the papers this morning. To this I add an exclamation point. If any of you talks outside this hospital about your or anyone else's treatment, you will have to deal with me and I will not be very pleasant.

"The third lesson begins now." Bernardo pointed to Arthur, an African-American. "Arthur, you and Jerry, sitting beside you, served together at the Tigris River POW Camp in Baghdad in 2003. What happened there?"

Arthur said, "What... happened?"

"Did I stutter?"

"Um, no."

"Then tell us what happened."

"Well, me and Jerry were Military Police."

"Anything else?"

"Um, no."

"I see." Then Bernardo pointed to Jerry. "Is Arthur right?"

"Yeah."

"Do you have anything to add?"

"Why are you picking on me and Arthur? Ask some of the others here."

"I didn't ask the others. I asked you."

"Well, we answered."

Bernardo stared at Jerry and then turned to a swarthy-looking man with a shaved head. "Gavin Scott, what happened to you at Tigris?"

"I was Military Police."

"Anything else?"

"Yeah."

"Tell us."

"No."

"Then why are you here? Sarah Harding wants to end this program anyway. So check out and go home. Save the government some money."

"Goddamnit, I might just do that."

"Then again, goddamnit, you just might not." Bernardo scanned the other men. "Gavin's going nowhere. Know why? Because Gavin's home is a park bench in Rochester, New York. Damn near froze his wonjees off last winter." Bernardo turned to Gavin. "However, you still got 'em. Doc counted two this morning during your physical."

"You've seen my medical records? You can't do that."

"Of course I can, and I did."

"I have a right to privacy."

"Not here. You gave it away when you signed that sheet of paper early this morning. We got us a smart lawyer. He hid your privacy waiver right there in plain sight." Bernardo turned. "Jerry, you and Arthur are luckier than Gavin. You live in houses except when—"

"Fuck you Bern—"

"Rapes!" shouted Arthur. He stood. "Yeah, rapes it was. In our assholes. They stuck their dicks in our assholes. They stuck them in our mouths. Over and over, switching back and forth. We ate our own shit. Whole fuckin' bunches of 'em made us do this. There. You satisfied?"

"Thank you, Arthur. Please sit down." One of the men had a coughing spell. Bernardo waited until it stopped.

"Everybody look at Arthur. He has some stories to tell. Why did you come here, Arthur?"

"To be in this... hospital."

"What's this hospital's name?"

"Lugar Veterans Administration Hospital."

"Which specializes in the treatment of the disease you carry."

"That's what they told me."

"What's the name of the disease?"

"It ain't gotta name s'far as I know."

"It's Post-traumatic stress disorder. PTSD. That's the name of your disease. You can now confront it. Arthur, does this make you feel any better?"

"Feel better?" Arthur sneered. "It can have all the fucking names in the world. Don't mean nothin'."

"Jerry, I can see that you've calmed a bit. Tell us more about Tigris."

"We were with the 800th Battalion Military Police at Tigris River in 2003. This was the prison where Iraqi POWs were led around with collars like dogs. I remember. Wish I didn't. They raped us and a bunch more."

"How many times were you raped?"

"Think I kept count on my friggen night stand with a magic marker?"

"Arthur, how many times were you raped?"

"I lost count. So did Jerry. Those motherfuckers called themselves Cradlers, whatever the hell that means. They raped us and prisoners."

Jerry cut in, "Know what they called us? Lambs. Me and Arthur were two of their Lambs."

"Arthur, who raped you?" asked Bernardo.

"Well... others."

"Can't rape yourself, Arthur, so it had to be 'others.' Who were they?"

"Some guys in our battalion."

"Were any of them officers?"

"Yeah."

"How many?"

Arthur said, "Several."

"How far up the chain of command did the Cradlers go?"

Jerry said, "We can't say."

"Do you mean that you don't know, or that you do know and for some reason won't tell us?"

Arthur said, "They ordered us to keep our mouths shut. They said it was for 'security' reasons. However, a lawyer in the JAG Corps said it was an illegal order and we can't be court-martialed for violating it. I told him me and Jerry are just grunts. Nobody'd believe us."

Father Bernardo walked to the table and lightly drew his hand across the sheet. Then he took a chair from a stack of them by the wall, placed it slightly inside the semicircle of chairs, and sat down.

"Arthur's PTSD is the birth child of parasites that entered and poisoned him in 2003. They've mutated to infect his mind, his body, his soul. Each of you has the same illness. Why? You were raped while serving your country... in most cases repeatedly and by gangs. The rapists were other soldiers in your units, or even your commanding officers. At first, you tried to fight back but you were overwhelmed by force or threats of injury or worse. You thought that you left the parasites over there and came home but you did neither. You tried to get on with your lives but you couldn't. All of you suffer from depression. Some of you have flashbacks. Most of you are divorced. Some of you abandoned your families. The parasites went inside you. You fought them, mostly with alcohol. A few of you graduated to stronger stuff, like meth and heroin. About half of you have been arrested for crimes ranging from public intoxication to drunk driving to assault. All of you have suicidal thoughts. A few of you tried to end your lives but failed. Each of you knows at least one other who tried but didn't fail.

"Arthur, you're a strong man. Why didn't you fight back?"

"I did, but there were too many of 'em. They said they'd hurt me, bad hurt me, if I didn't give in... if I told someone."

"Did you ejaculate?"

"No."

Bernardo pointed to another man. "Iggy, did you ejaculate?"

"No."

"What about you, Fred?"

"Yeah."

"Yeah what?"

"Yeah I did."

"Yeah you did what?"

"I fuckin' ejaculated. The bastards said it showed I liked it."

"Did you?"

"Fuck no."

"Do you know why you ejaculated?"

"No."

"Well, I do. Ejaculation is a normal response to stimulation of the prostate gland. The prostate lies against the rectum. A rapist's erect penis in the rectum stimulates the prostate… thus your ejaculation."

Five hospital therapists very quietly entered the room from behind the men and stood by the door. Only Bernardo saw them. He stood and invaded the semicircle a few more feet.

"All of you close your eyes and don't open them until I say so. Think back to when it happened. Take yourself there. You're in Baghdad, or Kabul, or Saigon, or on a bloody island, or Inchon, or in the jungle, or maybe on a ship, or anywhere. You're with your unit. You see them brave bombs and bullets, save each other's lives, including yours, hand candy to children, salute their officers, revere their flag, take snapshots with you in them, and you send these home. Sometimes, back at base, you see them on a video call with their children and watch them cry when it's over. However, it's their eyes. Always you study their eyes. Most people can behold a man's eyes and see his present. Some can see his past. It takes real talent to see his future. Each of you has this talent. You are experts at eyes. You saw theirs and predicted their future—and yours—for that night. Their eyes said they would take their pleasure of you.

"Arthur, Fred, Gavin—close your eyes and keep them closed.

"Later, you glanced into your wife's eyes and saw the divorce petition. You looked into your childrens' eyes and saw their abandonment. You drank on the job and one day your boss' eyes said you were fired and it happened a week later. You're in a rough bar, drunk and mouthing off. The other drunks' eyes say they don't like you and they let you know it when you stagger to your car. The cop's eyes are both sad and stern because he knows you and feels badly for you but must arrest you. In between these, you see the drunk tank, the courtroom, the prosecutor, and the judge. The prosecutor's eyes held scorn. The judge's eyes said this is your third DUI and you'll get a trip to prison."

Some of the men were crying. The therapists moved to the backs of their chairs.

"Make it come back. Make it come back big time." Bernardo paused. "Is it there? That sick nauseous tumor of rotten maggots in your gut? Yeah, you feel it. They're there. They're always there and they steal your food, drink your water, and suck at your body and spirit. You try to vomit them but you can't. You throw booze on them but they stay. You sob your tears at them but they won't melt. This very minute the tumor tears at your insides, knots your soul, despairs your life. You fight them every minute of every hour of every day. Sometimes you can push them to a distance and you tell yourself that they're gone but you know better. They come back. Always they come back."

Bernardo exited the semicircle and walked to the table.

"I'm not done. Keep your eyes closed. Each of you is sick. If you are to get well, you must get sicker so that you get a high fever. For without the fever, you cannot kill the parasites."

Most of the men were crying. Some were sobbing. More hospital people entered the room.

"We're almost done. Five hours ago, about half of you checked into this hospital. The rest of you made the motions but you hid safety nets in your luggage. You told yourself that it's nobody's business but yours and you by damn and sure as hell ain't gonna show it to this cockamamie priest in this cockamamie hospital.

"Now open your eyes."

Bernardo carefully removed the sheet from the table. On it were bottles of whiskey, bourbon, rum, and a various assortment of cheap wines. The Vodka bottles outnumbered all the rest. There was a Ziploc bag with an assortment of needles and marijuana. There was one gun.

"We searched your luggage and confiscated these. Gentlemen, each of you is now fully checked into the Lugar Veterans Administration Hospital."

The hospital workers handed towels to the men to dry their faces and blow their noses.

"You can leave this hospital anytime you want. We won't stop you. We might even encourage you. Every class has a few who leave and most of these make it home. A few disappear. Probably suicides. Too bad for them.

"As to you," Bernardo swept his arm across the room, "your crutches are removed. After you leave this room, we will destroy all these items except this one." Bernardo picked up the gun. "One of you packed this. It's a .45 Smith & Wesson Revolver, fully loaded. Darn good weapon and very illegal in this hospital. The owner won't get it back and he won't be prosecuted, but he'll have to endure a private chat with me."

Bernardo watched the hospital workers lead the men to the gym for their first workouts. Then he went to his office.

CHAPTER 48

Father Bernardo sat on the floor of the utility landing, lit a cigarette, and motioned Father Paul Kessler to the only chair. He marveled at Paul. The man was ninety-two years old, yet he climbed the steps and ladders up the St. Augustine steeple with vigor, strength, and few stops. It was Bernardo, over Paul's protests, who insisted on resting at the utility landing. The evening before, Paul had asked for Bernardo's help to investigate what he called 'strange goings-on' in St. Augustine Cathedral. Bernardo drove from Ferdinand to Dubain and met Paul in the St. Augustine sacristy after early morning mass. Paul said they were climbing the steeple to the Lookout Room but he wouldn't elaborate. Bernardo tapped the cigarette ashes into his left hand. "Well, we're half-way to the Lookout Room so it's unlikely I'll back out. Tell me what I'm looking for."

"Angels."

"Angels?"

"Yeah." Paul grinned "You think I'm senile and this is a wild-goose chase, don't you?"

"I'm withholding judgment on both."

"Oh Ye of little faith."

"Sometimes discretion is the better part of faith."

Paul paused as if to ponder Bernardo's comment, and then said, "I sometimes visit our 'nocturnal guests' who spend their nights in the back of the cathedral. One told me she'd seen angels."

"Really?"

"These folks see lots of things that aren't there. However, some of the others backed her up. They said the angels prayed."

"Well," Bernardo said, "I'm happy for them. Praying angels are better than snakes or skunks or little devils with red-hot pitchforks."

"I've seen the angels."

"Real ones?"

"I'm ninety-two, but I'm neither stupid nor blind. Two nights ago, I kept watch with the nocturnal company. The creatures were dressed in white but I neither saw wings nor heard a harp. I'm fairly certain they were human."

"So… you think we'll find one of these angel-humans in the Lookout Room?"

"No."

"Then why are we climbing to it?"

"To find something else."

"A person?"

"Maybe." Paul shined his flashlight in Bernardo's face. "Finish that cigarette. I'll stiffen up unless I keep moving."

Bernardo crushed his cigarette and they climbed to the Lookout Room. No one was there, but someone certainly had been. The two priests inspected empty cans, water jugs, and newly cut initials in the corner near the floor.

Bernardo said, "Paul, this isn't a goose chase and you're not senile."

"Oh Ye of partially restored faith."

"Yeah. Why would someone live in a church steeple?"

"To hide."

"Hide from what?"

"From people who want to kill him but who would never look for him in a church steeple."

"We did."

"Not to kill him."

Bernardo said, "This guy doesn't know that. He's dangerous. He could have killed us."

"Gosh, Bernardo, you're right. How can I make it up to you?"

Bernardo grinned and shook his head. "You're sandbagging on me, Paul."

"Gee, I've been forgetting things. Old age, you know."

"Yeah, right."

"A few of the nocturnal company said they'd seen a younger man with a full backpack crossing the altar and disappearing into the sacristy."

"Dressed in?"

"Black."

"Shouldn't we call the police?"

"No."

"Why not?"

"Our search isn't finished." There was Paul's half-toothless grin again. "I'm an old geezer so I know where to look. Better hope I don't die between here and there or it could be lost until the day the contractors arrive to rebuild the foundations that hold this church up."

"Does this church have foundation problems?"

"No. The men who built it 160 years ago knew and practiced their trades well. Keep your powder dry and have faith."

"I don't have a gun."

"Then all you have is faith."

They climbed down to the sacristy and stopped. Paul asked, "Do you know what a priest hole is?"

"Yeah. They started in Europe during the Thirty Years' war in the 1600s. Priests hid in them to avoid execution by the enemies of the church. They were never used in America."

"Ah, you Jesuits. You know so much and yet so little. St. Augustine parish was founded in the 1830s. They started construction of this cathedral in the 1860s. Catholics were not very popular in America... especially the German and Irish Catholics. The Know-Nothings and Ku Klux Klan persecuted them in the 1800s and 1900s. Then there were the World War One laws that prohibited the speaking of German in public. Priests at St. Augustine had no choice but to break the law and celebrate masses in German because their parishioners knew little English. Then Indiana went through that glorious decade, the 1920s, when the Klan controlled the state. In all this lives a secret. St. Augustine has a priest hole. It was closed off many decades ago to keep out vagrants. In the 1960s, a ninety-year-old parish priest passed the secret to me."

They wound their way down to near the bottom of the steeple. Paul stopped and put his finger to his lips. "From this point we whisper." They reached the bottom. There was a padlocked door to the outside but Paul wasn't interested in it. He walked behind the steps, reached up to some kind of lever device, and slowly pulled it down. A small portion of the wall turned inward toward what Bernardo could see was a passageway. He estimated the opening to be about four feet high and two feet wide. They entered. Paul handed the flashlight to Bernardo. "You lead from here."

"Why me?"

"I'm too young to die. Besides, I heard-tell Jesuits are 'Warrior Priests,' so it's fitting and proper that you take over."

Bernardo smiled and shook his head in mock disgust.

The passage was hewn roughly from the earth. Rock, bricks, mortar, and native timber bolstered the sides and ceiling. The floor was damp earth but, Bernardo could see, packed tightly from recent and frequent usage. The passage turned left and ended at a door. Bernardo saw light at the bottom. He turned to Paul behind him. Paul grinned, nodded, and whispered, "on three." Bernardo handed the flashlight to Paul and then turned back to the door. He put his left hand on the latch with his right hand above his shoulder. His fingers signaled the one and two. On three, Bernardo threw open the door and he and Paul entered.

The room was a square, maybe ninety feet on each side. Bernardo saw bunk beds along the sides and light bulbs strung along the low-hanging ceiling. Cafeteria tables in the center of the room supported everything from computers to fruit baskets to water bottles. Weapons occupied slots along the wall. There were twelve or so people dressed in white and two in black. One in white, a woman, was sitting behind a makeshift desk in the far corner of the room. Bernardo recognized the latter two, Jameel Shalih and Jayden Ramirez, from their police photos.

Ramirez and several of those in white reached for the guns.

CHAPTER 49

Polly sat at her desk in 7-12. There was a legal pad in front of her. On it, she had drawn layouts of the Fallout Shelter, written comments in the margins, and doodled the name of Johnnie Christiansen. However, no amount of pencil on paper could change the fact that she'd failed Johnnie, her Angels, Jesus, and the Angel Covenant. She had needed Johnnie on the mission against the Cradler, George Todrank, but made certain he suffered no harm. After the Las Vegas mission and securing Ramirez at 7-12, she'd carried out missions in other cities such as Seattle, Milwaukee, South Bend, Baltimore, and Sedona. She took each target out while Johnnie was safely hidden in their hotel room. Polly was with Johnnie at Piankashaw Rock when he'd saved Jameel Shalih. Then she'd let down her guard at her mother's treatment center and Johnnie, an innocent just like the fawn, was taken from her. Unlike the fawn, she could not rescue Johnnie by the simple act of lifting fallen tree branches. At this moment, Johnnie was most likely locked in a cell in the Fallout Shelter, terrified and oblivious to the reasons for his discomfort. But 7-12 was Johnnie's home. Garrett Jennings wanted its location and undoubtedly placed Johnnie on a harsh regimen of interrogation in order to get it.

Johnnie's loss forced her into the emotions of guilt and the intense drive to redeem herself from his kidnapping. It helped when she imagined reaching her hand from 7-12 in Dubain to Johnnie's cell at Oakenwald, caressing and reassuring him that he would be rescued, and all would be okay.

She watched as the Angels, Jameel Shalih, and Jayden Ramirez gathered around the computer table. The presence of both Shalih and Ramirez in 7-12 stemmed from a curious intersection of purpose, luck, observation, and timing. They'd saved Ramirez from Borgmann and then met him in Todrank's bedroom. The discovery of Shalih after Johnnie rescued him at Piankashaw had been more complicated. During their nightly forays into the cathedral, the Angels noted the occasional glimpse of another person genuflecting at the altar and then disappearing behind it. One night, Polly tailed the person up to the Lookout Room in the steeple. There, she surprised him. When he reached for a weapon, she leveled her .357 at him. It was a tense standoff until Jameel recognized her from Piankashaw Rock. Polly convinced Jameel that she and the Angels would hide and protect him.

Jameel and Jayden reunited, but there was a curious difference between the two. Where Jameel was soft-spoken, thoughtful, helpful, and highly effective with computers, Jayden was loud, obnoxious, and contrary, the very qualities that risked detection. On one occasion, Polly had to discipline Jayden with a threat to expel him from 7-12. Since then, he'd mostly sulked and had a tendency toward spiteful comments. Only Jameel liked and trusted him.

Curious, Polly rose, walked to the table, and stood outside the group.

Chartreuse, one of the Angels, said, "They've locked Johnnie in the jail. If Polly 'comes in' as Garrett Jennings demanded, Johnnie would be safe."

Malachi said, "Jennings will then lock up both Johnnie and Polly and then blackmail the rest of us to come in. If we come in, he'll jail us, too. Nobody wins but Jennings and the Archangels."

Ramirez spoke up, "Why should we do anything about Johnnie?"

Malachi turned on Ramirez. "You're not one of us. Johnnie Christiansen was here long before anyone heard of you. Don't forget that we're protecting you. You're not protecting us."

"Drop it, guys."

They turned and looked at Polly.

"Johnnie's my responsibility and mine alone."

"He is not," said Malachi. "One person is not enough. They will kill you, Polly." Then he turned back to the table. "Pull it up, Jameel."

Jameel entered the commands in Google 3D. A three-dimensional map of the southwest portion of Oakenwald appeared on the large screen.

Chartreuse said, "Too much foliage. Pull up the satellite feeds going back to winter."

Jameel did so and the Fallout Shelter came into view amidst the woods now denuded of leaves.

Malachi picked up a pointer and traced the approaches to the Fallout Shelter. "We can enter the woods from any angle. The challenges are the motion detectors and Archangels."

Chartreuse said, "We have to neutralize them. How do we do that?"

"They're probably arrayed in concentric circles," said Malachi. "I would guess at least two. The Archangels move within the rings. Our only chance is to locate the Archangels and detectors before we go in. Now, if you were Garrett Jennings, where would you place the rings?"

"We can't know," said Chartreuse.

"There's another way." Everyone turned to Jameel. "If I can hack into the Fallout computers, we'll find the detectors. Better yet, we can override the Archangels' commands. We shut down all the sensors except those on the outermost ring at its northwest side. We set off those... No! They're probably too smart for that. We—"

"Create several diversion points," said Chartreuse.

Polly asked, "Diversionary attack?"

"Right," said Chartreuse. "Only better. If Jameel hacks in, he can turn their surveillance against them." Malachi handed the pointer to her. "We use each ring and array ourselves in a semi-circle. We carefully time the sensor trips. The first trip will be on the innermost circle at this point. We've been 'discovered.' Thirty seconds later, we trip the outermost ring there. A minute later, we trip the second ring here."

Polly said, "The semicircle is to the northwest, away from the bisector and Old Dominion Road. I believe they'll fall for the diversions."

Malachi said, "My guess is there's a sixty-forty chance of success. How do we better the odds?"

"One person." Again, they turned to Jameel. "We get one person—a mole inside the Fallout Shelter," said Jameel. "We attack with the diversions. The mole then activates and unlocks Johnnie. Some of us melt away and the others secure Johnnie and the mole."

Polly said, "I know exactly how to get in. Smelly people."

"Smelly?" asked Jameel.

"You'll see. But first, Jameel, we have to know whether you can take over their computers and override their commands. Can you?"

He didn't get to answer as the door burst open and two men rushed in. For a moment, the angels stared at them and they stared back. Then several angels seized weapons and leveled them.

"Stand down!" Polly commanded. "Stand... down." The weapons lowered. "Our Jesus speaks again. These men save Lambs, just like we do. Fathers Bernardo and Paul, welcome to 7-12."

CHAPTER 50

Father Bernardo heard knuckle raps and looked up from his desk.

"Can I come in?" Gavin asked.

He motioned Gavin to the lone seat in front of his desk. Gavin had come for his Smith & Wesson. Bernardo wouldn't return it until Gavin successfully finished the program, and maybe not even then. Comorbidity of PTSD and psychosis was common. PTSD, psychosis, and a gun were a recipe for suicide or worse.

Bernardo asked, "What's on your mind?"

"I'm thinking about this morning."

Bernardo smiled. "Something's working, I guess."

Gavin hesitated. Bernardo waited.

"It was the first time I ever told anybody what happened to me."

"Why did you wait so long?"

"Who could I have told? My family? 'Um, mornin', honey. Sorry about last night. I couldn't get a hard-on cuz all I could think about was being raped in the ass.' 'Oh, hi, Joey. I can't go to your ballgames cuz I can't sit in the stands cuz I got hemorrhoids bad from being fucked in the ass. I'm really sorry.' Maybe my boss. 'Hey, boss ol' buddy, could you ask the company to get softer toilet paper in the stalls? That cheap ass wipe hurts cuz I done been fucked in the ass a whole bunch of times.'"

Bernardo almost smiled. The treatment of rape-induced PTSD sometimes had its own dark humor. "You couldn't talk there but you can talk here. I call it 'safe place' treatment. Probably, for the first time ever, you're in a place where you can say what really happened."

"I wouldn't have put it that way, but it makes sense."

"Did it help?"

"Maybe. Maybe not."

"However, you're not here to talk about PTSD."

"I want my gun back."

"I want the truth."

"About what?"

"About why you're packing."

Gavin snorted, "You said this was a safe place. It isn't. Not for me. Not for some of the others."

"Why not?"

"They're lying."

"Who?"

"Arthur and Jerry."

"About what?"

"They weren't raped. They're making it all up."

Bernardo hesitated, and then asked, "Can I get you something to drink? Coffee? Tea?"

"Think I'm goin' off the deep end, don't you?"

"Are you?"

"They were at Tigris in 2003, like they said. But they're Cradlers, not Lambs. They weren't raped. They did the rapin'."

"Hard accusation, Gavin."

"Hard truth, Bernardo."

"Gavin, let's start over. Is this okay with you?"

"Yeah, but only if you listen to me. Is this okay with *you*?"

"Yes."

"Good," said Gavin, "but you gotta go first. Tell me what you know about Tigris in 2003."

"I saw the photos. I listened to the news and read the papers. I remember all of it. But there's a piece I didn't notice until men in previous classes said that they, too, were raped and sodomized at Tigris. I suspected the involvement of officers, even though none of the victims ever talked about it. That is, until today, when Arthur said there were officers involved. Was he lying?"

"No."

"Why would he bring up the officers and the JAG lawyer if he and Jerry are Cradlers?"

"They're acting, Bernardo. They're good at it. They talk about those things as part of their cover and to build credibility with you and the other patients who don't know about them. Would you suspect them after they implicated officers?"

"No."

"I said nothing about officers, so you're thinking Gavin Scott is either sane and lying, or crazy and babbling."

"Gavin Scott is sane. I'm withholding judgment on the lying part."

Gavin shot up. For a moment, Bernardo thought he would dive over the desk. "You still don't get it!"

"Easy there, Gavin. Sit down. We'll get to the bottom of this."

Gavin sat.

Bernardo asked, "Did Arthur and Jerry—"

"Hell yeah! I was one of their Lambs! But—"

"But... what?"

"What he and Jerry are really doing is protecting their Cradler buddies up the chain."

"What chain?"

"The chain of command!"

"That may be so—"

"Goddamn it, Bernardo, it *is* so!"

"It doesn't explain why they're here."

"The hell it don't! They're carrying a message to me and any other Lamb in the class. 'Go through this rehab. Talk to the counselors. Eat healthy. Exercise. Tell the psychiatrists exactly what they want to hear so they give you Prozac and those other anti-psycho-hoobee-doobee-whatever pills. Maybe you'll come out of this all cured and happy. But if you say one word about what really happened at Tigris in 2003, you or somebody you love will die.'"

"Did they recognize you?"

"Of course they did. They recognized me when you called me out, and then again at lunch. They winked at me."

Bernardo leaned back and stared at the ceiling. "This doesn't explain the Smith & Wesson."

"I sure as hell didn't bring it for target practice."

"You brought it for protection against Arthur and Jerry?"

"Yeah."

"The names of patients are secret. How did you know Arthur and Jerry would be here?"

"I didn't. I figured they'd send a spy." Gavin left the desk and walked to a window, his back to Bernardo. He was breathing hard and his shoulders heaved several times. He lit a cigarette and took several long draws. It was against the rules to smoke on campus, but Bernardo said nothing because the cigarette calmed Gavin.

"Bernardo, I have two homes. One is with my family, and the other is the park bench. I stay mostly at the first and sometimes at the second. Know why?"

"Yes. Your wife threw you out."

"Hmmph. I was booted, but not by my wife."

"Then by whom?"

"Arthur and Jerry's employer."

"Who are officers in the chain of command?"

"No. I said they're protecting the chain, not working for it."

"Then who is their employer?"

"The Foundation."

"Who's the Foundation?"

"Google it. 'Foundation,' and 'secret,' and 'Jesus.'"

Bernardo punched some keys and clicked his mouse. "It's that fundamentalist group in Washington, D.C. Now I remember it."

"Yeah. Big Kahuna bunch of assholes. Breast beaters. Say they're Jesus people, but they're really politicians lookin' for more money and power. They do their real stuff mostly in secret so that they can preach Jesus with one hand and steal with the other. They got in trouble a while back when some of their members got caught with their pants down. The Foundation tried to cover it up, but several pissed-off husbands and wives went public."

"Now that you mention it, I recall that scandal."

"They put on that breakfast thing where all the bigwig hypocritical politician assholes get together and pray to Jesus."

"The National Prayer Breakfast."

"Yeah. That's what they call it. They stopped it for a few years after those Jesus-talkin' horny ying-yang's exposed their real stripes. They did go public for a while… even had a website. They took it down."

"Why?"

"To hide themselves! Do I have to spell it out for ya? Jesus is too good a gig for 'em. They went underground but continued to preach the hell outta him to everybody, even Muslims and Jews and those Indian people who worship cows and all. Russia's their biggest target because the Russians throw their queers in prison, and they love bribes. The real kicker is Siberia. It has more timber 'n diamonds 'n all those what they call precious metals, and so far no one to tap into them. The Foundation will change all that with Jesus-preaching, ruble-bribing, and mining companies controlled by them."

"Why hasn't the media grabbed ahold of this?"

"They're too secretive! Most Americans forgot about the scandals. Besides, how can you be against Jesus? Americans lost interest but they shouldn't have. I mean, it was thrown right out there. One of the members of the Foundation—I think it was that guy who served time because of that Nixon Watergate thing back in the seventies—he set up a 'born again with Jesus' thing in the prisons. He let it out there was a bunch of Jesus men in the government. The Foundation shut him up."

"So it's the Foundation that's protecting the Tigris 2003 chain of command. Why? What's the connection between the Foundation and the Tigris River Prisoner-of-War Camp in Baghdad in 2003?"

"The rottenness went all the way to the top of the chain at Tigris."

"The top?"

"Google 'Tigris River 2003 commanding officers.'"

Bernardo clicked the mouse and tapped the keyboard. He read the screen and then looked at Gavin. "Lincoln Kincaid commanded at Tigris in 2003. Was he—"

"You bet your sweet ass he was. The bastard loved mine."

"Is he a member of the Foundation?"

"He won't admit it, but he lived at the Foundation's palace—they call it Oakenwald—after he graduated from West Point and worked for the

Pentagon. He moved out when he got married. He admitted as much in that interview with that O'Malley lady a while back."

Gavin left the window and returned to his chair. Bernardo reached behind him to the small refrigerator and pulled out two Diet Cokes.

"They've threatened to kill my family… my wife, or one of my kids. Said they could make it look like an accident. To make sure I don't forget, every so often they order me to the park bench to play the drunken bum. I had to spend a week there this past winter. My wife was my lifeline. She brought me blankets, thermal underwear, layers of clothes, and food. A couple of times, at night, I sneaked back into my house and snuggled with my wife. It was she who kept my jewels from freezing off, by the way. I was back at the park bench before daylight. One day I thought if they're doing it to me, then they're doing it to others. My wife Googled the hell out of every Lamb I could remember."

"And?"

Gavin walked back to his chair, leaned over the desk, and in a hoarse whisper said, "They're dying, Bernardo. The Lambs. Know what else? On a hunch, she searched some Cradlers' names. Some of them are dying too."

"How?"

Gavin sat and sneered at Bernardo. "Measles epidemic. Yeah, that's it. Healthy men in their thirties and forties. They're dyin' of measles." Gavin wiped his eyes with his sleeve and leaned forward. "How the fuck you think they're dying? Accidents, suicides, disappearances. About thirteen months ago a Cradler in Sarasota was killed in a hit and run while he was crossing the street. No suspects. A Lamb from a little town outside Louisville and another on his ranch in Nebraska were killed. A Cradler was killed in Las Vegas—a blackjack dealer. George somebody. They found him in his hotel suite with his head blown off. You've heard of those murders at Camp Morgan. The dead guys are Cradlers. Some guy named 'Shampel' or something like that had gotten his hands on a gun. He killed two. The third, the warden, Borgmann, was hit in the stomach but survived. The killer disappeared. One of the female Lambs was found floating in a lake. On the plane yesterday, I was glancing through the paper when a Cradler's last name popped out at me. He'd disappeared from his home in Milwaukee. Cops have no clues and no suspects. The guy just vanished."

"I can understand killing Lambs. If any of them talks, there won't be any President Kincaid. But why Cradlers?"

"Because they're afraid that some of them might talk. You never know what a guilty conscience will do to a man, even a gang-rapist."

"A dead Lamb or Cradler doesn't talk. I get that. A blackmailed Lamb or Cradler is highly unlikely to talk. I get that. What I don't get is who decides murder versus blackmail?"

"I don't know. My wife found most of this on the Internet and I put two and two together. A man named Earl Thompson has been the head guy for years. He might decide... or the Foundation's board of directors... or maybe a small group within the Foundation that calls itself the Special Committee for the Propagation of Blowing Heads Off. I don't know. Who decides doesn't matter. It's how they decide."

"How?"

"We know they can't kill everybody, so there's got to be a list. Those who get to the top are on the 'kill roster.' Those who they think they can keep quiet with threats of killing their family are on the 'let live roster.' Problem is you never know when they move you up the list. But there's one exception."

"Who?"

"Me! I've moved up on the list."

"Why?"

"Because of you."

"Me?"

"Well, sorta you. You pushed me and I talked. I tried to doctor up the story, but I did a bad job."

Bernardo sat back. "My God, Gavin. I didn't know."

"It's okay, Bernardo. You couldn't have known."

"Do you think they'll make an attempt in this hospital?"

"Probably not. It's too visible, but you can't predict these fuckers. Now you know why I need my gun back. Can I have it now, please?"

Bernardo unlocked a drawer. He handed the Smith & Wesson to Gavin along with a pouch of ammunition.

"Thank you," said Gavin who then left.

Bernardo closed the door and called Polly Thompson on his cell phone. "I just had an interesting conversation with a man named Gavin Scott. He's a Lamb who packs a gun. Told me something I didn't know."

"What?"

"There are two Cradlers in this class who are spies for the Foundation."

"How long do we have?"

"This class gets discharged in twenty-eight days."

"Do you have photographs?"

"Yes. We take them when the men check in."

CHAPTER 51

Garrett Jennings sat in the black Ford Transit Wagon that was parked on an abandoned county road about a half mile from the Lugar V.A. Hospital.

He'd recorded Gavin Scott's meeting with the good Father Bernardo Estrada and Bernardo's call to Polly, and was now uploading them to Oakenwald. He lit a cigarette. Earl chastised Garrett. He said that smoking was 'impure.' However, Earl said many things, most of which were true, and only some of which Earl believed in. Garrett placed the impurity of smoking into the Earl Thompson category of true, but just outside the realm of 'what I really believe in.'

A few minutes later, Garrett saw movement in the passenger side mirror. Louis Cardova, a.k.a. Gavin Scott, approached from the back of the Wagon. "Did you get it all?"

"Yep. Just finished the upload to Oakenwald."

"Phone call?"

"Bernardo called Polly Thompson as soon as you left his office. They fell for it. Good work."

"It was easy, but thanks for the compliment anyway."

Garrett said, "I'm flying back to Oakenwald tomorrow afternoon. You stay here for the next phase. I suspect that Polly will attempt to take out Arthur and Jerry in the next few days. When she does, she'll expose herself."

***

She was dressed in black and hidden in the underbrush of a thick woods about twenty-five feet from the Transit Wagon. She ignored the mosquitoes flying around her in the heat and humidity. The warm humid breeze blew the leaves of the underbrush back and forth, so she could only catch glimpses of the Ford.

She had also recorded the conversation between Father Bernardo and Gavin Scott, and then detected the upload. She slowly stepped through the underbrush to within fifteen feet of the Transit Wagon. She knew the driver as well as the man who had entered on the passenger side. After they left, she emerged from the woods onto the road and its broken-up blacktop. She lowered herself on her legs but kept her back straight and her head high, the better to protect herself from anyone approaching. She picked up several cigarette butts, placed them in her pocket, and then again hid herself in the woods.

A vehicle made its way over the broken road. It stopped and she waited. There were three quick toots on the horn. She walked out of the underbrush to a Jeep and entered on its passenger side.

"Did they fall for it?" asked Father Bernardo.

"Down to the last syllable," said Polly Thompson.

CHAPTER 52

Garrett guided the Ford Transit Wagon out of the underground parking lot and turned onto the George Washington Memorial Parkway. He passed Arlington National Cemetery, took Interstate 66 east, and then Old Dominion Road. It was the beginning of rush hour. Traffic backed up and stopped when he reached Stratford Park. Homeless persons spent their days in the open areas of the park. Toward evening, after the park closed, most disappeared into the denser woods on the park's backside where the police were less likely to evict them. Garrett noted that the number of homeless had more than doubled since Sarah Harding took office. More and more made their way to Oakenwald to take advantage of JRP, the Jesus Rescue Project.

Garrett prided himself on the JRP. Before Garrett moved to Oakenwald, one or two homeless persons a month had wandered onto the Oakenwald Campus. Earl Thompson considered them pests, and he'd call the police and have them removed. Garrett suggested to Earl that the IRS auditors would look more kindly on Oakenwald's not-for-profit status if, instead of removing the homeless from Oakenwald, it provided them overnight accommodations in the Fallout Shelter jail, fed them, and offered them showers and clean clothing. Earl agreed and tasked Garrett and Polly with the project. Polly was unenthusiastic, so Garrett organized JRP on his own. Today, JRP cared for, on average, two to three vagabonds per night. Some had become regulars, and it looked like JRP would get at least one this evening.

He saw the squalid lady in the filthy red coat pushing her shopping cart on the sidewalk toward Oakenwald. Garrett called Joshua and said she'd arrive at the Fallout Shelter in about thirty minutes. "Make her take a shower if you can, and then launder her clothes."

Joshua said, "I'll try."

Garrett called Louis. "Anything moving?"

"No."

"Father Estrada's the key."

"I'm watching him."

"Good."

Garrett hadn't been truthful to Louis about his flight plan. Instead of flying out two days before, as he'd told Louis, he'd driven to the French Lick Springs Hotel in French Lick, Indiana, a casino town about thirty-five miles east of Dubain. He'd spent the night and most of the morning in his friend's suite, and then boarded the late afternoon flight from Louisville to Reagan. Garrett was both tense and relaxed, fearful and happy.

Garrett's phone wakened him. The clock showed 3:10 a.m. It was Rose. "Yes?"

"Garrett, lock down Oakenwald Hall now. There's no time."

"What?"

"I'm in the Fallout Shelter. The Angels attacked us here. They're probably still on campus."

Garrett shot up in his bed. "Where did they hit?"

"All over. They got inside. Lockdown—"

"How the hell did—"

"They hacked our mainframe."

"How?"

"We don't know."

"Why would they still be on campus?"

"They've got reason to attack anybody they can find."

"Why?"

"You'll see. Order the lockdown now. I've sent Joshua and Paul for you. They're armed. Wear black and holster your .45."

"I'm not a good shot."

"Garrett, there are four casualties."

"Good."

"No. Only one Angel. The rest are ours."

CHAPTER 53

The lady in red was led into the Fallout Shelter to a jail cell toward the back. On the way, she'd ignored the wave and smile from the young man in the second cell.

She accepted the food and bed but turned down the showers and laundry. At precisely 1:22 a.m., she rose and stripped down to her last layer of clothing, which was black. She inserted a wireless earpiece and tested reception. Polly ordered, "Check."

In turn, Kayla, Malachi, Jameel Shalih, Ramirez, and Chartreuse reported in. "Stand by. Jameel?"

"I'm in. Got the security configuration. Two circles. First is 125 feet from Fallout. Second is 250 feet out. Motion detectors at arcs every twenty feet. I'm picking up all locations—Kayla inside the van, Malachi at the southeast corner of the Old Dominion and Oakenwald Drive intersection, Chartreuse at the north side of the woods, and Ramirez at the southeast point."

Polly issued more commands. "Jameel, I am in cell five and Johnnie is in cell two. Unlock them." Polly's cell door clicked. Polly reported, "Unlocked. Jameel, maintain the first circle. Shut down the outer circle except for north and southeast."

"Done."

Polly: "Everybody else check in." They did.

At sixty seconds, Jameel: "First ring tripped."

Polly: "Move. Roger that. Roger that. Roger that."

Jameel: "Southeast tripped. North tripped once. Now twice."

Polly: "I'm picking up voices from down below. Move in. Repeat. Move in."

Polly left her cell. She ran to Johnnie's jail cell and opened it. "Johnnie, take my hand. Quick." There was no hand. "Johnnie, I said..." Polly grabbed his hand in the dark, but it was cold. She looked closer. Johnnie's toes were four inches from the floor. There was a noose around his neck and his head hung to the side. There was no pulse. Polly realized they knew she was coming. One of the Angels was a traitor.

Polly: "Abort! I repeat—take out anyone you see and abort!" She ran out the door and crouched. There were two shots to the north. Then two from the west. She saw movement in front of her and to her right and squeezed the trigger. One Archangel down. Two bullets whizzed past her head. She squeezed again. Second Archangel down. She ran toward the southeast and linked up with Kayla. Polly saw a flash from a tree. Kayla whirled and went down. Polly swept the tree stand with automatic fire. There was a grunt but no one fell.

Polly: "Kayla's hit. Meet Old Dominion. Repeat, Old Dominion." Polly threw Kayla over her shoulder and double-timed to the road. An engine was winding out to her right. There were no headlights but the white van came into view and screeched to a stop.

Polly ordered an Angel casualty count. Chartreuse responded, "Only Kayla."

"Archangel casualties?" Ramirez reported one and Chartreuse one. Polly reported at least two, maybe three.

Chartreuse asked, "Where is Johnnie?"

"We have to stop Kayla's bleeding." The others went to work. Polly moved to the front passenger seat.

Chartreuse persisted. "Where's Johnnie?"

"Johnnie's dead."

CHAPTER 54

Mattie Borgmann greeted Rhonda at the front door and led her to the back terrace that overlooked Patoka Lake. Kurt Borgmann, his back to the sliding doors, sat staring over the water. The Borgmann house was about one mile from Indiana State Road 164. It rested at the top of a hill amidst a copse of hickory trees. The hill gently sloped down about one hundred feet to the part of the lake called South Lick Fork. A deep forest of hardwood trees began at the shoreline on the other side of the lake, two miles away. It was unseasonably cool, and a gray overcast added to the darkness from the shade trees and the gloominess on the terrace. A half-empty Jack Daniels bottle and binoculars rested on a small table to Borgmann's left. A high-powered rifle with a scope lay on the table to his right. The glass in Borgmann's right hand was empty.

Rhonda stood with Mattie in front of Borgmann. "Kurt," said Mattie, "this is Rhonda O'Malley. She sang in the St. Augustine Choir right after you became director." Mattie turned to Rhonda. "Kurt so loves the choir. His doctors say he's well enough to go back, but he still tires so easily. Kurt, Rhonda is a reporter."

"I know who she is." Borgmann stayed rooted in his chair. His eyes left the water, focused briefly on Rhonda, and then moved back to the water.

Rhonda said, "Mr. Borgmann, I thank you for agreeing to talk to me. I hope I'm not intruding."

Borgmann said nothing.

"Kurt, please," said Mattie, "Ms. O'Malley is our guest. The least you can do is greet her."

Borgmann ignored his wife. He filled his glass and then resumed his stare at the water.

"Kurt?"

"The breeze is chilly, Mrs. Borgmann," said Rhonda. "Would you have a sweatshirt I can borrow?"

"Yes, of course."

Rhonda watched Mattie close the sliding door. Then she walked to the edge of the terrace where it dropped off to the ground fifteen feet below. A large sailboat was tacking about three hundred yards from the shoreline. Another, smaller sailboat lay anchored nearby. Several fishermen cast their lines from motorboats. Mattie brought out a large Indiana University sweatshirt, handed it to Rhonda, and then went back inside. Rhonda pulled the sweatshirt over her head as Borgmann motioned her to a chair. She produced a hand-held recording device and turned it on.

Borgmann said, "Thank you for the charade with Mattie. She'll learn the truth about me sooner or later, but by then I hope it won't matter."

Rhonda asked, "You called me. Why?"

"Are you armed?"

"No, but I see you are."

"Yeah. The rifle. Got a 9 MM Glock under my sweater. Have you heard of a group called the Angels?"

"Doesn't matter."

"Matters to me."

Rhonda said, "Yes."

"Have you heard of the Archangels?"

"Yes."

Borgmann reached under his chair and brought out a glass. "Wanna drink?"

"No."

"I take it you're familiar with the Foundation, and that it's running Lincoln Kincaid's campaign?"

"Yes."

"The Foundation sponsors the Angels and Archangels. Their jobs are to kill anyone who might reveal unpleasant facts about Lincoln Kincaid. I'm on their list."

"Why?"

"I'm a Cradler."

"Tell me something I don't know."

"No need to be a wise-ass, O'Malley. You're my only chance."

"Chance for what?"

"Staying alive! Goddamn it, O'Malley, don't you get it? The Angels keep a list. The Archangels keep a list. I'm at the top of both. The Angels want to kill me 'cuz I'm a Cradler. The Archangels want to kill me 'cuz I'm a Cradler and they don't want me talkin' 'bout Kincaid. I want a deal."

"What kind of deal?"

"Immunity, and a new home and identity."

"I'm not the police, the prosecutor, or the director of witness protection."

"I can't go to the police just yet. They'll arrest me and jail me."

"Of course they will. You're a rapist and a murderer."

"I can't protect myself in a jail cell."

"What makes you think you're safer out here? Someone with a high-powered rifle and quality scope can easily pick you off."

"It's six of one and a half-dozen of the other. I have weapons. I also have Mattie. They're less likely to kill me when she's here."

"You've placed Mattie on the front line to save your own ass? Ever consider they might kill her first and you second? Make it look like a murder-suicide?"

"I don't need your advice on personal protection."

"Apparently, you do. You want something from me so that you can 'stay alive' and then live in luxury on the government's nickel. You're an evil man. Quite frankly, I'd rather see you dead than alive. So tell me why I'm here."

Borgmann said, "I have firsthand info that'll destroy Kincaid. I have names, dates, places, ranks, victims, photos, and videos. I have it all, and I want to give it to you."

"Why?"

"I want you to publish your story as soon as possible. I'll be arrested, but the publicity should keep me safe. I'll demand protection. They'll have to give it to me."

Rhonda watched as Borgmann lifted the binoculars and scanned the lake. Then he slowly moved them across the woods on the other side of South Lick Fork. He laid them down and sipped his drink.

The first rule for reporters is to always have your facts straight. A violation of this rule could ruin a career and hand credibility to the objects of the investigation, in this case Lincoln Kincaid, Earl Thompson, and the Foundation. No doubt Kurt Borgmann possessed information that she either did not have or would confirm information she already had. No doubt he'd lie to save himself. She would test his credibility with a bit of misdirection, and ask questions to which she already had the answers. Andy said it was like cross-examination—never ask a question on cross that you don't already know the answer to.

Rhonda said, "You say you have information that will destroy Lincoln Kincaid and you're willing to trade it for your life."

"Yeah."

"Well, I already have it. There's nothing you can add. So," Rhonda stood, "I best be going. Don't want some sniper mistaking me for you."

"No, you don't have it. You've been investigating for months but you haven't published. That means your investigation is incomplete. So sit down."

Rhonda ignored Borgmann's command. "Where did you bury Ramirez?"

"I didn't. He escaped."

"Did he kill that guard… the one who was chasing him?"

"No."

"Then who killed him?"

"I did."

"I see. You pinned it on Ramirez to make him the subject of a manhunt. Either he'd end up dead and tell no tales, or he'd stay alive and tell tales no one would believe."

"Yeah."

"Do you know a man named George Todrank?"

"Yeah. He was with us at Tigris. He's dead. He was a dealer at Las Vegas… wouldn't keep his mouth shut when he was drunk. I believe the Angels murdered him."

"Jameel Shalih didn't shoot anybody, did he?"

"No, and it didn't happen at the Camp Morgan gate. We were at Piankashaw Rock. It's in the Hoosier National Forest."

"I know where it is. What happened?"

"I was pulling my knife across his throat when someone—a tall, weird-looking guy with braided hair—came out of the woods, shot me in the stomach and killed the other two. Then a dark-haired lady appeared. They were probably Angels. I played dead until they left, drug myself to the Hummer, and then drove back to Camp Morgan."

"Where did you hide the knife?"

"I didn't. Shalih took it."

"Isn't Kincaid your bosom buddy?"

"He was."

"Until you determined that the only way to save your own fat ass was to hand Kincaid to the wolves. I won't cry for either of you."

Rhonda sat.

"Lincoln Kincaid is twisted. He's sick. He lies. He abuses his family. He can't be president."

Rhonda jumped on it. "Such patriotism! What more can America ask from a rapist and murderer? First Nathan Hale—'I regret that I have but one life to give for my country.' Now Kurt Borgmann—'I don't regret that I have only one ass to save from my country.'"

"Let's talk about Lincoln Kincaid."

Rhonda asked, "Was Lincoln Kincaid one of the rapists?"

"He was the main rapist. The man just couldn't get enough."

"What about you, Kurt? Where were you when Kincaid 'just couldn't get enough?'"

"I was... with Kincaid."

"Is this all the information you have?"

"O'Malley, your stand up and 'I best be going' was a bluff. Since then you've been testing my credibility. I get that. But, tell me, would I have a chance at immunity if I gave false information to the police?"

Rhonda ignored the question. "You have information, you say. Where is it?"

"All the information I have is on three diskettes. They're inside the house."

"Why?"

Borgmann handed her the binoculars. "Zero in on the boats. See anything?"

"I see people."

"What are they doing?"

"Sailing and fishing. You can see the rods and reels."

"Look closer."

Rhonda saw that no one was holding or casting the rods and reels. Several with binoculars were facing toward Borgmann. All the people in all the boats were dressed in white.

Rhonda said, "The Angels are watching you. They probably know I'm a reporter and they can see you talking to me."

"They don't know what I'm telling you. Could be a line of shit for all they know."

"Have you seen any of the Archangels?"

"I don't know what they look like."

"That explains your search of the woods on the far side. Snipers? As in real snipers?"

"Yeah."

CHAPTER 55

Rhonda turned down Mattie's invitation to stay for dinner. Borgmann walked Rhonda to the front door and handed her a large manilla envelope. She opened it and saw the three diskettes.

On the drive back to Dubain, the import of her interview with Borgmann struck her in a manner outside all her experience. Under any other circumstances, the view of the reservoir, the waves, the smell of fresh water, and the boats—no matter the weather—would have united to awaken in her the feeling of her heart beating steadily and the sublime certainty of a power far greater than herself. However, she'd just left the presence of the man who'd partaken in the rapes of young soldiers at the Tigris River Prisoner-of-War Camp and helpless inmates at Camp Morgan, gladly aided others in doing the same, and then murdered to protect himself.

The second rule of investigative reporting is to remain detached and never lower yourself into the story. For a moment this escaped her, and she was willing to dump the rule of law—as had the Foundation—to satisfy her primal instinct with vigilante justice. At that moment, she would have been elated to watch Borgmann die slowly and painfully at the hands of the Angels or Archangels. It didn't matter which.

This shocked her.

She contrasted the interview with that of General Hernandez. Hernandez had honored the rule of law and received punishment for it. Yet, he faced his tormentors with courage and professionalism. Borgmann had dishonored the rule of law but now begged for it to save him. Was there room for justice? Did justice even exist? Was it a concept of which her part of the universe was ignorant?

She drove to her and Andy's house. When she came to his bed and started to lie down beside him, he jumped up. She hesitated while he turned on the nightstand lamp.

"Just what the hell do you think you're doing?"

"I think I'd like to sleep with you."

"I think I don't want you to."

"Andy, what's the matter with—"

"Nothing is the matter with me. What could possibly give you that idea?"

"Calm down, Andy."

Andy said, "The nerve of you! You accused me of ignoring you and then trying to jump into bed with you. Well, lady, that road goes both ways. I'm your husband, not your goddamn gigolo. The last time we slept together you ended up throwing it in my face. Fuck that. It won't happen again."

"Andy, I've never seen you—"

"This angry?"

"Yes."

"Well, I'm a sonofabitch! Gee, guess I'm psychotic. After all, I overwhelm you. I demand too much from you. I have too many sides. I'm a fucking fault line. You can't say no to me. I wear you out."

"I'll sleep upstairs."

"Good… fucking… night. Oh, by the way, and for the last time, I will not defend Jameel Shalih."

CHAPTER 56

Marian told the two men of her security detail to hide the limousine behind the barn and stay there until she returned. She walked up the concrete driveway and onto the porch of the home where Lincoln's parents and paternal grandfather lived. Their maid, a Filipino woman in her forties, answered the door and led Marian into the family room where Rachel and Jackson Kincaid, Lincoln's mother and father, and Benjamin Kincaid, Lincoln's grandfather, were watching a baseball game. Benjamin was ninety-two. Both Jackson and Rachel were seventy-three. Rachel was a bit plump, but her pride in her hair and dress had endured into her golden years. Jackson had thinned, but his thick hair remained, albeit now fully gray. Rachel and Jackson treated Marian with warmth and kindness and babysat the children when Marian was campaigning.

Rachel told family and friends that Marian was the daughter she never had. Marian, of course, had learned that Rachel was lying. She had a daughter, but threw her away to her clandestine lover, Earl Thompson.

Rachel said, "Marian! It's nice to see you in person for once and not on TV. Do please come in and take a seat. Can we offer you a drink?"

"I'll have a bottle of water, please. No glass." A bottle of water was less likely than a glass to betray her shaky hands. Marian thanked the maid and took a seat on an ottoman to the right of Rachel. She and Jackson were on a love seat, and Benjamin was on their other side in a rocking chair.

Jackson said, "Marian, you sounded tense on the phone, and you look tired. Is something wrong?"

Marian replied, "It's about Lincoln."

"Is he sick?" asked Rachel.

"Well, no. No. He's fine."

Jackson asked, "Then what is it?"

Marian wanted their help, but her request would hurt their feelings and perhaps add to her own pain. For a moment, Marian's courage left her, and she wondered whether her visit to Jackson and Rachel was wise after all. However, then the scene of little Gerardo and his wounded face and terrified tears came back to her. Nor could she lay aside the chill of Lincoln's words to her just that morning when she'd asked him to apologize to Gerardo. He said that he would not. "I am the head of this family, and I will rule over it. My orders and punishments in my house shall be unquestioned and un-challenged. You, Woman, and the children, will submit to me. There will be unpleasant consequences if you do not. Gerardo learned that lesson when he spied on me in your bed."

Marian said, "He's been... I don't know exactly how to put this... un-kind... to the children and me."

Rachel replied, "Unkind? Lincoln? In what way?"

"He's temperamental to me, and he shouts at the children for no reason. When I try to talk to him about these things he puts me off."

"It's the pressure of the campaign," said Rachel. "That nasty Republican lady… that senator from Maine… Josie Carter, has been attacking Lincoln something awful. You know, about the Foundation and his command at that awful prisoner camp—that one at Tigris River."

Benjamin swung his head from the game to Marian. "Woman, Josie Carter got her ammunition from your nosy reporter buddy in that inter-view." 'Woman' was Benjamin's way of belittling Marian. He scorned her for her college degree, her opinions, her life independent of Lincoln's, and her friendship with Rhonda O'Malley. For the most part, Marian ignored Benjamin.

Marian said, "Lincoln is handling Senator Carter's accusations quite well, and he has a large lead in the polls, so I feel it's more than the cam-paign. Lincoln has always been a light drinker. However, lately, he's been drinking heavily. I'm concerned about it."

Jackson said, "I'm sure you are."

"I'd be grateful if you and Rachel could talk to him. He respects you and might listen."

"Lincoln's drinking is none of your business, Woman," said Benjamin.

"Then, Mr. Kincaid, just whose business is it?"

"God's. If God wants Lincoln to drink less, then He and He alone will tell Lincoln."

"I disagree. Lincoln is my husband. His drinking and his treatment of our children and me are definitely my business. Besides, I haven't seen God around Lincoln lately. Have you?"

"I warned them," said Benjamin. "I told them you're uppity and mouthy, and that you don't know your place. No one listened."

"What place would that be?"

"Behind the men!" Benjamin exclaimed. "Cook, clean, have babies, smile into the cameras."

"You said 'no one listened.' To whom do you refer?"

"The Foundation, Woman. That's all you need to know."

"Is Lincoln in the Foundation?"

"Well... yes," said Jackson.

"Why did he lie about it in the interview with Rhonda?"

"Honey," said Rachel, "Lincoln didn't lie about the Foundation... he was protecting it."

Jackson said, "The public just doesn't know enough about the Foundation... how it's such a force for good in the world and how it carries Christ's Word to world leaders, even dictators who kill their own people. It must do these things behind the scenes, in secrecy. For example, I have it on good authority that it was Earl Thompson, and not the backward diplomacy of the US State Department, who got Ukraine and Russia to disengage their forces and stand down."

"How long has Lincoln been in the Foundation?"

"Since June 30, 1984," said Benjamin. "I arranged the meeting. It took place in our kitchen."

"Marian, Benjamin was already on the Foundation's board of directors," said Rachel. "He brought with him Fredrick Thompson, the Foundation's executive director at the time. It was a Saturday afternoon with Lincoln, Benjamin, Mr. Thompson, Jackson, and me. Lincoln had finished first in his high school class and had led the football team to the state championship. Many colleges had offered football scholarships to Lincoln. He was leaning toward Ohio State."

"However, Lincoln went to West Point," said Marian.

"Yes, honey. Mr. Thompson said it was best that Lincoln enter the military."

"Why?"

"He told Lincoln that a solid military career is a strong base for politics," said Rachel. "He said that Lincoln was a natural leader and could go far in life with the proper guidance."

"You mean the Foundation's guidance?" asked Marian.

"Well… yes," said Rachel.

"Just how far in life?"

"He said Lincoln could be a congressman, possibly a governor, and maybe even..."

"President of the United States."

"Yes," said Rachel. "We were so thrilled for Lincoln! It all turned out just as Mr. Thompson said it would. Lincoln will be the next President of the United States! And to think it all started right in our kitchen on a hot summer afternoon!"

Marian asked, "How did the Foundation 'guide' Lincoln?"

"It's rather complicated," said Rachel.

"It isn't complicated," said Benjamin.

Marian turned back to Rachel. "Money?"

"Yes, mostly for his campaigns," said Rachel.

"Connections?"

"Yes."

"Bribes?"

"Incentives," said Jackson. "A bribe is a crime, and the Foundation obeys the law."

"Wife?"

"Yes," said Jackson. "Fredrick Thompson set up that first meeting between you and Lincoln."

Stabs of adrenaline shot through Marian. She'd gone to Rachel and Jackson to ask for their help hoping that Lincoln might heed them, but the visit had morphed into sordid revelations. She recognized that this was no longer about Lincoln's nastiness and booze. It was about his truth. She saw that Benjamin sensed this but Rachel and Jackson had no inkling. They'd divulged secrets that had been hidden from her until now. She could not clearly define their motivations for doing so. Nevertheless, the circumstances in the room confronted her. She'd rolled the dice the minute she stepped through the front door. She had to change tactics to keep them talking.

She took no pride in rolling the dice again.

"So... the Foundation set up that first meeting between Lincoln and me. This was only after they'd investigated me. I suppose that was prudent. I have a handsome," Marian smiled, "although not perfect husband in Lincoln."

Someone hit into a double play. Rachel and Jackson moaned. Benjamin frowned. Marian didn't even know who was playing. She waited until the other team was running out on the field.

"Has the Foundation asked anything of Lincoln for all this help?"

"Yes, to become President Kincaid and rid the world of the sin of democracy once and for all," said Benjamin, "and to lead the world to the Kingdom of Jesus. Democracy is a sin because it violates the Bible and is prideful in the eyes of God."

Marian stared into Benjamin's rheumy eyes and saw in them the brushfire fanaticism of a man who was on the verge of getting what he had dedicated a long life to.

"I think I see it, Benjamin. Jesus will rule in love, peace, and dignity. There is no room for democracy, which is nasty, ugly, and brutish. However, unless Jesus himself comes back to earth, He has to rule through others."

Benjamin said, "Of course. God chooses them. He started three thousand years ago."

"Who are they?"

"Those he makes known to us."

"How does he make them known?"

"He puts them there. Your friend, O'Malley, would disagree, but Ponya of the Congo is one of God's chosen leaders. The only reason Ponya's there is because God put him there. It's as simple as that."

"I guess I know the answer already, but I have to ask—is Lincoln a chosen leader?"

Benjamin responded. "Of course. How much clearer can God make it? If you were a Jesus person, you would have seen this years ago."

"I was too focused on my own world, Benjamin. I suppose that has been my sin. Lincoln must be quite frustrated with me and this explains his drinking and displeasure. I have to make amends to him as soon as possible."

Rachel said, "You're starting to see it, Marian. I told them that you would and that they should have let you in on all this years ago."

"I'm not so certain," said Benjamin.

"So allow me another question, Benjamin. Like you, I'm concerned for my family and me. Where does the kingdom leave us?"

Jackson said, "Honey, God appoints his chosen people just like he does his chosen leaders. You, Lincoln, and the children are among God's chosen people, just like us. Make amends to Lincoln, like you just said, and then pray for him."

"Pray to Jesus or God?"

Rachel said, "Well, they're pretty much the same. However, our God, and yours, must be Jesus."

"Why?"

"Because he made a covenant."

"Oh? With whom?"

"With God, His Father, with the twelve disciples, and with himself."

"What kind of covenant?"

Benjamin said, "A covenant to bring about His Kingdom."

Marian thought for a few moments, and then said, "That makes sense. After all, the Kingdom cannot make itself."

Marian saw Rachel and Jackson smile at each other. She saw the glow in their eyes. The room swirled. She saw that the safety of her middle class American life was a delusion. She watched its facades falling away, not only for her, but also for her children, her friends, her colleagues, and everyone and everything she held dear. She felt a crushing need to run from the house, but she faced down the despair. She'd gotten a piece of the reality of her husband and his family, and she wanted more.

Marian said, "I like that we are God's chosen people. How does he make this known?"

Rachel said, "He has bestowed special graces on us."

Marian hesitated. Then it came to her. "By 'special graces' you mean something like, well, this house, and the Cadillacs in the garage."

"Of course," said Jackson.

"This was only an old farmhouse when I married Lincoln. You—Jackson and Rachel—have spent hundreds of thousands of dollars remodeling it."

"Actually," said Rachel, "it's closer to a million. We hired an architect and the best contractors. It's beautiful, don't you think?"

"Yes. When we leave the White House, I want a home like this. It's a combination of the modern yet hearkens back to an earlier time. The best is that you manage to retain that down-home scent of freshly baked turkey!"

"Thank you," said Rachel. "The maid is baking one now!" She and Marian laughed.

"You've worked hard for all this and for the money to travel the world as you do," said Marian. "My guess is that you've made shrewd investments. If you don't mind, I'd like some coaching from you. In what sectors did you invest?"

Jackson replied, "At first, oil, until the price collapsed, but we made out well because we sold our oil stocks and then bought short on Earl Thompson's advice. We're invested in Sherman Analytics, a defense contractor… made out quite well on its stock when the Iraq war came. I'll let you in on another secret and ask you to keep it that way." Jackson moved forward on his chair. "We are within a few weeks of wrapping up mining contracts with the Congolese government. Just recently, we invested in Russia's 'Siberian Project.' American companies are right now building living quarters in Central Siberia to house the workers."

"Workers?"

Benjamin said, "Yes, Woman. They need the miners to extract diamonds and precious metals and men to harvest the timber."

"Over the next ten years or so," said Jackson, "we intend to gift the stock to you, Lincoln, and the children."

"We never deal in paper," said Rachel. "Cash only. Benjamin says that checks leave a… oh, what do you call it...?"

"A paper trail," said Marian. "One that the FBI can use to prosecute the

Foundation."

Jackson said, "We follow God's laws, which are much higher than man's. We're criticized for this, but they don't understand that we are the chosen. The Jesus Equation has done well for us." Jackson swept his arms around the room.

"What is a 'Jesus Equation?'"

Benjamin said, "X Equals Jesus Plus Zero."

"Jesus plus zero? It makes no sense."

"Yes, it does," said Benjamin. "It brings out the real Jesus."

"Real Jesus?"

"Yes. The real Jesus was strong and tough, not this girly, long-haired hippie looking foolish in all those pictures."

One of the players hit a home run. Benjamin clapped his hands. Jackson and Rachel hooted. Marian gathered her wits as the others watched the player run the bases. The information she'd just received was overwhelming. However, there was more, and she would stay and get all of it. She sensed that it was time to drop the nice-lady tactics. She held the bottle of water in both hands to hide their trembling.

The TV noise died down and the next batter came to the plate.

"Will there be baseball in the Kingdom of Jesus?"

Jackson said, "Yes."

"How do you know?"

"We are the chosen. If we want baseball, there will be baseball."

"Will there be contracts in the Kingdom of Jesus?"

"No," said Benjamin. "We meet Jesus one-on-one, man-to-man. There'll be no need for contracts."

"Won't the baseball players—those who aren't God's chosen—demand them? Just like the players we're now watching?"

Jackson said, "Marian, the players will be so mesmerized by the love of Jesus, they'll gladly cooperate and play baseball, the game they love."

"Will there be courts of law in the kingdom?"

Jackson asked, "Marian, why all these strange—"

"Just answer my question, Jackson. If there are no judges and courts, then who will enforce the contract of a player who is not so, how do you put it, mesmerized by Jesus?"

Benjamin said, "Woman, we don't need that contract nonsense. Not now, not in the kingdom. Jesus can handle it."

"And, because we're still on earth, he'll do so through his chosen leaders. Am I correct?"

"Of course."

"Then what would a man like Ponya do to a baseball player who refuses to play without a written contract?"

"That," said Benjamin, "is up to Ponya."

"Who has the wonderful habit of killing people who disagree with him."

Marian stood and walked across the room to the fireplace. She grabbed the mantel and kept her back to the others.

"Marian, sweetheart," said Rachel, "it's not really like that."

"Yes, Rachel, it is really like that. The Foundation chooses the 'chosen people.' It has chosen Ponya, even though he's a genocidal murderer. Those in his country who are not chosen must obey him or be killed."

Benjamin said, "That's not true. Ponya will leave them alone so long as they do the will of Jesus."

"And the will of Jesus is whatever the Foundation says it is."

"Woman, that's not what I said."

"You don't have to say it, Benjamin. You... you use circular reasoning. To you, the ends justify the means. In effect, you are accountable to no one but yourselves. This Jesus Equation is mathematical nonsense. My God! The Foundation is monstrous! It condemns millions, like those whose spirituality is not that of the Foundation's Jesus—Hindus, Buddhists, Muslims... probably most Christians. What happens to people who won't give up democracy for the rule of Ponya or Trotsky or, God help us, Lincoln Kincaid? The list goes on and on. It's baseball players, school teachers, lawyers, farmers, technicians... homosexuals. Ordinary everyday people must submit or... die!"

Marian turned around and faced them. "You have it all down. You twist and manipulate. Lincoln didn't go to West Point because he loves his country... he went to get votes. I was chosen as his wife to have children who are nothing but props for the voters. You use cash so you can hide illegal contributions and probably bribes. You justify this with 'higher law' that you say is superior to the secular law. You use doublespeak."

"Doublespeak?" asked Rachel.

"Doublespeak. A lie is not a lie... it's 'protection.' A bribe is not a bribe… it's an 'incentive.' 'Prayer' means 'influence.' 'Chosen' means 'wealthy.' How many more are there? You can't answer because you're brainwashed with them.

"You and Lincoln kept me ignorant of the Foundation because you were afraid that I might take a stand against it, that I might leave Lincoln over it, and maybe even expose it. The children and I are no more than icing for Lincoln and the Foundation, and the next step to your Kingdom of Jesus. You people and your Foundation friends have been planning this for years! Lincoln has been the Foundation's sleeper agent. He will be the next president. Then he and your Foundation will tear up the Constitution and replace it with… with the pieces of the Bible that you yourselves choose!"

Rachel said, "Marian, please."

"Please? All this explains Lincoln's dysfunctions. Jackson and Rachel, you raised Lincoln with this madness... with your covenants, chosen people, the 'real Jesus,' 'X equals Jesus plus Zero,' whatever the hell that means... with this kingdom nonsense under which you will grant rights to no one but yourselves. Then you allowed the Foundation to do all these other things to Lincoln. Lincoln never had a chance. It was your job, Rachel and Jackson, to protect Lincoln from... from these... these bastards; from Benjamin, over there, and this Thompson guy."

Benjamin tried to retort. "Woman, we don't use foul lang—"

"Fuck you, Benjamin!"

Jackson said, "Marian, calm down."

"Calm?" Marian pointed. "You, Rachel, call me the daughter you never had. Well, that's a bald-faced lie. You tossed a daughter—her name is Polly Thompson in case you don't remember—so you could focus all your energy on my husband. You condemned her to a life of a professional assassin. She's very good at it, by the way. You must be so proud!"

Marian walked back across the room and stood in front of her in-laws. "Here's something you don't know. Your son, Rachel and Jackson, and your grandson, Benjamin, is a sexual sadist."

"He was cleared of all that in the Tigris River investigation!" exclaimed Benjamin.

Marian whipped on Benjamin. "I'm not talking about Tigris River, you miserable old bastard! I'm talking about my bedroom, in the governor's mansion."

Jackson said, "Marian, you must submit to Lincoln."

"Submit?" Marian retorted. "There's precious little submission when a man, Lincoln, fifty pounds heavier than me and many times stronger, gives in to his sick sexual cravings and all but rapes me. Yet, you say I must submit?"

Rachel said, "Let's pray for Lincoln."

"Lincoln needs more than prayer, Rachel. Yesterday, I had to take Gerardo to the doctor to be treated for bruises and abrasions on his face. It was your Foundation son, Lincoln, who put them there. He backhanded Gerardo to the floor in a fit of rage after Gerardo walked into my bedroom and saw me submitting to a fit of your son's perversions."

Marian ran out of the room to the front door. She opened it, stumbled down the porch steps, and began running down the driveway. Rachel, who'd followed Marian to the porch, cried at her back, "Marian, you must have faith in Jesus. He will enter Lincoln's heart and soften it toward you and Gerardo. You'll see."

Marian stopped and turned. Jackson and Benjamin stood behind Rachel. "You still don't get it, do you?"

"Get what?"

"Lincoln is a sociopath! He cannot be president. All the prayers and kingdoms and chosen people you crazies conjure up cannot help him."

"Marian, I'm sure that it's all a misunderstanding and that—"

"Has your husband ever raped you in the ass, Rachel?"

"Oh, my." Rachel put her hand to her breast. "No. Of course not."

"Well, my husband has... many times. And I can assure you... it isn't a misunderstanding!"

Marian turned and ran down the driveway and into the barn. She stopped at a stall and vomited.

CHAPTER 57

Rhonda sat on her couch and rested her feet on the ottoman. She drew a large circle on a writing pad. The circle represented a timeline. In the center of the circle she drew square avatars of Lincoln Kincaid, Marian, Ponytail, Jameel, and her informant in Kincaid for America, or KFA. She tapped her pencil, then added Polly, and then the Cradlers. The timeline started and ended at the top of the circle. She laid out the story's parts chronologically, moving clockwise. She placed the first scene, Lincoln Kincaid living at Oakenwald, at 1:00. The second scene was the day Marian introduced Rhonda to Lincoln Kincaid. At 2:00, she wrote "Marian in love with Creep." Tigris River, the Cradlers, and 'army's whitewash of Kincaid' appeared at 3:00. At 4:00 were the deliverances of Jameel and Jayden from Borgmann at Piankashaw Rock. She then added the names of the murdered people. She was running out of room and so had to make arcs of the circle and write scenes on additional pages.

She finished the timeline and then went to bed and tried to read a book. She gave up. Rolling onto her back, she put her arms behind her head and stared at the ceiling. At one time she'd thrilled in her investigation of the Foundation and the knowledge that she might write the story that could bring it and that bastard Lincoln Kincaid down. Both were villains and both deserved it. However, Stump was right. Undue familiarity with Lincoln Kincaid or the Foundation led to terrible forfeits. It wasn't concern for her safety that prevented sleep. Her restlessness arose from the guilty knowledge that she'd unwittingly dragged another into the plot of her story and perhaps made him a target. Not Stump. He readily joined and assumed the personal risk for the benefit of his newspaper. Not her source inside KFA.

It was Andy. 'Look up and get that scene in your head.' 'It doesn't have anything to do with me.' 'Yeah, Andy, it does.' There was her handwritten note placed in the front of the banker's box where Andy was certain to find it. 'Andy will defend Shalih.' Then there was her avowal to Jameel. 'Andy needs you as much as you need him.'

Stump had posed questions she'd been carrying since before she had left Andy. Why had she returned to Andy for help? Why had she been unable to escape Andy's circle? Had she even tried? Did she want to escape it? Why had she positioned Andy where he could be hurt by the crossfire between her and the Foundation? She didn't know. She'd never even thought of it until Stump threw it at her that night in his kitchen. She'd broken Andy's heart. Was she now manipulating him with it? Stump's assurance that she hadn't forced Andy to do anything and that Andy understood the risks had assuaged, but not erased, her guilt.

She recalled Stump's observation that she'd done Andy a favor by giving him an enemy. But the 'enemy' thing cut both ways—if she'd given an enemy to Andy, then she'd given Andy to an enemy. All this had eclipsed the pleasure she'd once felt and had replaced it with a sense of menace. They had to expose these people as soon as possible. They had to get the story out there.

Rhonda dialed Andy's cell phone. No answer. She tried twice more—still no answer. She left a message: "Andy, call me. It's important." Then she left the bed, opened a bottle of red wine, grabbed her notes, sat down at her computer, and started writing the story. Two hours later both the bottle and Rhonda were exhausted. She tried Andy again and left another message: "Call me. I... well... good night." She awoke the next morning with a hangover and with no call from Andy.

She went back to work on the story and finished it by mid-afternoon. She emailed it to Andy and Stump with a message that she wanted to discuss breaking the story into several smaller parts.

CHAPTER 58

Father Bernardo, Arthur, and Jerry stood before the altar in the Church of the Immaculate Conception.

Bernardo beseeched God. "These men are in pain born of the evil of others. Their faith has brought them to a hospital to relieve them of the pain. I have encouraged them to place their faith in you and undertake a journey that will allow more of your peace and joy into their hearts. They have done so. Their faith, coupled with my encouragement, now compels them on a journey to a place of peace, deep in a forest. The journey is long and arduous, but their faith is strong and durable. We ask you for safety and deliverance."

Then Bernardo led them in the Lord's Prayer. "Our Father, who art in heaven, hallowed be thy name, thy kingdom come thy will be done on earth as it is in Heaven..."

The morning warmed and the humidity appeared as haze above the trees. They stopped for water. Bernardo sat them in a circle facing each other, blessed the water in the canteens, and led them in meditation. "We let go of the noise inside us and replace it with the vision of a place of peace called Piankashaw Rock."

Jerry stopped. "A rock?"

"Have faith, for this is a special rock."

"Can we drink now?"

Arthur hushed Jerry. They closed their eyes and bowed their heads. After a few minutes, Bernardo said, "Lord, we now drink water to slake our physical thirst. Our spiritual thirst remains unsated."

They drank and continued on their journey along the Patoka River. The next stop was a railroad trestle over the river. Bernardo sat them on the bridge with their legs hanging toward the water. Then he blessed the energy bars. "Lord, we eat to sate our physical hunger. Our spiritual hunger remains."

They rested a few more times. At one stop, they smoked cigarettes.

Jerry said, "Father Bernardo, I apologize for my impatience with drinking the water."

Bernardo laughed. "I think God understands. After all, his son got thirsty in the desert."

"Does God," asked Arthur, "have anything to say about sating our lungs with cigarette smoke?"

"Don't think so."

They laughed.

The underbrush thickened and mosquitos bit them. Twice they spotted poisonous snakes. There was a copperhead under a downed tree and a cottonmouth resting on a rock beside the river.

"What if one of us gets bitten?" Jerry asked.

"Even snakes are God's creatures. If we leave them alone, they'll leave us alone."

They reached Piankashaw Rock and stood under it.

Bernardo explained, "This place was sacred to the Indians. It offered them protection from the winter winds coming from the northwest. Some years ago, men whose souls were torn by war lived under it. Most of them found peace, and most of them are buried in the cemetery by the river."

Bernardo heard their confessions. They sat in a row under the cliff's overhang, propped their knees, rested their heads, and closed their eyes. "Push out of your minds all but the presence of God. I shall do the same."

A few minutes passed. "Keep your eyes closed." Then Father Bernardo rose, reached behind a rock, and pulled out a Sig with a silencer. He aimed at the back of Arthur's head.

"Stop right there, Bernardo." Bernardo and the two men looked up. Gavin Scott was aiming the .45 Smith & Wesson at Bernardo. "Drop your gun, Bernardo."

Bernardo hesitated. "Gavin Scott, you lied!"

"I said lay down that gun."

Bernardo dropped the Sig.

Gavin said, "Jerry and Arthur, your meditations are done. Stand up."

Jerry asked, "Bernardo, what the hell's going on? Where'd you get that gun?"

Gavin responded, "The good Father hid it yesterday so he could murder you with it today."

"Bernardo, is Gavin right?"

Bernardo nodded his head.

"Why?" Jerry took a step toward him.

Bernardo said, "This man," he pointed at Gavin, "is not your friend. He is not my friend. He is a fraud. He is a liar."

Jerry looked at Bernardo and then shifted his gaze to Gavin. Behind him Arthur said, "Gavin?"

Gavin said, "Remember that first day when Bernardo preached to us about eyes and you saw the gun on the table? Well, Bernardo the priest didn't look closely enough into my eyes. He bought my story and actually returned this gun to me."

"Story?" Jerry asked.

"I told him that we three served under Lincoln Kincaid at Tigris River in 2003 and that you two were Cradlers and I was one of your Lambs."

Arthur said, "I don't remember you at Tigris."

"Of course not. I was never there. Bernardo fell for my story. I knew you two were Lambs, but I convinced Bernardo that you were Cradlers… that you were rapists. He brought you here so that he could kill you with no witnesses."

"Kill us?" asked Jerry. "Bernardo?"

Bernardo said nothing.

Gavin said, "You bet. I'm an Archangel from the Foundation. Bernardo here knows it well."

Jerry asked, "What the hell is an Archangel?"

"An Archangel's job is to kill Angels."

"Angels?"

Arthur said, "This is getting fuckin' weirder by the minute."

Bernardo said, "Arthur and Jerry, start running. It's your only chance. Archangels also kill Lambs. Look at him!"

Louis Cardova had raised his gun and was pointing it at Bernardo.

A female voice said, "Stop right there!" Polly Thompson approached from the north end of the cliff. She pointed a sawed-off shotgun at Gavin. Gavin turned toward her. Bernardo sighted Malachi and Chartreuse, each armed with an automatic weapon, sneaking from the south end of the cliff.

Polly said, "Drop that gun, Louis."

"Well if it isn't the mutineer herself, Polly Thompson."

"I said, drop the gun."

Louis laid the gun on the ground and sneered.

Polly said, "Now remove the guns hidden in your back waist and boot. Easy now."

Louis complied.

Polly held her gun on him. "This man's name is Louis Cardova. Like Bernardo said, he kills both Angels and Lambs. Maybe even the occasional Cradler.

"Louis, I warned Bernardo that you might try to infiltrate one of his classes. I'd shown him photos of you. He called me on the first day of this class and said you'd appeared. We played you from the beginning. You thought you'd fooled Bernardo. You hadn't. You already know that Bernardo called me just after you left and that your confederate, Garrett Jennings, recorded it. What you didn't know was that I was hidden in the woods not far from Garrett's Transit Wagon on that abandoned road. I saw you enter the vehicle. Then you drove away."

Polly motioned to Arthur and Jerry. "We planned all this. Bernardo had no intention of killing anyone. The Sig he pulled isn't even loaded."

Jerry checked. "She's right. Nice piece, but there's nothing in it."

Malachi and Chartreuse stood ten feet from each other and ten feet each from Louis Cardova. Both held automatic weapons on Louis.

Bernardo said, "Gavin, Louis, there's no cause for more death. Remove all your clothing, go to the river and swim to the center. No one will harm you. However, I have a question. What happened to the real Gavin Scott?"

Louis said, "Gavin Scott, he of the park bench, had an accident between his home and here and is now at a place where no one will ever find him." Then he turned to Polly. "You're a fool and a traitor, Polly Thompson. They'll hunt you down, and all I taught you will not save you.

"I will accept Bernardo's offer. I will go to the river. I will live to fight another day."

Louis began unbuttoning his shirt.

Polly gave the slightest of nods to Malachi. Malachi removed his backpack and took out a long rope. By this time, Louis was unbuckling his belt. He stopped when he saw Malachi approaching with the rope.

Bernardo said, "Polly, this isn't right. Let this man go. Jesus came to end 'an eye for an eye.' He said, 'Love your enemies.' Stop it now."

"Jesus demands justice for Johnnie. Louis Cardova hung Johnnie Christiansen in his cell. He shall die likewise."

Bernardo walked toward Louis.

Polly commanded, "Stop, Bernardo. Take Jerry and Arthur and leave this place immediately."

Bernardo said, "At least allow me to take Mr. Cardova's confession."

Louis sneered. "I hung Johnnie. He never so much as whimpered when I tied his hands and placed the noose around his neck. Polly there knows killing, don't you Polly? However, I have no sin. The Jesus Equation is all I need. So, Bernardo, I have no confession to give."

"Louis, please reconsider. The Jesus Equation is madness. It doesn't forgive sins. It makes them. Your soul is not cleansed. It is dark with mortal sin."

Louis thought for a few moments. "Okay, Bernardo." They moved downhill toward the river. Both knelt.

Bernardo whispered, "Run for the woods after I give you absolution." Louis' lips moved in a soft murmur. He suddenly chopped Bernardo in the neck and then bolted toward the woods. Chartreuse shot him in the lower legs. He fell, and then started crawling toward the woods. Polly sprayed his hands with bullets.

Bernardo lay unconscious.

Polly commanded, "Malachi, come here and tie the noose where Louis can watch you. Jerry and Arthur, see to Father Bernardo."

"I was… going to the river," Louis panted.

Malachi finished the noose and then looped the rope several times around a strong tree limb. Louis lay on the ground. Chartreuse tied his bleeding hands behind his back and dragged him to the noose. Louis, obviously in pain, said nothing.

"Four inches," Polly commanded. "Just like Johnnie."

Malachi and Chartreuse pulled the rope until Louis' feet were four inches off the ground and then tied it off on a tree.

Polly, Malachi, and Chartreuse gathered in a line and watched. Despite the wounds and loss of blood, Louis struggled against the rope.

CHAPTER 59

Rhonda packed a suitcase and then found the courage to call Andy again. She had begun to dial his number when an emergency message from Marian flashed. Rhonda hit callback.

"What is it Mar—"

"They published it!"

"Published what?"

"Lincoln's campaign published their autobiography of me. It's too late to stop it. They're already distributing it to bookstores all over the country. It's up on Amazon in hardcopy and Kindle."

"Why didn't… Lincoln could have stopped them."

"He's insane! All of them are insane!"

"Them?"

"I visited Rachel and Jackson's house. I got it all from them. They're the Foundation. They believe they are God's chosen people. They pounded all this into Lincoln since he was eighteen... told him he could be president. The Foundation ran his entire life. He's damaged. I can't help him. Nobody can help him. I'm leaving him."

"When?"

"Right now. Will you help me?"

"Yes, of course."

"Are you in Indianapolis?"

"Yes."

"Please come over here. We'll pick up the children at school and hide out at some hotel somewhere."

"No hotel. You'll hide out at our house in Dubain. There's room. I'm on my way."

On the drive over to the mansion, in spite of her best friend's anguish, Rhonda felt a strange sense of elation. They'd won after all. Marian's separation from Lincoln Kincaid, coupled with the publication of Rhonda's investigation, would be the death knell of would-be President Lincoln Kincaid, and severely damage, if not destroy, the Foundation.

She dialed Andy.

This time he answered. "What do you want?"

"Andy, there's not much time. Marian is leaving Lincoln. I'm on my way to pick up her and the kids. I plan to take them to the house. Can you prepare the guest bedrooms?"

"Marian Kincaid is dumping her husband? Hell yes, I will!"

"Give us about three hours. Would you make a batch of your special spaghetti for us? The kind I like?"

"Yeah."

"Thank you... Andy, there's one more thing. I have no right, really. But—"

"But what?"

"I want to come home."

"I know that. You just said you were coming down with Marian and the kids."

"Andy, listen to me. I'm coming home. Coming home to you. I want to take up our lives together. I love you, Andy. Will you take me back?"

"There's no taking you back."

Rhonda deflated. The semi-elation over the coming downfall of Lincoln Kincaid vanished. Marian and Stump had been right. In her ambition, she'd thrown him away.

"I understand."

"I have no need to take you back."

"Have you found someone else?"

"Have you?"

"No," said Rhonda, crushed that Andy hadn't denied that he had found another woman. "Can I live in the house with Marian and the kids? I'll take the rollout couch."

"No, you won't."

"I own that house too, and there is no legal reason I can't live in it. Please, Andy. I'll leave when Marian's situation is resolved."

"You need not take the rollout. You need not leave. You and I will sleep in our bed. I said there's no need to take you back because I never let you go. Come home. The door's open. It's always been open."

CHAPTER 60

It was drizzling.

Rhonda turned into the driveway of the Governor's Mansion and stopped under the portico. She and Marian loaded one large and three smaller suitcases in the trunk of Rhonda's car. Marian gave directions to Park Tudor, her children's school—east on 49th, then north on College Avenue to 71st. Rhonda backed out of the driveway onto North Meridian and then accelerated. Something caught her eye and she looked to the left to see Rose Cardova and two men rising from behind bushes, two houses north of the mansion. Then, between that and the third house, she saw Polly and Malachi frantically waving their arms in criss-crosses above their heads. Rhonda started braking and hit the button to lower the window. Just then there was a boom. The rear end of Rhonda's car jumped several feet off the pavement, seemed to hover for a moment, and then crashed down to the pavement. The brakes failed. Rhonda's ears roared. She heard a scream coming from her right. Her back, neck, and face turned cold. Was there a smell of burning hair? Then there was another scream, closer. Herself? Her eyesight clouded behind an aura of yellow, red, and black. Hot air scorched her lungs and she couldn't breathe. She was conscious of a struggle to her right but she couldn't turn her head to see. Now she felt cold and hot all over her body and wondered how that could be. Her hands stuck to the steering wheel. Her senses had slowed, it seemed, but her mind processed the blindness of her eyes and the odors of beef in a frying pan and pork on a grill. Then these went away. Something was wrong, terribly wrong, and no matter her struggles, she could not find it, know it, or stop it. Then she felt herself fading away.

CHAPTER 61

Polly drove east on Orchard Lane to where it dead-ended. She turned the white van around and parked off-road under the low-hanging trees away from the streetlights. Then she walked under an umbrella to the front door of the fifth house west of the dead-end. She knocked and the door opened. He wore a stained apron over jeans and a polo shirt. His dark hair was disheveled but his face was smooth. He stared at her, unblinking, with eyes that seemed shrunken, almost gnome-like. He shifted them to the driveway, but they lost focus, and he stared as though the image he sought existed in a nether world of his own making. Then he turned back to Polly.

Andy Balbach asked, "May I help you, Polly?"

Polly managed only a thank you. He led her through the house to the kitchen. There was a large pot on the stove and a loaf of Italian bread in a baking pan.

"Please, sit down." Andy pointed to Rhonda's side of the kitchen table. "That was her seat. I served her breakfast there."

"It smells nice in here."

"I made spaghetti for her."

Polly nodded.

"She liked my spaghetti."

"Yes."

"I'm the only one here. She won't make it."

"I..."

"Are you hungry?"

"A little bit."

Andy served her. "This is her favorite china. She liked pepper with her spaghetti. Do you want pepper?"

"Yes, thank you." She sprinkled it.

"Sometimes it made her sneeze. I'd laugh and she'd act mad."

Andy served Italian bread and a glass of water. Polly looked up at him expectantly.

"I'm not hungry just now," he said.

"Okay."

"I bought a bottle of her favorite red wine to surprise her. It's chilled. Do you want some?"

"Yes."

Andy opened the bottle and poured two glasses. Then he took his side of the table. "She was coming home."

"I know."

"I prepared the spare bedrooms on the third floor for our guests. She asked me to do that for her."

"That was nice of you."

"Sometimes she slept in the guest room."

"Yes."

"She was there when the earthquake hit."

"I remember that earthquake."

Andy said, "She talked about doing a story on earthquakes, but she ran out of time."

They fell silent while Polly finished the spaghetti.

"Do you want more?"

"No."

Andy poured more wine.

"Her favorite song was 'Danny Boy.' Our friend, Stump, said it was the Irish in her. She sometimes cried when she heard it. I should have sung it with her more often but... I didn't. Do you like 'Danny Boy?'"

"I think so."

Andy clicked the iTunes icon on the screen, and then chose the song. They listened without talking.

Andy said, "'Danny Boy' didn't work out for me."

"I don't understand."

"I should be in the grave."

"Why?"

"I like to imagine that she'd come and pray for me. I... I'm not very good at prayer. Do you think she might pray for me from heaven?"

"Yes."

"She believed in angels. Do you?"

"Yes."

"Do you think they were there when she died?"

"Yes."

"When we were in high school, we shot bottle rockets over Dubain. That night we made love for the first time under a maple tree. I think I'll bury her ashes under that tree. What do you think?"

"I've never buried anyone."

Andy cleared the dishes and ladled the spaghetti into Tupperware. "Do you like leftovers?"

"Yes."

"You can stay in the guest room if you want."

"That's very nice of you."

"Her bathrobe will fit you."

Polly poured the rest of the wine.

"Have you ever lost someone?" Andy asked.

"Yes. I tried to save him, but I couldn't."

Andy said, "She told me that you've killed people."

"I have."

"Do you plan to kill me?"

"No."

"I loved her so. Yes, indeed, I loved her so."

CHAPTER 62

Garrett Jennings rolled off Lincoln Kincaid and lit a cigarette. He offered one to Lincoln who first declined it and then changed his mind. The hotel prohibited smoking in their rooms, but Garrett didn't give a damn. What was smoking in a non-smoking resort hotel compared to all the other rules he'd broken, the kind associated with long prison sentences or worse?

They were in the master bedroom of the Presidential Suite in the French Lick Springs Hotel. They'd enjoyed their first meeting in this suite two months after Garrett had been 'cured.' That was quite a while ago, and they'd met in this suite many times since. The evening before, Garrett had held and comforted a sobbing Lincoln, devastated over the loss of Marian. Then they'd locked eyes, fallen into an embrace, kissed, undressed each other, and moved to the bed. They'd started gently, and then escalated to furious, almost violent, lovemaking.

They left the bed and moved to a couch in the main suite. Garrett switched the big screen television to CNN. Then his phone buzzed. They both saw it was Earl Thompson.

"Put him into voicemail," said Lincoln, "like I have."

"Can't. He'll get suspicious."

"He's always suspicious. The cold bastard will probably ask why I'm not campaigning. I don't want to hear this." Lincoln went into the bathroom.

Garrett answered, "Yes, sir?"

Earl asked, "Where are you?"

"French Lick Springs. Presidential Suite."

"Are you alone?"

"Yes."

"No one can find Kincaid," said Earl. "He isn't answering my calls."

"Mine either. I left him several messages."

Garrett heard the toilet flush.

"We have to find him, Garrett."

Garrett said, "Sir, Governor Kincaid has just lost his wife. He's entitled to privacy."

"Of course he is, but this is the most crucial point in his campaign. His numbers have soared since Marian died. However, that type of anguish can take away a man's good judgment. We don't want him sitting in some do-drop-in, redneck bar getting drunk and making a fool of himself. We have to get him back. He can have privacy as long as he is within our purview and under our control."

"I agree, sir. I'll find him."

"Good," said Earl. "Lincoln was scheduled for Florida today. Get it rescheduled as soon as possible after Marian's funeral."

"Yes, sir."

Earl hung up without a goodbye.

Garrett's instincts had been right all along.

He lit another cigarette, drew on it, and exhaled the smoke toward the ceiling. Earl knew. He knew that Garrett had just lied to him about being alone. He knew that Garrett was with Lincoln in the suite. He probably knew that Garrett and Lincoln had been lovers since shortly after they'd met.

Earl knew these things because he'd planned them.

Earl Thompson, the sonofabitch, had forced Garrett into a deadly game of political chess. Earl was quite the gamer. He'd rolled the dice when Garrett left his law firm to join the Foundation; not ordinary dice—they had rolled continuously since Earl threw them, were rolling still, and, Garrett estimated, would come to rest sometime over the next several days. When they did, they would come up with only one of three numbers—seven, eleven, or snake eyes… two ones. Seven or eleven was a win. Snake eyes was a loss.

Both Lincoln and Garrett had much at stake in the dice. If they came up seven or eleven, Lincoln would become Mr. President and Garrett a special White House aide. If they came up snake eyes, Earl would play his endgame—protect Earl Thompson and the Foundation at all costs. Like any smart gambler, Earl Thompson hedged his bets. He'd been laying the groundwork for both a win and a loss.

The point was that Earl had known about Lincoln's sexual proclivities for years, probably going back to Tigris River, probably even before that. Lincoln Kincaid had to be saved from himself, and Earl had tasked Garrett as the man to do it. There had been no assurance that Lincoln and Garrett would hit it off. However, Earl, along with nature and a bit of luck, had gotten what he wanted. The union of Lincoln Kincaid and Garrett Jennings, and their monogamy, would limit Lincoln's propensity for sexual violence to Garrett, thus all but eliminating his need for younger men such as Jameel Shalih and Jayden Ramirez. If Lincoln's need overpowered him, Garrett, Earl Thompson's ever-bright, ever-practical, and ever-resourceful assistant, would sate it himself.

Garrett mused that Earl had entered into a 'covenant' with Lincoln and Garrett without their knowledge or consent. However, this covenant was different in that it presupposed not a single goal, but two goals, one exclusive of the other, and Earl Thompson would choose which.

Whether by murder or blackmail, Earl silenced Cradlers and Lambs who might otherwise talk. He had silenced Marian Kincaid. The Foundation had tapped her phone. When Marian voiced her decision to leave her husband in the phone call to Rhonda, Earl Thompson saw both disaster and opportunity. Garrett recalled Earl's words after the confrontation with Marian Kincaid over her autobiography. Earl had mentioned a new covenant, although he never called it that. It would *"ensure the election of... Kincaid. Americans... so sympathetic." "...we may... tap into that sympathy."*

Marian's flight from Lincoln would have wrecked Lincoln's candidacy and exposed the Foundation. Her tragic death had removed those risks. There was a bonus—a week before Marian died, Earl had ordered the murder of Rhonda O'Malley. A dead investigative reporter who had gotten too close to the truth cannot write and publish stories that would take down Lincoln Kincaid with all the accompanying fallout. The friendship between Marian and Rhonda had propelled them into the same vehicle, which also led to Rhonda's death, another bit of Earl Thompson luck. Earl had ordered Rose to kill the two. Rose, more out of revenge for the death of her husband than any love she might have for the Foundation, accomplished the mission via perfect timing and a small C-4 bomb attached to the gas tank of Rhonda's car. She had detonated the explosive with her cell phone.

The shower started. The bathroom door opened and Lincoln asked, "Care to join me?"

Garrett declined. The door closed.

In contemplation of snake eyes, Earl had planned his endgame. Figuring prominently in it were the lives and times of Lincoln and Garrett. The Foundation would abandon Kincaid to his fate. Earl would tell the reporters that "Kincaid had covered up his sexual perversions with young men by blackmail and murder."

Though Earl said otherwise, he and the Foundation board never intended to elevate a homosexual, Garrett Jennings, to the position of executive director. They had better use for him.

***

The shower stopped. Lincoln emerged in his bathrobe, poured two scotches, and handed one to Garrett. They snuggled on the couch.

Lincoln asked, "What did the almighty Earl Thompson want?"

"He ordered me to find you."

"Anything else?"

"He was afraid you'd end up drunk in some cheap bar."

"Sounds like a good idea."

"Are you serious?"

"Maybe."

"Why?"

Lincoln thought before he responded. "I've never had drinks in a cheap bar. I might meet real people who need help, the kind that work and struggle, who are down on their luck and drowning their sorrows. I want to help *them*, Garrett, not the rich hypocritical bastards." Lincoln watched the news for a few moments, and then mumbled, "Maybe the people in a cheap bar will hand me truth."

Garrett turned up the television volume. Both CNN and Fox were reporting that the tension between Russia and Ukraine had receded when both countries agreed to pull back their troops ten miles from the border.

Garrett said, "Looks like Earl Thompson is saving his little war for you."

"I don't want it."

"You may have no choice. Wars happen and the President of the United States must deal with them."

"Yeah. I get that."

Fox announced that "Governor Lincoln Kincaid had canceled his campaign appearances pending the funeral of his wife. A campaign spokesman told Fox news that Kincaid's scheduled campaign swing through the south, including the swing state of Florida, would be rescheduled for a later time."

Garrett said, "We're rescheduling Florida."

"I won't go to Florida."

"It's a swing state."

"I'm aware of the swing states—Florida, Ohio, Pennsylvania, Michigan, Colorado, Iowa, Nevada, New Hampshire, Virginia, maybe even Wisconsin. I know so goddamn much. I know the histories of every blue and red state going back five elections. I can name every state Democratic Chairperson and the chairs in most of the counties. I know the names of every blue and red governor and their spouses, and even some of their children. I've memorized my canned speeches backward and forward. They're teaching me foreign policy. I'm now on Southeast Asia. Boy oh boy, it's all so goddamn interesting and so goddamn much fun."

"Lincoln, if the election were held today, you'd win in a landslide. It's the presidency, Lincoln… the fucking presidency. You have it in your hands."

Lincoln gulped his scotch and poured another.

"What's wrong?"

"I don't want it."

"Don't want what?"

"The presidency. I don't deserve it. They published Marian's autobiography. If I'd had the courage to stop them, she might be alive. I know about the Angels, Cradlers, Lambs and Archangels, the deaths, disappearances and murders, the Foundation's goals, and the sources of my parents' money. Did you know that Polly Thompson is my half-sister and my parents got rid of her so they could spend their all on me? Now she hates me and she should. My grandfather, Benjamin, is a pathetic fool who started all this for me. I was guiltier than hell at Tigris River. The Ferdinand V.A. hospital is treating some... some of the men I took advantage of. General Hernandez told the truth. The army ruined his career just to save my ass."

"Lincoln, how long have you felt this way?"

"It started when I met you, Garrett. Just a tiny bit. A sort of twinge that I didn't understand at the time. I started thinking seriously about it when I heard that Borgmann had murdered Shalih and Ramirez."

"They weren't murdered."

"It doesn't matter. They escaped by sheer luck. It was then that I started looking into myself. It wasn't pretty."

"Stop talking like that. You were made for the presidency."

"Programmed for it, you mean. Designed for it. I'm a wonderful machine that they want to make president, but nobody ever asked me, Garrett! Not my parents, not my grandfather, not Fredrick Thompson or his anointed son, Earl Thompson. Nobody. Not even you. Not even me. Most of the time I fooled myself into thinking I really did want to quarterback the Point to national rankings, take a cushy job in the Pentagon, and then be elected congressman, governor, and, finally, president.

"Today, I want to scream at them... I'm me, Lincoln Kincaid! Look at me. I'm a real person. I'm not a computer you can program. I'm not a raggedy doll on your strings. I can no longer stomach your criminal Foundation and all the nonsense about Jesus Plus Zero, and God, and Romans 13, and all that other blithering bullshit.

"I don't want to be your president! I want to be me... just me, goddamn it all to hell."

Garrett lowered the TV volume. "Do you really mean that?"

"I do. I want to raise my kids. I owe that much to Marian, and I can't think of anything I'd rather do more. For the first time in my life, I wouldn't be playing a character in a play written by others. I can be Lincoln Pennington Kincaid without the frills, speeches, and fakery. The Foundation be damned! Earl Thompson be damned!"

Lincoln started to cry.

Garrett took Lincoln into his arms. "Shh, shh, it's okay. It's okay, Lincoln. It's okay if you drop out of the race. Shh. Shh. It's alright. I'm here with you. You're safe, Lincoln. You're safe."

Lincoln fell asleep. Garrett slipped out of bed and checked his Smith & Wesson .45. It was loaded. He hid it in his suitcase beside his hammer. Then he removed the keys to his safety deposit boxes and fingered them and a flash drive onto the scapula he wore around his neck. The small drive was special. The business of listening devices went both ways. A month or so before, Garrett had tapped Earl's office and phone. He recorded the calls to and from Earl leading up to the murders of Marian Kincaid and Rhonda O'Malley. The first was a call from Benjamin Kincaid the day Marian had confronted Jackson, Rachel, and him in their home. The second was the quick conversation between Rose Cardova and Earl Thompson, shortly before the murders of Marian and Rhonda.

Garrett had downloaded those and many more Earl Thompson conversations onto the flash drive. It now hung next to the medal of Saint Rita of Cascia, the patron saint of lost causes.

CHAPTER 63

Andy partook of the rites of Rhonda's funeral with a strange sense of detachment.

Father Bernardo prayed the Catholic funeral mass. Father Paul, his own life so intertwined with the Balbach family and their history, served. There was the urn of Rhonda's ashes on the first step leading to the altar. Andy hadn't cried, hadn't shed so much as a tear, when the Beech Trees sang "Danny Boy." He would not do so now, in the last moments of the service, as the Beech Trees entreated the Lord to make all an Instrument of Peace. A part of him had died with Rhonda. He felt his losses, but a man doesn't cry at visions of his own funeral. He endures it.

The last notes echoed in the church, and Bernardo announced the eulogy. Andy stood, left the pew, and walked up the altar steps past Rhonda. Bernardo handed the microphone to him. Andy turned and faced the congregation. There was his family in the front pew slightly to his right. General and Louise Hernandez occupied the pew behind them. There was Rhonda's family, few in number, to his left. Behind them were Stump, Billups, Peachfuzz, and Clubby. He recognized Angels scattered about the church. The Honorable Everett Townsend, Judge of the Dubain Circuit Court, and the rest of the Dubain bar sat behind the Beech Trees.

Because of the over-capacity crowd, mourners snuggled tightly in the pews, and more stood in the aisles. The media had come forward. Fathers Bernardo and Paul faced him from their seats in a small pew on the left side of the altar. He found Polly Thompson standing in the back of the church forward of the basins of holy water. She had spent the night before at Andy's house. For a moment, he jumped back to that Fourth of July night—it seemed so long ago—at the Schnitzelbank. Polly was dressed in the red slit skirt, white blouse, and stiletto heels that Rhonda had worn that evening. He had chosen the outfit for Polly earlier that morning but withheld its history from her.

There emanated from all the pleas for comfort, for meaning, for closure. Help us, Andy. Take away our hurt. Make sense of eternity, of infinity. Convince us that our earthly lives are safe from the fraility of Rhonda's. You stand between heaven and earth, in God's light and with your eloquence. Only you can do this, Andy. Please.

Andy could not. He could affirm myths in the courtroom, but not here… not standing at the altar next to Rhonda's urn in St. Augustine Cathedral.

Andy started. "To embrace life, one must embrace death. Rhonda O'Malley lived that way. Thus, her life is more than an event of celebration, though celebrate we must. Her death is more than an event of grief, though grieve we must. Her courage is more than an event of admiration, though admire we must.

"Perhaps the measure of a life is the measure of its loss. This is the best any mortal can do.

"In all this, I have no opinion of God's will. I shall not so blaspheme or flatter myself.

"You ask of me words of comfort. I have no comfort. You ask of me words of understanding. I do not understand. You ask of me words of closure. There is no closure.

"I shall instead speak words of something infinitely more powerful and enduring than comfort, understanding, and closure. I shall speak of a life's purpose.

"Robert Frost, in perhaps his most famous poem, *The Road Not Taken*, speaks of two roads. I quote the last stanza:

> *I shall be telling this with a sigh,*
> *Somewhere ages and ages hence;*
> *Two roads diverged in a wood, and*
> *I—I took the one less traveled by,*
> *And that has made all the difference.*

"I'm not Robert Frost, and I'm certainly not a poet, so please permit me a measure of personal license to speak as I see his words.

"It's 1920. Frost, middle aged, is roaming the New England woods. Frost says it's late morning, but I like to think it's early evening in late fall. Winter is coming on. The sun nears the southwest horizon. The deep blue eastern sky is giving up stars. Mr. Frost encounters two roads and stops. They form a V and he stands at its tip. The road more traveled veers to his right and is familiar to him. It is straight and safe, and it leads back to his warm cabin and wholesome food and relaxing drink. The road less traveled by veers to his left, and he knows nothing of it or its destination. Yellow leaves swirl around him. His thin hair is messy… his eyesight strained. He is tired, thirsty, and hungry, and the wind chills his bones.

"He takes a step on the road more traveled by but then halts. He steps back and peers down the road less traveled by. He's timid and afraid. Ah, the cabin calls to him, and he to it.

"Then a great courage wells up in him. He says goodbye to the easy and safe road, and steps onto the road less traveled by. If the poem is taken literally, Mr. Frost was referring to himself as 'I' and that he survived the road less traveled by. He neither describes his journey on that road nor expounds on the difference that it made. Some say he hid these in his heart and assigns to the reader the burden of their discovery. Perhaps they are right, but it doesn't matter.

"What matters is that Frost journeyed on the less-traveled road.

"Frost, himself a gentle man, appeals to all that is courageous and decent and kind in us. However, he knows, as must we, that if we assume good in the universe, we must also assume evil. Frost encounters both on the road less traveled by. He throws away a life of comfort and ease and chooses to risk all. Curiously, he says, 'I shall be telling this somewhere, ages and ages hence.' We know that Frost, a mortal, will have left his earthly life long before the 'ages' arrive. But there is a second 'I.' Who is it?

"The second 'I' is we. 'We' includes Rhonda O'Malley. She could have turned onto the safer road of local news, opinion, and sports columns. I do not denigrate these, or those who write them. The point is that Rhonda chose the road less traveled by, the hard and exhilarating life of an investigative journalist. She turned her talents to uncovering uncommon good and uncommon evil. She searched and found the pieces and motivations of an evil that stalks us. She knew that good does not always prevail, that bad and evil triumph too many times. She accepted the risks of these without fear or hesitation.

"It is this that gave her life purpose. Robert Frost had nothing on Rhonda. Purpose was the difference for Mr. Frost. Purpose was the difference for Rhonda. She made her way on the road less traveled. It is not a nice road. It is narrow, curvy, and unpaved. Storms sweep it always. It has no signs, no markers or centerlines, and no speed limits. Danger lurks to the sides of this road and the traveler dare not leave it. The trek is one-way and the only escape is to reach the end.

"Rhonda encountered obstacles in the form of a group that calls itself, simply, the Foundation. She fought them and they fought back. No quarter was asked and none was given. Some might point to the urn of her ashes in front of me and say that Rhonda lost. She did not. She died not of a loss, but of a win. She triumphed, and because of this, the truth will come out. However, know now that the Foundation is evil. They cheat, they steal, and they kill. Certainly, they kill. The deaths of Rhonda O'Malley and Marian Kincaid attest to this.

"Frost would say that we are taking the safe road if we ignore the Foundation. The kicker is that he does not let us off the hook. Why? Because we live in an age 'hence,' and this is one of the times Frost sighs, speculating and doubting that we have the courage to take up his command to turn onto the road less traveled by. Let us not disappoint him.

"Let us, like Rhonda O'Malley, take the road less traveled by. Let us pick up where she left off. Let us live lives of purpose. Let us make 'all the difference.'"

CHAPTER 64

Andy, Billups, and Father Bernardo left the cemetery and returned to the Cathedral. They met Jameel Shalih and Jayden Ramirez at the utility landing.

Ramirez, holding a knife, asked, "What do you want?"

"First," said Andy, "I want you to give me that knife."

"Not a chance. This is Borgmann's knife."

"How did you get it?"

"Borgmann used it to slit Jameel's throat, but he didn't get the job done. Jameel took it."

Jameel asked, "What else do you want?"

Andy said, "To take you in."

Jayden said, "You ain't cops, and you ain't takin' nobody in."

"Do you know who I am?" Andy asked.

"Yeah, the hotshot lawyer who's gone off the deep end." Then he pointed to Billups. "Your buddy there is the queer, black-ass mouthpiece."

Andy said, "My late wife, Rhonda, and your friend, Polly Thompson, told us about you two."

Jameel said, "Yeah. Your wife found me right here. I held a gun on her from right where we're standing, but she made me put it away. She was good to me… brought me food. She said that you'd defend me, and that we needed each other. I didn't understand."

"Neither did I."

"I'm sorry she died."

"So am I."

Bernardo lit a cigarette and then held the pack out. Ramirez accepted one and let Bernardo light it. He took a draw and exhaled the smoke. Then he waved the cigarette at Andy.

"I know you mouthpieces. You get all the glory of taking us in and defending us. Whadda we get? A prison cell. Yeah. I been there. Me and Jameel can hide out anywhere we want. Ain't that right, Jameel?"

Jameel said nothing.

Ramirez added, "Besides, why should we trust a broken down lawyer and a queer?"

Andy said, "Jayden Ramirez, if you say 'queer' one more time, I'll smash your teeth."

"Yeah."

"Yeah, what?"

"Just try."

"I might."

"You'll lose your own teeth."

"Are you queer?"

Ramirez stiffened but made no advance. Andy waited, and then said, "Answer my question, Ramirez. Other 'queers' stuck it up your ass. You ejaculated and this means you liked it, didn't you?"

"You mother fuckin' lawyer."

"Answer me."

Jameel cut in, "I was with Ramirez. He didn't like it."

Andy said, "That's what I thought, but I want to hear it from him. Ramirez?"

"No. I hated it."

"So you agree."

"Agree? With what?"

"That there's one helluva difference between a homosexual rapist and a decent person whose sexual orientation is gay."

"Guess so."

"Good. Billups here is a good lawyer. He is married to his longtime partner. He won't use your asses for pleasure. However, he just may save them. You're charged with the murders of the guards and wounding Borgmann. If you're found guilty of the murders, you'll probably get the needle."

"Needle?" asked Ramirez.

"Capital punishment. You know, when the judge sentences you to death and the state kills you. Actually, Indiana uses two needles. The first needle puts you to sleep, if you're lucky. The second paralyzes every muscle in your body. Pray that the first needle works. If it doesn't, and you're awake, you will feel yourself slowly asphyxiating to death."

Jameel said, "We've murdered no one."

"The evidence that you did is strong. What are you gonna say? 'Hello there, jury of my peers, my name is Ramirez. I didn't murder the guard. Borgmann did. Then angels saved me.' 'Hello, my name is Shalih. I didn't murder the guards. Some angel ran out of the woods and killed them.' The jury will convict you and sentence you to death in record time."

They hesitated. Andy saw that he'd gotten to them.

Jameel got his voice back. "You... still haven't answered Jayden. Why should we trust you?"

"You shouldn't. We can't guarantee you anything. But, if you ask the prison warden at Michigan City—that's the north end of the state—he'll allow us to witness your executions. Might make it easier for you."

Ramirez asked, "You say this shit to all your clients?"

"No. I saved it for you."

Jameel said, "Jayden and me talked this over. Your legal system has done nothin' but get us raped and almost killed and now we are hiding in this friggen church. We're leaving for Idaho. It's a good place to hide."

"Good. Go to Idaho. Have a wonderful life." Andy motioned to Billups and the priest. They walked to the staircase and began descending.

"Wait!"

Andy turned. "What do you want, Shalih? Directions?"

"Can't we talk about this?"

"Nothing to talk about. You can go to Idaho, or Alaska, or Bumblenuts Egypt for all we care."

"Well... what'll happen if we turn ourselves in?"

"You'll be arrested and finger-printed. They'll stick their fingers up your asses and then check your mouth, ears, and any other bodily orifice they can find. They don't change gloves so you best hope they do your asses last. Then they'll turn hoses on you. The hoses are pressurized so you'll have to cover your ying-yangs or they might get blown off. When you're clean, they'll dress you in orange jump suits and throw your asses into separate cells."

"Then what?"

"Tomorrow or the next day you'll be arraigned. The judge will tell you what you're charged with and spell out the sentences if you're found guilty. He'll read you your rights—you know, all that technical stuff in the Constitution. Then he'll ask you if you can afford a lawyer and you'll say no, and then he'll appoint some fresh-out-of-law-school flunky to defend you. You can pretty much kiss your asses goodbye. They'll send you to a maximum-security prison for execution. It'll take another ten years for you to finish your appeals. All that time, you know deep down that the appeals will fail and you'll end up on a white sheet, hoping like hell that the doctor can't find a vein.

"In the meantime, Jobo'll be your cellmate. Now Jobo is forty pounds heavier than you and about a lifetime hornier. You'll be his bitch. Now, if that sounds like a life to you, we're leaving. No hard feelings. Say hi to Jobo."

Again, Andy, Billups, and Bernardo turned to leave.

"Wait! What'll happen if we hide?"

They turned around. Andy said, "They'll try you in absentia. Not a good thing. The courtroom will be empty except for reporters, and the prosecutor, and his witnesses, and your defense counsel, and maybe a witness or two. You'll be convicted of murder. Death or life. You hope for life but you'll probably get death. You'll be fugitives from justice. Tack on another ten. As far as I know, you can't get to Idaho without crossing state lines, so the feds will come in. You'll be tried in absentia in a federal court. Tack on another ten."

"How... how would the sentences work?"

"Let's assume you don't get the death penalty. Indiana will probably be first, which means you'll never make it to federal prison. If you do what Jobo tells you, you might live a couple of years. If you don't, Jobo'll stab you to death while you're sleeping. Jobo has maybe five life sentences so what's another life sentence to him? If, by a miracle, Indiana paroles you, the feds will throw you into a maximum-security prison. No golf course, but it doesn't matter. You're just pissants who don't play golf."

Ramirez stood frozen. Jameel looked like he would throw up.

Andy said, "Oh, and another thing… get ready for them."

Jameel asked, "Them? Who?"

"The guys who'll hunt you down. Maybe they're cops. Maybe they're bounty hunters. Doesn't really matter. You're in your Idaho cabin eating deer steak, sipping your home-brewed beer, and looking forward to screwing the two Indian women who've joined you. There's a knock at your door. You open, and there stands two beer-bellied men in cheap military uniforms with only half their teeth. Bounty hunters. They'll shackle you so tight you won't shit or piss until they unlock the chains around your waists. They'll take you to jail and collect their $200,000.00 reward for bringing in a couple of killers."

Jameel asked, "If we turn ourselves in, will all this Foundation and Lincoln Kincaid and rape come out at the trial?"

"Yes. If the jury believes you, they'll acquit. It's all part of democracy and the good old USA."

Ramirez said, "Fuck democracy. Fuck America. Where were they when we needed them? Why should we risk our asses for them?"

"Hmm. Maybe you shouldn't. America and democracy just might send you into Jobo's loving arms and then to the doctor with the needles. It's real cheap. No X-Rays, or MRIs, or rehab, or blood tests on execution day."

Jameel said, "Give me time to talk to Ramirez."

"Make it quick. We don't have all day."

They went to the back of the landing and whispered. Then they returned. Jameel nodded.

"Jameel, I can't hear your brain flopping. You have to talk. Yes or no?"

"Yes. We'll turn ourselves in. We want you as our lawyers."

"Fine. We'll defend you with conditions. Number one, you will tell us the truth. Number two, you will tell us *all* the truth. Everything. You will hold nothing back, even if you think it's not important. We decide what's important and what isn't. Three, you will treat the sheriff, his deputies, and all other police officers with deference and respect, even when they piss you off… and they will. Four, you will wear the jumpsuits, eat the food, sleep in the bunks, smell everybody's farts and puke, and not complain. Five, you will never try to escape. Six, you will never—ever—mouth off to the judge, prosecutor, or deputies. Seven, we are the lawyers. You are the defendants. We, and only we, do the talking. You will sit and look nice and innocent and say absolutely nothing until we say you can. Eight, you will talk about this case with no one but Billups and me—not your cellmate, not the drunks, not the deputies, or the FBI, or Homeland Security, or the media. Not even with each other. I guarantee that somebody will be listening and recording, and it will be used against you.

"Now, is there anything about this you don't understand? Shalih?"

"No, sir."

"Ramirez?"

"I get it."

"Good. Give me that knife. It's evidence."

Ramirez handed it over.

"There's one other point, and you listen real carefully—Andy Balbach, Joe Billups, and Father Bernardo Estrada are the only friends you have."

CHAPTER 65

Garrett entered the suite alone. He'd been in the weight room with Lincoln but declined Lincoln's invitation to swim laps in the pool. Before he could turn on CNN, Earl Thompson called.

"Yeah."

"Read the Dubain newspaper and call me back immediately."

Garrett pulled up his online subscription to the *Dubain Courier Journal*. The headlines shot off the front page.

Rhonda O'Malley Laid to Rest
Husband Drops Bombshell in Eulogy
Claims Organization Close to Governor Killed
O'Malley & Kincaid's Own Wife

© Copyright Dubain Courier Journal,
& Dubain Online News

Rhonda O'Malley, nationally recognized investigative reporter and native of Dubain, was laid to rest this morning in a moving ceremony capped by her husband's eulogy in which he all but openly charged a secretive organization known as the Foundation with murdering his wife and Indiana First Lady, Marian Kincaid. Ms. O'Malley had been investigating the Foundation and its ties to Indiana Governor Lincoln Kincaid, Marian Kincaid's husband. O'Malley first raised in a national broadcast interview with Governor Kincaid months ago…

Garrett skimmed through the rest of the article.

…Kincaid's campaign manager, Garrett Jennings, said that Balbach was probably still in shock from the loss of his wife… "the charges are baseless." Kincaid and his children are in seclusion at an unknown location.

The dice had turned up snake eyes. Garrett did not return the call to Earl. He had nothing more to say to him.

CHAPTER 66

Senator Josie Carter Lodge led Andy and Stump to her library and closed the door. Andy felt a pang when Josie hugged Stump and they exchanged kisses on each other's cheek. He felt better when Josie hugged him.

"Please, sit down," said the senator. "Andy, I offer my deepest condolences on the loss of Ms. O'Malley. Your eulogy was beautiful. Robert Frost is my favorite poet."

"Thank you, Senator."

"Please call me Josie." Then she turned to Stump. "I've subscribed to the *Dubain Courier Journal* for years. I have to keep up on Firmus... make sure he behaves. I can't have a former fiancé making up stories about me."

Stump laughed and touched her arm. "I don't have to make them up."

"Now, Firmus..."

"Josie, how many former fiancés do you have?" Andy asked.

"That's personal," said Josie. "However, Firmus knows."

Stump said, "Two. Mr. Franklin Lodge and me."

"Correct."

"Did you make the right choice?" Andy asked.

"Don't know if I made the right choice, but I do know I couldn't have made a wrong one."

"Great answer," said Stump.

"Thank you. Now, I know you two didn't come all this way to talk about my fiancés. Is this about Lincoln Kincaid and the Foundation?"

"Yes," said Stump. "We thought it best that we give you advance notice in person."

"Advance notice of what?" asked the senator. "Andy's eulogy and the *Courier Journal's* article about it have made serious allegations against very powerful people. You've already blown their cover. Is there more?"

"There is," said Stump. "Rhonda had been investigating Kincaid and the Foundation for months. She'd gotten too close. Marian Kincaid was, putting it gently, less enamored of her husband than she publicly showed. In a private lunch the day after Rhonda's interview of Lincoln Kincaid, she told Rhonda that she had serious doubts about her husband's fitness for the presidency. Turned out it wasn't a private lunch. The Foundation had bugged the room. Rhonda had been on the Foundation's watch list since before her interview of Kincaid. The lunch put Marian Kincaid on it. Eventually, someone—almost certainly the Foundation's executive director, Earl Thompson—put them on the elimination list."

"Is there proof linking all this together?"

"Yes," said Stump.

"Gentlemen, excuse me for a moment." Josie went to her desk. She opened and closed drawers and reached behind some books on a portable bookshelf. "Dammit, Franklin, where did you hide them this time?" She turned around to see Stump holding a pack of cigarettes and a lighter in his hands. Stump offered her a cigarette.

Josie said, "Firmus, the Surgeon General says cigarettes will kill you."

"I smoke on occasion. This is one of them. Besides, what does the Surgeon General know?"

"Thank you just the same."

"You're welcome."

Josie asked, "So, Firmus, you said there's more. What?"

Andy answered, "Rhonda had concluded her investigation and was about to blow the lid off Kincaid and the Foundation. She'd written three articles designed to be printed in a series. Stump is running them in the *Courier Journal* over the next week."

Stump said, "Josie, you need do nothing but sit back, watch, say nothing, and let this old flame do all the work."

"This will destroy Lincoln Kincaid," said Josie.

"It'll do more than that," said Stump. "It'll destroy the Democratic Party."

Josie said, "The Democratic Party will take its lumps, but it's shown a remarkable ability to come back from them."

"To a certain extent," said Andy. "We overcame the loss of the southern states to civil rights but it took decades. However, civil rights was simply a shift in policy for the Democrats. This is very different. It exposes duplicity and naked ambition by men who cared nothing for the country. The voters will skip disillusionment and move straight to anger. Anger lasts. The Democratic Party will be in upheaval for years."

Josie said nothing right off. There was an awkward silence. Andy and Stump held their peace. It was Josie's turn.

"Gentlemen, I want the presidency, but I want it on my own abilities and strengths. I believe I should earn it, not have it handed to me. I hope I don't sound presumptuous."

Stump turned to Andy with a smile and his hand extended. Andy peeled off a twenty dollar bill and handed it to Stump.

Josie asked, "What's that all about?"

"I bet Andy twenty bucks that you would say what you just said. He lost. I won."

Andy said, "I'm sorta glad I lost. It may be the best twenty bucks I ever spent."

"Let's get serious," said Josie. "Do you believe I'm presumptuous?"

Andy said, "No. You just did the math."

Stump said, "You didn't ask for any of this, Josie, but it is what it is. Kincaid will be forced out of the race. You'll destroy Sarah Harding in the primaries and defeat whatever Democrat takes Lincoln's place."

Josie nodded, and then crushed her cigarette. "How about we go to the kitchen? I'll brew coffee and cut some ham sandwiches."

They sat around the kitchen table. Andy said, "Seems like everything gets to the kitchen eventually."

Josie said, "People feel safer in the kitchen. When my kids were growing up, they'd sit at this table and admit to mischiefs that got them into trouble at school. I didn't have the heart to tell them that their teachers had already called me.

"I do have a confession of my own. I've prayed with some of the Foundation members."

Andy asked, "Why did you stop?"

"They pray to a Jesus who does not exist. However, at the same time, I feel badly for Lincoln Kincaid."

"Don't," said Stump.

"Our engagement, Firmus, will come out. Some'll say that Josie Carter Lodge's old boyfriend, by printing the articles, is, well, being loyal, or more."

Stump choked on his sandwich and drank some water.

"More?" Andy suppressed a smile. "Aren't you a happily married woman, Josie?"

"Damnit, Andy!" said Stump.

Then Josie saw the smile.

Stump had overcome his choking fit. "Maybe I'll start spreading rumors that my old flame has reignited, unless she promises to grant my one wish."

"That's blackmail!"

"Of course it is."

"Okay." Josie emitted a fake sigh. "What's the favor?"

"I want to sleep in the Lincoln Room."

"Firmus, the media will have a field day with that one."

"It'll be our little secret, Josie. Take it or leave it."

"I'll take it."

Andy envied them their little set-to. He'd seen another side of Stump since he and Josie met at the door. When their eyes locked, Andy felt like the third wheel. But he reveled in their lighthearted banter, and then joined in it.

"Stump, had you and Josie married, would you have turned Republican?"

"Absolutely not."

Josie said, "I believe him. We had some heated arguments back in the day."

"I always won."

"You did not, but sometimes I let you beat me."

Andy asked, "Why?"

"To spare the male ego… that's why."

Stump said, "Don't believe it, Andy. Josie's ego was ten times mine. It was the opposite. I let *her* win."

"Don't believe that, Andy."

"I'll withhold judgment."

Josie asked for another cigarette. "Do not, under any circumstances, say anything to Franklin about this."

"About what?" They turned to the door. Franklin Lodge entered with a load of groceries and placed them on the table.

Stump rose. "My friend, Frank, the winner." He and Franklin shook hands and Stump introduced Andy as another Democrat.

"Sometimes, Stump," said Franklin, "I wish you had been the winner."

"Oh, Franklin, cut it out."

Franklin turned to Josie, "Why have you allowed two Democrats into this house at the same time?"

"I want Andy to vote for me. I've already bought Firmus."

"Bought? That's ille—"

"Just one night in the Lincoln bedroom."

"Oh, that's fine," said Franklin. "Stump and I'll get out our Jack Daniels. He won't even remember sleeping in Lincoln's bed."

"What's this about my vote?" Andy asked.

"Will you vote for me?"

Franklin said, "Think long and hard before you answer, Andy. I still haven't made up my mind."

"Franklin, dear, get serious." She turned to Andy. "Will you consider it?"

"Maybe." Andy smiled. "I don't know enough about your positions."

Franklin rolled his eyes. "We'll be here at least a week."

"Just the basics."

"I struggle," said Josie, "with the role of the federal government in our system. Doubtless, it must handle those things the Constitution specifically assigns to it—national defense, regulation of interstate commerce, taxes, the powers allocated to the three branches, foreign policy, and the like. I also believe that the federal government must step in on matters that the states cannot handle themselves, such as environmental policy. I am uncomfortable, however, when the federal government invades the provinces of the states. What business does the federal government have in local schools?

Local gun laws? Healthcare?"

Andy responded. "Healthcare is a national issue. No state has an incentive to have a good healthcare system because it would end up with all the sick people in the country. The incentive is the other way, and that is to downplay and underfund healthcare."

"I get that, Andy, but I have a question for you. Why are you here today?"

"To give you a heads up."

"About what?"

"The truth about Lincoln Kincaid and the Foundation."

"Exactly. If the election was held today, he'd win. Would you want that?"

"Of course not, but your point is?"

"The federal government is one of limited jurisdiction. It's easy to say but hell to do. The question of the power of the federal government versus the states has bedeviled Americans for almost 250 years. We fought a civil war over it—albeit the main issue was slavery—and killed over a half million Americans in it. Yet, we're still debating it."

"I hope we never stop."

"Hmm," said Franklin, "we'll make him a Republican yet."

"Don't count on it," said Stump.

"Get serious, you two." Josie turned back to Andy. "Just how powerful should the federal government be? Power doesn't disappear, it flows. When the federal government invades the provinces of the states, it gains power at the expense of the states. In many ways, this can be a good thing, of course. I get your argument about healthcare, Andy, but there's another side to all this. You cannot always assume benevolent leaders. Indeed, we've elected some fools as president but the country has remained safe because we've spread power over two other branches, the Congress and the Supreme Court, and some fifty states plus territories.

"A president that steals power is, by definition, terrifying. We must assume that a Lincoln Kincaid slash Foundation will pull the wool over everyone's eyes and get elected. It's been averted this time. But what happens next time when there are no Rhonda O'Malleys and Marian Kincaids to stop it and the power of the federal government falls into the hands of someone beholden to the likes of the Foundation? You get a government that has the power and the inclination to do terrible things. These will be used against 'We, the people of the United States' and not for a 'more perfect union.' What happens to private ownership of guns? Will there be a national religion, like Sarah Harding's 'Christianity?' What's to stop them from mandating a computer chip in every person for 'health' purposes? They'll certainly rig elections because they control the means of holding them. I could go on and on, but I hope you get the point."

"I do."

Stump said, "You're starting to sound like Rhonda in her articles. It's like you met her."

"I did. Rhonda visited Franklin and me three days before she died. She sat right where you're sitting now, Andy, and gave me copies of her articles."

"Rhonda... here?"

"Andy, I apologize for sandbagging."

Andy said, "No apology needed."

"I need your vote, Andy, and, more importantly, your support. You know your way around Indiana politics. I can't lose Indiana and expect to win."

Andy responded. "Two conditions. The first is that you don't tell anybody and ruin my Democratic Party credentials."

They laughed.

"The second?"

"What is your vision for America?"

"Andy, there are those who self-righteously stand for a status quo America. We might admire their passion but we must abhor their blind subservience to Harding and the likes of the Foundation. America cannot stand still. It will either move backward under the comforting myths of reactionism, or move forward under the messy noise of democracy. It is this conflict—that between the sirens of illusion and the creed of true freedom—that constitutes the real social issue of our time. I am terrified of an America that is obedient and orderly. I am uplifted by an America that dares to disobey and disrupt. America must rebirth itself. Then, and only then, can we clean up the corruption of Sarah Harding."

"You have my support and my vote."

"Thank you."

Franklin cut in. "You should tell the rest of it, Josie."

"I shall. Rhonda told us about your marital situation. She also said that she wanted to go home to you but was afraid you'd say no. Then she asked us a peculiar question."

"What was it?"

"'Why is love so difficult?'"

"How did you answer?"

"I remembered the words of someone I'm very close to. It took years before they made sense to me. I said to Rhonda, 'Love is difficult and it often hurts. However, if you're lucky, you will have the difficulty, the hurt, and the love, for all your life.'

"She loved you, Andy. She still does. You shall carry the hurt, along with the love, until you meet her again… and you will meet her again. In the meantime, know that you must live in this life. Know that you can love again, in this life."

CHAPTER 67

Dubain Courier Journal & Online News

Editor's Note: This is the first of three articles researched and written by Rhonda O'Malley a week before she and Indiana First Lady, Marian Kincaid, were killed in a vehicle explosion. Her reports are a shocking exposé of Indiana Governor Lincoln Kincaid and a malevolent international organization called the Foundation. The articles have been edited for clarity but nothing has been cut. We stand by their authenticity and accuracy. We are mindful of the storms of protest and the fact that Lincoln Kincaid is in seclusion and mourning the death of his wife. We nevertheless proceeded to publication on the grounds of the people's right to know and the seriousness of the revelations. This morning, Indianapolis police stated that the deaths of Ms. O'Malley and Ms. Kincaid are being treated as homicides. They have made no arrests and have named no persons of interest.

Indiana Governor Lincoln Kincaid is the leading Democratic candidate for President of the United States. He is running on his record, which by any measure is very good. He reformed Indiana's tax laws, founded the hi-tech Hoosier Research Quadrant and upgraded Indiana's transportation infrastructure. He transformed Indiana's public school system into one of the best in the country. He attended West Point, graduated near the top of his class, and quarterbacked the football team into national rankings. He is good-looking, optimistic, charismatic, an inspirational speaker, smart, and savvy. He has a lovely wife and three adorable children.

He is also a liar, a rapist of young men, and a conspirator to blackmail and murder. Kincaid raped young American soldiers under his command at the Tigris River Prisoner-of-War Camp in Iraq in 2003. The army appointed General David Hernandez, US Army, Retired, to investigate Tigris River. He submitted a report that implicated Kincaid and other commissioned officers. However, the army excised Kincaid from the report and published another that exonerated him. Kincaid has continued to enjoy young men, procured by friends, most notably Kurt Borgmann, the long-time choir director at St. Augustine and now recovering from a gunshot wound in the stomach. Captain Kincaid and Borgmann served together at Tigris River. Later, Governor Kincaid appointed Borgmann as the warden of Camp Morgan, a minimum-security prison located east of Ferdinand, Indiana. In return for Kincaid's favor, Borgmann procured two inmates, Jameel Shalih and Jayden Ramirez, for Kincaid's pleasure. Kincaid enjoyed the two over a series of months at Piankashaw Rock, a lonely cliff formation in the Hoosier National Forest. Kincaid had worn a mask of sorts to hide his identity from Shalih and Ramirez. However, in a fit of rage, Ramirez ripped the mask away and both he and Shalih recognized him. His announcement as a candidate for president became their death warrants. Borgmann ordered their murders.

{Editor's Note: Ramirez is alive. He and Shalih have been charged with the murders of guards at Camp Morgan. Ramirez and Shalih turned themselves in to the authorities and are now incarcerated in the Dubain Security Center.}

Behind Kincaid is the Foundation. Kincaid lied on a nationally televised broadcast when he denied he was a member of the Foundation. He is a member, and the Foundation runs his campaign from Oakenwald, its campus in Alexandria, Virginia. It charges no dues and insists it has no formal membership lists or governing structure.

On the surface, the Foundation is a force for Jesus, a peacemaker among nations, the apex of benevolence. It teaches that the purpose of life is to love Jesus, to know that he cares for everyone, and not to judge. Its members include present and former senators, congresspersons, and members of administrations, foreign leaders, and wealthy businessmen. The Foundation enjoys non-profit organizational status. It seeks reconciliation among individuals and nations under the name of Jesus, champions the uplifting of the poor, and develops young peoples' groups, most notably Young Life. It mentors young people lost in America's ghettos. Its only public event is the annual National Prayer Breakfast, which has drawn the attendance of presidents from Eisenhower through Nixon, Carter, Reagan, the two Bush's, Bill Clinton, Barack Obama, and Sarah Harding.

This is the Foundation we see. It is benign, even inspirational.

There is a Foundation we don't see. It is terrifying.

This Foundation lurks beneath the surface and out of sight to all but its members. It is the temple gambler, a bandit of birthrights, sweet poison to young minds, and the neth-

erworld of cover-up, blackmail, and murder. The Foundation's goal is a new world order by way of a 'Kingdom of
Jesus' ruled exclusively by them and exploited solely for
their greater honor, glory, and wealth. It somehow justifies
all this with a bizarre theology composed of sinister twists
on random biblical passages and the nonsensical math
of their 'Jesus Equation,' $X = Jesus + 0$. The Foundation
adulterates Romans 13 to hold that God, and not voters,
chooses the world's leaders, and thus democracy is a sinful
affront against God and must be abolished. It manipulates
Acts 9:15 to ascribe to itself—and to itself only—the task
of spreading Jesus among world leaders. It holds that the
Gospels have Jesus all wrong in that he hung out with the
wealthy and powerful, and not the poor and downtrodden.
Therefore, it says that you reach the poor by way of the
wealthy and their generosity, and not government and taxes. It worships the privatization of government functions,
the better to weaken democracy, and shuffles contracts to
its friends to whom it teaches the ways and means of over-
charging and under-performing. It then spreads the wealth
among its members and those it has necessarily bribed to
gain the contracts.

Meanwhile, the Foundation has been pulling off one of the
most cunning bait and switches of all time. The bait, that
which we non-Foundationites see, is Lincoln Kincaid the
Good, Foundation the Benign, and Jesus the Son of God.
The switch is that which we do not see— Kincaid the Rapist, Foundation the Malignant, and Jesus the Exploited.

The tale of Lincoln Kincaid and the Foundation is a strange
twist on the biblical story where God lays his hands on an
individual, such as Moses, and bids him to carry out an
earthly mission. In Moses' case, the mission was to free
the Israelites from slavery. Substitute the Foundation for
God, Lincoln Kincaid for Moses, and the presidency for the

mission and you have the makings of the modern day story. The Foundation laid its hands on Kincaid when he was eighteen. They guided him through West Point, smoothed his way to a nationally recognized college quarterback, and then obtained commands for him first, in Pentagon Public Relations, and second, the Tigris River POW Camp. They gave him a home at Oakenwald, funded his campaigns for Congress, found him a beautiful wife, and managed his path to the Indiana Governorship.

The Foundation has no Jesus for sentimentality. They prevailed on Lincoln's parents to give up their second child, Polly, for adoption, so that they could focus all their emotional and worldly resources on Lincoln.

However, somewhere along Kincaid's journey to the presidency it all went wrong. Kincaid's sexual predilections for young men and boys and his recklessness in obtaining them gummed up the Foundation's plans and forced them into an unpleasant choice between no Lincoln Kincaid and Lincoln Kincaid the rapist. If the former, the Foundation would lose its investment in Kincaid and perhaps spend years searching for and developing his replacement. If the latter, the Foundation would be forced into the nasty businesses of cover-up, blackmail, and murder. They chose the latter.

CHAPTER 68

Dubain Courier Journal & Online News

Dubain At Epicenter of Firestorm

Dubain has become the epicenter of a growing firestorm that started after Dubain Attorney and widower of Rhonda O'Malley, Andrew J. Balbach, eulogized his wife and connected her death to the Foundation. It intensified upon the publication of the first of three articles written by Ms. O'Malley in which she denounced Lincoln Kincaid and the Foundation. A crowd estimated at one hundred people, including media and demonstrators, appeared outside the Dubain Security Center after they'd learned of the surrender of Shalih and Ramirez. As of this morning, all local hotels were full. Hotels in Evansville and the I-64 corridor are reporting an influx of guests. As of press time, demonstrators rallied at the Jerry Brewer football stadium and marched up and down Orchard Lane where Balbach's home is located. Local police estimated the crowds at 1,500 people with more pouring in. The demonstrators have been loud but peaceful. However, they appear to have spread to the French Lick Springs Hotel where, it is rumored, Lincoln Kincaid is hiding.

In a live TV broadcast, Reed Hanson of the Christian Coalition said that Mr. Balbach had forfeited his right to sympathy over his wife's death. "Balbach and O'Malley were separated when she died. Balbach is exploiting her death to destroy Governor Kincaid over a personal grudge, which began years ago at the wedding reception of Lincoln and Marian Kincaid. This is revolting." Many demonstrators agree. Some chanted "Kincaid Heaven Balbach Hell" and, in an apparent jab at Joseph Billups, co-counsel for Shalih and Ramirez and in a same sex marriage, many held up signs that said, "Adam and Eve Not Adam and Steve." In a rare show of unity, liberal Democrats joined with conservative evangelists in support of Lincoln Kincaid.

Balbach released a statement that "Shalih and Ramirez are brave young men who murdered no one."

It is not clear who is leading the demonstrators. It is rumored that they will surround both St. Augustine Cathedral in Dubain and the Church of the Immaculate Conception in Ferdinand tomorrow morning in bids to disrupt services.

There were calls for a boycott of the Schnitzelbank Restaurant frequented by Balbach. However, Kim Seaton, the Schnitzelbank's head bartender, said that the Schnitzelbank reported record sales with people waiting for up to two hours for a table. "This is the best publicity we've ever had. We're calling in all hands to handle the crowd."

CHAPTER 69

Andy and Joe Billups entered the chambers of His Honor Everett Townsend, Judge of the Dubain Circuit Court, for an on-the-record pretrial conference in the case of 'State of Indiana vs. Jameel Shalih and Jayden Ramirez.' Pamela Hearst, the Dubain County Prosecutor, and another man, Jacob Trocksley III, were present. The court reporter sat to the judge's left.

Judge Townsend said, "I have granted Pamela's motion to disqualify herself."

Andy asked, "On what grounds?"

"I have a conflict of interest," she said. "Let's leave it at that." She excused herself.

"I've appointed Jacob as the special prosecutor," said Judge Townsend.

Trocksley said, "Your Honor, I wish to be addressed as Mr. Trocksley."

"I'll note that."

There were three Jacob Trocksleys: grandfather, son, and grandson. Andy and his family had distasteful histories with all three. It started with grandfather, Jacob Trocksley One. One had lived with Andy's dad, Tim, and his grandfather, Ernie, at Piankashaw Rock in the 1960s. One was a Nazi in the Great Reich and a spy at Piankashaw Rock. He'd tried to kill Ernie and Tim and had a hand in torturing Andy's mother, Maria. One's real name was Kurt Getz, but somehow the Trocksley name stuck.

Along the way, One sired Jacob Trocksley II, Andy's professor of Constitutional Law in law school. Jacob II disliked Andy, and Andy didn't know why. He found out the hard way. Andy somehow pulled Trocksley as his thesis instructor. Andy wrote that secret societies, such as the Great Reich, are hidden parasites that threaten nations from the inside. He argued for amendments to the International Court Treaty to battle such threats. Andy set out his family's connection to the Great Reich in a footnote. It was a good thesis, but Jacob II barely passed him. It was then that Andy finally fathomed the connection between One and II.

After graduation, Andy walked unannounced into Jacob II's office and shut the door behind him. Witnesses said there was much shouting and many expletives from Andy. Right before he stormed out of the office, they heard Andy say, "That Piankashaw Rock Nazi bastard should have pulled out and let you run down your mother's leg. You know nothing about real law. How many asses did you kiss to get them to make you a professor of it?"

Andy despised Jacob III. He stood at just over six feet with blond hair and icy blue eyes, and wore nothing but expensive gray suits. The Indiana Supreme Court had admonished Trocksley for prosecutorial misconduct in two cases, one of which was Andy's. It was in Pike County, located immediately to the west of Dubain County. Andy had defended a woman on a felony drunk driving charge. The jury convicted and the judge sentenced her to one year in prison. Exactly two weeks after the sentencing, Andy received a call from the state forensics laboratory. They said that Trocksley had fudged the woman's blood alcohol level and she should never have been charged, much less convicted. The lab had first reported a BAC of .14, well over the legal limit of .08. However, they told Andy, they later discovered they'd confused another person's blood sample with that of Andy's client. It turned out that the client's actual BAC was .07. Trocksley knew of the problem, but withheld it from Andy and the court. Andy presented affidavits from the state's technicians in which they admitted the mistake and said they had made Trocksley aware of it. They had emails, texts, Skype sessions, and written letters to and from Trocksley as proof. The judge voided the conviction and released the defendant with the court's apologies. Then he held Trocksley in contempt of court for prosecutorial misconduct, perpetration of fraud on the court, and failure to disclose exculpatory evidence to the defense, and sentenced him to thirty days in jail. He stayed the contempt sentence, pending appeal to the Indiana Supreme Court. The Indiana Supreme Court not only admonished Trocksley, they upheld the contempt. The sheriff had to place

Trocksley in solitary confinement because of threats from other inmates.

Jacob III never smiled or laughed. He had the fanatic's incapacity for anything droll or whimsical. Once, during a break in docket call, Andy asked III if he was naturally as big an asshole as he acted, or did he take asshole pills in the morning. This drew laughs from the other lawyers. Trocksley, Andy later told friends, 'was not amused.'

Judge Townsend cleared his throat. "We'll first take up Jacob's motion to disqualify Andy and Billups as counsel for the defendants on the grounds of conflict of interest."

"The defendants," said Trocksley III, "cannot get a fair trial if they are represented by the same lawyers. Their cases are different and conflicting. Each should have special counsel appointed."

Andy turned to Trocksley. "I see you're up to your old tricks, Jacob. Since when have you been interested in a fair trial for any defendant?"

Judge Townsend said, "Andy, address your remarks to me."

Andy explained. "Judge, the facts are virtually the same for Jameel and Jayden. Both were inmates at Camp Morgan. Kurt Borgmann, the warden, and the guards repeatedly sodomized them. His buddy, Lincoln Kincaid, joined in the fun. The defendants recognized Kincaid when his mask was pulled off. Borgmann slated both of them for execution to protect Kincaid. Jayden escaped over the wall during the confusion at Camp Morgan right after the earthquake. Borgmann was in the process of slitting Jameel's throat when he was rescued by Polly Thompson and Johnnie Christiansen. They're described in the brief we submitted."

Trocksley asked, "Will they testify to this?"

"I can't say whether they'll testify to anything."

Judge Townsend noted the defendants' rights to remain silent and that the prosecution could not be privy to either defense counsel's trial plans or confidential and privileged communications between the accused and their lawyers.

"Jacob, your motion to disqualify is denied," said the judge. "Next is Jacob's motion in limine, by which he seeks to prohibit the defense from introducing certain evidence at the trial. I'll hear this motion in conjunction with the defendants' motions to order immunity for Polly Thompson."

Trocksley asserted, "Your Honor, the state's witnesses will testify that Shalih and Ramirez committed the murders and seriously wounded Borgmann and that these events occurred at the Camp Morgan front gate. On the other hand, the defense maintains that the shootings occurred at a place in the Hoosier National Forest called, according to Mr. Balbach, Piankashaw Rock."

The judge interjected, "Piankashaw Rock has been a landmark in Dubain County for well over two hundred years."

"Thank you, Your Honor. The defendants argue self-defense by way of a Polly Thompson who just happened to be there when Ramirez jumped over the wall and when Shalih was about to be 'executed.' Mr. Christiansen is alleged to be the shooter at Piankashaw Rock, which saved Shalih. Christiansen is deceased. The defense has listed Polly Thompson as a witness. All this is fantastical and inherently unbelievable. Its admission would therefore be unfairly prejudicial to the prosecution. My motion asks the court to exclude all evidence of Mr. Christiansen and Ms. Thompson. I might add that it is my belief that Mr. Balbach and Mr. Billups are fabricating this story."

"That's a serious accusation," said Judge Townsend.

Andy said, "Not really, Your Honor. Trocksley here is an expert on fabricated evidence."

"Balbach, you're a liar!"

"Am I? The Indiana Supreme Court has caught you twice. Are they lying—"

"Your grudge against my father is clouding your judgment and—"

"Not really. I hold a separate grudge just for you."

"Quiet!"

"Yes, sir," said Trocksley.

Andy just nodded.

"Your response, Andy?"

"Your Honor, Ms. Thompson will testify under oath that she was present when Jayden jumped the wall, and again at Piankashaw when Jameel was about to be executed. We will not discuss now her motives for being at either place at the times noted in the brief. However, we cannot compel her to testify because she'd be admitting, under oath, to complicity in what the prosecutor contends are four murders and one attempted murder. She will simply assert her Fifth Amendment right against self-incrimination and refuse to testify. If she doesn't testify, we will be in the unenviable position of arguing a phantom savior to the jury."

"I agree," said Judge Townsend. "Jacob?"

"Your Honor, I have wide discretion regarding grants of immunity, and I have no plans to grant anybody immunity in this case."

"I'm aware of your discretion," said Judge Townsend, "and I'm certain you're aware of mine. It is my job to ensure a fair trial for the defendants, and I have the power to grant immunity when the prosecutor refuses. It seems to me that Ms. Thompson's testimony is important. Moreover, Andy Balbach and Joe Billups have practiced before this court for years, and they have not, nor ever will, fabricate evidence. That is not to say that Ms. Thompson's testimony is true or even close to it. Even the best of lawyers can be fooled by witnesses, the police, and murder investigators, points that I'm sure you'll bring to the attention of the jury."

Judge Townsend cleared his throat. "The defense's motion for immunity for Polly Thompson is granted. She will have full immunity from any of the crimes she testifies to."

"Your Honor—"

"I've made my ruling, Jacob. Now, Andy's other motion seeks immunity for Kurt Borgmann. Borgmann himself seeks immunity, and it appears that he has demanded entry into the Witness Protection Program. Sounds to me, Jacob, like this man has something to say."

"Your Honor," said Trocksley, "I plan to depose Mr. Borgmann as soon as possible. After that, I'll make a decision as to his immunity."

Andy said, "Judge, it's very unlikely that Mr. Borgmann will testify even at a deposition, much less a trial, unless he is first given immunity. The prosecution is well aware of this and he should waste no time in granting immunity to Mr. Borgmann. In the alternative, we ask the court to grant the immunity."

Trocksley said, "I first want the opportunity to question Mr. Borgmann off-the-record to get an idea of what he can offer to the defense."

"Judge, Jacob is well aware of Borgmann's story. His off-the-record idea is a delay tactic."

"I'll allow it. The prosecution is ordered, however, to make sure the interview remains off-the-record. Jacob, Mr. Borgmann will have a free pass in the interview. Now, Borgmann's appearance anywhere near this court-house would cause a small riot. I will preside over the interview. If all goes well, the deposition will follow and I will preside over that. This will take place here in chambers after dusk.

"No one will record the interview. If we take his deposition, it will be sealed and there will be no copies until I order otherwise."

Judge Townsend then took up two more documents. "This is a defense subpoena for Governor Lincoln Kincaid to testify at trial along with a motion to grant him immunity."

"Your Honor," said Trocksley, "this is a naked attempt to smear Governor Kincaid with scurrilous lies in the middle of his race for president. I move to quash the subpoena."

"Denied. However, I will withhold ruling on the immunity issue."

"Motion to reconsider, Your Honor."

"Denied."

"There are no other motions before the court. However, I have some things to say. First, I will not tolerate aspersions on the honesty or character of any lawyer in this matter. Andy and Jacob, leave the bad blood at the courthouse door. I expect all of you to confine your behavior within the bounds of propriety and professionalism. I remind you that you are profes-sionals in a highly sensitive case.

"Second, I am issuing a gag order. None of you is to talk to the me-dia, directly or indirectly, about anything involving this case." He turned to Andy, "This means no more statements about the innocence of Shalih and Ramirez."

"Yes, Your Honor."

"Is there anything else?"

"Yes," said Andy. "Borgmann asked for protective custody for obvious reasons. So far as I know, he is not under protective custody, and he should be."

Trocksley said, "I can assure you, Mr. Balbach, that we're working on that."

"Your Honor, protective custody delayed is protective custody denied. Every minute Borgmann is unprotected is a minute someone could murder him."

Andy turned to Trocksley. "Jacob, it doesn't take a rocket scientist to arrange protection. Your motives for delay are, at best, questionable, and, at worst, despicable. You shouldn't be working on it. You should have already done it."

Judge Townsend ordered Trocksley to do so immediately.

The lawyers walked out of chambers into the hallway. They stopped.

"I don't need a protective custody lesson from you, Balbach."

"Apparently you do. And know this—the subpoena to Kincaid is only the beginning. We'll issue subpoenas to every sonofabitch connected in any way to the attempted murders of my clients. You can file all the motions to quash and make all the objections you want. I'm content to leave the rulings up to Judge Townsend. Mr. Ramirez and Mr. Shalih are the defendants, but your Foundation—don't even try to deny your membership—and Lincoln Kincaid, and all the rottenness they stand for will, be on trial."

CHAPTER 70

Billups drove Andy to the Schnitzelbank. "We both can use a drink."

After wading through demonstrators on the sidewalks outside the Schnitzelbank, they found seats at the bar. Some of the demonstrators were in the barroom and began haranguing Andy and Billups.

Kim admonished them. "You have the right to demonstrate on the public sidewalks outside. You may not do so on Schnitzelbank private property. You can enter the restaurant just like any other customer as long as you follow our rules. If you don't, I'll throw you out."

Kim poured drinks for Andy and Billups.

Andy said, "Kim, I loved your comment in the paper yesterday about the protestors driving record sales."

Kim laughed. "Wish I wouldn't have said it. It's gotten worse. Today, the restaurant and our catering business are overwhelmed. We've had to turn people away. If this keeps up, I'll have to draft you and Billups as bartenders."

"I can pour beers," said Andy, "and do the whiskey highballs. Billups'll do the fancy drinks."

"Billups is a redneck tea-partier who can't pour water over ice."

"How many times do I gotta tell you guys that I can't get a red neck?"

"As many times as we call you a redneck," said Kim.

Billups said, "I was right about Kincaid all along. You liberals wouldn't listen because you think you're smarter than everybody else."

Kim retorted, "We also have eyesight. I see one helluva lot of conservatives out there on the barricades."

"Well, I'm a smart conservative."

"'Smart conservative' is an oxymoron."

Andy smiled. The other bartenders and some of the patrons around the bar laughed at this exchange. Those in agreement with Billups also laughed after they saw him smiling and the knuckle bump between him and Kim. "Good dig, Kim. I hand it out, and I know that them what hands it out gotta be ready to take it back."

Kim leaned in between Billups and Andy. "Some in here don't think all this is funny. They're not laughing."

Andy said, "Fuck 'em if they can't take a joke."

The door opened and Pamela Hearst entered. She joined Andy and Billups. "Thought I'd find you two here." She ordered a double vodka on the rocks and downed a third of it.

Andy said, "Thanks, Pam, for sticking us with Trocksley."

"I had no choice."

"How's that?"

"I got phone calls in the middle of the night warning me away from the case."

"From whom?"

"They wouldn't give their names."

"What did they say?"

Pam looked down at her drink, and then gulped another third of it.

"Pam, what's wrong?"

"They threatened my two children. They told me where they attended school and even gave me the names of their teachers."

Andy said, "Did you report it to the po… Oh Jesus!"

Andy ran to the parking lot and called Clubby. "I just heard that the Foundation is threatening families. We—"

"It's under control, Andy," said Clubby. "Mom and Dad got several anonymous calls. I've moved them, as well as Shelly and Terri's families, into my house. It's crowded but we're having fun. I've placed motion detectors, cameras, and floodlights around the house."

"What about—"

"We got the guns out and we have plenty of ammunition. Whoever these people are, they'll stop at nothing. You're bound to be on their kill list. Grab Remington and get over here where we can protect you. I've hired a friend of mine—a former cop—to be your bodyguard when you're at work."

Andy's panic over the safety of his family receded. "They won't harm me. I'm too visible."

"So were Rhonda and Marian Kincaid."

"I'll think it over."

"Goddamn it, Andy, there's nothing to think over. Get your ass over here!"

"Thanks, Al." Andy terminated the call.

CHAPTER 71

Dubain Courier Journal & Online News

Editor's note: This is the second of three articles researched and written by Rhonda O'Malley a week before she and Indiana First Lady, Marian Kincaid, were killed in a vehicle explosion. We stand by the article's authenticity and accuracy.

To understand the Foundation and Lincoln Kincaid, one must understand their mantra, the Jesus Equation. This is no mean feat. In words it is "X equals Jesus plus Zero." At first glance, it is the stuff of crackpots. The "Plus Zero" to a mathematician means nothing. After all, anything plus zero equals that anything. $2 + 0 = 2$. So why is it there? The Jesus Equation comes into focus only when the Foundation's mindset is factored in. The "plus Zero" strips Jesus of the Gospels and exposes Him to "X." The equation then becomes "X = Jesus." What is "X?" Some call it a "covenant" among a small group of people to achieve greatness. This is one of the labels favored by Earl Thompson, the executive director of the Foundation.

The Equation is not about math and numbers. It is about the Foundation's self-serving theology. Perhaps the best analysis of its meaning is to focus not so much on what is in the Equation, but what is not— God and the Holy Spirit, the other two of the Christian Trinity. The Foundation eliminates these. This is no accident and the Foundation proves so when it says that they are not Christians like everybody else. The mere term, *Christian*, they hold, is too narrow for them. Instead, they place themselves above Christians by calling themselves *followers of Christ*.

On the one hand, *Christians* believe that Christianity is spawned by a heritage of thousands of years of history, scores of hard lessons, and the teachings of Jesus in his Sermon on the Mount, all of which are in the Bible. On the other hand, *followers of Christ* believe that the biblical heritage taken as a whole is messy, time consuming, and a nuisance. Their focus is on the future, in which lays the Kingdom of Jesus, and so they escape the biblical heritage of Christianity by simply eliminating it. This is where the real work of the Jesus Equation starts. Using "X" as a variable, the Foundation bastardizes Jesus into Dark Jesuses, as many and with such powers as it needs or wants. None of the Foundation's Dark Jesuses was born to a virgin in Bethlehem two thousand plus years ago, none was crucified and rose from the dead, none made water into wine and multiplied the loaves and the fishes, and none presents to the world anything that is good, decent, or redeemable.

The Foundation's Dark Jesuses are many and powerful. There is a Dark Jesus of a New Order who demands a worldwide Kingdom of Jesus and tasks the Foundation with its attainment and then leadership. There is a Dark Jesus of The Foundation. This Jesus is about power, obedience, and judgment, and not love, gentleness, and forgiveness. There is a Dark Jesus Who Hates Homosexuals. The Dark Jesus of Women relegates females to second-class status where they are expected to produce babies and tasked to cook, clean, and serve men. There is a Dark Jesus of Cash Only to the exclusion of checks, credit cards, and bank accounts, the better to evade paper trails of money laundering, bribery, fraud, and hucksterism.

The Foundation knows, of course, that it cannot attain the world kingdom in one roll, and so their first victim is the United States of America. Makes sense. If you win America you win America's economy and its Military Industrial Complex. You then use the economy to blackmail and bribe weaker nations, and America's military to gain your first conquests—read Mexico, Canada, and South America. Then you move on from there. However, Americans say, it can't happen here. They are wrong. It can and it is.

Today, the Foundation is on the cusp of electing as president its stealth candidate, Lincoln Kincaid. Like Hitler, they will use democracy to get into power, and then destroy it to stay in power.

CHAPTER 72

Andy left the Schnitzelbank and drove home. He worked his way through the police cordon that kept protestors fifty feet from his house, parked on the street, and waved at the officers as he stepped onto his front porch. When he opened the door, he smelled cooking. He walked to the kitchen and stopped. There stood a woman, her back to him, stirring the contents of a cooking pot. She was dressed in Rhonda's favorite casual skirt and white blouse, and even her dark hair looked like Rhonda's.

Andy said, "Hello."

She turned around and smiled. She wore Rhonda's makeup, dark red lipstick, and bracelets, and sipped from a glass of Rhonda's favorite wine.

"The doors were locked," said Andy. "How did you get in?"

"I parked behind the empty Wood Products factory building and walked through the woods to your back door. Then I picked the lock," Polly said.

"You've been on the third floor."

"Yes. These are Rhonda's clothes. I hope you don't mind."

"If I do?"

"I would return them to the third floor and leave."

Andy turned toward the steps to his bedroom. He stopped and turned back to Polly. "What are you cooking?"

"Lentils with kidney beans."

"Smells good. Do you cook often?"

"Yes, beginning about six months ago. I have to feed my Angels."

"Please pour a glass of wine for me."

They ate supper at the kitchen table. Polly sat in Rhonda's chair. Normally, Andy disliked the beans, but Polly had cooked them in a special way that he found quite tasteful. Andy asked for seconds, and then thirds. "This is very good, Polly."

She blushed at the compliment.

Andy said, "It's given me an appetite, the first since..."

"You don't have to say it, Andy."

"Thank you. It's... it's very hard."

Polly reached across and folded her hands over Andy's. "I'm sorry you lost her. You know grief. I'm just learning it."

"Are you sure you want to?"

"You have life, Andy. I want life. I want to feel its pleasures, and pains, and everything in between. Rhonda and Marian lifted me onto life's road and helped me navigate it. They expected nothing in return. They were my first real friends."

They finished eating, cleared the table, and washed and dried the dishes side by side in silence.

***

Someone shook Andy awake. He rolled over. It was Polly, clad in a long beige nightshirt and black panties.

"Can I sleep with you?"

"No."

"Andy, I just don't want to be alone. That's all."

He moved over so she could slip in beside him. They fell asleep with their backs to each other.

Polly woke before Andy. During the night, Andy had rolled over. She felt his body spooning against her back, his right arm encircling her just below her breasts, and his morning erection pressing against her buttocks. She remained still. She wanted to.

CHAPTER 73

Andy picked up the phone. "You and Billups in my chambers," ordered Judge Townsend.

The judge's secretary led them to his office. There sat Jacob Trocksley III, looking like he was about to vomit. The judge directed Andy and Billups to chairs.

Judge Townsend started, "Mr. Trocksley informs me that he has offered Kurt Borgmann full immunity in return for his testimony against Lincoln Kincaid and others. Borgmann has accepted the immunity." He let that sink in. Then, "Jacob has something else to say."

"I've reviewed the deposition that Borgmann gave us. He confirmed the stories of Shalih and Ramirez."

Andy asked, "Do you still believe Borgmann's statement that Kincaid was not involved in the murders?"

"Absolutely. Borgmann said that Garrett Jennings, Kincaid's campaign manager, issued the kill orders."

"Jacob," said Andy, "I'm proud of you for figuring all this out. After all, it was right there in front of you the entire time."

"Andy," said Judge Townsend, "let's hold back the sarcasm. This is not an easy moment for Jacob."

"Um... Judge, he'd rather be addressed as 'Mr. Trocksley.'"

Billups cut in. "Andy, zip it."

"So why are we here?" Andy asked.

Trocksley continued, "I have no evidence that refutes Borgmann's testimony. I have no choice but to dismiss with prejudice all charges against Jameel Shalih and Jayden Ramirez."

***

Andy was surprised to find reporters waiting for them on the courthouse steps. He made a short statement and answered a few questions. Then he turned to watch Jacob III's discomfort at the questions directed to him. However, Andy noticed, Trocksley made it a point to play up Borgmann's role.

Afterward, Andy asked Trocksley if he'd alerted the media.

"Certainly not."

"However," said Andy, "the word on Borgmann is now out there and he's not protected."

"I already told you that we're working on that."

"Yeah... you're working on that."

"What are you driving at?"

"We have Borgmann's sworn testimony. Yet, I can't help but think that your job gets much easier if Borgmann just... well, disappears."

"My father was right, Balbach. He—"

"Jacob, please address me as 'Mr. Balbach.'"

"My father said that you really deserved an 'F' on the thesis, but he passed you so you could graduate."

"Really? What's his favorite Scotch? I'll send him a liter in gratitude for his kindness."

Trocksley turned and walked away.

Andy and Billups met with their clients and escorted them from the Dubain Security Center.

CHAPTER 74

Dubain Courier Journal & Online News

Editor's note: This is the last of three articles researched and written by Rhonda O'Malley a week before she and Indiana First Lady Marian Kincaid were killed in a vehicle explosion. We stand by the article's authenticity and accuracy.

The social contract is between government and its people. It's all the laws, rules, regulations, and actions of government of, for, and on behalf of the people. The social contract undergoes constant change, shifting according to the political persuasions of those in power at a given time.

Sarah Harding's social contract is not pretty. It favors the wealthy and powerful over the weak and vulnerable. It passed massive income tax breaks to the wealthy, raised the taxes of the middle and working classes, and cut school, health, college, and environmental programs. It is running enormous deficits and thus growing the national debt toward the breaking point. It loves all things military. It has

funded expensive weapons systems that the Pentagon itself says it has no use for. It takes away the vote and steals
elections. It creates fear of terrorism, immigrants, and smart
and educated people. It increasingly rewards those who
cheat, lie, and steal.

What is the social contract planned by Kincaid and the
Foundation? We need only look to their "Manifesto," a
highly secret document that maps out their plans for America and beyond. It is an eight-year plan based on the supposition of at least two terms for Lincoln Kincaid. The social
contract embedded within is ghastly. Let us live it.

Kincaid and the Foundation are in power. They tear up the
Constitution and hold a convention of the states to draft a
new constitution that is more amenable to "modern times."
The president has dictatorial powers while Congress and
the courts are rubber stamps. There is no bill of rights. You
have no freedom of speech, freedom of the press, or freedom
to hang out with whomever you choose. There is no due
process of law or equal protection under the law. Gone are
the rights to remain silent, effective assistance of counsel,
confront witnesses, and trial by jury. You vote, but only for
the government's candidates. The overriding theme of national defense is pounded into you by the government-con-
trolled press. They invent crises—whether of terrorism or
from a foreign country—that frighten you because you cannot know the truth. The president has channeled your fright
into a New Patriot Act. If you had any rights before the new
Act, you have none after it. The government chooses your
enemies. National defense is national hysteria.

Beware the knock on your door in the middle of the night.
They have come for you, or someone you love, or your
guns, or your books, or anything. You trust no one because
you can't—not your spouse, not your kids, not your in-
laws, not your neighbor, not your best friend—no one, be-

cause any of them could be a government informer. They persecute homosexuals, immigrants, African-Americans, and Jews, and force you to do the same.

They've outlawed abortion and many Americans applaud this. At last, they say, there is protection for the unborn. However, there is this uneasy feeling that Kincaid and the Foundation don't really give a damn for the unborn. They do give a damn about turning the unborn into babies so that sixteen or so years later they will have a steady supply of soldiers for their armies.

You still have your Facebook, Twitter, Instagram, Google Plus, YouTube, Snap Chat, and all other social media. You still have email, Hangouts, and Skype. You have all the amenities on the Internet that you have now, such as search engines and online banking. But meet your newest and best Internet friend, your government. You dare not post anything that smacks of criticizing the government.

They lie to you. They lie so often and with such sincerity that you may come to believe the lies even though you know they are lies. They target your children. The ABCs of education as you know them are long gone. The state determines your kids' lessons and how they're taught. There is no homework. Your children recite Christian prayers daily in their classrooms, and revel in the 'glorious history' of the United States without all the tittle-tattle of slavery, mistreatment of the Indians, segregation, the rise of crime, and corruption. Corporal punishment is back, and you know this because your kid comes home from school with welts on her butt and slap marks on his face.

The inalienable rights of life, liberty, and the pursuit of happiness are, indeed, alienable. You have no middle class security. You work at and love the job they give you. Your union is long gone. Your social security, 401(k), and Medicare ac-

counts have been appropriated by your government, probably to enter into more defense contracts—*read* more money
in the pockets of Foundationites. Your parents live with you.
You've read the president's decree outlawing guns for all but
military personnel. Some Americans rebel at this and they
take themselves and their guns and hide in the mountains.
The story dies in two days but you wonder what happened
to these folks and you dare not ask. Have faith. One day the
government, well into the cliché that a picture is worth thousands of words, releases pictures of them. Some hang by
their necks. Others lay on the ground with caved-in skulls.
Still others, held up by ropes tied to a post, are bullet-ridden.
Emblazoned on each photo is "Enemy of the State."

Meet your friendly neighborhood government.

You watch your sons and daughters begin military training
at age ten and you must show how proud you are. Then you
watch them march off to fight and die in wars instigated
by the sociopaths who run America. At first, the fighting is
close to home. Your government has conjured a giant conspiracy of Hispanic immigrants whose purpose is to foment
rebellion against the United States and win back US states
it lost in the Mexican-American War of 1846-7: California,
New Mexico, Arizona, Colorado, Nevada, Utah, Colorado,
and a few midwestern states for good measure. They manufacture "border incidents" and regale you with accusations
of terrorism via bombs, executions of American citizens,
and rapes, and they have their fine spanking war with Mexico. Right next door. Very convenient. Mexico surrenders.
Then you look north to Canada and below Mexico to South
America. After that, your guess is as good as anybody's but
your government's. You hear names of places like Middle
East, Russia, Great Britain, Europe, Australia, and so on.
Your soldier-kids stop writing you and you know they're
dead, but your government tells you otherwise.

This is the Foundation's Social Contract with America.

"Wait a darn minute!" you say. "What's left for me? They have their Jesus Equation and Dark Jesuses. They have America and its weapons. They are the new chosen. What do I have? God. I have God! Yeah! He's with me always. Told me Himself. I can put my faith in God. I have a soul because God exists. I have free will because I have a soul." Fine. You pray to God. You pray like hell that He brings back the America you once knew, one with a real Constitution and Bill of Rights, with courts to enforce them. You pray for the return of the freedom, the noise, the politics, and the damned politicians, the taxes, the exasperations, the crazy elections, all of it. You promise God that this time you'll stay informed and vote at every election.

However, God doesn't answer your prayers. You beseech him again and again, but He says nothing. Then the truth hits you. God no longer exists because the Foundation has turned him into a zero. You can't un-zero God because you lied to yourself when you said it can't happen here. You didn't think through the Jesus Equation and you and tens of millions of others fell for the bait and switch. It's too late to change the math.

For you, there is left only determinism, a fancier and longer word for fate, a state of existence into which your life is locked into the absolutes of predictability, manageability, manipulability, and malleability. It is a life void of romance, the rule of law, good and bad, sin and virtue, courage and cowardice, joy and sadness, fear and confidence, victory and defeat, morality and immorality, happiness and sadness, pain and pleasure, life and death, love and hate.

There is left for you only the commonality of all creatures—instinct and the primal impulse to survive.

There is left for you only a Zero God.

CHAPTER 75

Lincoln Kincaid had no way out.

Garrett and Lincoln had locked themselves in their suite at the French Lick Springs Hotel. Garrett overheard other guests in the hallway talking about the barricades the Indiana State Police had erected at every outside entrance. Instead of storming the suite, the police patiently waited, handcuffs at the ready, to arrest Lincoln when he emerged. But Garrett sensed that, at some point in the standoff, the police would lose their patience and arrest Lincoln in the suite. There would be a knock on the door, a demand to open it, and then a charge through it. No doubt, the police knew that Garrett owned a Smith & Wesson .45 and held a license to carry it.

Garrett switched back and forth between CNN and Fox News, both of which were broadcasting live from the front of the hotel. The cameras scanned a bedlam of reporters, news cameras, demonstrators, and the just plain curious. Everybody, it seemed, craved a piece of Lincoln Kincaid. Most could sate their curiosity with a mere glimpse of him. Others would not be so generous.

As though proving Garrett's point, Fox shifted to a live interview of Special Prosecutor Jacob Trocksley III on the Dubain County Courthouse steps. "...dismissed all charges against Jayden Ramirez and Jameel Shalih based on the sworn testimony of Kurt Borgmann. Borgmann turned state's evidence against Governor Lincoln Kincaid. Kincaid faces multiple counts of rape and two counts of conspiracy to murder Jameel Shalih and Jayden Ramirez."

Ironic, Garrett thought, that Trocksley had taken the assignment to protect Kincaid by convicting Shalih and Ramirez of murder, only to have the gods of justice turn on him. Now, he could look forward to prosecuting Lincoln Kincaid on the testimonies of Borgmann, Shalih, and Ramirez.

Garrett glanced at Lincoln and identified the undercurrents of shock and denial, the personal defenses Lincoln had erected to shut out the reality that his life was over. At some point, the defenses would crumble. Garrett would protect Lincoln for as long as he could. There was no other option, save one, after that.

Then, CNN announced that they were joining General David Hernandez, who was making a statement. "...to investigate the goings-on at Tigris River... under the command of Captain Lincoln Kincaid. Prisoners of war and American servicepersons, men and women, were repeatedly overpowered and raped. Captain Lincoln Kincaid participated in the rapes. The report I submitted includes this. The army revised the report to clear Kincaid of all charges. I have released copies of the report I submitted. Mine is the truth. The army's is not."

Garrett muted the TV and Lincoln leaned forward. He said, "It all started in my parents' kitchen. I was eighteen. We bought in because it sounded so wonderful, and for so many years it was. Most assume that it began coming apart in that interview with Rhonda O'Malley. In truth, it had already started months before, when the illusions that protected me turned against me. I realized that the Foundation wanted to use me for their own agenda and would blackmail me into supporting it.

"That kitchen had long gone, Garrett. Sometimes I wondered whether it really happened. I hold no grudge against Rhonda. Maybe it was meant to be.

"I loved Marian but I... wasn't always good to her and the kids. She told my mother that I was a sociopath. But I'm not. I'm not a sociopath. Do you think I am?"

"No, Lincoln. You are a good man with a conscience. Marian probably made the statement when she was angry."

"Well, according to my mother, she was. Then there's Polly. My parents threw her out as an infant, but I just know she blames me for it. I... did something... horrible to her at a Young Life Camp.

"I talked to Ponya again and again. He assured me that those in the safe zone were, indeed, safe. He seduced me but I was willing. I ignored his history of atrocities. I tried to stop him but it was too late. So many innocents... and I gave him the weapons to do it!

"Apologies. I have many. It's the best I can do."

"Lincoln, get your mind around this—others forced their dark aspirations on you. It backfired on them. Take satisfaction in that."

"There is little pleasure for me in others' misfortune."

Lincoln's protection zone was fading. Garrett would push him back into it. "I've made inquiries, Lincoln."

"Oh?"

"Actually, more than inquiries. I purchased a cabin and some acreage in the Idaho wilderness under an alias. We'll live out the rest of our lives there. Just you and me. Nobody will arrest you, and you won't face trial or prison. I've contacted friends who will smuggle us there. It'll be our private hideaway until the statutes of limitation have run on the crimes you're accused of."

"But I am guilty of those crimes! Should I not pay the price?"

"Many are guilty, Lincoln, and most of them will pay nothing."

Lincoln lowered his head for a few moments. "Do good people know they're good? Do bad people know they're bad?"

"These things are left to God."

"Thank God!"

They laughed.

"Are you serious, Garrett? I mean about Idaho?"

"Of course."

"When do we leave?"

"Soon. Maybe a few days."

"How do we get past the police at the entrances?"

"Where did you hear that?"

"I didn't. C'mon Garrett. I'm smart enough to know that the police aren't dumb enough to let me escape this hotel."

"There is an underground passage from here to the West Baden Springs. I read about it in a book I found in the historical section of the French Lick Public Library. The book was old, yellowed, and tattered, the kind that hadn't been opened in a long time. At the time, Indiana had outlawed gambling of any kind, but the hotel had other ideas. The owners dug the tunnel in the 1920s so gamblers could flee from police raids. It starts in the lowest level cellar here and ends in a cellar there. I found the entrance a month or so ago. It's been bricked shut but some have loosened. It'll be easy to knock out a few and wiggle through."

"But wouldn't the cops block the entrance here and exit there?"

"Only if they know about them and they don't. They sealed the entrance in 1958. That's three generations of cops ago. I doubt whether this generation has ever heard of it."

Lincoln said, "It's a risk but it sounds doable."

Lincoln had bought into all of it. Garrett loved Lincoln, and for that he would spare him the truth and carry the dread alone.

"Let's take a shower together, Lincoln."

They emerged from the shower, dried each other with towels, and then went to the bedroom. Lincoln said, "There's something I have to know, Garrett. I love you. Do... do you love me?"

"Yes, Lincoln, I love you."

"I had to hear you say it."

"We found each other, Lincoln."

They kissed.

"There's so much I want to do, so many things I want to experience—ride horses, fish, plant a garden, hike, camp, explore, add to our cabin… learn how to fly an airplane."

Lincoln's sincerity touched Garrett. They made love and then lay in each other's arms. Right before falling asleep, Lincoln said, "I'm almost free. Help me, Garrett. Help me get free all the way."

"I will, Lincoln. Sleep now."

Garrett buried his fear. It was the best he could do for the man he loved.

***

Garrett awoke and, for a minute, it was as if none of it had happened. However, pleasant dreams while asleep do not match reality while awake. The lawyer in him thought it through. There were two governments and two sets of laws—the State of Indiana and the United States of America. Indiana prosecutes those who violate Indiana law. The USA prosecutes those who violate federal law. Garrett had broken federal, but not Indiana laws. Lincoln had violated both. No doubt, the USA had already seated grand juries to indict both Lincoln and Garrett.

However, Earl Thompson had violated a host of federal laws—bribery, foreign corrupt business practices, tax fraud, racketeering, wire fraud, money laundering, and more. Would the USA also indict Earl Thompson? It would, if there was sufficient evidence and the motivation to go forward. Rhonda's articles and research, along with Borgmann's confessions would deliver the evidence. The high profile of Earl Thompson and his Foundation and all its 'works' afforded the motivation. Earl would not be able to avail himself of the Foundation's legal cover. Garrett would see to that.

In any event, Earl Thompson's murderous ways had not ended. However, this time, Earl—and not Garrett—would give the orders.

CHAPTER 76

It was overcast and there was no moon. Jameel, on the passenger side of the pickup truck, looked over to Jayden Ramirez, who was driving, and then checked the rowboat on the bed of the truck. They'd stolen both.

"Jayden, let's not do this."

"I already told you a dozen times I'm gonna get that sonofabitch Borgmann. I'd murder Kincaid, too, if I had the chance."

"Jayden, Borgmann will get his no matter what we do."

"No, he won't! Get that through your head, Jameel. Borgmann will testify with immunity. That means they can't touch him as long as he testifies. Then he'll go into witness protection. They'll set him up down south, near the ocean, probably on a beach. He'll eat the best food, drink the best booze, and fuck the best boys. All of it on the government's ticket."

"And we'll be punching a cash register for minimum wage in the Bumfuck Egypt Kinko Ginko Convenience Store."

"Sometimes things just work out that way."

"Not this time."

"We're free and out of jail. I wanna keep it that way."

Ramirez had no reply. Jameel saw he'd get nowhere with him. Jayden had planned Borgmann's murder in detail. He said he'd gotten the idea from Polly and that Christiansen kid in Vegas when they'd killed Todrank—make it slow and make him suffer. First the knee caps and then the shoulders. Make him bleed and suffer. Then shots through his hands and a knife in his thigh. Make him beg for his life. Finish him off with a bullet to the head but make sure he knows it's coming.

Jayden turned onto an old logging road that ended near the water. They unloaded the boat, rowed across South Lick Fork, and landed directly below the Borgmann home. It was brightly lit, both inside and out. They donned black ski masks, made their way to the terrace, and reached the sliding door. It was open. Ramirez entered the home, but Jameel hung back.

"Never took you for a chicken shit, Shalih."

"Never took you for a murderer, Jayden."

Jayden entered the home. Jameel watched him disappear down the hallway. Jayden returned a minute later. He was angry.

"Somebody beat us to it."

"To what?"

"What the fuck do you think?"

"Is he dead?"

"You bet your sweet ass he's dead."

"I want to see him."

This time they entered the home together. The only sound came from a television in the bedroom. Kurt Borgmann lay on his back, his eyes wide open and staring at the ceiling. There was a gun in his hand and congealed blood around him. The back of his skull was spread over the pillow and the wall behind the bed.

Jayden whispered, "Nobody beat us. He killed himself."

Ramirez rolled his eyes at Jayden.

They pushed the boat into the water, jumped in, and rowed back across the lake. There they loaded the boat and were soon on the highway to Dubain.

Jayden pounded on the steering wheel. "Goddamn it, this is the second time I got there too late. Somebody killed him before I could!"

Jameel looked at Jayden. "It was a suicide. He killed himself."

"What fuckin' planet you live on, Jameel? It was staged."

"How do you know?"

"I just do."

"Then who?"

Jameel said, "Probably the Foundation. Borgmann dead means no Borgmann to testify against Kincaid."

"That leaves only us."

"Yeah, it does."

"Maybe somebody will kill Kincaid."

"That's wishful thinking."

CHAPTER 77

Rose and the Archangels threw open the door of 7-12, surged into the room with their weapons drawn, and stopped. They saw, not Angels, but an old priest on a stool reading a book, swathed in unnaturally bright light.

He looked up and smiled. "Hello. My name is Father Paul. Can I help you?"

Rose asked, "Is this the place the Angels call 7-12?"

"Yes."

"Where are the Angels?"

"They are not here."

"Will they return?"

"It is their home."

***

It was early morning. Andy parked the Coachman RV on the street in front of his house. The Angels had spent the night there after fleeing 7-12. Andy had been reading a book in bed when Polly called.

"Imogene Thompson called me a few minutes ago. She'd overheard a phone conversation between Earl Thompson and Rose Cardova. Earl said he'd received information from the Foundation's spy inside the Angels that we were hiding under St. Augustine Cathedral. We have to vacate 7-12 right now. Can we spend the night at your house?"

Andy couldn't say no.

Polly greeted him on his front porch. But this was the old Polly, she of the blank smile and no-inflection voice whom he'd met on the Riverwalk in February.

Polly said, "We're prepared to leave."

"Have you identified the spy?"

"I'm narrowing it down. I'll have it before we get there."

"Are you taking your weapons?"

"Yes."

"Do you plan to use them?"

"I hope we don't have to."

"Polly, you can't use them. You must stay on the side of the law, even though your father has not. Promise me this."

"The most I can promise is that we will use the weapons only for self-defense. That's lawful, is it not?"

"Only if you have no other reasonable means of protecting yourself."

Polly led Andy into his house. The Angels' quizzical eyes shifted to Andy for a moment, and then back to Polly. They had also detected her regression.

Two Angels carried the leftovers from the large batch of spaghetti Andy had cooked during the night.

The Angels filled the Coachman and left.

***

Andy hit the answer phone button on his steering wheel. It was Bernardo.

"Andy, Paul left the rectory last night but hasn't returned. I'm worried."

Andy told Bernardo to call Stump and meet at Al's house.

Andy then called his brother. "Al, there's an emergency. The Archangels are probably holding Father Paul in 7-12."

"Who the hell are the Archangels and what the hell is 7-12?"

"I'll explain when I get there."

CHAPTER 78

Garrett took the call from Earl Thompson in the bedroom with the door closed.

"What do you want?"

"I'm in the boardroom with the directors. They've just voted to expel Lincoln Kincaid from the Foundation and to no longer support him for office."

"Gee, what a shock."

"No need for sarcasm."

"Cut through the crap, Earl. I'll ask again—what do you want?"

"I think you already know."

"Damn," said Garrett. "I was right all along."

"What?"

"I was born in the dark, Earl Thompson, but I wasn't born last night. You planned all this long ago."

"Garrett, listen to me."

"Why did you allow Rhonda O'Malley to interview Lincoln?"

"I don't understand—"

"Don't give me the 'I don't understand' bullshit, Earl. You heard me. We were aware that O'Malley had been investigating Lincoln and the Foundation for months. I monitored her as you ordered and told you that she had a source inside the Foundation who was feeding her the goods on Lincoln Kincaid. You laughed at me. Then you sent him to O'Malley on national television and she nailed him, just as you'd intended."

"That's nonsense."

"That's truth, you conniving bastard. You started your endgame with that interview. You knew Lincoln was gay. You knew his family life was a facade. You saw that Lincoln Kincaid's activities at Tigris River and Camp Morgan would blow up on him, and then you. But you needed help, so you dug a little deeper and found me. You knew I was gay before you hired me. You knew the treatments wouldn't work. You knew about Lincoln and me. You brought me into the Foundation and used me as the vessel to Lincoln's destruction. You played me, Earl."

"Nobody will believe—"

"You couldn't allow Lincoln to withdraw from the race in dignity. No, that would have made you look bad because your old man, and then you, had laid your hands on him. Instead, you folded your hands in false prayer to your false Jesus and gave Lincoln enough rope to hang himself. He did, and so the failure was on him and not you, or your father, or that old bastard Benjamin Kincaid."

"Garrett, there's not much time—"

"Go to hell, Earl Thompson. You knew I was close to sniffing out your true intentions regarding Lincoln. You feared what I might do. You published the false Marian Kincaid Autobiography and feared what she might do. Instead, you murdered her and hinted at the sympathy factor to me. But the sympathy for Lincoln would not survive the truth of Lincoln. You murdered her, not for sympathy, but to shut her up and throw me off the scent. It worked with Marian Kincaid. It didn't fool me.

"Rhonda O'Malley's demise with Marian was just icing on the cake. It saved you the trouble of planning and executing her murder. But she fooled you. She'd already written the articles and her friends published them."

"Garrett, you must protect the Kingdom of Jesus!"

"To hell with your fucking kingdom! It doesn't exist and never will. Polly escaped you. If I had her courage, Lincoln and I wouldn't be holed up in this hotel surrounded by police and media."

"The Foundation gave much to Lincoln Kincaid."

"That's laughable. You didn't give, you stole—wife, children, youth, self-respect, freedom, everything that makes life worth living."

"I'm not afraid of a couple of queers."

"You'd better be afraid of this one."

"Garrett, I have to know. Will you—"

"How many?"

"What?"

"Do you have more Lincoln Kincaids in the pipeline? You're too smart to put all your Foundation eggs in one Kincaid basket. You have more on the way. How many farmhouse kitchens have you visited in the past twenty years, Earl?"

"I'm sure I don't know what you're talking about."

"I'm sure you do. So I'll just take your answer as a 'yes.'"

"Garrett, let's get back to the subject at hand."

"You tipped them off."

"Them?"

"The police and the media. They assumed Lincoln was with his children in seclusion until you told them he was holed up in this hotel with me."

"I deny that."

"Of course you deny it, Earl. It's what you do. Deny, deny, deny. You have to apologize and order me."

"What?"

"Say you're sorry and order me to do it."

"What are you driving at?"

"I have to hand it to you, Earl. You're good. The smartest sociopath I know. But your life is barren. You've lost all your family and most of your friends. In time, you'll lose everything. Why? Because you have no vision beyond money and power, Earl. You feel nothing for anyone, but you're damn good at acting otherwise."

"Garrett, I admit that I haven't always been honest with you. I apologize for that and the 'queers' remark."

"Your apology warms my heart. But that's only the first half. Ordering me is the second."

"Garrett, we're counting on—"

"Order me."

"You know what you have to do."

"I will do nothing unless you order me to do it."

"Okay, I will. I order you to handle the situation."

"That doesn't cut it. Maybe I can help. I'll state the order and you say either yes or no."

The phone went silent for several seconds. Then, "Begin your statement."

"Are you, Earl Thompson, ordering me, Garrett Jennings, to carry out a mission?"

"Yes."

"And that mission is to never allow Lincoln Kincaid to leave this room alive?"

"Yes."

"Lincoln must die?"

"It's the best for—"

"Answer yes or no."

"Yes."

"And you order me to kill him."

"Whatever," said Earl.

"Excuse me?"

"Yes. I order you to kill him."

"Who?"

"Lincoln Kincaid."

"There you go, Earl. Wasn't so hard now, was it? Here's my response—I'll think about it. However, if I do, I'll do it for him, not for the Foundation, not for the board, and certainly not for you. And, by the way, Earl Thompson…"

"By the way… what?"

"Go fuck yourself."

Garrett mumbled a prayer of thanks to Saint Rita, and then slipped the flash drive back onto the scapula. He had recorded the entire conversation.

CHAPTER 79

They hid the RV in Stratford Park amidst the darkness and heavy rain. Polly, Chartreuse, and Malachi got out. Polly ordered the rest to remain in the RV until they received a phone call from her.

The three marched abreast toward the loading dock. Chartreuse flanked Polly on the right, and Malachi on the left. They stopped thirty feet from the dock and waited. The doors to the building opened. Five Archangels walked to them, their automatic weapons pointed at the three Angels. Their leader, known to Polly only as 'Alpha,' spoke.

"We've been expecting you."

"Of course you have," said Polly. "Oakenwald is our home. We return in peace and goodwill. As you can see, we're unarmed."

Alpha said, "Pardon me if I don't take your word for it." He ordered an Archangel to handcuff Polly and Malachi, and then search them. He reported no weapons, went back to his place in the line, and raised his automatic rifle.

Polly asked, "I suppose your spy, Alpha, is the one of we three who is not handcuffed?"

Alpha nodded at Chartreuse. She went to his side and he handed a gun to her.

Polly said, "Chartreuse, we trusted you with our lives. You trusted us with yours. What happened?"

Chartreuse said, "You abandoned your father, a great man. You abandoned the Foundation and all it had done for you. You cast away the glory and promise of the kingdom. You ingested the poison of doubt over a harmless earthquake and a couple of deer. Then you force-fed the poison to the rest of us. You halved our mission when you terminated a covenant and concocted another. You had no authority to do either. Your 'new' Jesus is disgusting, worse than your disobedience and selfishness."

"I admit to disobedience, but… selfishness?"

"It was always about you, Polly, and no one else. You got your way, always bossing me. 'Do this, Chartreuse, do that, Chartreuse.' In the end, you failed. You are pathetic, Polly."

"The pathos is yours, Chartreuse. You delivered us as they asked. They have no more use for you, and they won't forget that you twice changed sides. They intend to kill us. They will kill you, too."

"Chartreuse," said Alpha, "Polly is lost in her illusions. You are safe with us."

Polly asked, "What now?"

"Your father and the board are waiting. We will march both of you in front of them and they'll pass judgment."

"Malachi was only following my orders. Let him go."

Alpha said, "He waged war against the Foundation, thereby committing treason. Just like you, Polly, just like all your Angels, excluding Chartreuse."

"Your Angels," said Chartreuse, "will not receive the phone call you promised. They're either dead or about to be."

Polly deadpanned. "There's no need for a phone call. You fell for it." She nodded left and right.

There was a poosch sound and an Archangel lost half his head. Chartreuse dove to the ground where Malachi kicked her in the stomach. Alpha turned, and in a crouching run headed toward the entrance. Angels appeared from every direction. Ramirez made it to the door and prevented Alpha from closing and locking it. He, Malachi, and other Angels rushed inside. Someone hit the emergency siren. There was a flurry of gunshots and screams from inside Oakenwald Hall. Then the shooting stopped. One of the Angels unlocked Polly's handcuffs.

Polly entered. She saw two Archangels in pools of blood. One Angel, entangled with the body of an Archangel, lay dead. It was Malachi.

Four Angels joined her. Ramirez kicked in the door of the boardroom and announced, "Archangels."

CHAPTER 80

Earl Thompson hung up the phone and turned to the board. "Garrett and Lincoln have no way out. I believe Garrett will do the job."

The security siren pierced the air. There was muffled shooting and human cries. Earl flipped a switch and the siren stopped. The door to the boardroom burst open but nobody appeared. Someone yelled 'Archangels' and announced that they were coming in.

Earl smiled. "We're safe."

However, Angels, not Archangels, entered. They carried automatic weapons and filled the room.

Earl ordered, "Put down those weapons."

None of the Angels spoke or moved.

"I'm calling security." He picked up the phone. "We've been taken captive in the boardroom." Earl waited. "Hello? Anybody? Alpha, are you there?"

Polly entered. Behind her were Chartreuse, Alpha, and two other Archangels, all bound, gagged, and chained together. "I believe these are the people you're looking for, Father. All the others are in 7-12, waiting for us to walk into their trap."

"I order you to remove yourself and your... your henchmen from this room."

"Your orders mean nothing. One, they're Angels, not henchmen. Two, you double-crossed them with a spy. Three, you killed Johnnie and now Malachi, their friends. Four, they have guns and you do not."

Polly directed the Angels to stand the board members against the back wall of the boardroom. "Pat them down for weapons."

Benjamin Kincaid protested that he was ninety-two years old and could not stand for any length of time.

"Then sit on the floor, you fool."

"Stop this, Polly. Stop it now. I am your father."

"You're not her father!" In walked Imogene. "You've never been her father. You've never been my husband."

"I've never feared a drunk."

"You should have feared this one."

Polly saw that Imogene had unnerved her estranged husband.

Earl sputtered, "The Kingdom of Jesus and... you're part of it. Lincoln Kincaid... let us down."

Imogene said, "Those words—'kingdom' and 'Jesus'—are venom from your mouth. This was never about a kingdom or Jesus. It was about ever more money and power for you and your friends. You succeeded for a while, but in the end you have failed. In a way, I pity you, Earl. Your entire life's work is in ashes, and there is no rising from them.

"You're evening is full of surprises, Earl. Here's another. I played a part in destroying you."

"How? It was you, Imogene! You were Rhonda O'Malley's mole."

"Never suspected a drunk, did you? Big mistake, Earl."

Polly said, "Your kingdom is over. A new kingdom shall arise, and none of you," Polly swept her arm toward the board members, "will be part of it."

The switch of topics back to the kingdom resurrected her father's composure. "You're a foolish woman, Polly. Do you really believe that the kingdom belongs in that backward state of Indiana?"

Polly responded, "Backward? You've never been there, yet you pass judgment on it. Someone once said that the only knowledge worth having is what you gain after you already know everything. That someone was you. You forget—or never believed—what you preached."

"You know nothing about starting a new kingdom."

"Yes, Father, I do know. In that way, I'm something like you."

The Angels buried the dead in the woods and imprisoned Earl, the board members, the remaining Archangels, and Chartreuse in the Fallout Shelter.

CHAPTER 81

An old, banged-up van, hand-painted black, turned onto South Newton Street and headed north toward St. Augustine Cathedral. It slowed at the cathedral and signaled right onto Orchard Lane, heading east and away from the cathedral. It turned around in Andy Balbach's driveway, pulled several feet forward, and then stopped. No one entered or exited either the house or van. Five minutes later, the van drove west on Orchard Lane toward the cathedral but stopped a block away from it. Two persons with scoped, high-powered rifles left the van. One headed toward the neighborhood south of the cathedral, and the other headed to Kundek Cemetery north of the cathedral. The van then circled around the streets of Dubain and eventually turned onto the street that bordered the north side of Kundek Cemetery. It parked at the gate. The engine shut down. No one exited.

***

Andy left Clubby's house and sped to his own. He ran into the house, loaded Remington with five shells, and chambered one. He donned a raincoat and then drove to within two blocks of the cathedral. By now it was dark and raining heavily. Andy found his way to the bottom of the steeple and hid behind the bushes.

He'd taken on the mission of rescuing Father Paul and avoiding the risk of losing another brother, Clubby.

He'd argued with Clubby against activating the Dubain SWAT team. "There's only one escape from 7-12. It's a passage that starts at the bottom of the steeple and ends at 7-12."

"Yeah, right," Clubby had replied. "These people have automatic weapons and they're holding Father Paul hostage. They're highly trained, nasty, and deadly. Do you expect them to free Paul, lay down their weapons, walk to the officers, and announce, 'You have a beautiful town and cathedral and please arrest us, thank you very much?' No, they'll come out shooting. I'm sure they have lookouts hidden in the grounds around the church. Probably a sniper or two."

"No, Al. These people think we're small-town country yokels. There'll be only one guard hidden near the entrance."

"Can you guarantee that?"

"No."

"Didn't think so. We have to trap them in this whatchamacallit 7-12. A shootout in the passageway will get people killed. If we engage them at the entrance, they'll pin us down with automatic fire and not give a hoot-in-hell about their bullets killin' innocent people."

Andy asserted, "If you and the team are going in, I'm going with you."

"Not a chance, brother. You're not trained, and you'll get yourself killed."

"No, I'll survive because I understand these people. You do not. You'll lead the team into hails of bullets, and you'll get yourself killed."

"You seem pretty sure of yourself, Andy. Where do you get this inspiration from?"

"From a place you'd never understand."

Andy worked his way to the southeast corner of the steeple and peered around it. His intuition, the piece of him that Al would never understand, was wrong. There was no Archangel lookout.

Then all the floodlights in the parking lot went dark. Andy turned the corner and entered the passageway. He stopped ten feet from the door to 7-12. He heard only mumbles of conversation.

Then he felt a blow on the back of his head.

His intuition had failed him.

***

Stump sat next to Bernardo. There were ten members of the team in the van, including Clubby, the team's leader and the van's driver. Bernardo would take responsibility for Father Paul after the team rescued him.

Stump worked his laptop computer. "I can't pull up the phone's location and the calls go directly into voicemail. Andy's cell phone is off."

Clubby vented his anger. "Goddamn it! Andy's gone ahead against my direct orders. He's fucking up the whole works. He'll end up a hostage with Paul. If the Archangels don't kill him, I will."

The other team members—five men and four women—said nothing. This was their first mission, and Stump saw through their bravado to their terror. Funny, he thought, that the Dubain SWAT team, like soldiers entering combat, had two sets of questions—those you ask aloud and those you dare not. The first were the type of 'What happens if?' 'What do we do when?' 'Who is the first one in?' 'Where is their lookout?' Clubby had answered the former when he briefed them on the mission in the Dubain Police Station. The rest gnawed at each member. 'Will I chicken out?' 'Have we trained enough?' 'Can we trust Clubby's judgment?' 'What if I'm wounded?' 'What if I'm killed?' 'Just how good are the Archangels?' 'Why should we risk our lives for a ninety-two-year-old priest who got his own ass in the Archangel sling?'

Clubby, still cussing his brother, parked at the north gate of Kundek Cemetery. The snipers reported seeing no one. Clubby and the remaining team put on Kevlar armor, helmets, and night-vision goggles. All carried automatic weapons, ranging in make from M-16s to Uzis. Each carried a pistol in a special holster designed for quick access. These were a mixture of Colt .45s and 9mm Glocks. One carried a Sig Sauer P220.

Stump watched them form the standard snake line with Clubby at the point. They passed the Balbach family plots and then disappeared into the rain and darkness. Stump entered commands on his computer. All the lights around the cathedral, including those on All Souls Point, went dark.

Stump turned to Bernardo. "I'm not in the mood to bury anybody, especially another Balbach. Say the best goddamn prayer you can think of."

CHAPTER 82

A glass of water rested on the floor beside Rose. Remington lay propped against the wall about ten feet away. Andy was in 7-12 on a chair. Rose Cardova and a male Archangel, Raphael, stood in front of him. Andy felt blood running down both sides of his head and face. His lips were swollen. One eye was blackened shut and the other saw mostly stars due to blows to his head. Two teeth lying on the floor explained the taste of blood in his mouth. However, the pain radiating from his broken left shin overrode all. Raphael held the baseball bat that, Andy was certain, would soon break his other leg or maybe his skull and neck, or maybe everything. There were plenty of bone targets in Andy's body.

Father Paul, unharmed, sat on another chair several feet from Andy and next to a table. Andy thought he saw a knife laying near Paul but couldn't be sure.

They'd tied Andy to his chair but had not bothered with Paul.

Rose repeatedly demanded, and Andy repeatedly denied, knowledge of the Angels' location. Rose promised to release both Paul and Andy when Andy talked. Andy had not talked. Thus the beatings. He played for time, certain that Rose would kill both him and Paul if he caved and that Clubby and his team were on their way. But when?

Rose repeated, "The Angels killed my husband. Where are they?"

Andy repeated, "You killed my wife."

Raphael delivered another blow to Andy's head. "Answer the question, Balbach."

It took a few seconds for Andy's open eye to focus on Raphael. "I don't know." He saw Rose nod at Raphael. Raphael raised the bat. Andy shut his eyes.

Paul interjected, "Stop! He doesn't know."

Raphael lowered the bat.

Andy managed to turn to Paul and subtly blink with his open eye. Paul blinked back. Andy saw his lips move. It looked like 'To'… something. To what?

Rose turned to Paul. "I'm sure he does know. He and Polly Thompson were screwing before his wife even died." Then she turned back to Andy. "Where is your lover, Polly?"

"Pro… Probably with… other Angels."

Raphael fisted him in the gut. Andy doubled over until he caught his breath.

"Rose Cardova," said Paul, "I know from personal experience that the Balbachs are tough folks. If Andy does know—and I'm sure he does not—he won't tell you."

"We'll see," said Rose, "we have all night."

"You don't. Andy and I are in here. Others know this and either are, or will be, out there." Paul nodded toward the door. "Get out while you still can."

"Why the rush? We," Rose pointed to Paul, and then Andy, "have hostages, and," she pointed at the automatic weapons, "have far superior firepower."

"I wouldn't bet on it."

Andy got it that Paul, too, was stalling. But for how long? Then Andy remembered the stories about Paul's 'sixth sense.' The only variable was time. Had Paul mouthed, *two minutes*? Andy had to go with it. One minute had passed. He'd have to stall for one more. He rolled his eye and dropped his head to feign unconsciousness. A glass of water splashed hard against his face. Andy moaned but lifted his head.

"Where are the Angels?"

"They're… at home."

"Your home?"

"No," said Andy, "your home."

"My home?"

"Oak… Oakenwald."

"You lie!"

"No." Andy saw the bat rear back. "…gave themselves up. Call… Earl Thompson."

Rose turned to Raphael. "Get me a phone."

Later, Andy would see it in slow motion. Raphael stood up. Andy turned his head toward Paul. Paul reached back to the knife, lunged toward the back of Andy's chair, and pushed both over. The door banged open and two objects flew over Andy's head. Both flash-banged. Partially deafened, Andy heard someone scream. Himself? He felt something tugging at the nylon ropes that held his hands. Father Paul? They came free. Two more objects struck the wall to his left and fizzed. Tear gas. His eyes filmed over and he could hardly breathe.

Andy fought against unconsciousness. Andy, you will. You will!

People, kaleidoscopic and dressed in armor, helmets, and goggles, charged into the room, spitting bullets from automatic guns and pistols. Andy saw Rose Cardova, dim but somehow glittering, shooting from the back of the room. Andy turned and saw Remington against the wall. He crawled toward it, dragging his broken leg. He never thought that a human could feel this much pain. Yet, he grabbed Remington and rolled partially to his right. He clicked the safety off, raised Remington from the floor, and pumped five shells toward Rose.

He felt Remington slip from his hands. Then all went black.

***

Andy woke up in a room that smelled of disinfectant. There was a breathing apparatus over his nose and mouth. A cast wrapped his broken leg. He remembered that someone had carried him from 7-12 and that he felt like he was suffocating. There was an ambulance siren, then doctors and nurses, and then voices and beeping.

Clubby, Stump, and Bernardo stood over him. Andy pulled the mask away. "Who?"

Clubby said, "Later, Andy. Rest now. They're calling in a dentist to fix your teeth." Clubby tried to push the breather back over Andy's nose and mouth. Andy managed to push it away.

"Who?"

Clubby leaned over him. "What do you mean?"

"Who? Paul?"

"Paul has broken ribs, but they say he'll make it."

"Who?"

Bernard nodded at Clubby.

"Andy," said Clubby, "Two SWAT team members were wounded. They're in surgery but the docs say they'll be okay."

"Arch... angels?"

"Three dead. One wounded."

"Dead... Cardova?"

"Yeah."

"How?"

"Twelve gauge shotgun shells in her face and stomach."

"Remington?"

"It was the only shotgun in the room."

Andy tried to roll on his side but Clubby held him back. Andy felt tears and then Clubby stroking his forehead.

"Andy, you and Remington saved lives, including mine. It's over, Andy. It's over."

CHAPTER 83

Garrett unwrapped the .45 and hid it along with his hammer under the night-stand. He'd spoken the truth to Earl. He'd lied to Lincoln. Lincoln's life was shattered and no number of apologies would fix it. There was no cabin in Idaho and no friends to smuggle them there. There was no secret passage. Lincoln would not attend Marian's funeral. He'd never see his children again.

***

Garrett and Lincoln lay together in bed. Lincoln was asleep. Garrett rose, removed the pistol and hammer, and quietly closed the door behind him. He sat at his computer and hacked into the Foundation's bank accounts. He smiled. The fools had not yet changed the passwords. They would pay… literally.

A foundation gives away money. The Foundation annually contributed small amounts of 'shade' money to various causes as cover and to retain its not-for-profit status.

Today, the Foundation would turn from tax-dodger and become a real foundation.

He transferred one million dollars to the International Gay and Lesbian Rights Commission. He made other gifts of various amounts to Greenpeace, the International Commission on Human Rights, the American Civil Liberties Union, Doctors without Borders, the V.A. Lugar Hospital in

Ferdinand, and the United Fund for Relief of Victims of the Congo War. He created a trust fund for Lincoln's children and transferred three million into it. He had just spent over fifty percent of the Foundation's available cash.

He thought about his own money. He transferred one dollar to the Foundation, care of Earl Thompson, and gave the rest to his family in Florida.

He next tapped into the Foundation's bylaws and inserted a clause: "No Foundation money is to be spent on the legal defense of any Foundation member who is suspected of committing, or otherwise charged with, a crime."

He drafted a letter to George Peabody, Director of the FBI.

> Dear Director Peabody:
>
> I wish to admit criminal activity and exonerate others from it. All the crimes committed or allegedly committed by or on behalf of the organization known as Foundation, Inc. and Kincaid for America have been perpetrated by the Foundation's Board of Directors, the members of the organization called 'Archangels,' and me. Certain other people, however, Polly Thompson, Garrett Jennings, my wife, Imogene Thompson, Lincoln Kincaid, and all individuals of the organization known as 'Angels,' are, or will be, suspects. None of these was involved in any way with the Foundation's criminal actions. All are innocent.
>
> Sincerely,
> Earl Thompson
> Executive Director
> Foundation, Inc.

Then he wrote to the Attorney General, United States Department of Justice.

Dear Mr. Fitzgerald:

> Enclosed is a flash drive of conversations between Earl Thompson and others in which Mr. Thompson engages in, admits to engaging in, or incriminates himself in, criminal activity. This includes murder. There are more recordings

of Mr. Thompson on my personal cloud. I printed the user-name and password on the inside of this envelope.

In addition, while working as an associate attorney at the Washington, D.C. law firm of Jones & Revis, and then for the organization known as Foundation, Inc., I became aware of criminal activity involving money-laundering and bribery. I have stored proof of these in a lockbox under an alias, Gary Johnson, at the First Federal Bank of Virginia in Richmond, Virginia. The key is located in my apartment under a loose brick in the fireplace.

Sincerely,
Garrett Jennings

Garrett removed the flash drive from his scapula and placed it in the envelope. He buzzed the front desk to arrange for mailing the letters.

The bedroom door opened and Lincoln stepped out.

"What are you doing?"

Garrett answered, "I'm resigning from the Foundation effective immediately."

"Can you come back to bed?"

"I'll join you in a few minutes."

Lincoln asked, "What's with the gun and hammer?"

"There was some pounding on the door."

Lincoln went back to bed. Garrett had another idea. He ordered one hundred large pizzas with all the toppings to be delivered to the people, media, and police surrounding the hotel—courtesy of Lincoln Kincaid. He paid with the Foundation's credit card.

Then he lit a cigarette, sat back, and smiled at what he'd just done.

There was one last job. He felt no fear. He was at peace.

In this mood, he entered the bedroom. Lincoln was dozing, his face turned toward Garrett's side of the bed. Garrett grabbed the hammer and smashed in Lincoln's skull. He waited a few minutes and felt for a pulse. There was none.

Then he placed the barrel of the revolver in his mouth, angled it upward, and pulled the trigger.

CHAPTER 84

Andy folded the cardboard covers on the banker's box and stored it in the attic. He closed the front door and began walking to Kundek Cemetery. It was late afternoon on an Indian summer day. The leaves had changed color, and most had fallen. It had rained the night before, cleansing the air. The sky was navy-blue. He reached the gate at the bottom of Kundek Cemetery. And there he stopped.

The Coachman RV and a Ford Transit Wagon were parked along the street that bordered Kundek Cemetery's west side. A woman, her back to him, stood under the maple tree at Rhonda's memorial stone. Further up the hill were three children and two adults in dark suits. Andy met the woman.

Polly Thompson smiled. "We attended Lincoln Kincaid's funeral this morning."

"Are those the Kincaid children?"

"Yes."

"I watched a bit of the funeral on TV," said Andy. "I never cared for Lincoln Kincaid, but I see now that he was used by fanatics. I hope he's found peace and forgiveness."

Polly said, "I was the luckier of the two of us. I got out and saved myself. Lincoln never had that chance."

"Are you going back to Oakenwald?"

"Yes, for now. I have much unfinished business there."

Andy said, "It seems that Earl Thompson and others are missing. I wonder what happened to them."

"They're in hiding."

"I wonder where?"

"Probably in a safe place."

"Will you move back to Indiana?" Andy asked.

"I haven't decided. We both have much thinking to do."

"I don't. This is my home."

"I didn't mean it that way. Will you marry again?"

"No."

"That seems final."

"I cannot have another Rhonda O'Malley. There's only one of her, and she's gone from my sight."

Polly stared into Andy's eyes. She grimaced, and then softened.

Andy turned and walked to Rhonda's memorial stone. He'd buried her ashes beneath it. Andy knelt and began pulling dead flowers and weeds from around the stone. Polly helped him.

"Rhonda was my friend," Polly said.

"Yes. She was like that."

"She loved you, Andy."

"We talked a few minutes before she died. She was coming back to me. Why did they have to kill her?"

"Because she was a brave woman who would not back down."

Still kneeling, Polly moved closer to Andy and placed her arm around him.

Andy said, "I loved her. God help me, I loved her so."

"I've learned to pray. I'll pray for both of you."

Polly released Andy. She gathered the children and the two Angels. Andy walked them to the Transit Wagon. He kissed her on the cheek and they left.

Andy returned to Rhonda's grave and sat with his back against the maple tree.

"Where are you now?" he asked.

Then maybe, faintly, almost a whisper in the breeze, "I await thee, my Andy, my love. Make sweeter my grave."

At first, haltingly, through tears, and then stronger, mellower, sweeter, Andy hummed "Danny Boy."

ACKNOWLEDGEMENTS

Thanks to Jeff Sharlet, whose excellent work alerted me to the danger of secret, fanatical groups very like the one in this story. To Janalyn & Crew, and Celine & Beverly, my two foster mothers. To Ian Graham Leask, my writing coach, and friend. To Rick Polad, whose patience in overcoming my stubbornness and copy editing several versions of my work was beyond the call of duty. And to Gary Lindberg, entrepreneur, who has created a fabulous home for new authors.

ABOUT THE AUTHOR

 Tommy Birk is a lawyer in his hometown of Jasper, Indiana. His first book, *Beneath the Rock*, was self -published, but as a result of a swarm of terrific reader reviews, was acquired by Calumet Editions. *Zero God* is his second novel, and he's hard at work on his third.

DISCUSSION QUESTIONS

1. What is fascism?

2. How is fascism framed in Zero God?

3. Although communism is never mentioned in Zero God, what is the difference between it and fascism?

4. Many Americans hold that fascism "can't happen here." Can it? If so, how would it come about?

5. Are there any signs that the United States is edging closer to fascism?

6. How would Zero God appear if it were written in another genre?

7. How would Zero God alter if it were written in the first person?

8. What is the role of humor in a thriller/suspense novel?

9. What is the true difference between liberalism and conservatism? Do parts of them overlap?

10. What are the major elements of the Social Contract?

11. What is the role of investigative journalism in a democracy?

12. Some seismologists hold out the possibility that the New Madrid fault line will produce an earthquake in the range of 7.5 – 8.0 on the Richter Scale in the next 50 years. What would be the effect of such an earthquake on the Midwestern United States?

13. The Logan Act is a federal law, passed in 1799, that makes it a felony

for a private citizen to engage in negotiations with a foreign power on a dispute between that power and the United States government. Does the Logan Act still make sense?

14. The American military's dirty little secret is rape in the ranks. What, if anything, is being done to expose the secret and decrease the incidence of rape? The military now allows LBGT's to openly serve. What effect will this policy have on the incidence of rape?

15. What, exactly, should be the role of the federal government?

16. Some Americans zre weary of the messiness and noise of democracy. What do you say to them?

17. Americans have seen privatization of government functions over the past twenty-five years or so. Where has it been successful? Unsuccessful? What are the motives of those who promote it? Pure, or something less?

18. What is the relationship between Andy and Polly at the end of Zero God: Lovers, friends, allies, enemies, ambiguous, or something else?

CPSIA information can be obtained
at www.ICGtesting.com
Printed in the USA
BVHW041450210123
656725BV00001B/106